DARK PLACES

Jon Evans has backpacked through some of the roughest territory on earth, including China, Mauritania, Indonesia, Zimbabwe, South Africa, New Guinea, India, Nepal, and the Balkans. In between treks, he divides his time among the United States, Canada, and England. Visit his website at www.rezendi.com.

Jon Evans

An Imprint of HarperCollins*Publishers*

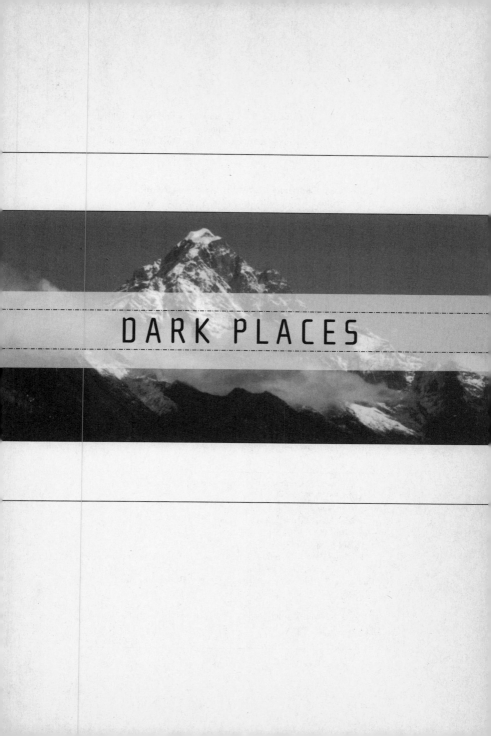

DARK PLACES

DARK PLACES. Copyright © 2004 by Jon Evans. All rights reserved. Printed in the United States of America. No part of this book may be used or reproduced in any manner whatsoever without written permission except in the case of brief quotations embodied in critical articles and reviews. For information address HarperCollins Publishers Inc., 10 East 53rd Street, New York, NY 10022.

HarperCollins books may be purchased for educational, business, or sales promotional use. For information please write: Special Markets Department, HarperCollins Publishers Inc., 10 East 53rd Street, New York, NY 10022.

FIRST EDITION

Designed by Jennifer Ann Daddio

Title page photograph /
Part One photograph © Joseph M. Duraes

All other photographs courtesy of Getty Images

Library of Congress Cataloging-in-Publication Data

Evans, Jon, 1973–
    Dark places / Jon Evans.—1st ed.
        p. cm.
    ISBN 0-06-059423-3
    1. Americans—Nepal—Fiction.   2. Himalaya Mountains—
Fiction.   3. Wilderness areas—Fiction.   4. Serial murders—
Fiction.   5. Backpacking—Fiction.   6. Hiking—Fiction.
7. Nepal—Fiction.   I. Title.

PS3605.V365D37 2004
813'.6—dc22
                                                                2003056889

04 05 06 07 08 WBC/RRD 10 9 8 7 6 5 4 3 2 1

TO MY SISTERS

The dark places of the earth are full
of the habitations of cruelty.

—PSALMS 74:20

"And this also," said Marlow suddenly,
"has been one of the dark places of the earth."

—JOSEPH CONRAD, *HEART OF DARKNESS*

ACKNOWLEDGMENTS

I would like to thank:

My parents and sisters.

My agents—especially Vivienne Schuster at Curtis Brown UK, and also her compatriots Euan Thorneycroft, Carol Jackson, and Tally Garner, Deborah Schneider at Gelfman Schneider, and Liza Wachter at Rabineau Wachter.

My publishers—Carolyn Mays at Hodder & Stoughton, Michael Shohl at HarperCollins United States, Iris Tupholme at HarperCollins Canada, and Frederika von Traa at de Boekerij.

My first circle of readers—Nathan Basiliko, Judith Cox, Linda Howard, E. Anne Killpack, Sarah Langan, Allegra Lundyworf, Max Pentreath, Horst Rutter.

Gavin Chait for making an appearance. Peter Rose and Neil Katz for overpaying me in New York so I could move to Montreal and write. Rick Innis for finding me a job after that money was gone. The Tom sisters—Donna, Linda, and Winnie—for keeping me entertained in Montreal, New York, and Toronto. My cousin Rachael Nicholson for putting me up, and putting up with me, in London.

And, finally, the Truck Africans: Ally, Amanda, Andrea, Angela, Brian, Caz, Chong, Gavin, Jo, Jorge, Heidi, Mattias, Michael, Mick, Naomi, Nick, Patsy, PK, Sam, Shirray, Tim, Tony, and Wendy. Long may you run.

ONE

NEPAL,
OCTOBER 2000

ABANDON

Remember, I told myself only minutes before we discovered the body, *this was supposed to be fun.*

I had thought I would enjoy carrying a heavy pack up fifteen thousand vertical feet of uneven stony trail. Now I was too miserable to laugh at my own idiocy. Every step prompted a jolt of pain from the infected blisters on both heels, and my brittle knees ached and popped like a sputtering motor. My pack straps had carved a pair of red furrows into my back, each one filigreed by an itchy fungal infection. I had a nagging headache, shortness of breath, and nausea, a textbook case of low-grade altitude sickness. But what really made the whole situation unbearable was my traveling companion's attitude.

"Isn't it fantastic?" Gavin said, as I trudged behind him. "It's just extraordinary. I've been looking at it for three days now and I never get bored of it."

The *it* in question was the Annapurna Range of the Himalaya, the glorious snowcapped mountains that surrounded us, and even in my irritable state I couldn't argue with his superlatives. Every time I looked around I felt like I had stepped into a fairy tale. But I would have preferred to

appreciate its grandeur from the window of our lodge, preferably while eating *momos* and drinking an entire pot of lemon
tea, rather than following Gavin to inspect the abandoned
village. He had browbeaten me into coming with him, knowing that I didn't have the mental strength to argue. Probably
thinking that I would thank him later.

I'll thank him with a two-by-four, I thought. *I'll show him my
gratitude with a ball-peen hammer*. Even without my pack,
which I had left back at the lodge, each motion felt like a sac-
rifice. Step, breathe, step, breathe, stop, breathe, repeat.

"Acute mountain sickness, my foot," Gavin said. "I feel
fantastic. I've never felt better in my life. I think I'm suffering
from acute mountain wellness."

"How nice for you," I muttered.

"Paul! Is that snow?"

I looked up from my feet. Gavin pointed excitedly at the
shadow cast by a tall boulder, where a thin layer of the morning's frost had not yet thawed. He was from South Africa,
and never in his well-traveled life had he seen snow up close.
I was originally from Canada and found the idea of a snow-
less existence nearly incomprehensible.

"No," I said. "Sorry. Just frost."

"Oh. Pity."

We moved on. The abandoned village was located on a
ridge that jutted out above the Marsyangdi river valley like a
peninsula. A few dozen low, small buildings of dark rough-
hewn stones welded together by frozen mud. It seemed
insane to me that people had lived up here. It seemed insane
that anyone had ever even *considered* living up here. Not even
the yaks came this high. Nothing grew but lichen, a few particularly stubborn strands of grass, and a thin knee-high
layer of vicious thornbushes. The wind howled ceaselessly,
numbing my exposed skin, and even with the sun at its
midpoint I could still see my breath. And the effort required
to quarry those hundred-pound stones, probably from the

Marsyangdi riverbed far below, and bring them up to this godforsaken overlook—mad, I thought, absolutely barking, as the Brits on the truck used to say.

Gavin hemmed and hawed over one of the buildings, inspecting its joints and shining his Maglite flashlight inside, while I stood behind and tried to catch my breath. I had been trying all day, and I was beginning to fear that it had gone for good.

"Imagine being born here," he said, and I tried but failed. Some cultural gaps are simply too wide to jump.

He led the way through the village. We must have gone right past the body without noticing it. For a little while we stood on the edge of the cliff, which dropped a hundred sheer feet before easing off a little and tumbling down to the dry riverbed a thousand feet below. By now we were accustomed to precipices. I had lost track of how many times during the previous week I had scrambled across steep drops on narrow and treacherous trails.

Eventually I grew bored of contemplating my own mortality and turned around, intending to return to our lodge. Then I saw him. A fellow backpacker, sitting with his back against one of the village buildings, facing us. Even from a hundred feet away and with the cold, dusty wind in my eyes I could tell there was something badly wrong with his face.

"Whoa," I said, and narrowly prevented myself from taking a fatal step backward in surprise. "What the hell?"

Gavin turned to look, and said, "Fucking hell."

We advanced without really thinking about it. About halfway there I realized that the man was dead. Not just dead. Killed. Unless he had thrust a pair of matching Swiss Army knives into his own eyes. The red handles protruded from his eye sockets like antennae.

The victim was tall, white, probably midtwenties, typical backpacker, wearing a blue jacket over a thick green sweater, jeans, and battered hiking boots. There wasn't much blood, but I could smell it in the air like iron. Most of it was pooled on top of his head, dark brown muck filling a dent so large and misshapen that his thick dark hair did not conceal it. The liquid congealed on his cheeks was pale, almost transparent.

Gavin muttered something astonished in Afrikaans. I looked around. Nobody there but the two of us and the cold wind and the mountains. We could see the trekking trail about half a mile away, and the two Gunsang lodges facing one another across it, but they seemed as deserted as this long-abandoned village.

I felt newly vibrant, energetic, ready for action. The sight of the dead man had cued adrenaline to wash through me like some kind of mythical cure-all. My aches and pains had vanished. My head was clear. I felt as if gauze had been lifted from all of my senses; I had never seen so clearly, so distinctly. The body's instinctive fight-or-flight response can be a wonderful thing. I can understand how daredevils get addicted to it.

I crouched a few inches away from the body, examining it carefully, conditioned not to touch anything by years of cop shows and detective novels. Another flush of energy coursed down my spine like electricity. Every hair on the back of my neck stood to attention, like an army under review. My skin actually crawled. Until that moment I had always thought that was just a melodramatic expression.

Even my nausea had, ironically, faded away. I felt more fascination than revulsion as I examined the body. His arms hung loose by his sides. A tan line revealed that his watch was missing. He hadn't shaved in a few days. His mouth was slightly parted as if in contemplation. I avoided looking at the eyes.

"Christ almighty," Gavin said.

"Yeah," I said.

"The knives are a little unnecessary, aren't they?" he

asked, his accent much harsher than usual. "I mean, Jesus, they practically cracked his skull in two."

"Yeah," I repeated.

Nightmare, I told myself. *Just another nightmare. You'll wake up any moment now.* What I was seeing wasn't real, couldn't be real. My subconscious had mixed the past and the present into this lethally horrible cocktail and was serving it up to me as I slept.

It would have been a comforting belief. But it wasn't possible. Dreams often seem real, at least while they last, but sane people cannot mistake reality for a dream. No matter how much we might want to.

Gavin dropped to his knees next to me and touched the corpse's arm experimentally.

"Don't," I said. It seemed like a violation.

"Why not?"

I searched for a justification. "We should leave the scene alone."

He gave me a don't-be-stupid look. "For who? The Nepali police? Somehow I doubt they've got a crack homicide investigator in the district."

Which was true. Fingerprinting, DNA testing, forensic analysis . . . there would be none of that here. Just a bunch of minimally educated Third World policemen here to rescue stranded tourists and fend off Maoist insurgents, not to investigate murders.

Gavin touched the stone wall the corpse slumped against, then its arm again, then the wall. He looked worried.

"What are you doing?" I asked.

"He's still warm," Gavin said quietly.

"What?"

"Warmer than the stone, at any rate. Feel for yourself."

I paused for a moment, then I did just that. The arm felt cold and clammy to my touch, but there was no denying that it was noticeably warmer than the ground or the wall. We looked at each other for a moment, then rose to our feet and looked around us uneasily.

"Let's just make sure we're alone here," I said, very calmly.

"Good idea," he agreed, equally calm.

We walked through the village again, senses on high alert. I dug into my pocket for my own Swiss Army knife but decided to leave it there. It was a small knife, though sharp as hell, but more to the point, walking around with a bared blade would have seemed like an admission that the world had gone terribly wrong, an admission I wasn't yet ready to make. Far better to pretend this was just another travel encounter, another anecdote for the journal and boozy late-night retellings.

It didn't take long to determine that there was no one else in the village. We returned to the body and stood there for what felt like a long time, staring at it and at each other, trying to work out what the things were that we should do.

"Do you recognize him?" Gavin asked.

I had just been searching my memory. If the man had died today, then we had probably seen him before. Trekkers on the Annapurna Circuit moved in packs, all in the same direction at roughly the same speed; the scenery changed, but our neighbors remained the same. But this was high season, with more than two hundred people a day passing along the trail, and it is hard to recognize a frozen and mutilated face. I shook my head. We stood there a little longer.

"We should take pictures," I said eventually. "For evidence. Before we disturb anything."

Gavin nodded and dug into the camera pack he kept with him. He had a serious camera, big as a brick, with lenses and various attachments, and he assembled it into what I presumed was the ideal homicide-evidence configuration and shot a roll of film from various angles. I took a few snaps

myself with my cheap point-and-click. I think we were both
relieved to have something vaguely constructive to do.

When we were finished we looked at each other and without speaking approached the corpse again. I guess we had
decided that we were the best investigators the murdered
man was going to get up here. I tried to call fragments of fiction to mind, to remember what real detectives did. They
looked for hairs, blood, anything that might give you a DNA
sample of the killer. None of those were apparent. The victim's fingernails were dirty but not bloody. He didn't seem to
have put up any resistance. Detectives looked for fingerprints, but that was going to be beyond us. The killer's prints
might be all over those Swiss Army knives or that blue
waterproof jacket, but I doubted they had fingerprint pow-
der anywhere in Nepal this side of Kathmandu. Maybe not
even there.

Looking at the jacket I saw a familiar red tab on it and
shook my head in dismay. "He's Canadian."

"How can you tell?" Gavin asked.

I fingered the red tab. MEC, it read. "Mountain Equip-
ment Co-Op. Canadian travel gear store." Somehow this
made it personally offensive, that the victim and I had bought
our jackets at the same store.

"He doesn't have a pack," Gavin observed. "Maybe it's
back at one of the lodges here."

"Maybe," I agreed. "Let's see if he's got any ID . . ."

He nodded. We reached clumsily around the dead man
and dug through his pockets. Nothing there but a few Nepali
rupees. The body was stiff as a board. We gingerly prodded
under his shirt and his jeans to see if he was carrying a travel
wallet. Around his waist was a beige Eagle Creek security
pouch much like the one I wore. But it was empty.

"His watch is gone," I pointed out.

"Right," Gavin said. "Maybe it was just a theft. Probably
a Nepali, if so."

"Maybe . . ." I said doubtfully.

"*Ja,*" he said. "I don't think so either. Those knives . . ." He shook his head. "That's just sick. I don't think a Nepali would have done that. I work in the Cape Flats, you know, I've seen a fair few murdered men before, but I've never see one done like this."

"I have," I said, but so softly that he did not hear me.

Laura, I thought. *It's just like Laura. It's just like Cameroon.*

HEAR YE, HEAR YE

We went back to the two Gunsang lodges, rickety wood-and-stone buildings that faced off across the trail like sumo wrestlers waiting for the signal to begin. There was nothing there; no pack, no people, nothing but the bored proprietors waiting for the rest of the day's batch of lodgers. Gavin and I were the first and so far only trekkers to stop there for the night. Gunsang wasn't on the Lonely Planet Trail, so the vast majority went from Manang straight to Letdar without stopping. The only reason we had stopped was because I felt sick and wasn't eager to go up another thousand feet. And because we both appreciated that it wasn't on the Lonely Planet Trail.

We asked the lodge owners, both stout Nepali women with impassive faces, who like all lodge owners spoke enough broken English to communicate. No Canada-man had stayed in Gunsang last night; just a group of Dutch in one lodge, and the usual mélange in the other, one German man, one Frenchwoman, and a Kiwi couple. Conclusion: Either the dead man was coming from the other direction, downhill from Letdar to Manang, or he had left Manang much earlier than Gavin and I. Which was entirely possible. We had begun the day's trek well after first light.

We left the lodges and stood on the trail between them. The midday clouds were thick above Annapurna, and its heavenly vista was almost entirely concealed. In the distance we could see a pair of trekkers approaching from below.

"Right," Gavin said. "I guess it's pretty obvious what we do."

"Split up?" I asked.

"*Ja*," he said. "One of us goes to Manang and tells the police. In case they can't identify him, the other goes to Letdar and tries to find out who he was."

"Sounds good," I said. "I'll go to Letdar." There was no sensible reason for me to be the one to go there; I just didn't want to deal with the police. Besides, in the real world, Gavin was a legal-aid advocate for poor South Africans. This bearer-of-bad-news thing was right up his alley.

He looked at me narrowly. "You sure? I thought you had AMS."

I shook my head. "I feel fine now. Actually I feel great."

"Izzit?" Gavin asked, a South African expression that basically translated to *really?* "Well, it's an ill wind. All right. You think you can get there and back to Manang before sunset?"

I thought it over. If I left my pack behind I'd make good time. After nine days of carrying forty pounds on my back, walking unencumbered felt almost like flying. On the other hand, it was already midday, who knew how long I'd have to stay in Letdar, and up here the sun dropped like a stone.

"I can get back to Manang tonight," I said. "Probably late night, but that's no problem."

Gavin shook his head. "I don't think you should do that."

"Don't see why not," I said. "I've got plenty of layers with me, and I'm not about to get lost, the stars and moon are so damn bright up here you can practically read a news—"

"That's not what I mean," he interrupted.

"Then what do you mean?"

"I mean I'd hate for the body count to increase at your expense."

"Oh," I said, and then "oh," again. It hadn't even occurred to me in a personal-risk way that there was a bona fide murderer out there who might not appreciate our attempts to identify the victim and find out what had happened to him. I managed a wavering grin and said, "Right. Self-preservation being my personal specialty, I'll spend the evening in cosmopolitan Letdar."

"Right," he said. "See you tomorrow." And we went our separate ways.

My heels burned, my knees ached, my back itched, my pack felt like an anvil, but I had grown accustomed to my various agonies, and God knew I had a lot to think about. The trail wound upward, ever upward, through fields of lichen and bramble, hugging the bottom of a massive slope of jagged red rock. The notion of someday going downhill felt like a myth. At one point a faint subtrail separated itself and veered nearly straight up that slope, so steep that I doubted even the sure-footed mules and horses of Nepal could navigate it. I wondered where it went. All the way to Tibet, probably. We were less than twenty miles from that border.

It was strange, trekking on my own. For the first time I began to understand just how far from civilization I had come. The constant presence of other Westerners, the nights spent in halfway-civilized lodges with hot water and hot food, and the well-marked trail had made it very easy to think of the trek as just another hike. In fact, this was one of the most remote places I had ever been. I was a seven-day walk from the nearest road, seven days of much tougher hiking than I had expected, and I would soon be higher above sea level than any place in North America outside of a few Alaskan peaks. The Coke bottles in the lodges up here had Chinese characters on them, because it was cheaper to smuggle them in on yaks from Tibet than to carry them up from Kathmandu.

I wasn't surprised that there was no one else on the trail. Western trekkers followed a rigid schedule, setting out in the morning and arriving at their destination by midafternoon, and I was well behind today's last stragglers. A few days ago I would have expected to pass Nepali porters or mule trains, but up here there were no actual Nepali villages, so the traffic had dwindled to a handful of porters carrying goods to and from the few clusters of lodges built for us tourists.

Not for the first time I wondered what the Nepalis thought of us, of the Westerners who came en masse from halfway around the world to walk through their backyard. Europeans, mostly, but a fair number of Americans and Canadians as well. Mostly around my age, late twenties and early thirties, traveling solo or in twos and threes, but I'd seen a fair sampling of gray hair and wrinkles as well, and several organized package-tour groups of twenty or thirty. During high season around three hundred Westerners a day would march past any given point on the trail, and even during the worst of the winter, or the height of the monsoon season, a few hardy souls trickled along. I wondered if we all seemed inexplicably insane to the Nepalis. The appeal of carrying a heavy pack from village to village through the world's most mountainous territory for two full weeks was not always immediately obvious. The Annapurna Circuit was a relatively civilized trek, no tents or outdoor cooking required, lodges and beds and hot food available every night and several times each day along the trail, but it was still a harsh and demanding journey. I doubted most Nepalis, or Westerners for that matter, had the slightest understanding of why we trekked. I wasn't sure I understood myself. Testing yourself physically, immersing yourself in the exotic and welcoming culture of Nepal, experiencing something as far away from a daily Western urban rut as could be imagined, those all had something to do with it. But I thought mostly it was the purity of the place that drew us all. Looming mountains, untouched forest, wild rivers fed by towering waterfalls, and the simplicity of traveling only by putting one foot in front of another, walking until you arrived at a village that hadn't changed much in the last few centuries. That was all there was to life when you were trekking. Everything else was unnecessary.

I was surrounded by some of the world's highest mountains, but clouds had drawn in, and I could not see above the snow line. These weren't the typical mountain clouds, the vapor that forms above snowcapped peaks after the sun has heated them, then expands throughout the day, so that you only get the postcard views for the first hour or two after dawn. These were storm clouds. I wondered if there was snow on the Thorung La, the narrow pass that marked the apogee of our trek. More than a few inches, and they shut the pass down. Maybe the dead man didn't need us; maybe his murderer would be trapped by the fickle Nepali weather.

It was just like Laura. Just like Laura's murder in Limbe, Cameroon. That was unbelievable. What were the odds? The odds were astronomical. I felt like there was something going on, something unexplained, something more mysterious than a single murder. If only I had a good conspiracy theory to hang my hat on. But it was pure chance that we had decided to wander around that broken-down abandoned village, pure chance that we had stumbled on that slumped corpse.

I wished we hadn't. For two years I had been trying to drive the memory of Laura out of my mind, or if that was impossible, at least trap it in a cage and tame it. And now, when I felt I was so close, when on good days I could look at the pictures of her I kept buried in my closet without tears clogging my eyes, there was this reminder of how her body had looked on the black sand of Mile Six Beach. It had taken months, after we had found her there, before I could close my eyes without that sight superimposed on my eyelids.

I forced myself to think of something else, anything else. I tried to imagine what had happened to that nameless Canadian victim. There hadn't been a struggle. He must have been ambushed from behind. Or maybe it was somebody he knew. And somebody either very strong or swinging something very heavy, from the way his skull had nearly cracked open like an egg.

And then the victim had sat down neatly with his back to the wall, the way we had found him? That didn't seem likely. Toppling over seemed more likely. The killer must have dragged him over to the wall, arranged the body. I couldn't remember seeing any bloodstains on the ground. On the other hand, I couldn't remember looking for any either. It couldn't have been far away from where he was found though. And then the knives, I was somehow convinced that they must have come last, some kind of horrifically depraved signature. Just like the knives in Laura's eyes.

Could it be the same person? Obviously it couldn't be. Obviously it didn't make any sense that I, of all the people in the world, should just happen to follow the same killer's trail twice, two years apart, on two different continents. The very notion was ridiculous, was completely implausible, was . . . *unscientific*. But I couldn't help holding it up in my mind and turning it around. Couldn't help wondering if I would recognize any of the faces in Letdar.

And what would I do if I did? That was the real question. What would I do?

Burdened by my pack and my contemplation, I
didn't get to Letdar until about an hour before sunset. It
wasn't a village, just a collection of a dozen lodges. Two more
were under construction, a backbreaking proposition up
here near the vegetation line. Every plank, every brick, every
pot and pan had to be carried up here on the backs of prema-
turely wizened Nepali porters. I wondered if they resented
the white tourists whose presence led to their toil, or whether
they welcomed the work. Probably no, to both. Probably
they didn't think about us at all; they just shouldered the
loads and unquestioningly took them where they were told
to go.

Nearly every bed was already occupied, which explained
why new lodges were under construction. Adam Smith's
invisible hand at work. I got a wooden bed frame, sans mat-
tress, in a dormitory room with five others at the Churi Lattar Lodge. The dinner hour had just begun, and I was
famished, but I knew I had to get to all the lodges before
night fell and all the trekkers retired to their sleeping bags. I
wished, for neither the first nor the last time, that Gavin had
not been overcome by the desire to explore that abandoned
village.

It had gotten cold enough that nearly everyone was in the
common room, seated around low wooden tables, eating garlic noodle soup and drinking lemon tea, waiting for their dinner orders to emerge in random order from the kitchen. I put
an order in for *dhal baat*, knowing it would be at least an hour.
Then I walked to the doorway and looked around at the
assembled masses. About thirty people, various groups, various languages. Usually common rooms roared with conversation, but altitude sickness and sheer exhaustion had drained a
lot of the joie de vivre from this crowd. Which made my job

easier. But not easy. I had always hated public speaking, always hated calling attention to myself in front of strangers. Still. A man had died, and I had a job to do, and that had to trump my stage fright.

I took an empty teacup and a sugar spoon and banged the spoon against the teacup. It made a hollow empty sound that did not carry. I took another empty teacup and clashed the two cups together as hard as I dared, and this worked much better. A hush fell over the room and thirty pairs of confused, expectant, and irritated eyes turned toward me.

"Listen," I said, trying to project, plowing ahead before I had a chance to get embarrassed and tongue-tied. "This is important. My friend and I found a dead body today, back in Gunsang. A trekker. We're pretty sure he's Canadian, we're pretty sure he died today, and we're pretty sure that he was murdered."

There was a long pause during which I feared irrationally that they would laugh at me and turn away; and then a half-dozen voices asked, with varying accents, "Murdered?"

"Murdered," I repeated. The room had fallen silent, and they were staring at me with utter fascination. "His pack is gone, his ID is gone, and his watch is gone. My friend has gone back to Manang, to the police. We don't have any idea who the dead man is. What I want to know is if any of you knew him."

"Tell us what he looks like," a burly German demanded.

"Dark hair," I said. "He was wearing a blue jacket from a Canadian store, a green wool sweater, and jeans."

Silence. I looked around the room, really looked, for the first time. To no avail. No faces I recognized, no guilty or shifty expressions, nothing but genuine surprise. A few expressions of sympathy, or dismay . . . but mostly fascination. They wanted to hear more, I could tell, but they had nothing to add.

"All right," I told the crowd. "I'm going to go ask at the other lodges. If any of your friends are sick or sleeping, ask them when you can. I'm staying here tonight. And do me a favor, if *ðhal baat* comes out for dormitory bed six before I get back, save it for me."

The crowd stared at me expectantly. I searched for a pithy end to my speech and came up with, "Thanks. I'll be back later."

Exit, stage center, out through the door. And for once I hadn't felt my usual awkwardness and embarrassment when talking to a crowd. Because I knew I had them in the palm of my hand. Nobody was going to catcall a dramatic revelation of Murder on the Trail.

For some reason I was angry with the people in the lodge, and the way they had reacted. A man was dead, a man who had walked the same trail they had for the last week, and there had been no sympathy, no grief, no cries of "That's awful!" There were no voices volunteering to help in any way they could. Just amazement, fascination. As if it was part of the scheduled entertainment. Another notch on their travel belts, that they had walked with a murdered man. Another story for their friends when they returned to their safe European or American homes. He wasn't really a dead man to them; he was another element in their life-enriching trip, just another Travel Experience, like an animatron on a Disney ride.

And it wasn't just them. I felt some of that myself. Would I have reacted so casually, so clinically, if I had found a dead man with knives in his eyes back in California or Canada? Like hell I would have. But I was here on an adventure. Until today a safe, tame, communal adventure, but an adventure nonetheless, and I was treating the murdered man as just another episode in my journey. I felt like I had co-opted his death, that it was no longer his own.

It was in the seventh lodge, after I had described the dead man for the seventh time, that the silence was bro-

ken by a voice from the back. "We know someone like that,"
the voice said, an Australian voice, its tone alarmed. "His
name is Stanley. We were expecting him here, but he never
showed up."

The voice belonged to a woman named Abigail, who was
traveling with a German man named Christian and a younger
Aussie girl named Madeleine. I sat down next to them. The
rest of the room listened expectantly.

"What happened?" Abigail asked, and she, at least, was
genuinely upset. I told her most of the story, leaving out any
mention of the knives.

"Fucking hell," Madeleine said. "God. I can't believe it. I
can't believe I was traveling with someone who was murdered today."

"Can you tell me anything about him?" I asked them. "I'm
going back to Manang tomorrow to talk to the police. His last
name?"

They looked at each other, tried to call it to mind. Christian nodded abruptly. "Goebel," he said. "His last name is
Goebel. I saw it at the checkpoint in Chame." Every day or
two on the trail we had to sign in at a police or Annapurna
Conservation Area checkpoint, mostly to keep track of
trekkers who got lost or stumbled off cliffs. "It's a German
name, that's why I remember."

Stanley Goebel. The dead man had a name.

"We met him in Pisang," Abigail said. "Three days ago.
He was Canadian, yeah. He was traveling on his own. I don't
know. He seemed like a good bloke. He worked in an auto
factory somewhere near Toronto. He was only in Nepal for a
month."

"He didn't have much money," Madeleine added.

They fell silent. They didn't have anything else to add. I
grew irrationally angry again, this time at the paucity of their
epitaph. *He seemed like a good bloke. He didn't have much money.*
That was it? That was all they had to say? Abigail and Chris-

tian at least seemed upset. Madeleine watched me with that awful wide-eyed fascination.

"All right," I said. "I'm staying at the Churi Lattar. If you think of anything else, could you come and let me know?" I sounded to myself like a detective on *Homicide: Life on the Street*. I should give them my card, that was what Pembleton and Bayliss did. "I'm going to go check the other lodges, to see if anyone else knows anything."

And to get away from here, because no offense, I know we only just met, but I can't stand your company anymore.

And, maybe, to see if I recognize anyone in the other lodges.

But I did not recognize anyone, and nobody else knew anything. I returned to my lodge famished and exhausted. Some kind soul had saved my *dhal baat*, and never have rice and lentils and curried vegetables tasted so good. I had a second helping, drank a pot of lemon tea, returned to the dorm room, peeled my boots off, and curled up in my sleeping bag.

Sleep came hard that night, and it wasn't because of the hard wooden bed or my snuffling dormitory companions. I didn't want to be alone. I wanted a warm body next to me. No; more than that. For the first time in a long time I allowed myself to admit what I wanted more than anything, what I knew I would always want more than anything. I wanted Laura next to me. Laura and her quick laugh, her mane of long dark hair, her gentle touch. Laura who I had loved and who had loved me. Laura who had been dead for two years.

Nicole had told me, on the night the tribe of the truck disbanded, that one day I would get over it. Wise and wonderful Nicole. We had camped by the side of a dirt road, just outside Douala, a city popularly and accurately known as the armpit of Africa. It was late, the fire had burned down to ash and glowing embers, and almost everyone had retired to their tents. Only my closest mates had stayed up. Nicole, her husband, Hallam, Lawrence, Steve. Thinking about it now I realized they had stayed up primarily to keep an eye on me. I was in bad shape, those first few weeks. I guess they thought I was a danger to myself.

"It'll get better," she had said. "You'll get better. I know you probably can't believe that right now, but . . . Just believe that it's possible. You'll get over it. We'll all get over it. I know that sounds callous and horrible, and maybe it is. But it's true. Remember that."

I had remembered. But I thought that, for once, wise and wonderful Nicole might have gotten it wrong.

I didn't want to think about it anymore. I didn't want to think about anything anymore. I dug out my Walkman, put in my Prodigy tape, and blasted it into my ears as loud as I dared. All I wanted was to exterminate all rational thought, but somehow it eventually put me to sleep.

RETRACE AND RETREAT

I woke an hour after dawn. At home this would have been a sign that something was seriously wrong with me. Here on the trekking trail it meant I had slept in. All of the other dorm beds were already vacant. Where there is no electricity, I had discovered, even so-called night people fall into a dawn-to-dusk routine within a matter of days.

I hadn't washed yesterday, but the solar showers on the trail didn't warm up until midafternoon, and I dreaded the thought of the icy downpour I would have to endure at this hour. I could probably talk the proprietor into heating a bucket of water for me, but it seemed like a selfish waste of valuable firewood. *Manang*, I thought. *I'll shower in Manang.*

I went through my morning ritual of smearing antibiotic cream on my blisters and covering them with patches of a long bandage roll that I had bought in Chame. The bandage was made in India, and the glue had an irritating habit of dissolving in the middle of the day, but it was better than nothing. At this point I was using the antibiotic cream primarily for its placebo effect; the blisters were open, nearly purple, and angry red streaks radiated from them like a child's drawing of the sun. But at least they hadn't gotten any worse today.

A few other stragglers were hurrying to get on the trail. I had overheard in Manang that there was a bed shortage in Thorung Phedi and Thorung High Camp, the next stops after Letdar and last before the Thorung La, and the last few to leave Letdar each day would likely have to turn back and try again the next day. I was almost relieved to be going the other way. The appeal of trekking lay largely in its Zen-like contemplative pace. The idea of having to rush to beat the crowds was just fundamentally wrong.

I ate a breakfast of tasty *tsampa* porridge and lemon tea, stifled a groan as I shouldered my pack, and started out back down the trail, back toward Manang. I felt wonderful. My altitude sickness had vanished. It was good to be going downhill. The air was crisp and clean, and the mountains loomed around me like glorious visions of some faraway fantasy land, like a Tolkien landscape. Yesterday's clouds had vanished, and there seemed to be more snow cover on the peaks. I wondered if the Thorung La was open. If it shut down for more than a day or two, there would be a backlog of trekkers occupying every bed within miles, and it might take all season to clear the bottleneck.

I had left my watch back in the city of Pokhara, but I guessed it was about two hours back to Gunsang, and another two to Manang. Back there by noon, mission accomplished, Stanley Goebel's name acquired. I walked and wondered what had happened to his pack. His killer had presumably taken his passport, wallet, and watch, but his pack? That would make sense, if the killer was Nepali; he could sell the pack and many of its contents back in Pokhara or Kathmandu. But I didn't think so. I thought the killer was one of us, a fellow trekker, and that Stanley Goebel's pack had been flung over the edge of the cliff near where he had

died. It would have fallen a long way, well out of sight. I wondered if it would ever be discovered.

If I was right, and the murderer was a Westerner, then he
had probably spent last night in either Letdar or Manang.
Nepali merchants clad in jeans and flip-flops took but a single
day to go from Manang over the Thorung La to Muktinath,
but only an extremely fit and well-acclimatized Westerner
could do the same, it was at least three days' journey for most
trekkers. Manang or Letdar then. And Manang had an airstrip and regular dawn flights, weather permitting, back to
Pokhara. That made sense. The killer was probably back in
Pokhara's balmy climate. Hell, he could be halfway to India
by now, or in Kathmandu, waiting for a flight out of the
country.

I gave up on contemplation and focused on walking. It
was easy to turn my mind off up here, to reduce the entire
universe to the placement of one foot in front of the other. I
was going downhill, but the wind was in my face, numbing
my skin. I pulled my hat down low on my brow to mitigate
this and trudged onward, mind empty, happy simply to walk.

I don't know what it was that alarmed me. Maybe I
caught a sideways glimpse as I turned a corner. Maybe I
heard something. Maybe it was that sixth sense that tells you
when someone is watching you. Whatever it was, it made me
stop and turn around and look down the trail behind me.
About a thousand feet away the trail rounded a bend in the
red stone slope it followed, and there I saw a single human
figure, following my path.

Nothing unusual in that. Someone with bad altitude sickness who had decided to descend in order to recover. Or one
of those rare hardy souls who had gone clockwise around the
Circuit, a much more difficult route because there were no

lodges for a long way on the other side of the Thorung La. Or a Nepali porter heading back to Manang for another load. I kept walking.

But after about a minute I could no longer deny the alarm bells ringing in my head, even though I did not know what had cued them. I turned around again and squinted at the figure. It stopped, and a moment passed when we looked at each other across a distance. Then the figure resumed its travel toward me, moving at a quick walk. And I realized that he or she was not carrying a pack.

Everyone carries packs up on the trail. Trekkers carry their backpacks, or are joined by Nepali porters who carry them in their place. Other Nepalese either ride horses, if rich, or carry wood or stone in one direction and empty Coke bottles in the other, if poor.

I paused for a moment. I felt very cold all of a sudden, and I wanted to turn and run. Instead I dropped my pack to the ground for a moment, spent a moment rooting through its top pocket for my binoculars, and raised them to my eyes. I'd hardly used them at all on this trip, had kicked myself a couple of times for bringing them with me. Now I was very glad to have them.

The figure was tall, male, wearing sneakers, gray slacks, a green jacket . . . and a ski mask. He looked big and fit, and he was moving with purpose, and he was looking right at me as he walked.

Lots of people had ski masks, you could rent or buy them in Pokhara or Kathmandu, for the subzero temperatures and high winds on the day you crossed the Thorung La. And it was cold today, and windy. But not *that* cold and windy.

And I was all alone on this remote trail, fourteen thousand feet high, in the back end of nowhere, half a world away from home, amid mountains so rugged and wild they were barely claimed by any country. The kind of place where people can vanish without a trace.

I stared through the binoculars, the pit of my stomach beginning to tighten into a cold knot, and as I stared, he waved. A jaunty, how-ya-doing wave of his hand. He grinned at me from beneath the ski mask. I shivered. I didn't like that grin at all. He was moving even faster now. There was something about his body language, the tilt of his head, the angle of his torso. He didn't look like he was walking aimlessly down the trail. He looked like he was very specifically walking toward me.

I replaced the binoculars and hoisted my pack automatically and resumed my journey down the trail. *This is ridiculous*, I told myself. *You're not being chased by a killer. That doesn't happen to people. Not in real life.*

Oh yeah? I shot back. *I bet that's what Stanley Goebel thought.*

It seemed insane. The notion that it was not a trekker coming toward me (*with no pack and a ski mask on*) but a murderer bent on doing me harm. I told myself that I couldn't really take the idea seriously. But I was walking much faster, as fast as I could without turning it into a jog, and the pit of my stomach had tightened into a cold, slippery knot. I glanced over my shoulder. He was gaining on me.

It does happen, I realized. *It happens every day all over the world that people are killed by other people. And I think it's beginning to happen to me right now. I think the man behind me is here to hunt me down and kill me.*

I didn't know what to do. I tried to think of something, anything, and failed. I just kept walking, too mentally paralyzed to do anything else. I could feel myself beginning to sweat like a pig despite the cold. I desperately forced my mind into some kind of rational order, made myself think of some kind of alternative to walking like an automaton.

Stand my ground and fight? I hadn't seen any weapon. I looked over my shoulder again, as if expecting to see the figure brandishing a sword. He was even closer now, maybe five hundred feet. I picked up my pace to a near-trot but knew that unburdened by a pack he could easily catch up to me. Whatever had crushed Stanley Goebel's skull hadn't been at the murder scene. No bloody rocks lying around. Maybe the figure had an iron pipe tucked inside of his jacket. An iron pipe and a pair of Swiss Army knives. My heart was pounding like a machine gun.

Drop my pack and run? That was the sensible thing to do, but I didn't want to do it. I felt like I would be starting something. He would run to catch me. Then I could no longer pretend that it might be a harmless encounter with a harmless man. I wanted to put that moment off and keep some hope of denial as long as possible. And he would probably catch me. He was in better shape than I was, I could tell that much, and he was wearing sneakers, not hiking boots. Another danger sign. Wearing sneakers on these frequently treacherous trails, especially at this frigid altitude, only made sense if you needed speed.

Drop my pack and scramble up the slope, throw rocks down at him? Also a desperate move. And it would get me away from the trail, away from any hope of rescue.

Still trapped by fear and indecision, I rounded another bend and saw the sweetest sight in the world. The leading wave of trekkers heading to Letdar. A line of trekkers as far as the eye could see, stretched out in twos and threes and fours. I had bemoaned the crowds, the hunt for spare beds, the overpopulation of the trail since the moment I had set foot on it. Now I took it all back.

A wild plan came to mind. I'd stay here, drop my pack, wait for him, pretend I was going to stand my ground. He'd get here just as the first few trekkers arrived. I'd get them to help me overcome him, and we'd drag him back to Manang, I'd come back not just with Stanley Goebel's name but with his killer as well. Drunk on the apparent brilliance of my plan, I shrugged my pack to the ground and turned to face the masked figure.

Who had already turned back. Maybe something in my body language, some physical sign of relief, had given it away. Maybe it wasn't even the killer after all, merely a trekker with sensitive skin out for his morning walk who had just remembered that he had forgotten his pack—although that didn't seem likely. But by the time the first trekkers reached me, he was out of sight. I considered going after him, trying to deputize the newcomers into helping me catch him, but concluded that they would just think altitude sickness had driven me mad. Besides, we weren't going to catch him, he had sneakers on and no pack.

It took me three attempts to put my pack back on because I was shaking violently with fear and adrenaline. I took my hat off and mopped at the sweat on my face and began to walk weakly down the trail. Trekkers nodded and said hi to me as they passed. They probably thought I was going back down because I was sick. I looked sick. I felt sick, sick and overwhelmingly relieved. I'd only been afraid in that way once before, in Africa, when I was sleeping outside and hyenas approached our camp. The raw primal fear of being *prey*.

I walked very fast down the trail, past the endless knots of trekkers, thinking furiously. My first theory was wrong, he hadn't gone to Manang. I wondered why. He could have been far away from the scene of the crime by now, but he went to Letdar instead. Maybe he just wanted to finish the trek, to go over the Thorung La. Maybe he was a traveler just like anyone else here, with a side order of homicidal mania.

I knew roughly where he was now. Which didn't really help. I didn't know which direction he was going. Lots of trekkers wore green jackets, even assuming it wasn't one of those reversible ones that were different colors on each side, and I hadn't seen his face. He would probably just disappear into the crowd of trekkers and cross the Thorung La tomorrow or the next day. Maybe even today.

I was trying to come up with some plan to catch him when I realized I was in Gunsang. I looked over to the abandoned village and saw about half a dozen Nepalese standing around a familiar figure—Gavin, in his battered brown coat. The police, I realized, he'd brought them here, to the body. I walked back to the scene of the crime.

{ 4 }

THE OFFICIAL WORD

The police consisted of five men carrying rifles and one man with a uniform, a handgun, and a laminated cardboard identity card that said ROYAL NEPAL POLICE FORCE. His name was Laxman. He shook my hand and left me to stand next to Gavin as they investigated the crime scene. The investigation consisted of crouching and looking at the body, going through the victim's pockets, and then removing the Swiss Army knives and wrapping the corpse in a large sheet of opaque white plastic presumably brought expressly for this purpose.

"If you had any faith in the Nepali police force," Gavin said, "I'm sorry to tell you that it has been badly misplaced. At first they wanted to arrest me. Even locked me up overnight. Eventually I talked them out of that. Then they decided it was the Maoists. Then they tried to call Kathmandu on the satellite phone. The satellite phone is broken. So they decided it wasn't the Maoists after all. It's a suicide."

"Suicide?" I asked incredulously.

"Right. Any kind of murder up here would be very bad for tourism, you understand. I'll bet once he gets in touch with Kathmandu they'll be very upset that he ever suggested the Maoists. You see, what happened was that he poked his own eyes out and was so maddened by the pain that he beat his head against the wall until it broke. Or something. They decided on this without even leaving their office, so they weren't inconvenienced by the realities of the crime scene. I insisted they come up here to look at him." He shrugged. "You can see how effective that was. Did you have any better luck?"

"Good and bad," I said. "His name is Stanley Goebel." I took a deep breath. "And I think whoever killed him came after me this morning."

Gavin turned and stared at me. "Izzit?"

I told him the story as the Nepalese shouldered the body, wrapped in plastic like a carpet, and three of them carried it draped over their shoulders back toward the trail. Laxman crooked a finger at us, and said, "You must follow." We fell in line behind him and began the trek back to Manang. I wasn't sure if Gavin believed my pursuer was the murderer or not. I was beginning to doubt it myself. Maybe I had just panicked.

"I doubt we're going to make it onto Laxman's Christmas card list," Gavin said. "Troublemakers, that's us. How dare we report a murder to the police?" He shook his head. "If you're right, he's just a few hours behind us, and here we are walking the other way. And just no point in trying to tell them otherwise, believe me. Like a brick fucking wall. They make the Old Rhodeys back home look like models of open-mindedness."

We walked on in silence, following the body, as if part of a highly unconventional funeral procession. I wondered how many dead bodies had been carted up and down this trail. Thousands, probably. It was an old trail, hundreds of years old, once upon a time the trade route used to carry salt from Tibet down to India. At least that was what the Lonely Planet guidebook said. And if you couldn't trust Lonely Planet, whom could you trust?

Manang was the biggest town on this side of the
Thorung La, with a population of maybe a thousand people.
The townspeople lived in a maze of narrow, uneven, cobblestoned alleyways that wound their way around gray stone
buildings three or four stories high. Yaks and mules and
horses wandered the shit-strewn streets, mostly tethered but
some free to roam. South of the old stone town was a cluster
of large wooden trekking lodges, each capable of holding a
hundred or more people. Manang got double the business of
anywhere else on the trail because trekkers generally spent
two nights here in order to acclimatize to the altitude.

The Marsyangdi River ran right by Manang, spanned by
a pair of wire-mesh bridges, and above it loomed an alpine
glacier that seemed close enough to touch. Between the
Marsyangdi and the town the ground was divided into farming lots by century-old walls of heaped rock. Potatoes grew
here, and cabbage, and precious little else. There were trees,
but they were low and misshapen. I had noticed that logs from
pine trees that grew up here burned for ages, because pine
grew so slowly at this height that it was dense as hardwood.

There was a satellite dish, which had impressed me when
I had first arrived, but I gathered from what Gavin had said
that it did not actually work. Power lines were draped over
much of the town, but the nearby microhydro plant had been
out of commission for some weeks, and even though there
was an airstrip just an hour south of the city the repairman
had not yet flown in from Kathmandu to fix it. But each of
the major lodges showed bootleg Chinese laserdisc copies of
Kundun or *Seven Years in Tibet* every night on a generator-
powered television. Progress, of a sort.

Laxman took me to the police headquarters, an old stone-
walled room containing a desk and several chairs, wood pol-

ished smooth by decades of use. He appeared to have had his fill of Gavin, who took it upon himself to follow the other police to see what happened to the body. Laxman sat down at his desk, withdrew an enormous leather-bound book, and opened it about halfway. The page he was on was half filled with crabbed writing. He took up a pen and began to write, and I realized that the book was Laxman's official police journal. I sat down opposite him and waited. I was nervous. They had originally arrested Gavin, locked him up for a night—who was to say they wouldn't change the official story again and pin the crime on us? Not much we could do if they did.

After some time Laxman put down his pen, looked at me, and said, "Passport."

I dug my travel wallet out and passed it to him. He flipped it open, glanced through it, then looked up at me sharply. "The South African says your name is Paul. But your passport says it is Balthazar."

"Oh—but—yeah—it is," I stuttered. "I mean, Balthazar, that's my legal name. But everyone calls me Paul. It's a short form."

He gave me a hard, unbelieving look, and I began to wonder if my parents' fondness for baroque names, which had already caused me untold grief in grade school, was about to land me in a Third World jail. But he simply nodded and made another note in his book.

"I am sorry your friend is dead," he said abruptly.

I was going to protest that he wasn't my friend, but decided not to confuse matters any more than necessary and simply nodded.

"I am very sorry your friend chose to kill himself," he said, emphasizing the last four words.

"He didn't kill himself," I said. "There's no way. That couldn't have happened. Somebody—"

"I have to fill out an official report," he interrupted.

I stared at him.

"I write this official report, and I send it away. To my superior officers in Kathmandu. And at the bottom of this official report goes my signature. Mine. You don't sign it. The South African doesn't sign it. I sign it. Do you understand?"

"Yes," I lied.

"And what this official report will say is that your friend killed himself. Do you understand *that*?"

"He didn't kill himself," I said again. "That's impossible."

"Of course he didn't kill himself," he said. "I am not a complete idiot. But that is what the official report will say."

I opened my mouth and closed it again and looked at him for a little while. Then I said, "I don't understand."

"I am not stationed here to solve white man's murders," he said. "I am stationed here to help rescue trekkers who break their leg, to keep an eye on Tibet, and to kill anyone I know is a Maoist. Now if a Nepali killed your friend, that would be different. Then I would have to do something. I would have to find the man right away. If I could not find him, I would still have to find *a* man. And he would be arrested quickly and sent to rot in jail. But both of us know what happened here. One trekker kills another, what do I care? Do they live here? Do they care about my people? If I say, yes, this a murder, maybe there is a scandal. It gets in the newspapers. It gets in the Lonely Planet. People wonder, should I come to Nepal, should I go trekking? And I do not like trekkers. I think you can see that. I do not like you. But my people need your money. So to risk that, to find one trekker who kills another? What reason do I have? Soon he will be gone back to his own country. Let his own police find him when he kills again. If two Nepalis go to your country, and one kills the other, do your police rush to capture the other and put him in one of your jails? I do not think so."

"They certainly do," I said hotly, though I was not nearly as convinced of this as I tried to sound. "Our police treat everyone the same, and they *definitely* never ignore a *murder* in their backyard."

"I do not think that is so," Laxman said. "You are from Canada, yes? I have been to Canada. I was a Gurkha, you know. Do not think of me as some ignorant man who has never been away from Nepal. I served twelve years in the Indian Army, and I trained once in Canada. I do not believe what you say. I wonder if you believe it."

"That's why you locked Gavin up," I said disbelievingly. "So the guy who killed him had time to get away."

"Quite," Laxman said. "Now go away. Continue with your trek. Cross the Thorung La. Trek all the way back to Pokhara. And then, please, go back to your own country without making any more trouble in mine. We have quite enough trouble here without importing it. Thank you. You may go."

After a little while I stood up. He wasn't incompetent. He certainly wasn't stupid. He just didn't want the hassle, and there was no way I could force it on him.

"Naturally," he warned me, "if you repeat anything I said here, I will deny it and find a reason to arrest you."

"Naturally," I said sarcastically. And I went. What else could I do?

I spent a little time looking for Gavin, but after a while I gave up. It was still early, and I could have gone back to Gunsang, but I decided to spend the night in Braka, a little village twenty minutes' walk toward the airfield. There was a lodge there called the Braka Bakery and Super Restaurant, and it lived up to its name. And I was in no mood to travel any more today. All I wanted to do was shower and eat and read and sleep and start anew tomorrow. And leave poor Stanley Goebel behind.

I was another forty pages into *War and Peace* when Gavin joined me.

"I got a double room again," I said.

"Good," he said.

"What happened to Mr. Goebel?"

"I had his body inspected."

I blinked. "Inspected? By who?"

"By one of the good doctors of the Himalayan Rescue Association," he said, and paused to order seabuckthorn juice, an intensely tangy drink made from a local berry, from the lodge waitress.

I had forgotten that there were three Western volunteer doctors in town, treating trekkers and locals alike. Just two days ago we had gone to their altitude-sickness lecture, held in a cabbage patch just outside the building they occupied.

"What did they say?" I asked.

"She told me that it couldn't have been suicide," he said dryly. "I'm ever so glad that we got that settled. And she confirmed that a Stanley Goebel had signed the attendance register at their altitude-sickness clinic two days ago."

"That's it?"

"Not entirely. She determined that he was killed by a stone. Fragments in his skull or something. And that the knives . . . that was done after he was already dead. And she agrees that he died within the last couple of days. She tried to look for fingerprints on the knives and jacket . . ." He shrugged. "Not exactly her area of expertise. But she thinks the knives were wiped clean."

"Is she going to talk to Laxman?"

"They don't have to," he said. "He came and talked to us. And made it very clear to all concerned that our opinion was as valuable as a fart in a hurricane, and that if he so desired, he could have us expelled from Nepal or possibly jailed for interfering in a police investigation."

"Pretty much what he said to me," I said.

"To her credit Dr. Janssen didn't seem particularly intimidated. But I don't think it really matters whether she says anything or not. Whether we say anything or not."

I nodded, slowly, thinking it over as he poured himself a glass of juice. He was right. Even if Laxman suddenly morphed into a highly motivated Sherlock Holmes, Stanley Goebel's killer was going to walk. No evidence of any kind. Even if it had been him on the trail behind me, an event I was beginning to think of as an attack of paranoia rather than that of a murderer, that simply narrowed him down to one of the throng in Letdar or Thorung Phedi tonight. They could have locked down the villages and interrogated every traveler and it still wouldn't have helped.

"So I reckon there's only one thing we can do," Gavin said.

"What's that?" I asked.

"Sweet fuck-all." He raised his glass in a mock toast. "To Stanley Goebel, unlamented and unavenged. There but for the grace of God go all of us."

I clinked my lemon tea against his seabuckthorn juice, and we drank to the dead man.

UP, AND DOWN AGAIN

In the dream I was climbing Mount Everest. There was a blizzard, but I knew I was on Everest, almost at the summit, pulling myself up the vertical Hillary Step on a fixed line. It seemed remarkably easy, and I felt a giddy sense of triumph. *Eat your heart out, Jon Krakauer*, I thought. I was almost near the top, where two figures waited for me. I recognized them, two old friends, but couldn't call their names to mind. I pulled myself up farther, near to the top, where the line was anchored around a rusty iron pole, and the blizzard thinned out and I saw them clearly. Laura and Stanley Goebel. They stared down at me with knives in their eyes. I felt myself slipping, and when I looked down I saw that frostbite had turned my fingers the blue of glacial ice. I tried to pull myself up to the top, and slowly, one at a time, my fingers fell off my hands and tumbled down into the swirling snow. It didn't hurt at all. I tried to hold on with my thumbs, but they too snapped like icicles and fell away, and I plummeted back into the blizzard. For a moment everything went dark, then I was lying on my back in a snowbank and the sun shone brilliantly into my eyes. *I made it*, I thought. And then a man wearing a ski mask crouched over me. And I couldn't move. Ice had formed around me, trapping me in the ground. Something glittered in the man's hand.

"Paul," Gavin whispered urgently, shaking me awake. "Time to go."

I made guttural noises, opened my eyes, lifted my head. I was cocooned in my sleeping bag, fully dressed, with only a razor-narrow slit open to let in the thin subzero air. Thorung High Camp, I remembered. That was where we were. Except Jim-Bair-the-American had rechristened it Thorung Death Camp.

"What time is it?" I asked.

"Nighttime," he said. "Dawn in about half an hour. Get your kit together. I'll order you some tea."

He left. Normally I would have rolled back into the sleeping bag and gotten another hour's sleep. But today was the big day, today we crossed the much-discussed Thorung La. I pulled myself together, put my boots on, and assembled my pack by Maglite. The two other occupants of the room still slept. The gravel floor crunched under my feet as I stumbled toward the door and made my way outside. I left the pack against the wall of the long low bungalow and walked to the outhouse. My breath formed thick clouds in the air. Up above, the sky was stuffed full of stars, impossibly clear and bright. Around me was the stark lunar landscape of sixteen thousand feet, lightly dusted by snow. Snow for Gavin at last, hurrah.

I swallowed down three cups of tea, bought three Snickers bars as the day's trail food, filled my water bottle from the High Camp's jerry cans, and we were on our way as dawn began to stain the eastern sky. Gavin made the first snowball of his life and threw it at me. Both his technique and his aim were terrible, and I demonstrated to him how it was done.

After that we settled down and just walked. It was a steep hike, but not as steep as yesterday's near-vertical climb from Thorung Phedi to Thorung Death Camp. And after almost two weeks of trekking, my uphill muscles were things of iron. I'd had a headache the previous night, but that day, climbing to the Thorung La, I felt terrific, vibrantly alive. Many of the Death Camp inhabitants had seemed suicidally miserable last night. I was glad to have had the benefit of an extra two days' acclimatization around Manang. Even so, I had felt the hypoxia. I had tried to play cards, but I couldn't add or remember the scores; had tried to read, but couldn't focus for more than a sentence at a time. In the end, like everyone else I simply waited to grow tired enough to fall asleep while drinking loads of garlic soup and lemon tea. The HRA doctors had told us that hydration was key to minimizing altitude sickness. According to Nepalis, garlic and lots of it was the cure.

One of them seemed to have worked. I was breathing quickly, but not panting, and moving at a steady pace. Gavin, who was awesomely fit and seemed to thrive as the oxygen grew more depleted, walked faster and took fewer breaks than I, and soon disappeared into the distance. Suited me. We got along well, but we were both ready to sever our weeklong travel partnership. Both of us were loners at heart.

My dream had not dissipated, which was unusual. Usually I forget my dreams completely within moments of waking. This one had resonance. They had warned us at the HRA cabbage-patch lecture that we might have strange and vivid dreams up here, and I guessed discovering a dead body and maybe being pursued by a killer was bound to contribute to that.

I still hadn't decided whether the masked man was a killer or not. It didn't make any sense that Joe Random Trekker would go for a walk with no pack and a ski mask, then abruptly double back just as I happened to turn a bend and see that the trail was no longer empty. But it didn't make any sense that he would return from Letdar to track me down either. So I'd found out his victim's name. So what? How did that threaten him? Why wouldn't he just keep going up the trail? He had committed the perfect crime. He didn't need to track me down; it only put him in more danger. Unless he thought I had found out something else, something that would identify him. But I couldn't imagine what that would be.

For that matter—I stopped all of a sudden, not to take a break, but because my thoughts were racing in this thin air, and a question had occurred to me for the first time. Why had we found the body at all? The killer had presumably thrown Stanley Goebel's pack, and the rock he had used to kill him, over the cliff near where the murder had taken place. Why wouldn't he have disposed of the body in the same way? What possible reason did he have to leave it there to be discovered?

Maybe somebody had come along, who would have seen him, after discarding the pack and rock, before discarding the body. Possible. It seemed unlikely, but possible. But why wouldn't he have gotten rid of the body first?

Did he *want* it to be discovered? Was there some sick psychological thing with the knives where he wanted the world to see what he had done? Did he want the world to see Stanley Goebel disfigured? But Abigail had said he was traveling on his own. The killer was presumably either a complete stranger or a very recent acquaintance. So why this hateful mutilation?

Another trekker passed me, and I resumed my slow trudge upward, thinking. Laura's body could have been disposed of too. Or at least hidden out of sight, in the rocks and weeds. Instead it was left draped on the black sand of Mile Six Beach like a bloody flag. Why call attention to it?

What was the connection? There had to be a connection, I decided. Two murders so similarly perverse, of travelers in Third World countries; two perfect, unsolvable crimes; they had to be connected by something other than my presence. But I could not even begin to think of what the connection might be. And I felt like I shouldn't even try. I shouldn't think any more about Laura. I had been thinking about her for two years. It was past time to let her go.

About an hour after leaving Death Camp we got to a tea-house that was reportedly midway to the top. I ate a frozen Snickers bar with some difficulty and paid a full U.S. dollar to wash it down with lemon tea served in a small metal cup. My hands were cold, even inside the two layers of gloves I had rented in Pokhara, and I removed my gloves and warmed my fingers on the cup, thinking uncomfortably of my dream. Water has a much lower boiling temperature at that altitude, so the metal did not feel uncomfortably hot.

I climbed onward, past a gaggle of French package tourists wielding ski poles, who were necessarily moving at the speed of their slowest member, past six-inch iron bars engraved with apparently random numbers that protruded from the thin snow cover to mark the path. The sun had risen behind us and the snowcapped peaks all around us glittered like diamonds. The only colors of the landscape were dark gray earth and white snow. It was astonishingly beautiful, like walking through a Group of Seven painting. I tromped slowly but steadily in the thick dark gravel, moving at a constant comfortable pace. An old seabed, I remembered. Aquatic fossils are found at the summit of Mount Everest. Long ago, before India plunged into the Asian continent and forced the folds of the Himalaya high into the sky, this very earth I walked on had been deep beneath the sea.

I passed a cairn on the left side of the trail; an American tourist, according to the headstone, who had died here not so long ago. It didn't say whether it was a blizzard or altitude sickness that got him. Or a killer.

And then I looked up and saw a blaze of color ahead. Strands of triangular Buddhist prayer flags by the hundred, red and yellow and green and blue and white, festooned the apex of our trek. Anticipated, feared, spoken of in hushed tones for two weeks now, the Thorung La.

There was a teahouse here — rebuilt every year, according to the guidebook, after being destroyed by the winter — and a crowd of triumphant trekkers milled about and took each other's pictures. I wasn't really in the mood, but I got a Dutch girl to take my picture against the sign that reported that I had reached the altitude of 5,400 meters, aka 17,500 feet, the same height as Everest Base Camp. I ate another Snickers bar, had another metal cupful of the most expensive lemon tea in Asia, and tried to work out why I felt so disappointed.

The rocks on the other side of the pass were brown and beige, and if I squinted I could make out a green patch far below. Muktinath, I presumed. An oasis in the desert Tibetan Plateau, according to my Lonely Planet guidebook, politically Nepali, but in terms of culture and ethnicity and geography, it was part of fabled and mysterious Tibet. I took one last look around at the clean, stark panorama and began the long trek down.

Downhill was hell. When I finally arrived in Muktinath I thought my knees were going to buckle and collapse. I staggered past the series of temples on the edge of town, walked up to the first lodge I saw, and asked for a bed. But they were full. I went to the next, and the next, and the next; it was the fourth that had a spare bed. I collapsed on it, surprised at the paucity of lodging, for I knew I had to be part of the leading wave. Most of those crossing today would have begun at Thorung Phedi, a good hour below Death Camp.

I made myself get up and washed myself with a bucket bath. There was no hot water, but I was beyond caring. I shaved with a broken fragment of a mirror. I wanted to wash my clothes, but the communal tap nearest my lodge was being used by a Nepali family to fill a series of large buckets, so instead I went to the police checkpoint to sign in. The bored policeman flipped through my passport, stamped my trekking permit, and gestured to the ledger. I wrote down my name, nationality, passport number, etc. Gavin had already checked in. I flipped through the last few pages of the ledger, thinking to myself that somewhere here was the killer's name.

And then I saw it. Eight pages and two days ago. Stanley Goebel, the entry read. Passport number and all.

I stared at it until a pair of trekkers came up behind me and the policeman motioned me to make way. I stared at the ledger as they went through the procedure. Had Stanley Goebel's killer taken his identity? Used his passport? Or was Stanley Goebel alive and well, was the dead man someone else? Had Abigail the Australian been wrong? Or had she lied?

I wanted a picture of that entry, and I had my camera on me, but I could easily imagine the policeman being sticky about letting me take one; so after the two trekkers had left, I took my camera out, set the flash to on, and asked the policeman if I could take his picture, idly flipping the ledger back to the appropriate page. He puffed his chest out proudly, and I snapped a shot of him—and, apparently accidentally, a shot of the ledger as I lowered the camera. I wasn't sure it would turn out, but it would have to do.

I hobbled back to my lodge, my mind churning. I ordered fried noodles with cheese and vegetables and wrote in my journal until the food arrived. I didn't realize how hungry I was until the plate was before me. After it was empty I went back to my room to give my legs a rest, intending to track down Gavin later at whatever lodge he was at and tell him the news.

But I didn't do that. Instead I closed my eyes and opened them again well after dawn.

My legs were fine the next day. Unless I tried to go even the slightest bit downhill, in which case bolts of agony shot through my knees and quadriceps with every step. I knew within moments of getting out of bed that I wasn't trekking out of Muktinath that day. That, and the soon-discovered fact that this side of the Thorung La was the easy half of the Annapurna Circuit and thus overpopulated with groups of twenty or thirty pudgy German package tourists, explained why it was hard to find a room in Muktinath. I wondered what happened to those who came late over the pass. I didn't envy them, finally arriving at what they thought was their destination after one of the most physically grueling days of their life, only to find out that there was no room at the inn, and they had another hour to go before reaching the next group of lodges.

I could walk around town, albeit slowly and stiffly, and I looked for Gavin, but he was gone. And maybe that was for the best. Why rehash it? Yes, the appearance of the name Goebel in the Muktinath ledger was mysterious; and yes, in the back of my mind I'd had the idea that I could send my picture of it to the HRA doctor who had examined the body, whose name Gavin could tell me, to compare to the handwriting used when Stanley Goebel had signed in to the Manang ledger; but really, what was the point? Regardless of the name, a man had been murdered and his murderer had gotten off scot-free. There was no point in sifting through the ashes of those two cold facts.

And yet. It was all the whys that bothered me. Why was there a murder in the first place? Why the knives? Why was the body not hidden? Why had the masked man followed me on the trail? And now why this confusion over the name? And the most fundamental question: Why was it all so much like the murder of Laura Mason in Limbe, Cameroon, more than two years ago?

It had been a typical night on the truck. No, scratch that; it had been a good night. There had been no rain.

Chong and Kristin and Nicole had cooked and cleaned. There
was plenty of firewood for once, and we had a big bonfire, and
Steven and Hallam and I had passed the guitar back and forth
and sung songs. A few curious locals had squatted and stared
at us, but not the huge crowds we had sometimes drawn in the
desert and in Nigeria. Limbe was a pretty regular stop for
overland trucks and its inhabitants fairly cosmopolitan.

After dinner Laura and Carmel and Emma and Michael
went swimming on the black-sand beach. I wasn't in the mood
to swim, so I stayed with the rest. We played guitar and
passed joints around and everyone got a little high. We remi-
nisced fondly about the epic meal we had had in Nigeria, the
spacecakes in Dixcove, the FanIce in Ghana. Food was
always a popular topic on the truck. We talked about whether
we would find a way across to Kenya by land. At that point
we were still hopeful. There was talk of going through Chad.

Eventually it got late. Carmel and Emma and Michael
had returned. I assumed Laura had come back to our tent
and gone to sleep. I decided to accompany Hallam and
Nicole for a midnight swim before joining Laura in the tent.
Hallam took his midsized Maglite to light our way, even
though the moon was bright and it hardly seemed necessary.
When I first saw her I thought it was a dead animal, a big dog
or something, lying in a puddle. It wasn't until five or ten seconds of Hallam aiming the light at her that my mind finally
clicked and identified her. I think it was the same for Hallam
and Nicole. Whoever had killed Laura had stripped her
naked and gutted her like an animal, and she had died with
her hands on her belly, pathetically trying to keep her insides
from spilling out. She had been gagged with a black rag. And
there were knives in her eyes.

The next day I could walk and I trekked through the
Arizonian desert landscape, in the shadow of Dhaulagiri, the

world's seventh highest mountain, to the medieval village of Kagbeni at the end of the remote Mustang Valley. The following day I walked along the nearly dry bed of the Kali Gandaki River to the town of Jomsom, even bigger than Manang. I did not want to trek anymore, and Jomsom had an airstrip. I bought a plane ticket with Buddha Air. The next morning I made my way through the Kafka-esque chaos of the Jomsom airport, where they had demolished the old building and not really gotten around yet to constructing another. I boarded a prop plane, overloaded with bags of the apples grown around Jomsom. The engines were so loud they gave us cotton wads to stick in our ears. The plane carried me from the Wild West desert of Jomsom, over conifer forests, and deciduous forests, and hills terraced into rice paddies, and subtropical jungle, and back to the city of Pokhara, five days' worth of trekking compressed to twenty-five minutes. My Annapurna Circuit was complete.

6

LIFE ON A
LONELY PLANET

Trekking is wonderful, but it was good to be back in civilization. Pokhara's Lakeside district was like Disneyland for backpackers; nothing but restaurants, bars, bookstores, souvenir shops, supermarkets, pharmacies, trekking outfitters, massage parlors, music stores, banks, camera shops, travel agencies, Internet cafes, and about a hundred lodges armed with running water and reliable electricity. I could have parachuted into Lakeside naked but for my passport and ATM card and been fully outfitted for travel within twenty-four hours.

I went to the Sacred Valley Inn, took a room, repossessed the gear I had deemed inessential-for-trekking from their locker, and had a long hot shower. I ate pepper steak and drank wine and read a two-day-old *International Herald Tribune* at the Moondance Cafe, which wouldn't have looked out of place in any First World country, except for its affordable prices. I traded my copy of *War and Peace* and a hundred rupees for a bootleg copy of Peter Matthiessen's *The Snow Leopard*. I took my trekking pictures into a camera shop to be developed.

And then I continued my investigation.

I began with the police, and as I expected, they were no help. They had not heard that a man had died on the trail. They would not contact their compatriots in Manang to see if there were any new developments. I should wait for the official report to be filed in Kathmandu before doing anything. It wouldn't be more than a few months.

After that I called the Canadian embassy in Kathmandu.

"Welcome to Canada, *bienvenue au Canada*," a disembodied voice said. "For service in English, press one. *Pour service en français, appuyez le deux.*"

I pushed nothing, having learned long ago the best way to avoid voice-mail mazes. After a little while a telephone began to ring and a real-live woman answered it.

"Hello?" she said.

"Hello," I said. "My name is Paul Wood. I'm a Canadian citizen. I'm calling from Pokhara. I'm calling because I want to know if you've been told that a Canadian man named Stanley Goebel was found dead while trekking in the Annapurna district."

"One moment, please," she said, as if she got this kind of call all the time and was going to transfer me to an extension specifically reserved for death confirmations. I went into the limbo of hold.

"Hello?" a man said eventually. "Can I help you?"

I repeated my spiel and went into hold one more time.

"Hello?" a different man said. "Are you calling about Stanley Goebel?"

"Yes, I am," I said.

"And who are you?"

"My name is Paul Wood, I'm a Canadian citizen."

"And what is your interest in the matter?"

"I found the body."

There was a pause as the man absorbed that. Then he said,

"Well, thank you for calling in, but the Nepali government has already informed us about Mr. Goebel. His family has been notified and his body is on its way home."

"What exactly did the Nepali government inform you of?" I asked.

I think he could hear the edge in my voice, and he began to erect a bureaucratic wall to hide behind. "Their final report has not yet been filed," he said cautiously, "but they have informed us on an informal basis that Mr. Goebel regrettably committed suicide."

"Is that so. Well, I'm calling to inform you that that is regrettably not the case. Mr. Goebel was murdered."

"I beg your pardon?"

"Murdered," I repeated. "Violently killed. Somebody smashed his head in and stuck knives in his eyes, and the Nepali police are lying through their teeth about it because they can't be bothered to deal with a murder. I have pictures that prove this."

"Mr. . . . what was your name again?"

"Paul Wood."

"Mr. Wood," he said. "I've read the Nepali report myself, and it quite definitively states that Mr. Goebel obviously killed himself, and it makes no mention of any *knives* . . ."

"I am the person who found the body," I said, speaking each word slowly and distinctly. "I'm telling you that the Nepali report is a pack of lies."

"I see. Mr. Wood, obviously I can't accept those claims unless they are confirmed by the Nepali police."

"The police don't want to do anything with it."

"Mr. Wood . . . Obviously we appreciate that you're calling in to help us with this tragic case, but if you don't have any evidence of what you're saying, then there's very little we can do. The only official document here is the Nepali report, and it says quite clearly that the death was a suicide."

"The only *official document*?" I said incredulously. "That's what you care about? Whether or not I have official documents? I've got pictures, and they show beyond question that he was murdered."

"Now, of course if you'd like to get in touch with the Nepali police to aid them with their investigation, I can put you in touch with some of the relevant officials, who I'm sure would be very interested in whatever photographs you have. As I said, their report isn't final yet, and can still be amended—"

"What's your name?" I demanded.

After a long pause he said, very grudgingly, "My name is Alan Tremblay."

"All right. Mr. Tremblay, I have just told you that a fellow Canadian citizen was murdered in cold blood up there, that the Nepali police are covering it up, and that I have photographs that prove this. Do you understand that that is what I was saying?"

"I understand, but our policy is to accept the Nepali government's official report and investigation instead of poorly substantiated phoned-in claims of murder from random travelers."

"You understand fine but you just don't give a shit, is that it?"

"Mr. Wood, I think that is completely uncalled for. I am perfectly willing to connect you with some Nepali police officials if you would like to assist them in their—"

I hung up.

I was still fuming when I returned to the 1-Hour Photo Development shop and picked up my pictures. I stopped at a cafe and bought a Coke, a little surprised that my addiction to lemon tea had abruptly vanished now that the trek was over, and sipped from it as I flipped through the pictures. Monkeys, rickety bridges, towering waterfalls, tiny villages, prayer wheels, mana walls, mule trains, mountains mountains and more mountains, fellow trekkers, me upon the Thorung La. And those three shots of the dead body, a little overexposed. And my shot of the Muktinath ledger. It had come out perfectly and I could make out the Goebel entry very clearly.

A brain wave hit me, and I paid for my Coke and went to the Pokhara office of the Annapurna Conservation Authority. We had had to sign in here to get our trekking permits. The office was quiet, and the man behind the desk didn't mind if I looked through their ledger to see when my friends had begun their trek. I flipped back through two weeks of entries and began to pore over them. And found Stanley Goebel's entry, in neat handwriting, only a half-dozen places ahead of my own. He must have stood practically next to me in line that morning.

His handwriting in this ledger was very different from that in the photo. Clearly the work of someone else.

So, after killing Stanley Goebel, the murderer used his name, and presumably his passport and trekking permit, to check in to Muktinath. For no conceivable reason. Hell, the checkpoints were in practice optional, you could walk right by them if you wanted to and nobody would demand that you check in.

No conceivable *logical* reason, that is. But then there was no conceivable logical reason to kill him in the first place. Maybe he wasn't traveling alone, maybe he started his travels out with a friend, and they had a falling-out, and the friend decided to follow him and kill him? Maybe he was killed by somebody who got his kicks by killing people and pretending to be them for a while? *Who knows what evil lurks in the hearts of men?* I thought. Clearly this was a case for the Shadow, not for me.

I was about out of options. Nepal didn't care. Canada didn't care. I felt like at the very least I had a responsibility to

write all this down, document what had happened, tell somebody about it in case it ever happened again. I thought of
Interpol. I wasn't sure what they did, but I knew they were
some kind of international police force. But what exactly
were they going to do when the Nepalis were stonewalling?

In desperation I decided on the last refuge of the conspiracy theorist: the Internet.

The Internet cafes that littered Pokhara had come to
a communal arrangement that kept Internet access prices at
seven rupees per minute, about six U.S. dollars an hour,
approximately ten times the price in Kathmandu. It was
unabashed OPEC-style cartel capitalism, and I had to admire
it, though I wondered how they kept members in line. If
somebody tried to boost their business by competing on
price, did the cartel take him out back and beat him with a
stick?

I sat down at one that competed on quality instead, with a
relatively high-speed ISDN line instead of the slow staticky
phone connections used by most. The computers were
newish, probably made in India, and came with headsets
used to make scratchy inaudible telephone calls over the
Internet. I launched Internet Explorer and then I typed into
the address bar: *thorntree.lonelyplanet.com*.

The enormous power wielded by the Lonely Planet
publishing empire over backpacking tourism has to be seen
to be believed. With the stroke of a pen their writers can turn
hot spots into ghost towns, or draw thousands of travelers to
what had been a backwater. They can determine with a single
well-chosen word whether lodge owners and their families
will be wealthy or bankrupt within the year. They have de
facto control over all budget travel in developing nations:

who goes there, when, where they go, and what they do. Experienced travelers talk of "the Lonely Planet effect" when a hitherto unmentioned place or activity they recommend leads to a deluge of travelers, the sprouting of a hundred lodges and souvenir shops, and a wave of overcommercialization and traffic that almost inevitably destroys whatever quality prompted the recommendation in the first place.

Of course this is not their fault. The fault lies with the hordes of travelers who follow their Lonely Planet bible faithfully without once venturing away from its safety blanket; and with the world, for having so many budget travelers and so few magical places that can be accessed cheaply and conveniently. All Lonely Planet does is publish guidebooks better than the competition's. As a result fully 90 percent of travelers in developing countries rely on them for guidance.

Since guidebooks are only updated every year or two, and destinations change more rapidly than that, Lonely Planet maintains a website where they provide recent updates on the hundreds of countries they cover. They also provide a forum called the Thorn Tree where Lonely Planet travelers can talk to one another. The Thorn Tree seemed like the best place for me to tell the world what I had found. After all, despite my many reservations, I was a Lonely Planet traveler myself. It seemed right that I should tell my people what I had discovered. It was the best I could think of to do.

I logged on as "PaulWood" and created a new topic in the Indian Subcontinent area, entitled "Murder on the Annapurna Circuit." Thinking, *That should get their attention.* Then I wrote down what had happened as simply and shortly as I could. I didn't mention the knives—it seemed gratuitous to do so. I didn't mention being pursued on the trail. I didn't mention Cameroon. I described finding the body, discovering his name, the stonewalling of the Nepali police, the Muktinath ledger, the unhelpful Canadian embassy. I ended with a warning to those in the region that there was a real live murderer on the loose and a plea for anyone who knew anything else to get in touch with me and/or post what they knew here.

I wasn't concerned about Laxman's warning not to cause more trouble. For one thing I doubted too many official Nepali government sources read the Thorn Tree. For another it barely qualified as trouble. A few thousand people would read it and shake their heads in surprise and dismay, assuming the LP Web editors did not censor it in the first place, and in a few weeks the topic would disappear, the Thorn Tree was a busy place. At best it might be shrunk to a one-line mention in the "Dangers and Annoyances" section of the next edition of LP's *Trekking in the Nepal Himalaya*. And that would be the final resting place of Stanley Goebel.

By the time it was finished it was night and I was tired. I went to bed in my comfortable double room in the Sacred Valley Inn, and another wave of longing came over me all of a sudden, a deep, aching, desperate wish that I lived in a parallel universe where Laura had never been murdered, that she was here with me, that I could hold her warmth in my arms and nestle my chin on her shoulder and smell the clean sweet smell of her hair. I was glad I was so tired. The memories were too painful to dwell upon.

When I woke up I showered and brushed my teeth and went straight to the nearest Internet cafe. I didn't really think there would be any responses yet, but there might be. I tapped my fingers impatiently as I listened to the screech of the dial-up protocol handshake, a sound as ubiquitous and recognizable around the world as a pop song.

There were three responses, each one very brief.

```
Anonymous       What can I say but "holy shit"?
10/27 08:51     Y'all watch out up there. Maybe
                The Bull changed continents...?


JenBelvar       What is The Bull?
10/27 11:08


Anonymous       Alleged serial killer on the
10/27 14:23     African trail. Read the boxed
                text in "Africa—the South."
```

It didn't mean anything that the first and third poster
were anonymous. About half the Thorn Tree posts were from
users who didn't bother logging in. Maybe they were the
same person, maybe not. It was a place to exchange information, not identity.

I stared at the screen for a long time. Specifically at the
phrase *serial killer*. I hadn't articulated it before. Then I went
to the biggest bookstore in Pokhara. On a rack full of the latest LP books they had no less than two copies of *Africa—the
South*, wrapped in plastic, which seemed bizarre to me—how
many people fly from Kathmandu to Johannesburg? I talked
them into letting me open the plastic and read it for a few
minutes in exchange for two hundred rupees.

7

THE TALE OF THE BULL

Boxed text, page 351, 1998 edition of Lonely Planet's *Africa — the South*:

THE BULL

As this book went to press a rumour had spread like wildfire that there is a serial killer targeting backpackers in Southern Africa. It is true that there have been several murders of budget travelers in the region within the past few months, but our investigation leads us to believe that they are not connected.

The rumour states that a man who calls himself The Bull is roaming the region, finding lone travelers, accompanying them to out-of-the-way spots, then murdering them and mutilating their eyes. The Bull is said to be a European backpacker, not an African resident, and is alleged to have left a trail of bodies from Cape Town to Malawi and back again.

The facts are that four independent travelers have been found murdered within the last three months: two in South Africa, one in Mozambique, and one in Malawi. In both of the South African cases the eyes of the victims were in fact mutilated. However, our investigation indicates that a murder on the Mozambican coast and a murder in rural Malawi took place on consecutive days in June of this year, which is difficult to reconcile with the work of a single individual. Furthermore, the fact that there is a name associated with the rumour, particularly one as colourful as "The Bull", leads us to believe that there is some myth mixed with the grim reality of these murders.

Lonely Planet urges all travelers to take all reasonable precautions wherever they go, to stay informed of local conditions via the Updates section on lonelyplanet.com and the word on the trail, to choose their travel companions carefully, and to avoid hitchhiking and traveling alone whenever possible. Even though we do not feel the evidence indicates that there is anything to the rumour of The Bull, Southern Africa includes politically unstable states and a significant minority of its population lives in desperate poverty. While South Africa is politically stable and relatively highly developed its crime rates in certain poverty-stricken areas are alarming. Travel safe.

I read it three times. Then I read it again.
Mutilating their eyes. The eyes of the victims were in fact mutilated. The Bull.

I rented a boat and went paddling about on the pretty lake that adjoins Pokhara. It helped me expend some of my nervous energy. It helped me to think rationally again, to organize my thoughts into what I knew and what I suspected and what might be.

The undisputed facts: Laura had been killed in Cameroon. Stanley Goebel had been killed in Nepal. Two other backpackers had been killed in South Africa. All of those killings involved eye mutilations. The two South African murders were already rumored to be the work of a serial killer. A traveler, not a local.

LP hadn't said specifically what kind of mutilation had been performed. But I had a pretty good guess. It hadn't said that the other two African killings had *not* involved mutilation — and those murders had occurred in Malawi and Mozambique, countries as poor and undeveloped as they come, and it wouldn't surprise me at all if this information simply wasn't available.

And how many had not been reported murdered at all? How many Stanley Goebels were out there, officially suicides or accidents?

It wouldn't be the first time a madman preyed on travelers. There had been that psychopath in Australia, not so long ago, who had tortured and murdered seventeen backpackers before one got away and reported him to the police. But this would be the first one who actually went traveling to find his victims.

No, that's not necessarily true; he might just be the first one who was *noticed*. It was so easy to commit murder in these circumstances. It was stunning how easy. Third World police who really don't care, an endless supply of victims who deliberately seek out remote locations on their own, amid a constantly shifting crowd of travelers who meet and leave each other, appear and disappear without word or notice, always en route to somewhere else. With a cool head and a cruel heart it would be the easiest thing in the world.

Except Lonely Planet didn't believe it. Primarily because two murders had occurred on consecutive days. But was that really the case? They had occurred in Malawi and Mozambique — could the information that came out of there really be relied upon? Might one or the other in fact have happened a few days earlier or later? Had someone confused the date of discovery with the date of the murder? It was possible. It was entirely possible.

From Southern Africa to here. It occurred to me that I knew someone who had traveled from South Africa to Nepal and had been intimately involved with this murder. Gavin. But no, that made no sense. He had the best alibi in the world; I doubted we had spent more than an hour or two apart from one another after we met and joined forces in Tal, five days before Gunsang. And he certainly couldn't have killed Stanley Goebel, he was with me all day. With an accomplice . . . ? The *Scream* solution? No. Ridiculously complicated, didn't make any sense. And besides, I knew Gavin. If he was sick in the head, he sure concealed it well. He had struck me as one of the most moral people I had ever met.

I shook my head violently as if to empty it of thoughts and tried to paddle around and around the little island in the lake without thinking. My best ideas usually come to me when I'm not actively seeking them.

Cameroon, I thought. That had to be the key. Nepal and Southern Africa were stuffed full of thousands of backpackers marching lockstep down the various backpacker trails. But Cameroon was in fucking Central Africa. Lonely Planet hadn't published a book on Central Africa for ten years because there wasn't much there except blood and bullets. Cameroon was relatively civilized compared to the Central African Republic or either of the Congos. In fact until Laura's death it had been shaping up as one of my all-time favorite travel experiences. But there were no hordes of Lonely Planeteers there, that was for sure. A few particularly adventurous French tourists, a bunch of grizzled oil expats, and the odd overland truck trip like ours.

I tried to line up the dates in my mind. I remembered, because it had irritated me greatly, that the latest *Africa — the South* edition had come out just after I had left that area. That meant the June deaths mentioned therein had occurred while I was in Africa. In fact they had occurred while I was in

Cameroon. In fact they must have occurred within a couple of weeks of Laura's murder, because we had found her body on the night of June 15.

Which, first of all, made the whole serial-killer theory hard to swallow. Mozambique to Malawi to Cameroon? Three murders, in three very distant and undeveloped African countries, within the span of two weeks? Possible but very hard to believe. And, much to my relief, the timing made a more specific theory, that it had been someone on the truck, completely impossible. Nobody on the truck had left Cameroon before the end of June, of that I was certain. Which cleared the three candidates I had had in the back of my mind.

Maybe there was no serial killer. Maybe The Bull was just a rumor after all. Maybe it was all just an awful coincidence, and I was overwrought because I had had the terrible bad luck of discovering two dead bodies in two years. I told myself that that was probably the case. I told myself again and again. I was still telling myself that on the flight back to California.

TWO

CALIFORNIA

8

SLAVE TO THE GRIND

The return to the real world is always traumatic. When traveling every day is fraught with *intensity*, every meal and bus trip and squalid hostel room an adventure, every new place a fresh assault on the mind and senses; whereas in the real world you can go weeks without raising your head from whatever rut you have dug for yourself. I called the transition from one to the other "decompression." In this case, moving from two months in high-intensity South Asia back to low-intensity San Francisco. And like decompression from scuba diving, if I didn't do it carefully, I just might get the bends.

Still, it was nice to see my old haunts again, even if they were coupled with the bewildering did-the-last-two-months-really-happen? sense that absolutely nothing had changed since I had gone, that my two months of Asian travel equated to a single California day. It was good to eat breakfast at the Pork Store, to have coffee and play chess at the Horseshoe Cafe, to wander aimlessly up and down the West Coast beach, to lie back in my own bed and listen to my favorite music, to cycle across the Golden Gate Bridge into the hills of Marin. And San Francisco is a beautiful city, a wonderful place to return to, even if it had been overrun of late by too much money and too many people and dot-com dreams of avarice.

Thankfully that particular house of cards was in midcollapse when I returned. "This town needs a recession," I had snorted more than once in the previous year, and it looked like I was getting my wish. Many of the hundreds of dot-com companies in the area had been founded on little more than a wing and a prayer and an astonishingly stupid idea, and every day more of them shut their doors or laid off half their staff. While in Asia I had received a half-dozen e-mails from friends or acquaintances informing me, often with curious jubilation, that they were newly unemployed. And while apartment prices weren't yet descending from the stratosphere, they were in a holding pattern for the first time in years.

I wasn't worried about my job, even though I was a programmer for an Internet consulting company. I knew times were going to get leaner as the dot-coms that had flung ridiculous sums of money at us for the last year were winnowed out, but we had a pretty good portfolio of real customers as well, and I was very good at what I did. Even if it all fell apart I had a pretty good nest egg saved up thanks to my decision to accept a cash bonus in lieu of stock options during the previous year, a decision that was much mocked by my friends at the time but seemed prescient now that the company's stock had dropped 80 percent in six months. The lease on my pleasant Cole Valley apartment expired in three months and the landlord had already let me know that I could renew it at the same price if I wanted to. Life was comfortable.

Comfortable. Not the same thing as good. I can't say that life was good, or that I was happy. I had friends in the city, but no close friends. My work was diverting and paid ridiculously well, but I didn't really enjoy it. More and more I got the feeling that life was somehow drifting away from me just as I should be ready, in my late twenties and established at last, to reach out and grab it.

The truth was that I traveled so much, that I insisted my employers give me four months unpaid leave a year, because even though on paper I was one of the most fortunate people on this earth, healthy and wealthy and privileged, I was unhappy in the real world, and I did not know how to make myself happy. The truth was that the last time I was happy, really happy, was in Africa.

Two and a half years before I went to Asia I joined an overland truck trip with the audacious goal of driving all the way from Morocco to Kenya in five months. We went a long way, we went across the Sahara and along the Gold Coast to Cameroon, but we did not drive all the way across Africa. This was in part because a large war broke out in the Congo, and in part because one of our number was murdered on a black-sand beach in Cameroon. Laura Mason. The girl I loved.

Until then it was a weird and wonderful experience. There were twenty of us on the truck, all of us complete strangers traveling independently. It was no catered, guided tour. Our vehicle was thirty years old, army surplus, and we counted ourselves lucky if it broke down only every other day. The company had hired a driver, a mechanic, and a courier to go with us, but within a few weeks they too were just part of the group. Everybody cooked, everybody cleaned, everybody went to the local markets for supplies, everybody worked, everybody got filthy digging the battered old truck out when it got stuck in soft sand and mud, something that happened more than I care to remember. We met in Morocco, which is a tourist trap in a good way, and after a few giddy drunken get-to-know-you weeks there, we went south, where nobody goes. And we drove across the Sahara Desert.

Twenty perfect strangers, thrown together in a grueling and hyperintense situation. We had a major breakdown in the middle of a minefield in the no-man's-land between Morocco and Mauritania. We huddled together on the floor of the truck as we drove through forests of trees bristling with razor-sharp eight-inch thorns in southern Mauritania, clawing at us through the open sides of the truck like that scene from the *Wizard of Oz*. We watched all of our tents and possessions pounded flat by a freak near-hurricane in Mali and spent two days recovering what we could. We suffered the attentions of Bamako's street hustlers. We trekked through Dogon Coun-try just as it was hit by a heat wave, carrying our packs twenty kilometers a day in 130-degree heat. We endured through the eight hours and seven different inspections of the Nigerian border crossing, dealt politely but firmly with the drunken men with guns who demanded outrageous bribes. We took three days to travel the forty kilometers of the Ekok-Mamfe road, a swamp of mud with potholes as large as our truck.

Everyone got sick. Everyone got fed up, everyone got angry, everyone snapped. And we spent every waking hour together whether we liked it or not. And I know it doesn't sound it, but looking back, it was fantastic. We were either going to fragment into screaming hostility or gel into one tight group, and, miraculously, we gelled. We had our squab-bles, had our screaming matches, had our irritable black sheep, but somehow we became a kind of family.

And then one of our sisters was killed.

I returned to California on a Thursday and returned to work on the following Monday. Long experience had taught me to give myself a few days to deal with the jet lag and the decompression. The bends, like I said. I'd gotten them in a big way when I had come back from Africa to Toronto and gone to work the next day. After two hours in the office I had quit my job on the spot.

I swiped my security card at the door and walked into work, past vaguely familiar faces, and sat down at my desk in the hipper-than-thou, open-floor-plan office. It was a good desk, near to the fridge and foozball table. I felt like I had never left, like my entire trip had been a Sunday night's dream.

I sat down before my laptop and cleared the screen saver. The to-do-before-travel list I had left open two months previously was still on the screen. I had 743 new e-mail messages in my work in-box. I dumped the first 650 into a read-later folder and worked my way through the most recent. The project I had been working on, which had been "almost complete" when I had left, was still in beta testing. They wanted me to add a small collection of new features that wouldn't take long. There was another project "almost out of the sales pipeline" and once the specs were written I would be its lead developer. And there was a patronizing buzzword-laden e-mail from the CEO, dated last week, informing us that he keenly regretted laying off twenty people but had great faith in the company's vision and execution. Also, the company was embarking on a cost-cutting plan and cans of Mountain Dew would now cost fifty cents instead of nothing. Snapple, seventy-five cents.

"Paul!" Rob McNeil said, clapping me on the shoulder, and I brightened up almost immediately. He had that effect on people. Rob was one of the company's graphic designers, and one of my favorite people to work with: talented, professional, and easygoing. "You're back! How was your trip, man?"

"Yeah," I said. "Pretty good. How's things here?"

"Interesting question, cogently put. Read the principal's e-mail?"

"Yeah. Can you loan me seventy-five cents for a Snapple?"

"First sign of the apocalypse, boyo. Twenty down, four hundred to go. This is official Résumé Burnishing Week for everyone in the office. Mark my words, 40 percent of today's Web traffic will be to Monster-dot-com." He sat down and shook his head ruefully. "You know, I don't really mind that management has made more incredibly stupid decisions than fleas on a St. Bernard. It goes with the tie, you know? Lack of oxygen to the brain. What I mind is that they think we're even stupider. He writes like he's writing to fucking children."

"But they think we are children," I said. "Idiot savants anyway. Me know language of magic machines, you draw pretty pictures. Daddy, can I have a Snapple? Mommy, you promised me my stock options would vest today!"

He grinned. "That's right. And I don't know about you, but I'm thinking about taking my toys and going home."

The first thing I did, after working through my e-mail and meeting with my manager, Kevin, was go back to the Lonely Planet site and see what the word on the Thorn Tree was. I had avoided checking it since my return to California. I wasn't quite sure why. I supposed it was at least in part because I had been trying to get the whole subject out of my mind and avoid obsessing about it on an hourly basis. But now that I was back at work it somehow seemed safe, as if the banality of my job could neutralize any dangerous thoughts or emotions.

```
Rakesh219        I am Nepali and I say you are a
10/29 19:03      liar. Our police are good people
                 and would not do these things. I
                 always liked people from Canada
                 but now I think that you are
                 liars. I think maybe you murdred
                 this person yourself. Go home to
                 Canada if you think Nepalis are
                 so bad. People like you are
```

always coming here who think
they can tell us what to do
because we are poor. I think you
white people make us poor so can
come here and do bad things to
people and our temples. Everybody
knows that you are weak and all
your women are whores and all
you men sex each other. I hope
more of you come here and get
killed.

JenBelvar   Folks, please don't think the
10/30 11:15   guy above (Rakesh219) is
               representative. Nepalis are the
               nicest, friendliest people in
               all of Asia, if not the world. I
               guess there's one in every
               crowd, especially on the Net.

               The Kathmandu Post had an article
               on Mr. Goebel today. They said
               he was a suicide. I don't know
               what happened but it sounds
               awful and my heart goes out to
               his family and to the people who
               found him.

Anonymous   I met Stanley Goebel in Pokhara
10/31 01:42   just a couple weeks ago, before
               he went trekking. We had a beer
               together and he was a great guy.
               I can't believe some sick fuck
               killed him. But I sure can buy
               the cover-up. Yeah, the Nepalis

are great, but everyone knows
their government is massively
corrupt.

Anonymous   The Bull was just a rumour,
10/31 08:51   people ask about it all the time
                 in the Africa trail, and there
                 weren't any more murders after
                 the ones in the book. And before
                 everyone gets paranoid let me
                 just remind you all that the
                 number 1 killer of backpackers,
                 by a really huge margin, is
                 traffic. Worry about crazy drivers
                 not crazy serial killers.
                 Especially in South Africa—those
                 taxi drivers are nuts!

GavinChait   I'm the South African that Paul
11/01 11:03   Wood mentions, who found the
                 body with him, and I'd like to
                 verify for the record that
                 everything he wrote is true. I'm
                 in Pokhara for the next two days
                 and staying at the Gurkha Hotel
                 if anyone there knows anything
                 or wants to know more.

Inga   I met the girl who was killed in
11/02 05:07   Malawi a couple of years ago just
                 before she died. People there
                 were totally freaked about The
                 Bull, and a lot of people said
                 they'd heard about other people
                 killed who weren't officially

```
           murdered. It sounds just like the
           story here and it's scary. Sure,
           there weren't any more deaths
           after the Lonely Planet book came
           out, but what if that's just
           because the guy (OK, or girl,
           equal opportunity mayhem here)
           read the book and decided to cool
           it down and move somewhere else?
           I think maybe there's some
           sickhead out there who goes
           traveling to kill people.

Anonymous  Hey, everybody needs a hobby.
11/02 18:06
```

That night I met most of my San Francisco friends for an unofficial reunion dinner. Rob and Mike and Kelley and Ian and Tina, people I worked with, and Ron and Toby, who like me hailed from Toronto and like me had been brain-drained down here by the almighty American dollar. We ate at Tu Lan, a hole-in-the-wall in the worst area of the city that serves the best Vietnamese food on the planet.

Everyone talked about layoffs, recession, the collapse of the stock market, and the hubris of last year's paper multimillionaires, mostly with a relieved sense of *schadenfreude*. We had spent the last two years in an environment where the subtext was that you were a total failure as a human being if you weren't a millionaire by age thirty, and I think everyone was grateful to have that kind of pressure off their shoulders.

They didn't ask about my travels other than vague "how was the trip?" questions. I answered equally vaguely. I had learned over the years that almost nobody wants to know. Nobody wants to know the war stories, nobody wants to hear about the irritations and frustrations of travel, or about the madnesses and cultural events you've witnessed, and they really don't want to know about the wonderful experiences that you had and they did not. Experienced travelers want to know, and close friends want to hear you tell it, but these were neither. Of course they would have listened to the story of Murdered Man's Body Found on Trail, but I couldn't bring myself to do that, couldn't reduce him to an anecdote. Not yet anyway.

We ate, we drank, we smoked, we talked, we laughed, we exchanged catty comments about mutual acquaintances and friends at work, we speculated about whether our waiter was gay, we had a good time. I had a good time. I really did. I enjoyed it. But I kept looking around and wondering why these people were my friends. Was it just by default? Just because we happened to have met one day at school or work, and found each other's company acceptable, and met each other again often enough that we grew comfortable in each other's presence, and now we called that friendship? They were good people, all of them, and I enjoyed their company. But was it any real mystery why none of them were *close* friends? Were any of them really my tribe?

Did I even have a tribe? I pondered that as I sat on the N-Judah subway/streetcar back home. My family, never close, had fragmented around the continent. I could not remember the last time my sisters and my brother and my parents and I had all been in the same room. I had had close friends in high school, and they still lived back in Canada, and when I visited there we all acted like we were still a band of brothers. But of course we knew we weren't. Time and distance had worked their inevitable decay, and I had grown apart from them, and they from me. We called each other friends only to honor the memory of the friendship we once had.

There was my Africa tribe, the tribe of the truck. But they were almost all Brits and Aussies and Kiwis, mostly living in London, and a tribe six thousand miles away is in many ways

worse than no tribe at all. And I'd seen them only once after
Cameroon. I'd felt then that our bond was unchanged, even
stronger, that Laura's tragedy had in some way sealed us
together. But was that really true? Was I just romanticizing?
And if they were my tribe, why wasn't I in London right this
very minute?

Maybe I belonged to the tribe of people who have no
tribe. Maybe I would stay in that tribe forever. And maybe
almost everybody I knew belonged to that tribe too, and we
all spent half our social energy hiding it from one another.

I fell asleep desperately wishing for Laura.

I started falling for Laura, or more accurately
started admitting to myself that I had fallen for her the
moment I saw her, the day both of us nearly died for
chocolate-chip cookies. A day that didn't take place in any
country on this earth. It says so right in my passport. The
French- and Arabic-language stamps report that I left
Morocco on April 14 and entered Mauritania on April 16. It
was the day between, the fifteenth of April 1998, that we
afterward called Cookies to Die for Day.

The only way to go overland from Morocco to Mauritania
is in a military convoy that leaves twice a week. At first I
assumed this was just paranoid bureaucratic convention. I
changed my mind when we drove past the first shattered
Land Rover. We saw a good half dozen of those, plus a few
heaps of metal that might once have been motorcycles, the
half-buried skeleton of a truck that looked disturbingly like
ours, and occasional piles of bleached camel bones. Once we
saw an actual land mine, unearthed from the sand by the
desert wind. It looked like a rusted, Frisbee-size can of tuna.

On our second day in no-man's-land Big Bertha broke
down. Big Bertha was our Big Yellow Truck, thirty-year-old

army surplus, never designed to cross the Sahara where the omnipresent sand wreaks endless havoc on every moving part of any machine foolish enough to enter. For the umpteenth time Hallam and Steve donned their overalls, peeled back the cab, and dived into the grease and machinery. After a little while Steve emerged to warn us, "It'll be a few bloody hours. Unless it's a few fucking days."

Big Bertha was physically divided into the cab, which held three people comfortably, and the body, about thirty feet long, where we passengers rode. Between the cab and the body was a six-inch gap where the main table and assorted tools were stored. We entered the body via a retractable iron staircase in the middle of the left-hand side. Those stairs took you up to "second class" or "the mosh pit," a flat wooden floor with inward-facing benches on either side that extended toward the back of the truck. To the left of the entry staircase, two more steps went up to "first class," three rows of padded double seats with an aisle in the middle. At the very back of the truck was a big wooden cabinet that contained our packs and, beneath them, the safes for our valuables. Instead of windows there were thick transparent plastic sheets attached to the roof of the truck, which we could roll down and lash to thin vertical steel bars, spaced about two feet apart, that ran around the perimeter of the truck. In the desert we kept the sides open. With the plastic down the truck quickly became an oven.

Not a cubic inch was wasted. Overhead lockers hung above the benches. There was storage space beneath the seats and benches. Food supplies were under the mosh-pit floorboards, engine parts below first class. The bookcase, tape player, and frequently broken fridge were at the front of the mosh pit opposite the stairs. Compartments accessible from the outside of the truck held twenty jerry cans of water, extra fuel, more tools, firewood, the stove, tents, folding chairs, cooking gear, etc., behind locked iron gates. The roof held spare tires and firewood. In all, Big Bertha would have been one of the most impressive expeditionary vehicles on the planet, if only her engine didn't falter and fail at least twice a week.

Broken down in the middle of a minefield, in the middle of no-man's-land, in the middle of the Sahara Desert. It sounds desperate and romantic, but at the time it was teeth-grindingly boring. Melanie's thermometer told us it was 115 degrees in the shade. Too hot to read, too hot to play cards, too hot to do anything but sit and be miserable. So I decided to go for a walk.

Not quite as stupid as it sounds. We had finally left the trackless desert behind and were driving on a hard-packed, semipermanent trail. From the roof of the truck we could see down the trail to the military checkpoint where the rest of the convoy waited, maybe two miles away. It seemed perfectly safe so long as we didn't venture off the trail. And no matter how many times I read page seventeen of *Walden*, I was too hot and too far away from New England to understand a thing.

I closed the book and looked around. A dozen people looked at me listlessly from whatever shade they had managed to improvise for themselves.

"Anybody want to go for a walk?" I asked.

There was no response. I felt a little like a visitor in a hospital's terminal-cases wing. The only life came from the few, Michael and Emma and Robbie, who occasionally raised their Sigg water bottles and used the tiny hole in the screw-top to drip a little water on themselves. It didn't really help. The only thing that cooled you down was the spray bottle, but Hallam had forbidden its use until we took on water in Nouadhibou.

"Nobody?" I said dolefully.

A voice emerged from the raised seats at the front of the truck. "I'll come."

I turned my head and looked at her. She smiled at me. I smiled back.

We had spent nearly six weeks in Morocco, but this was only our second real conversation. Our first had been in Marrakesh, just before her two-week fling with Lawrence ended, almost a month ago. One of the weird things about truck life was that you were always but always in a group. With twenty people constantly crammed together, one-on-one conversations with anyone but your tent partner were rare.

We set out to the south, hatted, sunblocked, carrying a liter of brackish desalinated water apiece. For a little while we walked in silence.

"I really like the desert," I said. "I guess I knew I would. I mean, my favorite movie was always *Lawrence of Arabia*. But I didn't know just how much."

"I do too," she said. "Although I was expecting more, you know, Hollywood, *English Patient* desert than this."

Up until that day the Sahara had consisted mostly of plains pounded absolutely flat by sun and wind, punctuated by straggling chains of rock and tufted with thornbushes and cacti. But then even that hardy vegetation had begun to dwindle away. We didn't know it then, but Hollywood desert, the windswept fields of enormous dunes between Nouadhibou and Nouakchott, was only two days away.

"But it's amazing," she continued. "It, not to be all hippie on you, but it feels like it's alive. You know? It's the most blasted, dead place there is, but it feels . . . present."

"You can be all hippie on me," I said. "I don't mind."

"Okay. Good. And you can be all cynical on me if you like."

"Do you think I'm cynical?" I asked.

"I think you'd like to be. But you never will."

"Why not?"

"You're too nice," she said.

"Oh."

We walked on a few paces.

She said, "That was intended as a compliment, in case you're unclear."

"I know," I said, smiling sheepishly. "Thanks."

"Sorry. I'm crap at being praised too. I never know what to do."

"I know!" I exclaimed. I'd often thought that, but never heard anyone else say it. "What are you supposed to do? You can say thank you insincerely, and then you look like you're just being polite and don't really care, or you can say it sincerely and make a point of it, and then you seem insecure, or . . . I don't know."

"Maybe we should just stick to taking the piss out of each other," Laura suggested. "We're all pretty good at dealing with that."

"You Brits are."

"Really? Is it very British?"

I raised my eyebrows. "Are you kidding? You guys are miles, light-years, more sarcastic than the worst of my friends back home. In Canada you'd all be ostracized in seconds. One look, and boom. National silent treatment."

"Would you really ostracize me? Poor little old me?"

"Well . . . no. I'd still talk to you. But nobody else would. You'd have to rely entirely on me for translation."

"Would you still talk to me if I told you Canadians were rude? And wimps when it gets cold? And crap at ice hockey? And"—barely keeping a straight face—"secretly you all wish you were American?"

I grinned and put on a mock John Wayne drawl. "Listen, lady, you better know where I draw the line. And I draw it way back over thataway. And you know what you find on this side of that there line?"

"What do I find?"

"Trouble. Trouble with a capital *T.*"

I half noticed that we passed two piles of large flat rocks on the right-hand side of the trail, spaced about thirty feet apart from one another, but paid them no mind. We were too busy entertaining one another and gaping at the landscape. The desert had changed its look yet again. Here the sand had been densely packed by the wind, then baked by the sun into near-sandstone. The result was a huge field tiled by a fractal pattern of cracks, occasionally interrupted by puddles of soft sand, or by swooping, curving forty-foot ridges worn smooth as glass by the wind, all of it colored the rich gold of a lion's pelt.

Our trail was marked by deep tire ruts that could have been gouged decades ago. Occasionally it disappeared into patches of soft sand fifty or a hundred feet wide before reemerging. As we crossed one of those patches, I saw a flicker of movement in the distance, and I stopped and squinted.

"Look," I said. "Camels." A half dozen of them, barely visible.

"One hump or two hump?" she asked.

I shook my head. "Too far to tell."

"They could be horses," she said.

I looked at her.

"You know," she said, "with big growths on their backs. Hunchback horses. That happens. A ship carrying a whole circusload of hunchback horses might have crashed on the coast here and released them into the desert. And maybe it was years ago and they've survived ever since by sneaking up on convoys like ours and ambushing them at night."

"I don't think that's very likely," I said sternly.

She blinked at me innocently.

"But," I said, "they could be people wearing camel suits.

You know. Soldiers. Saudi Arabian soldiers who got lost because they didn't make the eye slits big enough. They might have just taken a wrong turn in the Sinai and wound up over here."

She nodded. "That's possible too."

"But from this distance you just can't tell."

"I guess just to be safe we shouldn't really call them camels," she said, her lips quivering with repressed laughter. "We should call them Unidentified Dromedarial Objects."

I nodded very seriously. We managed another two seconds of sober looks before both of us burst into laughter.

The rest of the convoy, a dozen civilian vehicles escorted by three military jeeps, waited for us at the checkpoint. Europeans, mostly, in Land Cruisers and Land Rovers brought across from Gibraltar, plus four crazy Germans on fully decked-out motorcycles, two Belgian girls cycling around the world, and a half-dozen multinational hippies in a Volkswagen van that looked older than me. There were also a few African families driving back home in battered but serviceable Renaults and Peugeots.

The rest of the convoy seemed even more bored and bad-tempered than our group. The checkpoint itself was a brick pillbox just big enough for four soldiers dressed in jungle camouflage suits and carrying AK-47s. Like all the soldiers, they were Arabic and not black. There had been more and more black faces as we moved south through Morocco, but rarely among soldiers or officials.

A French couple approached us and demanded that we tell them what was wrong with our *camion* and how long it would take to fix. They had to repeat it five times before my rusty high-school French decoded what they were saying. "*Trois heures, peut-être plus,*" I said with a casual shrug, annoyed by their hostile tone. The French pair muttered with frustration and retreated back to their Land Rover, casting occasional angry glances our way.

The Moroccan and Mauritanian soldiers who escorted the convoy were within earshot of the conversation but paid no attention. They maintained the African relationship to time. Things happen when they happen, if they happen at all.

Laura and I decided to abandon the convoy and walk up the hill above the checkpoint, larger by maybe a hundred feet than any other hill in sight. The view from the top was incredible. An endless stark sea of golden desert extended to the horizon in every direction. Our Big Yellow Truck looked as small and unimportant as a Tonka toy.

"You know what I'd really like?" Laura said, after we had our fill of gaping and sat down. "I'd really like to take a shower and eat some ice cream. But not at the same time. And if I could only have one I'd pick the shower."

I nodded. "Between the sand and the sweat I feel like I grow a new layer of crud every day."

"And you don't have to deal with a bra," she said, looking down at herself. "You blokes get to walk around topless all day. You can only imagine our troubles."

"Another victory for the grand patriarchal conspiracy."

We smiled at each other. After a moment she closed her eyes, lay back on the ground, and tipped her Tilley hat over her face. I sat and watched her. I wasn't exactly ogling her but I was very aware of her presence. Even encrusted in sand, her long dark hair pulled into a ponytail, she was pretty. She wore sandals, khaki shorts, and a white shirt, and just beneath the brim of her hat I could see the small smile that was her default expression. She was a naturally happy person. I liked that about her. Just being near her made me happy, right from the start.

"Cookies?" a voice from behind asked.

I turned around and looked. A goateed man grinned down at me and held out a bag of Spanish chocolate-chip cookies.

They seemed so out of place in the middle of the Sahara that for a moment I wondered if the man was a mirage. But he was real, and the cookies were delicious. I couldn't remember the last time I had tasted anything so sweet. Laura devoured three, closing her eyes to savor the taste. We used the last of our water to wash them down, and our Spanish angel, Fernando, offered to fill up our water bottles from his own, claiming he had plenty of water. After a moment we accepted.

"Oh my," Laura said, after a sip. "Real water. Clean water." I nodded blissfully. For five days we had been stuck with safe but foul-tasting desalinated water from the town of Dakhla, and Fernando's water tasted like champagne by comparison.

We sat and chatted with Fernando for a little while, talking mostly about football and the girlfriend waiting for him in Senegal. His English was uncertain, and it didn't take long for the conversation to peter out. The sun was beginning to sink from its apogee and I was growing tired from our constant exposure.

"Should we go back?" Laura asked, moments before I was about to suggest the same thing.

"Yeah," I said. "Time for a siesta."

We rained thanks on Fernando and began the walk back. As always it seemed three times as distant as the first leg. But with Laura by my side the time shrank away nearly to nothing.

"Hey," I said, about halfway back.

"What?"

"You're a lot of fun."

She smiled at me. "Thank you," she said. "So are you."

We walked in pregnant and slightly awkward silence for a little while, glancing at each other without saying anything. I was trying to work out if anything she had done during our expedition counted as flirting or whether she was just being friendly. Later she told me that she was pondering the same thing in reverse.

Then two hoarse, desperate voices called out, and we looked up in surprise. Just a few hundred feet away, right where those two piles of rocks met the side of the trail, was one of the military convoy's jeeps. The two men inside were shouting to us in French. I couldn't make out what they were saying. Laura and I looked at each other, worried — they were were clearly alarmed by something — and hurried toward them. We were only twenty feet away when I realized, from the position of the jeep between the rocks, that the soldiers had not driven on the visible hard-packed road that we walked on. Instead they had taken a longer and much fainter path I only now noticed, which ran from those two rock piles — trail markers — to where the convoy waited.

"Oh shit," I said. I turned around and looked behind us, wide-eyed.

"What is it?" Laura asked.

"Nothing," I said. "Come on." I consciously made myself hurry to the jeep before allowing myself to fully understand the implications. Laura followed.

"No walk there! No walk!" the soldier nearest us said loudly, anger and worry jostling for space on his face. He pointed to the trail the jeep had followed. "Road!" He pointed to the road behind us, the stretch of obvious road between jeep and the convoy, the length of which we had just walked twice. "No road!" he exclaimed. "No road! Minefield!"

"Oh my God," Laura said.

We stared at each other wide-eyed for a moment. Then, to the soldier's great disapproval, for no real reason, we both began to laugh.

"You could have died," Robbie said, his voice faint with enormity, when we returned to the truck and told our story to the assembled masses.

Laura and I looked at each other. Then Laura turned back to Robbie.

"Believe me," she assured him solemnly, "those cookies were to die for."

When I woke up I believed, for half an instant, that Laura was there, with me in Cole Valley, still alive. That hadn't happened for almost a year. But the moment of realization had lost none of its power to hurt.

I went to work. At work I checked the Thorn Tree. There was only one new entry.

```
BC088269      Ha ha ha
11/04 06:01   The Bull is real, I am The Bull
              and I'll stick knives in all
              your eyes
```

Random juvenilia by some mental twelve-year-old, I thought, and shut the window.

Then I sat bolt upright and opened it again.

Knives in all your eyes. Nobody had mentioned that. Nobody knew about the Swiss Army knives except me, Gavin, and the Nepali police. Of course the LP article had mentioned mutilation. But I went back to the Thorn Tree and carefully reread that new entry.

What I saw the second time turned my spine into an icy river. It was the sender's name, an apparently random collection of characters. *BC088269*. I thought I had seen it before. And I thought I knew where.

I got up and walked out of work and took the N back home. So I missed an hour of work. Let them fire me. This was important.

I went into my house and dug into my stack of travel pic-

tures, waiting to be filed into albums. Near the top was the
picture I had taken in Muktinath, the picture of the false
ledger entry the killer had made in Stanley Goebel's name.
His name and his passport number.

His passport number was BC088269.

Of course it wasn't definite proof. It just meant there was
someone who knew Stanley Goebel's passport number and
the details of what had happened to him. But for me it was
the straw that finally broke the skeptic's back. It was the final
piece of inconclusive evidence that made me certain that
there was more to this iceberg than just the tip. It made me
certain that there was some kind of connection, that these
deaths could not be coincidental one-off events. That there
was somebody out there stalking and killing travelers on the
Lonely Planet trail.

The Bull is real, I am The Bull.

It was such a relief to be certain.

But now that I was certain, what exactly was I supposed
to do?

9

SNIFFING THE PACKETS

I still didn't have any hard evidence. An overwhelming mass of circumstantial evidence, sure, but no smoking gun. And even if I did, what was I supposed to do, go to the FBI? The State Department? Get them to issue a vague travel advisory telling Americans to be careful out there?

There was Interpol. Whatever they were. I would try to find out.

The media? The *San Francisco Chronicle* or the *New York Times* or maybe even *Larry King Live*? That might work. I had enough for a pretty good story. I even had pictures, although no paper in the world was going to run a shot of a dead man with knives in his eyes. I wished I'd taken a picture at the ACAP office, of Stanley Goebel's original handwriting, for a before-and-after shot. Maybe they could get in touch with his next of kin and get a sample.

And yet. What good would that do? A story would run in a newspaper one day, and maybe a snippet on CNN. A bunch of people would read it and ooh and aah. And it would be a warning so vague that it was useless. "Be careful if you go backpacking in the Third World because it looks like there's a serial killer somewhere on the planet." Yeah, that would save lives, that would have The Bull shaking in his hooves.

However. It occurred to me that if BC088269 was in fact The Bull, then I knew one more thing about him. I knew that he was out there on the Net. And the Net was something I knew a great deal about. More than most people. More than most techies even. In fact I was an expert.

Maybe, just maybe, if he had been careless, I could find him.

I put off the most promising lead, partly so I wouldn't lose hope quickly and partly because I'd need to do some social engineering in order to follow it, and spent the rest of the day searching through that vast maelstrom of disordered information called the Internet.

You probably think there's a lot of stuff out there. You have no idea. There's the static Web, company websites and online health databases and government reference materials and a zillion vanity pages and all the other stuff you already know about. Search engines such as Google and AltaVista track these pages reasonably well . . . if they know about them. Every search engine runs an automated "spider," which goes to every page in its database, then every page that those pages link to, and so on and so forth—but even so there's huge amounts of "dark matter" out there, pages that have no links to them and consequently go unnoticed by the search engines.

Then there's the dynamic Web, sites that display different information with every passing day, or for every user, or depending on some kind of context. Newspapers are the most obvious example. The Thorn Tree is another. Spiders have a lot of trouble with the dynamic Web and capture only a small minority of what's available. Consider snapshots of Times Square, taken every ten minutes; they'd tell you everything about the billboards, but very little about what happened on the video screens. Spiders are like that. The huge Lexis-Nexis database stores every article from every Western periodical, but misses out on countless zines, pamphlets, and minor foreign papers, and charges a small fortune for access. Fortunately, we had an account at work.

And that's just the Web. Most people think the Internet is what appears in their Web browser. Us techies know better. Think of the Net as a sixty-five-thousand-lane highway. The whole World Wide Web runs on but two lanes. Most of the lanes are nearly empty, or used only to keep the whole network running, but some of them are as busy as the Web; e-mail, obviously, but also Usenet, instant messaging like AIM and ICQ, IRC, MUDs, Napster, File Transfer Protocol, and even older protocols such as Gopher and Telnet, the dead languages of the Net, its Latin and Greek. There were even a few ancient BBS systems still out there, to which you actually had to dial directly.

Much of the data out there, probably most, simply cannot be searched, is effectively invisible except maybe to the FBI or National Security Agency. Most of what can be searched is readily available through two or three sites, say Google and MetaCrawler and Lexis-Nexis. But there is a small fringe of information that is available only if you look very hard and very carefully, using exactly the right words, on one or two of the lesser-known search sites.

I did not intend to leave any stone unturned. I searched NorthernLight and Mamma and HotBot and AltaVista and Inktomi and GoTo and Ask and About and DejaNews. I searched Reuters and the Associated Press and Dow Jones and AfricaNews. I searched conspiracy sites and hacker sites and travel sites and serial-killer-fan-club sites and travel advisories and international-security companies. I searched for various combinations of: "The Bull" and "serial killer" and "traveler" and "backpacker" and "Laura Mason" and "Stan-

ley Goebel" and "Lonely Planet" and "murder" and "eye mutilation" and "knives" and "Swiss Army knives" and "BC088269"
and "Malawi" and "Cameroon" and "South Africa" and
"Nepal."

And in the end I didn't come up with much. More than
nothing, but not much. Articles in British papers about
Laura's death, telling me nothing I didn't know already. A
reference to my own Thorn Tree article. And a massive pile of
useless and irrelevant information. There were, however, two
palpable hits, and one maybe.

First of all was an article from the *South Africa Mail &
Guardian:*

> *Is there a spectre haunting the Baz Bus?*
> You've seen them everywhere since the end of apartheid:
> American and European backpackers lured here by the promise
> of beaches and safaris and cheap ganja. But lately the talk in
> the Baz Bus and the beachfront hostels has a taken a decidedly
> grim turn. A rumour, documented in the new edition of the
> Lonely Planet guidebook most use as their bible, suggests that
> a serial killer is preying on their ilk.
> On May 22, Daniel Gendrault, 25, French, was found
> murdered in Cape Town. On May 31, the body of Michelle
> McLaughlin, 31, Scottish, was discovered in Kruger Park. On
> June 13, the remains of Oliver Jeremies, 19, German, were
> found in the ocean near Beira, Mozambique. On the night of
> June 14, Kristin Jones, 25, English, was killed in rural Malawi.
> While the Lonely Planet guidebook suggests that the quick
> succession of the last two dates meant that they could not be
> the work of one man, the Mail & Guardian has found that
> Oliver Jeremies was most likely killed several days before he
> was discovered.
> The most salaciously grotesque element in the rumour is

that the killer, invariably called "The Bull" though no one knows why, carves out his victim's eyeballs and keeps them as a souvenir. The police have confirmed that the eyes of the Cape Town and Kruger Park victims were mutilated but will not provide details. The authorities in Mozambique and Malawi cannot provide any details on the murders there other than those found in the sketchy official reports.

There have been no more deaths in the six months since, but the rumour continues to spread, and even though it seems that "The Bull" has left the region—if he ever existed—his mention in the Lonely Planet guide will certainly keep it alive for years until the next edition appears.

South Africa's hoped-for luxury tourist boom has never materialized, but since the end of apartheid we have at least managed to lure intrepid twentysomething backpackers by the thousand. They may not splash out dollars like the middle-aged Americans our tourist office seeks to attract, but a whole industry has grown up around them, and the reports they take back to Europe have a real effect on our overseas image. The crime crisis has already put a dent in their numbers during the last two years, and if the rumours of "The Bull" are taken seriously, we could soon see the Baz Bus running half-empty.

Still more intriguing was an old Usenet conversation from the DejaNews archive:

```
Date: 13 September 1995, 13:08:16 EDT
Newsgroups: alt.serial-killers, alt.perfect-
   crime
Subject: Killer on the road
From: anon@penet.fi (Anonymous Remailer
   Service)
Reply-To: dev@null.com
```

Two questions for you armchair psychos out
   there:

1. How would you commit the perfect murder?

   It wouldn't have to be anyone you knew. The
   goal here is just to commit a murder of any
   random human being. The victim has to be
   healthy and strong, to keep it challenging.
   But it doesn't have to be anyone in
   particular. How would you do it so that
   the risks are eliminated or minimized?

2. How would you commit the perfect group of
   murders?

   Note that this is very different from the
   first question. Here you have to kill an
   arbitrary number of people. Say 10-12 of
   them. Otherwise the same rules as above
   apply. But obviously you can't just keep
   pushing people off the same cliff or
   someone's gonna get suspicious. You can be
   either a mass murderer or a serial killer.
   What do you do? I guess my Subject: line
   makes my opinion obvious, but I'd like to
   know what the rest of you think.

   Taurus

Date: 13 September 1995, 23:01:08
Newsgroups: alt.serial-killers, alt.perfect-
   crime

Subject: Re: Killer on the road
From: gplaine@golden.net (George Plaine)
Reply-To: gplaine@golden.net

anon@penet.fi (Anonymous Remailer Service)
   wrote:

>1. How would you commit the perfect murder?

   It's a pretty good question but I think
   mystery novelists have beaten it to death
   over the years. There's basically 2 ways
   to commit the perfect murder:

   —make sure nobody thinks its a murder
   (generally an accident)
   —make sure somebody else takes the fall
   (generally by dressing things up as a
   murder-suicide, but there's tons o'
   variations out there)

>2. How would you commit the perfect group of
   murders?

   This is way more interesting...A big
   accident like a collapsed building or a
   bomb attributed to someone else sounds
   good. Serial killer, that sounds like a
   hard gig. Even if you're driving around
   picking people up and disappearing them,
   every crime and disappearance goes on
   record, and every little mistake you might
   make catches up with you. I think one big
   bang is the way to go.

Date: 14 September 1995, 14:51:56
Newsgroups: alt.serial-killers, alt.perfect-
   crime
Subject: Re: Killer on the road
From: solipsism@innocent.com
Reply-To: bgates@microsoft.com

gplaine@golden.net (George Plaine) wrote:
>anon@penet.fi (Anonymous Remailer Service)
   wrote:
>>2. How would you commit the perfect group
     of murders?
>
> [. . .]Serial killer, that sounds like a
hard gig.
> [. . .] I think one big bang is the way
to go.

People used to have a lot of success (if you
can call it that) by hitching or by picking
up hitchers, but that's a lot harder these
days. Cell phones, car locators, cameras on
highways and every ATM machine, DNA testing—
it's not easy being a psychopath anymore.

I think it's probably easier to kill a single
random person in a rural setting, eg bumping
them off a cliff, but easier to be a serial
killer in a dense urban place like New York
or LA or Chicago.

But what do I know, I haven't killed anyone
yet.

Date: 14 September 1995, 13:08:16 EDT
Newsgroups: alt.serial-killers, alt.perfect-
   crime
Subject: Re: Killer on the road
From: anon@penet.fi (Anonymous Remailer
   Service)
Reply-To: dev@null.com

solipsism@innocent.com wrote:
>gplaine@golden.net (George Plaine) wrote:
>>anon@penet.fi (Anonymous Remailer Service)
   wrote:
>>>2. How would you commit the perfect group
   of murders?
>>
>> [. . .]Serial killer, that sounds like a
   hard gig.
>
> Cell phones, car locators, cameras on
   highways and every ATM
> machine, DNA testing—it's not easy being a
   psychopath anymore.

You're making the assumption that the
killings take place in a First World country
with a well-funded police force. Why think
that? You could go off to Asia or Africa or
pick some random tribesmen there and they'd
fit the criteria. Or, better yet, go on a road
trip through Central America or someplace
like that, kill someone in every country, and
just make each one look like one of those
death-squad things. You could even pick off

fellow travelers. I think it would all be
miles easier in the Third World.

Also it has occurred to me that there's never
been a documented truly random serial killer.
I'm talking Leopold & Loeb-style, picking
people truly at random rather than because
they fit some fucked-up need or psychological
profile. Maybe this is because there's never
been one. Or maybe it's because only the
nonrandom killers get caught.

Taurus

Taurus. Which of course means: *The Bull*.

And finally there was one very cryptic IRC log fragment,
which apparently had been automatically saved to file when
the IRC session had crashed, and by chance the old Unix box
that had hosted the session had its log files open to the Web
and to directory browsing, and HotBot's spider happened to
have stumbled across it in passing:

NumberThree: Frankly I'm kind of bored with
the term _serial killer_. Maybe I should
lobby for a new one. _Sequential homicide
artist_or something.
NumberTwo: Artist? That's a pretty fancy-
shmancy name to pin on The Bull's tail...
NumberThree: If Kafka could have a hunger-
artist...Maybe all of The Bull's stuff should
go up for an exhibition somewhere. You know,
a real-world place, an installation.

<u>NumberTwo:</u> And everybody who comes in to see
it gets killed?
<u>NumberThree:</u> Hey, everybody knows that you
have to suffer for Art.
Seriously, what I think is th
##
NO CARRIER

All very interesting, of course. The *Mail & Guardian* confirmed that the four African deaths could have been one person's work—but it seemed very unlikely, if the *M&G*'s dates were correct, that they could have gotten up to Cameroon for June 15. But there was no reason to think the dates were correct. It was Africa; all information should be considered wrong until definitively proven correct.

The Usenet conversation was highly suspicious but inconclusive and not terribly helpful except that it confirmed that someone who called himself Taurus had been thinking pretty hard about this as long ago as 1995. He'd used the Finnish anonymous remailer service, since taken down by that country's authorities, and didn't seem to have any language idiosyncrasies, so there was probably no way to track him.

And the IRC fragment . . . that was just weird. But then the Net is a weird place. It was entirely possible that this was a discussion of some MUD role-playing game, or strange California art commune, or (judging from the names) a *Prisoner* fan club, or something even less comprehensible and completely irrelevant. But it still gave me the chills. *Sequential homicide artist.*

All very interesting, but not particularly useful with respect to the goal of finding who and where The Bull was. It was time to move on to the prime lead. That post to the Thorn Tree. It could have been made from any Web browser on the planet, and the Thorn Tree allowed you to take any name you liked, so long as it wasn't already used by someone else, without verifying it in any way. Apparent anonymity. But I knew that the Web's anonymity was a myth if you weren't careful; and with a little help and a little luck, that Thorn Tree message could be traced a long way toward its sender.

10

CONNECTION ESTABLISHED

First of all I went to lonelyplanet.com and dug out their list of offices and phone numbers. It was a pleasant surprise that their website was hosted and run from Oakland, just across the San Francisco Bay from me. But it made sense. The Bay Area was the center of all the world's Web traffic. I'd heard estimates that 40 percent of the data on the Internet was routed through the region.

I needed Lonely Planet's help, so I called their Oakland office and asked for their Web editor. I told her secretary that I was investigating a story. I wish I could say that when she answered I felt some frisson of significance, a feeling in the pit of my stomach, but the truth is I just felt sexist surprise that their Web editor was a woman.

"Talena Radovich," she said, brisk but friendly. "What can I do for you?"

"Hi. My name is Balthazar Wood," I said. I had come to realize over the years that a twenty-dollar name subconsciously impresses people in official situations. I knew it was going to be tough to convince them, and every arrow in my quiver would help. "I'm working on what you might call a complicated investigation, and I'm calling to ask for your help."

"And who do you work for?"

"I'm not really working for anyone," I admitted.

"Julia said you were a journalist . . . ?"

"In a sense. A story of some kind will probably come out of this. But there's a lot more to it than that."

There was a pause, then she said, with a hint of suspicion, "Maybe you should tell me what you're talking about."

"Yeah," I said. "But I warn you, it's pretty complicated and probably pretty hard to believe. Do you have some time right now, or do you want to talk later?"

"I have some time right now."

"All right," I said. "Here goes. Here's the nutshell version. When I'm finished with it you're probably going to think I'm completely crazy, but please bear with me and let me fill in the blanks, okay?"

"Okay," she said. She sounded curious. That was good.

"All right. Two weeks ago I was in Nepal, on the Annapurna Circuit, and I found the body of a dead man. Not just dead, but murdered."

"Murder on the Annapurna Circuit," she said when I paused for breath. I thought she might have a slight accent but I couldn't be sure. "The Thorn Tree article."

"That's right, I wrote that," I said gratefully. It made it much easier that she had read and remembered what I had already written. "What I didn't write there was that two *years* ago, in Africa, a friend of mine was murdered in the same way. There's boxed text on The Bull in your Africa South book, I don't know if you've read that—"

"I wrote it," she said.

"It says that—you what?"

"I was one of the researchers for that edition, I wrote the section on The Bull."

"Oh," I said. "I thought you were the Web editor."

"Most of us spend a few months every year on the road doing research and updates."

"Oh. Wow. Sounds like a pretty good job."

"Beats working. Where exactly are you going with this?" she asked.

"I'm going to the part where I sound like a crazy conspiracy freak," I said. "I've been doing a bunch of research and I've got a whole pile of evidence that is totally circumstantial but which makes me believe, basically, that The Bull is real, that he killed my," I hesitated, "my friend Laura in Africa, and he killed this guy in Nepal, and he's still out there."

"Oh," she said. "Okay, yeah, that's pretty freaky all right. Why are you calling me?"

"Because I think one of the responses to what I wrote might actually have been written by the guy. And I happen to be something of an expert on Internet software, and I'd like you to let me look through your server logs so I can maybe track down where he is."

"Um . . . Mister . . ."

"Wood. Balthazar Wood."

"Mr. Wood, shouldn't you be calling the FBI or something? What we do, you know, what we do is we publish travel guidebooks, and investigating serial killers, that isn't exactly our strong suit, you know? And . . . this is the weirdest phone call I've had in a long time."

"Sorry about that."

"So why aren't you calling the FBI and getting them to subpoena us?"

"The FBI only investigates crimes on American soil," I said.

"Oh, yeah. They said that on *X-Files* last night."

"Also I don't think any Americans have been victims yet."

"But, come on, there's got to be *somebody* official you can call. At least somebody other than me."

"If you've got any ideas I'd love to hear them," I said.

There was a long pause.

"Okay," she said eventually, "this is totally *nuts*. First of all, Mr. Crazy Conspiracy Freak, I want to meet you face-to-face, and it's gonna be in a crowded public place because no offense but this whole subject as you might imagine kinda totally freaks me out, and you're going to bring me this huge pile of evidence you say that you've got. Then, in the unlikely event I don't think you're just some sort of maladjusted psycho-ward case, then I'll go to the folks here and we'll talk things over. And I'm telling you now I'm pretty sure they'll say no. But if you're convincing enough, I'll at least talk to them."

"Thanks," I said. "Thank you. That's what I was hoping for."

"Where do you want to meet?"

I thought it over. "I don't really know Oakland . . . is San Francisco okay?"

"That's where I live," she said.

"Okay. Do you know where the Horseshoe Cafe is?"

"Lower Haight?"

"That's right. When is good for you? Sooner the better for me."

"Tonight at eight," she said. It wasn't a question. "I'm five-foot-ten and I have a nose ring and purple streaks in my hair."

"It's the Lower Haight," I pointed out. "You may have to narrow it down a little further than that."

She had a good laugh, low and throaty. "I'll be wearing black, does that help?"

"Enormously," I said. "I'll be the old guy with a serious beard and huge folder of old newspaper clippings and no sense of personal hygiene, sweating and twitching nervously in the corner with my back to the wall."

"The man of my dreams at last."

"Seriously, I'll be wearing . . . hum . . . you know what? I'll have a beat-up copy of *Trekking in the Nepal Himalaya* with me."

"Sounds good. See you at eight."

"All right. Bye."

I resented her on sight. She seemed like one of
those people who was accustomed to everything good in life
coming to her at the snap of her fingers. She was tall, athleti-
cally lean, and extremely pretty, shoulder-length black hair
with royal purple streaks, eyes blue as glacier ice, an aristocratic face, pale perfect skin punctuated by a silver nose ring.
The other guys in the Horseshoe kept giving her sidelong
looks, and if we had met in any other circumstances, I would
have been a tongue-tied ogler. Plus she had my generation's
ultimate dream job, Internet editor/Lonely Planet writer, and I
thought I could tell just by looking at her that she had the
hippest apartment in town and a string of fellow Beautiful People friends and probably two or three generations of money in
her family. She was nice enough. Don't get me wrong. Maybe I
just resented her because she was so far out of my league.

She swaggered in and sat down across from me. The table
was an old Galaga video game half obscured by the remains
of my *Trekking in the Nepal Himalaya* and my folder full of
printouts and pictures.

"What did you think of that one?" she asked, nodding to
the book.

"Actually I thought it was the worst book you guys have
ever done," I said. "No offense. But lots of people on the trail
had a different book that was a thousand times better."

"Yeah," she agreed. "The Trailblazer Guides one, right?
That is a lot better. We're seriously revamping ours for the
next edition."

"I've forgotten your name," I admitted.

"Talena Radovich," she said, and we shook hands primly,
as if meeting at a wedding.

"All right," I said. "Here's what I've got." I pushed the folder over to her. "The last page is a time line I wrote out that connects all the events."

Sep 1995	"Taurus" suggests on Usenet that the perfect serial killer would go to the Third World and kill there.
22 May 1998	Daniel Gendrault found murdered in Cape Town. Eyes mutilated.
31 May 1998	Michelle McLaughlin found murdered in Kruger Park. Eyes mutilated.
8 Jun 1998 (approx.)	Oliver Jeremies killed in Mozambique.
13 Jun 1998	Oliver Jeremies's body washes up in Beira.
14 Jun 1998	Kristin Jones found dead in Malawi.
15 Jun 1998 (midnight)	Laura Mason murdered in Limbe, Cameroon. Swiss Army knives are left in her eyes.
16 Jun 1998 (1:30 A.M.)	Laura Mason found dead by myself, Nicole Seams, and Hallam Chevalier.
1998	Rumor of "The Bull" begins to spread.

Nov 1998	Rumor of "The Bull" published by LP.
18 Oct 2000 (morning)	Stanley Goebel murdered in Gunsang, Nepal. Swiss Army knives are left in his eyes.
18 Oct 2000 (noon)	Stanley Goebel found dead by myself and Gavin Chait.
20 Oct 2000	Stanley Goebel's name and passport number BC088269 entered into trekking checkpoint in Muktinath.
26 Oct 2000	"Murder on the Annapurna Circuit" message posted to the Thorn Tree.
4 Nov 2000	Someone claiming to be The Bull posts to the Thorn Tree with the name BC088269, referring to knives in eyes. Neither i) the passport number nor ii) the information about the knives was known except to i) myself and Stanley Goebel's family ii) myself and Gavin Chait and the murderer.

She read very quickly, which I suppose becomes an editor.

"Is this everything?" she asked when she was finished. Her tone wasn't dismissive, she just wanted to know if there was anything else.

"Not quite," I said. I hesitated for a moment and decided

not to talk about maybe having been pursued on the trail by the killer, on the grounds that it might seem a little too histrionic. "I have some pictures. One is a shot of the entry in the Muktinath ledger. The others are of Stanley Goebel's body. They're pretty disturbing and you might not want to look at them."

She held her hand out. I gave her the pictures. She flinched at the second one but studied it, and the other two like it, carefully. Then she handed them back.

"Okay. Jesus fucking hell. Let's go next door. I need a drink." She did have an accent, but I couldn't place it. Eastern European maybe?

I gathered my possessions and we went to the Mad Dog in the Fog, a quasi-British quasi-alternative pub next door. It was a weekday night, so the music wasn't deafening and there was even a free table. I ordered a double scotch on the rocks. So did she.

"I didn't know about Jeremies," she said. She sounded guilty. "There was no way I could have known. I went to Beira myself and nobody said anything about him being days dead when they found him. The police in Mozambique are no help, believe you me. I even called his family, but they weren't talking. And I had a fucking deadline to meet. I had to fight a small war with the chief editor to get the warning in the book at all."

"I'm not blaming you for anything," I said, surprised. "Nobody is."

"*I* might." She shook her head. "Maybe. I got a lot of questions though. Like, you say nobody knew about the knives and the passport number. What about the police there?"

"True," I said cautiously. "They knew. But they had no motive to—"

"No. But let's . . . cast a wide net here. I don't want to go off half-cocked." She sipped her Scotch. "I hate this Johnny Walker shit."

"Then why did you order it?" I asked, almost relieved to have a change of subject.

"Because I can't afford anything good. Okay. And you got the time of the rumor screwed up. The rumor was all over South Africa when I got there, everyone was talking about it, and that was two days before McLaughlin was found. The eye mutilation thing and everything."

"Waitaminit," I said. "Before?"

"Before."

"Who starts talking about serial killers when only one person has been killed?"

"The serial killer," she said. "Who else? Unless he hired a PR agency."

"That's nuts."

"So is he," she pointed out.

"Could be a she."

"Right, that happens a lot," she said sarcastically. "But for the sake of argument, let's just call him a he. Anyways. There's still one totally huge Mack-truck-size hole in your otherwise pretty theory, you know."

"Yeah," I said. "I do."

"June 8 in Mozambique, June 14 in Malawi. Possible. But June 14 in Malawi and June 15 in fucking *Cameroon*? Come on."

"Yeah," I said. "I was thinking maybe he did it deliberately to confuse things, he raced to the airport in Malawi, flew to Harare, flew to Cameroon, and the next day went right out and—" But she was shaking her head as if I was suggesting Wings was better than the Beatles.

"Okay," I admitted. "That part doesn't make sense to me either." It wouldn't make sense to anyone who had ever traveled in Africa. "Unless maybe the June 14 date is wrong. If you move it back to June 13 or June 12, it starts becoming kind of possible."

"Then he's only got four or five days to get from Mozambique to Malawi and find some fresh meat . . . but, okay, maybe just maybe. I got a vague idea that that June 14 date is pretty solid, but I'm not sure off the top of my head. I've still got my notes, I'll look it up. I take it you're sure about the June 15 date?"

"Very," I said shortly. "Okay. What about the knives? Did that happen in the south?"

"I don't know. It was all locals who found the bodies there, and I never talked to them directly. The police probably wouldn't have told me who they were either. All they said was that the eyes were mutilated. They wouldn't say how. I knew a policeman in Cape Town; if he still works there, I'll ask him."

"Great." I swigged from my scotch. "Huh. Jeez."

"What?" she asked, and I met those blue eyes directly for the first time and had to look away in a hurry.

"It's just nice to be able to talk to someone else about this," I said. "And, you know, even if I'm wrong, to be taken seriously. I'd started to wonder if I was just losing the plot and going paranoid."

"You've definitely got something serious here. Can I take this?" She put her hand out on the folder. "And the pictures? I'm going to try and talk my editor into giving you access. You still might be wrong, but we're going to take you seriously."

"Thank you," I said. "Thank you very much."

11

TRACEROUTE

The next day I finished all the work I had by noon and spent the rest of the afternoon surfing the Web and playing foozball. There were a lot of people with time to play foozball. Not a good sign. Kevin reassured me that the Morgan Stanley project I was due to lead was just "hung up on the dotting the t's and crossing the i's stage." He sounded like he even believed it. If he hadn't, I would have begun polishing my resume.

Just before I logged off and went home I got a crushingly disappointing e-mail:

```
From: talenar@lonelyplanet.com
To: BalthazarWood@yahoo.com
Subject: Your proposal
cc: editorial@lonelyplanet.com

Dear Mr. Wood,

We have considered all the information you
have sent us and we regret to inform you that
we have decided not to assist you in your
investigation.
```

While we appreciate how serious your suspicions
are, we feel it would be irresponsible of us to
assist you without evidence that shows beyond
any reasonable doubt that your theory is
correct. While you have amassed an impressive
collection of circumstantial evidence, there
remain unexplained holes in your time line of
events and there is no "smoking gun." Our
stated Thorn Tree privacy policy is that we
will never reveal information about a user
without their consent, and any violation of
this policy without being compelled by a
subpoena could leave us open to damaging
lawsuits. In short, so long as it is possible
that you may be wrong, we do not wish to
participate in what may be a wild-goose chase.

We do regret our lack of cooperation and hope
that you understand our motivation. If you do
acquire any new and compelling evidence,
please let us know.

Sincerely,

Talena Radovich
Web Editor
Lonely Planet Publications

I restrained myself from punching my laptop. It wasn't
the computer's fault. "Shit," I said. "Fuck. Shit fuck shit fuck
shit fuck shit fuck." It didn't make me feel any better.

I went home to my apartment, turned on the TV, and
went up into Deep Cable to find the most brain-dead programming that I could. I was sick of thinking. I was beginning to think of lobotomies with longing.

About ten minutes into *Married ... with Children* I got a phone call.

"Balthazar? Hi. It's Talena."

"Oh," I said. "Yeah. I got your e-mail."

"Right. Let's pretend that you didn't."

I tried to figure out what she meant and failed. "What?"

"I talked it over with the board, and they're all very sympathetic and might even be willing to violate the privacy policy without a subpoena if you happen to get a videotape of the guy confessing his crimes."

"That's big of them."

"But first of all they don't want to violate their policy, and second of all they don't want to discourage people from traveling, unless they have hard evidence. Actually what they're worried about is that you'll go to the media. You can never tell what stories take off, and if yours does, we might be selling a lot fewer books for a while."

"Well, you can tell them that their worst fears are about to come true," I said, trying to make it sound like a threat.

"I could. However. That's what the *board* thinks, and instructed me to tell you."

"I don't understand why you're calling me. And how did you get my number?"

She sighed patiently as if talking to a child. "The miracle of call display. And I'm calling you to tell you that the board and I think differently. That I think probably being onto something is good enough. So I'm personally going to help you."

"Really?"

"Yes, really."

"Help me how exactly?" I asked.

"What kind of help do you want?"

"I want the logs off your Web server."

"Then I'll get them to you," she said.

"You could be fired."

"Only if you tell someone."

"I won't tell anyone."

"I know. Now tell me what you want me to get. Web-Trends printouts or what? I'm computer-friendly but I'm not a techie, so you'll have to give me explicit details."

I switched off the TV, sat down, and walked her through the details of where she could find the files that I needed. I heard her typing as I talked, presumably transcribing my instructions. She didn't ask any questions.

When I was finished, she said, "Got it. I'll get them tomorrow. What's your address?"

"My address?"

"Your address. So I can bring you the floppy with the files. Like you said, I could get fired, so e-mail's a wee bit too insecure for my liking."

I gave her my address.

"All right. Tomorrow at eight. Be there."

"I will," I said.

"Bye."

"Talena?"

"Yes?"

"Thank you."

"My pleasure," she said. "See you tomorrow."

After she hung up a thought occurred to me. I went to my study, sat down at my laptop, and logged on to the Thorn Tree. There were no new entries to my conversation, so I added my own:

```
PaulWood      BC088269:
11/06 19:45   you think you're pretty smart,
              don't you?
```

With any luck I'd bait him into giving us new data.

I checked my e-mail. There was a new message from

Carmel, an Aussie girl from the truck, telling me how much she hated her new job in Sydney, and asking me how Nepal had been.

Good question, I thought. *But are you sure you want to know the answer?*

I wanted to answer. I wanted to send an e-mail to all of the tribe of the truck, telling them everything I had found and everything I suspected. These were the people who would understand what I meant, and what it meant to me. Maybe some of them could even help me find out what was going on. Like Hallam and Nicole. Before driving our truck across Africa he had been a paratrooper, and now he was a security consultant, and she had one of the keenest minds I had ever encountered. Or Steven, with his dubious jailbird past and host of shady connections. This was a job for people like them, not for a mild-mannered computer programmer.

But, really, what good would it do? Other than a meaningless moment of catharsis, what was the point in telling them what I had seen and discovered? What could they really find out that I couldn't? Why remind them of Laura's murder, and trouble them with this sick, unsolvable mystery that seemed somehow connected to it? It didn't seem right to unleash it on their minds just because I couldn't stop it from preying on mine. All it would do was drag a bunch of horrible old memories out of the mud. I had gone through too much of that myself recently to want to wish it on others.

Talena showed up right on time, dressed in jeans and a purple sweater, a floppy disk in her hand. I took it from her and said, "Thank you."

I expected her to turn around and walk away, and there was an awkward silence for a few seconds, before she said, "Aren't you going to invite me in?"

I blinked and said, "Oh. Okay."

"I am risking my job for this," she reminded me. "Least you can do is let me shoulder-surf."

"Oh. Yeah, sure. No problem."

She followed me in.

"Nice apartment," she said.

"Yeah," I said, and then sheepishly, "Sometimes it's a little cleaner . . ."

She laughed.

"Do you want a drink or something?" I asked.

"Let's just get to work."

"Right." I led the way into my study, where my laptop sat on the desk, connected to a cable modem. She sat next to me and I had to remind myself to focus on what I was doing. She was even prettier than I remembered, she moved with athletic grace, her jeans and sweater were both tighter than absolutely necessary, and she wore something that smelled like fresh strawberries. I couldn't help but think that it had been four months, since a drunken encounter with a giggly blond girl named Amy I had met at a party, since . . .

"So are we meditating before we begin or what?" she asked.

"Um, yeah. Just planning," I lied, inserting the disk. "I warn you, this could take a while and will probably be very boring."

"That's okay. Just keep me informed about what you're doing. And use English words and no acronyms."

"I see you have dealt with my kind before."

"More than the amount necessary to have a full and happy life."

"Very funny. Well, the first thing I'm doing is checking for the exact time that Mr. BC088269 posted to the Thorn Tree." I went on the Web, logged in to the Thorn Tree, scrolled down to his message. "It was 06:01 on November 4. I'm going to assume that the Web servers are using the same time zone as your database server —"

"They are," she said.

"Okay. Next we look at the log files." I opened them up in

UltraEdit. Each one consisted of hundreds of thousands of rows of text, each row a long stream of data unintelligible to anyone uninitiated in the secrets of my field:

```
64.76.56.49, 11/4/00, 0:00:19, ARMSTRONG,
64.211.224.135, 2110, 438, 22573, 200, GET,
/dest/
206.47.24.62, 11/4/00, 0:00:19, COOK,
64.211.224.135, 109, 502, 32090, 200, GET,
/prop/booklist.html
129.82.46.82, 11/4/00, 0:00:21, MAGELLAN,
64.211.24.142, 78, 477, 11505, 200, GET,
/cgi-bin/search
206.47.244.62, 11/4/00, 0:00:23, MAGELLAN,
64.211.224.135, 0, 567, 28072, 304, GET,
/dest/europe/UK/London.html
```

. . . and so forth and so forth, one for every time anybody looked at a Lonely Planet Web page that day.

"And this means something to you?" she asked.

"It does."

"What does it mean?"

"Well . . . each line represents one request. One page that some user out there wants served to them. And each line tells me the IP number of the user's computer, the date and time, the server computer name, the IP number served, how much time the whole request took, how many characters the user sent, how many characters the server sent, whether it all completed successfully, whether the user was getting or sending information, and the page they wanted."

"Uh-huh. And this is useful?"

"Maybe. First of all let's get all this into Excel. Text is

hard to work with." I called up Microsoft Excel and ran its import wizard on the four log files, turning them into malleable spreadsheets, which I cut-and-pasted together into a single file. A very large file.

"You guys are popular," I observed. I sent an impressed look over my shoulder and met those electric blue eyes again.

"A million hits a day," she said proudly.

"Right," I said briskly, making my head swivel back toward the computer. "Yeah. One point two three million on November 4. Good thing I've got a monster machine here or this would take forever. Okay. Yeah. All right, first thing, let's get rid of everything that isn't within a two-minute window when that message appeared." I sorted the entries by date and wiped everything except those between 6:00 and 6:02. This reduced things to a manageable twenty-two hundred hits. "Next, let's get rid of everyone looking at your main site instead of the Thorn Tree." I pinged thorntree.lonely planet.com, found out that it was 64.211.24.142, and got rid of all requests to different servers.

"That's still two-hundred-odd possibilities," she said. "I thought you'd actually be able to look at the messages they posted."

"No such luck. But we're not done yet. Anyone actually posting a message would use an HTTP POST method, not a GET, you use GET if you're just reading." I eliminated all the GETs, and this reduced the spreadsheet to only three rows:

```
116.64.39.4, 11/4/00, 0:06:01, MAGELLAN,
64.211.24.142, 3140, 9338, 32473, 200, POST,
/cgi-bin/post
187.209.251.38, 11/4/00, 0:06:01, COOK,
64.211.24.142, 2596, 1802, 31090, 200, POST,
/cgi-bin/post
109.64.109.187, 11/4/00, 0:06:01, HEYERDAHL,
```

```
64.211.24.142, 0, 2847, 72, 500, POST, /cgi-
bin/post
```

"Easier than I thought," I said.

"So we've got three possibilities?"

"Actually, no. See that 500 on the last line?" I pointed it out. "This means that there was a server error, so whatever was sent never made it up to the Thorn Tree."

"So it's one of the first two."

"Right. But see that 9338 in the first one, and 1802 in the second? That's how many bytes went from the client to the server. That means the first one was a pretty long message. And the message our friend sent was . . ."

". . . pretty damn short."

"Exactly."

"Okay," she said. "So we found the right line. I still don't get what that gives us."

"That gives us the IP number of the computer he used to send it. One-eight-seven two-oh-nine two-five-one thirty-eight."

"And every computer on the Internet has its own number?"

"Well . . . no." I saved the spreadsheet, just in case, expelled the floppy, and handed it back to her, avoiding her eyes. "That was the way it was originally supposed to work. But it's more complicated than that. Basically as a rule of thumb any computer that's permanently on the Net has its own IP number. Unless it's behind a proxy server, or . . . well, there's a lot of issues. So this still might all be useless. On the other hand it might take us right to him. I can get a look at the router chain we go through to get to that machine from here, that might give us some idea where it is." I opened up a telnet session to my Unix account, typed in

```
traceroute 187.209.251.38
```

and examined the lines of cryptic gibberish the computer spat
out in response.

"Shee-it," I said. "That, I was not expecting."

"What?"

"That message came from Indonesia."

"Really?"

"Looks like it." I pointed at the last few lines of the trace-
route response.

```
17 Gateway-to-hosting.indo.net.id
(187.209.251.31) 641.612 ms 587.980 ms
590.526 ms
18 Quick-Serial-b.indo.net.id (187.209.251.2)
869.458 ms 669.086 ms 608.886 ms
19 187.209.251.38 (187.209.251.38) 620.897 ms
643.124 ms 588.700 ms
```

"See that dot-ID at the end of those last few lines? Each
country has its own code. CA for Canada, UK for the United
Kingdom, and so forth. ID means Indonesia."

"Indonesia is a big place," she said doubtfully.

"So it is," I said. "Let's see if we can't zoom in a little." I
typed in:

```
whois 187.209.251.38
```

and the computer responded

```
IP Address: 187.209.251.38
Server Name: WWW.JUARAPARTEMA.COM
Whois Server: whois.domaindiscover.com
```

"What's that? Whois?" Talena asked.

"Basically it goes out and gets the name that goes with the
IP number," I said. "If any."

"Computers have names?"

"Kind of," I said. "Between each other they just use the IP number, but they figured out a long time ago that that would be hard for people to remember, so there's a system called the Domain Name Service that matches names to numbers. So you can just type in lonelyplanet-dot-com instead of sixty-four dot two-eleven and so forth."

"How does that work?" she asked. "Is there a big white pages or something?"

"Pretty much," I said. "It's a complicated descending hierarchy, but basically there's thirteen really big computers that work as the master white pages. What this just told us is that the name we're looking for is juarapartema-dot-com, and that it was registered by a company called domaindiscover-dot-com. Registration's turned into this big complicated mess, but basically if we go there we should be able to find out more . . ."

I navigated to domaindiscover.com and searched for juarapartema.com:

```
whois: juarapartema.com

Administrative Contact, Technical Contact,
Zone Contact:
Mak Hwa Sen
Internet World Cafe
Kuta Beach, Bali, DKI 33620, ID
[82] 29 9210421
root@juarapartema.com
```

"Gotcha," I said. "Kuta Beach, Bali. Now what the *hell* are you doing there?"

"Let's take a break," she said. "I'll take that drink now."

"Okay," I said. She followed me out to the kitchen. I opened the fridge and glanced in. "I've got beer and . . . um . . . water."

She laughed.

"I just got back from traveling," I said defensively.

"Yes," she said, "and you're a guy."

"I do have some Glenfiddich," I said, remembering that she drank scotch.

"You do? Then you're playing my song."

I drizzled some nectar of the gods over ice for both of us, and we sat down on the couch. I felt surprisingly comfortable next to her. I'd never been able to relax around beautiful women—every moment I spent near them felt like part of a high-stakes job interview—but with Talena I felt perfectly at ease.

"It's a little scary that you can do this," she said. "So everything everyone does on the Web can be tracked down?"

"It depends," I said. "Like, if you're using AOL you're actually probably pretty safe from this stuff, because everyone on AOL looks like they're on the same machine. On the other hand the AOL people know everything you do. Yeah, as a rule, most of the stuff you do can be watched."

"And when they tell you this is a secure connection, they're lying?"

"No, that's completely true, those are probably impossible to break into. But they'll still know what machine you're using to connect."

"Well. Call me freshly paranoid."

"If you really want to there's ways around it though," I said. "If he'd been careful, if he'd gone through Anonymizer or Zero-Knowledge or SafeWeb or something, we'd never be able to reach him."

"What are those?"

"Sites you go through that basically clean up everything you do so you're anonymous."

"But how do you know they're actually doing that?" she asked.

"You don't," I admitted. "I mean, you can run tests and so on, but to a certain extent you have to take it on trust. Doesn't really bug me though. I mean, I've got nothing to hide."

"You've got everything to hide," she said, "believe you me."

"Meaning what?"

"Meaning . . ." She visibly decided to avoid the subject and shook her head. "Meaning I don't trust the powers that be to know anything about me they don't have to, is all. So our friend The Bull is in Indonesia. What do you think that means?"

"I think it means he's still on the road," I said.

"Yeah," she said. "And you know what else it means?"

"I'm afraid I do."

"Means somebody else might wind up with knives in their eyes in a week or two. Unless we do something."

"Do something? Like what do you have in mind?"

"Beats the fuck outta me. That's the problem," she said, and emptied her Scotch. "Have you eaten? I'm starving."

"Me too," I lied.

We went to Crepes on Cole, just a couple blocks from where I lived. By unspoken mutual agreement we didn't talk about The Bull. Instead we talked about everything meaningless that either of us could think of. Favorite obscure movies. Most overrated rock stars. The decline and fall of the Great American Novel. Best long walks through San Francisco. What to do if you're pursued by rabid deer while biking through Marin County. Ten ways to spot a New Yorker on Market Street. Why the best neighborhoods always have the worst neighbors.

I think we were both surprised by how well we got along—a lot of the laughter was of the "I can't believe you like that too!" variety. She wasn't nearly as stuck-up and snobbish as I expected. Maybe a little bit, but when you're young and beautiful and you have the world's coolest job in the world's coolest city, a little bit goes with the territory. She lived in Potrero Hill and suffered through an hour-long commute to and from work, torpedoing my initial guesses about her perfect apartment and moneyed family. "LP mostly pays you with fun and prestige," she said at one point. "The dollars are pretty fucking nominal."

The only awkward pause came when I asked her where she was from. She grimaced, and said, "All over," in a distinct let's-change-the-subject tone. But we somehow got from there to the topic of proposed new Ben & Jerry's flavors, and the moment was quickly forgotten. When the waitress leaned over and politely told us that they were closing soon, both of us were surprised and glanced at our watches to double-check. Eleven o'clock had sneaked up a lot faster than either of us had realized.

We split the check and walked to the corner of Rivoli and Cole, where her bike was parked.

"Well," I said, "I'm glad you came over. That was fun."

She flashed me a million-watt smile that made my spine wobble. "Yeah, it was."

"So . . ." I said, as always drawing a blank on what I should say or do at this point.

"Yeah. We should talk about the whole . . . thing. I don't know. I feel like we have to do something, but I don't know what."

"Me too. Me neither."

We looked at each other for a moment longer.

"Well," she said. "I should go. Long bike ride home. Let's sleep on it. I'll call you tomorrow night, okay?"

"Sure thing," I said, and I watched her bike away, reluctantly abandoning all the fantasies in the back of my brain that involved her staying. Well, abandoning them for tonight. I didn't really think we were ever going to happen, but that never stopped a guy from dreaming.

12

CONSOLIDATION AND RESTRUCTURING

I got to work, logged in, read my e-mail, and realized I had absolutely nothing to do. Suited me fine. I pointed Internet Explorer to *www.interpol.com* and began to read.

About a half hour later I had given up my hope in Interpol. They seemed like a fine enough organization, sharing information and police techniques around the world, but they didn't run from country to country chasing international terrorists the way the movies made it seem. More of a bureaucracy than anything else. They specifically said on their site: To report a crime, don't contact us, go to the National Contact Bureau for your country.

What the hell, it couldn't hurt. I compiled all the information I already had, except for the bit about the Lonely Planet Web logs—didn't want to get Talena in trouble—and sent it the USA's NCB. I figured it would get read once and forwarded to the e-mail equivalent of the Dead Letter Office, or Psycho Conspiracy Theorist Office, but at least I had tried.

Just as I finished, Kevin came over to my desk.

"Paul," he said, "can I see you in my office? Something's come up."

"Sure," I said, guessing that the Morgan Stanley contract

was finally official. "Should we wait for Rob? I think he's at lunch." Rob was due to be the lead designer on the project. Actually I hadn't seen him all day, but that was typical. He was an artiste and played up his impetuosity for all it was worth.

"No," he said, "this doesn't involve Rob."

I went into his office and sat down as he closed the door.

"All right," he said. "Well. Look, Paul, everyone knows you're a brilliant programmer."

"Thanks."

"So brilliant that we've allowed you continue with your rather unorthodox work schedule of, is it four months vacation a year?"

"Four months unpaid leave." Was this one of their biannual attempts to convince me to work all year?

"But as you know the company's been going through difficult times lately. The bottom's really dropped out of the market, and we've been burning money like water."

I was going to bring his attention to the amusing mixed metaphor but decided against it. Instead I switched to rah-rah-rah mode and said, "But the Morgan Stanley contract is going to save our bacon, right?"

"Yesterday," Kevin said, "Morgan Stanley assigned the contract to Quidnunc."

"Ah." One of our competitors.

"This has left us in a bind where we simply have too many employees and very few billable projects. As this was not totally unexpected, we have assembled a contingency plan that we are now putting in motion. As a result of losing this contract, market forces are forcing us to significantly restructure the size of the organization. We predict that this is a temporary expedient, only lasting until this anomalous market downturn is corrected."

I began to get an uneasy feeling in the pit of my stomach. "Kevin—"

"It's important to realize that our growth paradigm will not in the long run be affected by this and we view it as a hiccup. However, in the interim we have been forced to make some very difficult decisions with a view toward consolidating our operations—"

"Kevin, are you laying me off?"

He tried to look me straight in the eye, I'll give him that, but at the last second he failed, and, staring at the desk, he said, "Yes."

"Okay," I said.

"Paul, I'm really sorry, I fought as hard as I could for you, but the top brass—"

"I'm not just saying okay," I interrupted. "I actually mean it. In fact I'm happy to hear it." And I was too. In fact I realized I was smiling. I felt as if a huge weight was ballooning away from my head. Unemployment! I felt like I was being paroled.

"Really?" he asked.

"Absolutely."

"Why?"

"Middle management like you will never understand." I meant it as a tease but I think he took it as an insult. Ah, well, he had, after all, just fired me, I could live with him thinking I'd taken a shot at him.

"What about Rob?" I asked.

"Him too."

"Severance package?"

"Four weeks pay and one month free COBRA health coverage. Here." He gave me a manila envelope from a frighteningly tall stack on his desk.

"That sounds fair. Am I supposed to sign a contract saying that I won't sue you or something?"

"Jeez. We never thought of that. Do you think you could . . ." he began.

"Kevin," I said. "I'm not suing you, but I'm not signing anything either. Anything else?"

"What about the Palm Pilot we gave you?"

"I threw it into the San Francisco Bay," I said. It was the truth.

"You—what?"

"Can't stand the things," I explained.

"Oh," he said. "Well. I guess we'll just write that one off. Your laptop's here?"

"It sure is," I said, very glad that all of my important notes and correspondence were backed up on my Yahoo! account. "I'll just leave it."

"Okay. Well. Thanks for taking this so well."

"My pleasure. Are you supposed to escort me out of the building now?"

He looked miserable.

"Ah, jeez, you are too." I shook my head. "Just watch your own back. I've heard that in some places the last guy to get the ax on a day like this is the guy who just fired everyone else. Spares the place a lot of bad blood, or something."

This was a total lie but it was worth it for the frightened expression that crawled over his face. I followed him out of the building feeling a little guilty about it. But only a little.

I walked out of the office, crossed Mission Street, took the little pathway that led to Market Street, intending to go down to the Muni station and go home. Just at the corner of Market and Montgomery I stopped dead in my tracks so abruptly that an Asian woman nearly collided with me. I barely noticed her furious look.

I stood there for what felt like a long time. I think maybe it really was a long time. Maybe half an hour. People gave me strange looks. Probably because I was dressed normally. Part of San Francisco's charm; if I had covered myself in silver paint or mummified myself in leather strips, nobody would have paid me the least bit of attention, but a tranced-out yuppie like me, that was man bites dog.

I guess I flipped out a little just then. It was a whole bunch of things. Partly it was being newly unemployed. It's something that rattles you, a lot, even if you have money in the bank, even if you know you can get a new job in a matter of days, even if you're actually happy about it. And I was happy about it. I was happier than I had been for months, but I didn't understand why. That rattled me too.

I had never been so free, not in my whole life. It was terrifying.

I don't know why, but I felt like there were an infinite number of roads leading from the corner of Market and Montgomery, and the one that I chose would define my entire life. That half hour felt pregnant with . . . . whatever you want to call it. Doom. Fate. Destiny.

I could get another job. I could stay here. I liked Talena, and Talena liked me, and she hadn't said anything about a boyfriend. I thought there might be possibilities there. I could stay and try to teach myself how to be happy. It couldn't be that hard, could it? Lots of people seemed to manage it.

I could move to London. Move to my tribe, or at least find out once and for all whether they were in fact my tribe. Maybe a change of scenery was just what I needed. Maybe my problem was that I was never meant to live in America, and I could never be happy here.

I could go home to Canada. I could work for a year as a volunteer teacher in some godforsaken village in Chad or Suriname or Bangladesh. I could move down to L.A. and start writing screenplays. I could move to Zimbabwe and join my cousins on their farm. I could go to the South Bronx and begin a romantic Dostoevsky-esque death spiral of drugs and violence and empty sex with crack whores. I could become an Antarctic explorer, or a professional scuba diver, or a Cirque du Soleil acrobat. I could enter the Shaolin Temple and become the baddest motherfucker in the whole wide world.

The man who killed Stanley Goebel was in Kuta Beach, Bali. He might be the same man who killed Laura.

I reflexively told myself to stop thinking about Laura. I had done enough thinking about Laura. I had done more deep, wrenching thinking about Laura than I ever would have if she had not been murdered and we had gotten married and spent the rest of our lives together. I had loved her, and I had lost her, and I had to get on with my life. She was dead. A man had killed her. For a long time I had nursed a suspicion that her killer was someone I knew, someone on the truck. But I could let that suspicion go now. I was free of it at last. One thing this whole Stanley Goebel thing had made clear was that, since I knew for a fact that everyone on the truck had been in Cameroon while The Bull was stalking Mozambique and Malawi, there was no way that anyone on the truck could be The Bull. And that meant that Laura's murder had been nothing but a random act of senseless violence. It proved that her killer was John Doe, faceless, anonymous, unknown.

Wait.

Did it?

Or was there another possibility?

I turned away from the Muni station and walked back along Market Street. I entered the American Express travel office at the next corner.

"Hello," I said to the lady behind the desk. "I want to go to Bali."

"And when would you like to go?" she asked.

"Today," I said, living out a fantasy I had long had, and

despite the emotions flickering and straining within me, a
toxic maelstrom of suspicion and anger and confusion and
loss and the need to do anything rather than nothing, I managed to enjoy the look of surprise on her face.

It all worked like a charm. There was a flight from Los
Angeles to Denpasar that left at 10 P.M. Shuttle flights went
from SFO to LAX every half hour. It wasn't even that expensive, two thousand dollars return, not so bad for a last-minute
ticket across the Pacific. I could afford it. I scheduled the
return flight for three weeks later.

I went home. I packed. I called SuperShuttle. I wanted to
check the Thorn Tree, but my laptop had been repossessed,
so I went to the nearest copy center and checked from there.
And indeed:

```
BC088269        As a matter of fact I am pretty
11/07 08:02     smart, Mr. Wood. A lot smarter
                than you're going to look when
                I'm through with you.
```

I felt triumphant. I'd lured him into a conversation. I
wrote back:

```
PaulWood        Spare us, OK? I'm talking about
11/07 16:51     real murders here. I don't have
                time for a juvenile full-of-
                shit wannabe like you. You say
                you're The Bull? Then tell me
                this, what color jacket were
                you wearing up on the trail?
                You know what I'm talking
                about. Or you would if you were
                for real.
```

Then I went back home and called Talena at work. She'd just left. I called her at home. She wasn't there yet. I left her a message telling her to call me right away. I waited in the study, for her phone call or the SuperShuttle van, whichever got there first.

The phone rang. I picked it up.

"I called my friend in Cape Town," she said. "The South Africans were the same as the others. Swiss Army knives in their eyes. He's reopening the case and he's going to talk to your friend Gavin and call Interpol."

"Great," I said. "I'm going to Indonesia."

"You're what?"

"I'm going to Indonesia."

"When?"

"Tonight," I said.

"Tonight? Are you crazy?"

"Maybe."

"What the fuck do you think you're playing at, you idiot?"

"Hey," I said, more than a little hurt. I was doing this, I suddenly realized, in part to impress Talena. "I got laid off today, I got nothing better to do, I'm going to go down there."

"And do what?"

"Find him," I said shortly.

"Yeah? Suppose you do. And then what?"

"And then I'll know who he is."

"No, you dumb shit, and then you'll be dead, because in case you've forgotten, you're a *computer programmer*, and you're chasing a fucking *serial killer*, and he already knows who you are, and he's going to fucking murder you if you find him. You're being the worst kind of macho moron. Cancel the tickets and stay here."

I chose to ignore her advice. "Listen," I said, "he sent another message today."

"I know. I saw."

"Could you try to check to see if it came from the same place? If you remember anything about what I did?"

"I remember fine, I already checked, it came from the same place," she said. "Now tell me you're going to cancel the tickets."

"I'm just going to go there and see what I can find out," I said.

"Balthazar," she said quietly. "You stupid *shit*. You think I want to find you with knives in your eyes?"

"Call me Paul."

"All right, Paul. Tell me this. Suppose you do find him. Then what exactly are you going to do?"

"I don't know," I said.

"You think you're going to kill him because he killed your friend?"

"I don't know," I repeated.

"Because I'm telling you now, you're not the type."

"How do you know what the type is?"

"I've seen a lot more murder victims than you ever have, you . . . Look." She abruptly switched from angry hectoring to pleading. "I grew up in Bosnia. I was there for the war. I've met enough nice guys who wound up dead for one lifetime. Take it from me, you're no killer. And I know you're a guy and that sounds like an insult, but it's not, I like you for it. And believe me, *please* believe me, chasing him down to Indonesia is the worst and stupidest thing you can do right now."

For a moment I started to wonder if she had a point. Traveling halfway around the world to track down a serial killer in order to impress a woman I had just met—that was just maybe not the height of good judgment, especially when she was so obviously unimpressed. Even though things were in motion, the ticket purchased and my ride to the airport en route, I might have reconsidered if that had been the only thing driving me.

But Talena wasn't the main reason I was going. Not by a

long shot. For the first time ever I felt like I was actually doing something other than grieving in response to Laura's death. Call it the unrequited need for closure. Call it being sick and tired of life pushing me around, and wanting to do some pushing back. Call it revenge. Maybe Talena was right, maybe this was the worst, stupidest, least rational, most insane thing I could do. I didn't know. But I did know that it felt miles better than doing nothing at all.

"I gotta go," I said. "SuperShuttle is here."

"No, Paul, *don't* be a total fucking—"

"Wish me luck," I said. "I'll be in touch."

THREE

INDONESIA

13

TOO MANY AUSTRALIANS

The flight passed in a haze of bad food and bad movies and bad company. I didn't really mind. Sometimes I felt that as I had gotten older the only thing I had really gotten better at was waiting. Twelve hours on an airplane? No problem. I dozed, watched movies, read the Lonely Planet guide I'd bought at the airport, stared out from my window seat at the endless metallic sheen of the ocean. I had an emergency-exit row and the extra space to go with it, for which I was very grateful, as they don't make economy-class seats for men six feet tall. I didn't really think. There didn't seem to be any need for it.

The twelve hours passed in a flash, and then I was outside in Indonesia's sweltering heat, walking down steep stairs from the airplane to the tarmac. I passed a McDonald's and a Hard Rock Cafe on the taxi ride from the airport to the beach, and found a comfortable bungalow room for two dollars a night.

Kuta Beach was awful. Green, and pretty, and it boasted a terrific beach, but awful all the same. It reminded me of Fort Lauderdale. The population consisted largely of noisy, obnoxious, drunken, college-age Australians. Generally I like

Aussies, but not this batch. Indonesian men wandered around with hateful eyes and briefcases full of cheap knock-offs for sale, watches and perfume and rings and Zippo lighters. Indonesian women walked around, barely clad, offering five-dollar "massages" to the Australians. And watching the Aussies I could see how the idea that all white men look alike and all white women are easy gets around the Third World.

I sat on the beach and watched the sunset. It was spectacular. But it was half ruined by the company. One drunken batch of Aussies played rugby on the beach, shoving the Indonesian hawkers out of their way, knocking one woman and her cargo of bright sarongs sprawling onto the wet sand. Another group passed a huge hash pipe around. At the beachfront cafe where I sat there were two men sitting at tables with prostitutes. One was a fat bearded man in his twenties, strutting and beaming as if the presence of two twenty-dollar-a-day whores showed that he was the most desirable man on the planet. The other was a wrinkled, white-haired man with two girls who looked about thirteen.

It occurred to me that The Bull was not so different from a lot of other travelers. Some people go traveling to explore, or to experience; but a hell of a lot go to exploit. Many Third World travelers are there at least in part because poor countries offer cheap drugs, cheap sex, complete anonymity, and police who happily turn a blind eye in exchange for a small contribution. The Bull took it a little further than the drug tourists or the sex tourists, he got his kicks from murder, but the general idea was the same.

I was no angel myself. I had lost track of how many countries I had gotten high in. Sure, soft drugs should be decriminalized, but in the meantime it was hard to argue that I was somehow helping a country by contributing to the violent gangs that invariably control the drug trade. I'd never slept with a local girl, the idea made me morally queasy; but I'd met and traveled with lots of people who had. It wasn't exactly prostitution, the way it was usually done, just an accepted trade-off; the local girl sleeps with you for a week or two, and you buy her a lot of gifts. It wasn't just men either, I'd met muscle-bound Africans with temporary European girlfriends who were, shall we say, not conventionally attractive. Sometimes it was genuine romance. Sometimes it was a harmless fling. Sometimes it was exploitation. The line was much too fine, and rationalization much too easy, for my liking. I was sure the fat bearded man was already telling himself that the two beautiful women at his side were there mostly because of his powerful physical magnetism.

I finished my beer, watched the sunset, listened to the ocean. I was exhausted, drained by a day's travel and by jet lag. I wanted to sleep, but instead I went out and found the Internet World Cafe. It was fair-sized, about twenty machines. There was nobody there that I recognized. I'd spent the flight alternating between fear that I wouldn't be able to find the killer and fear that I would. Now that I was here it was the first fear that dominated. There were literally thousands of tourists in Kuta Beach; even if my theory was correct and I would recognize the killer, what were the odds that I would just happen to bump into him?

I logged in and checked the Thorn Tree, but no response from our boy yet. Talena had sent me an e-mail telling me I was a complete idiot and she'd be damned if she'd help me and I better send daily updates. I sent one back telling her I'd gotten in and everything was fine, went back to my bungalow, and got a much-deserved night's sleep.

I had come to Indonesia because I had resurrected the theory that Laura's murderer was somebody on the truck. Originally I had written that off because the dates didn't fit, there was no way a trucker could have been involved in the

Southern Africa killings. But now I wondered: What if Laura
had been a *copycat* killing? What if somebody on the truck
had heard about the Southern Africa killings, from a phone
call or an e-mail, and decided to respond in kind? What if
Laura's murder hadn't been random at all? What if she was
killed by somebody she knew, who dressed it up to look like
the work of the serial killer allegedly in Africa?

What if it had been one of us?

I could think of three candidates. Three people I had traveled with, gotten drunk and gotten high with, cooked with,
sweated blood with, who I had seen sick and angry and
embarrassed and ecstatic and giddy, who I had spent nearly
every day with for four solid months; three people I could
still envision as killers. Lawrence Carlin. Michael Smith.
Morgan Jackson.

If true this would explain a lot. Especially if the same person who killed Laura had killed Stanley Goebel as well, if
Goebel had been a victim of the copycat—call him The Bull
II—rather than the original killer. That would explain why
he came after me on the trail. Because he knew me and I
knew him. He feared I had seen him in Letdar or seen his
name on one of the checkpoint ledgers. I wished I'd looked at
those more closely. So it also explained why he switched to
using Stanley Goebel's name and passport.

Of course there were still a few holes in the theory. First
of all, how would he have known the vital detail of the Swiss
Army knives when apparently nobody knew this but the
South African police, who weren't telling? And if Laura's
death had been a crime of passion, which I thought possible—Lawrence, in particular, had had a brief fling with her
early on in the trip, before she and I came together, and I
thought had never really gotten over it—why would the same
person have gone on to kill a total stranger in Nepal two
years later? And what were the odds against my stumbling
onto a crime committed by the same man?

Actually those odds weren't as awful as they first looked. It is an enormous planet out there, people who say "it's a small world" obviously haven't seen much of it, but the backpacker trail makes up a pretty small and navigable part. It wouldn't be the first time I stumbled into someone I knew. In Thailand in 1999 I had bumped into a girl I knew from England on Thanon Khao Sanh, and the very next day met a guy I'd traveled with briefly in Zimbabwe. The Lonely Planet is a shrunken planet. And it shrinks even further depending on the type of traveler you are. Anyone who spends four months on a truck in West Africa is an adventure traveler, who likes struggle and challenge, prefers *doing* over *seeing*, and is too poor to buy his or her own Land Rover. There are a finite number of places in the world that suit the budget adventure traveler, and the Annapurna Circuit is one of them.

All of which might lead me to The Bull II, if he existed. There weren't many places around Bali for an adventure traveler. The drunken beach-bum culture in Kuta Beach? Definitely not. Culture and dances and art in Ubud, a little farther north? No. In fact the only Bali possibility mentioned in my SFO-purchased *Indonesia: A Travel Survival Kit* was a live volcano named Gunung Batur, in the middle of the island. You could climb to the top of it and fry eggs on the hot rocks there. I thought that might be exactly the kind of thing The Bull II was into. Because I thought he and I might be into exactly the same kind of thing.

Not counting killing random strangers, of course.

It was three days after the cookies-and-minefield incident that Laura and I finally came together. The night Robbie got lost in the desert. Damn fool went for a walk and got caught out by sunset. Then, instead of staying where he was, he kept walking, trying to find us. It was an hour before

Emma, who was at that point Robbie's girl, realized he hadn't gone for a nap. We all rushed out to look for him before Hallam could stop us and impose some kind of organization on the search.

Our camp that night was in the shelter of a U-shaped sand dune. Most of the others ran out toward the mouth of the U calling Robbie's name, but Laura and I, who had been spending a lot of quietly nervous time near each other in the previous three days, slogged up the dune, sliding two steps back for every three steps forward, until we reached the top. Our idea had been that maybe he had his flashlight with him and we could see him from the top.

The moon was nearly full that night, which in the Sahara means you can easily read a newspaper by its light. We could see a long way. But there was nothing but the desert wind, so fierce that contrails of sand were visible six inches above the dune, so loud that it swallowed up our cries of Robbie's name as soon as they left our lungs. Laura raised her hand to protect her face from the wind, and without even thinking about it, I stepped between her and the wind and put my arms around her protectively. She looked up at me, her eyes wide, and held me tight.

"I hope he's okay," she said. I could barely hear her over the wind's howl.

"He'll be fine," I said. "He'll stop when he realizes he's lost. Hallam will find him."

A few seconds passed, then I lowered my head those final two inches and kissed her for the first time.

It was the headlights that interrupted us, I don't know how much time later, the headlights of the Tuareg Land Rover that had miraculously stumbled across Robbie wandering through the desert five miles from our camp and, even more miraculously, tracked us back to this particular sand dune. After returning our lost sheep, they camped beside us, and Laura and I spent most of the rest of that night beneath their big canvas tent. It was one of my favorite memories, sitting with my arms wrapped around her as we and the Tuareg nomads in their sky-blue robes sat around their fire, sang songs from our respective homelands, and ate grilled chunks of a dead lamb that stared at us accusingly from the back of their Land Rover. It was a good night. It might have been the best night of my life.

Three suspects.

Lawrence Carlin because he had carried an ill-concealed torch for Laura long after she dumped him, and he was a menacing figure we had nicknamed the Terminator only half in jest, a man so tightly coiled that it was easy to imagine him snapping.

I thought maybe we had seen him snap, just once. In Nouadhibou, during a long, hot, hungry wait outside the passport office, a cloud of flies descended on the truck, so thick they actually obscured the sun. They didn't bite, but they crawled all over us, feasting on our sweat, buzzing and twitching. It was enough to drive you mad.

It drove Lawrence into a killing frenzy. A quiet, emotionless, expressionless killing frenzy that must have lasted ten minutes. He stalked barefoot up and down the truck, smashing flies into unidentifiable blotches with his sandals, paying no attention to the catcalls which slowly diminished into a silence that was both awed and a little bit frightened. Under those circumstances, believe me, ten minutes is a very long time. It was funny, yes; we often mocked him about it afterward, yes; but it was also genuinely scary.

For a long time he didn't like me. That was understandable. From his point of view, I had stolen his girl. Their breakup had been amicable enough, and they were only together two weeks, and he was always polite to both of us, but I often sensed cold hostility beneath the courtesy, and on several occasions I noticed angry glances directed at me. Little things. Perfectly understandable. But still.

In Cameroon, after her death, he and I became close friends. Grim friends, joined by mutual grief and shock, but close friends all the same. The others helped me, supported me, those nights I got desperately drunk and maudlin; but Lawrence actually joined me. Some nights he seemed as torn up and despairing as I did.

Maybe because he had a guilty conscience.

Michael Smith, despite all his charm, because of an incident that occurred in Ouagadougou, popularly known as Wagga, the capital city of Burkina Faso, quite a pleasant place despite being the fifth poorest country in the world. He and I were walking down the road, a pathetic-looking small boy scurrying alongside us, trying to sell us a model car made of meshed wire. You saw them all over, small boys with model cars. As by this time both of us were old Africa hands we ignored the small boy completely. Until we turned a corner. The small boy, on the outside of our turn, had to sprint to keep up with us, looking up at us and pleading for our custom in soft broken French as he ran. He never saw the oncoming car.

There was a wet thump a little like a water balloon hitting pavement. Then the small boy lay dazed on the ground, blood oozing from his mouth and his left leg. And Michael laughed. He laughed as if he had just witnessed a Buster Keaton comedy routine, not a malnourished child's serious injury.

I stopped and stared, not knowing what to do. The car—a Mercedes with tinted windows, almost certainly belonging to a government official—reversed slightly then drove around the fallen body and away. I took a step toward the victim but Michael grabbed my arm and pulled me back.

"What—what are you doing?" I demanded.

"We have to go," he said. "They'll blame it on us. They'll call the police. We'll be arrested, we'll have to pay off everyone and their dog, it'll be whole *days* of hassle."

Other passersby began to congregate around the boy, who hadn't moved except for a couple of spastic twitches. A small pool of blood thickened in the dirt around him. The Africans looked at us darkly and muttered to one another. I didn't know what they were saying, but I could tell from their tone of voice that they were moving from shock to outrage in a hurry.

Michael stepped into the street, tugging me along, and waved down a taxi.

"We can't just leave him," I protested feebly.

"There's nothing you can do," Michael said, his voice irritated.

He pulled me into the taxi. And to tell you the truth I didn't really resist.

He was probably right about what would have happened. He was probably right about my inability to help. It wasn't that that put him on my short list of potential murderers. It was that laugh, that instinctive amused laugh, when he saw the car smash into that little boy.

Morgan Jackson because he was the Great White Hunter, friendly but utterly without empathy. He told stories about hunting wild pigs for sport in his native Australia, relishing every gruesome detail. He left the truck several times, alone, for up to a week, and never told us much about where he had been when he got back.

He was fun to be around, and he seemed to like me and Laura. But if he didn't like you, he made it pretty clear that he didn't much care whether you lived or died. And with Morgan you knew it wasn't just an expression. If I had been with Morgan instead of Michael that day in Wagga, he wouldn't have laughed. He would have kept walking without paying the wounded child any notice at all.

One night in Ghana, I remember, we hacked the campsite out of the bush with machetes, a job Morgan took great pleasure in. Around the fire that night the talk turned to the wildlife in West Africa. More precisely to its nonexistence. There were allegedly a couple of hundred elephants in Ghana, but for the most part the denizens of West Africa's game parks had all been killed and eaten during the region's periods of drought and famine.

"Must have fucked you off to hear that," Robbie said to Morgan. "The Great White Hunter comes all the way here and there's no animals left to hunt."

"Not a problem," Morgan said.

"Why not?"

Morgan smiled. A toothy predatorial smile. "I can always hunt Africans," he said. "If I feel the need. No shortage of them, now, is there?"

After a moment we collectively decided it was a joke, just another outrageous Morgan quote, and we laughed. Uncomfortably, but we all laughed. Except for Morgan himself. He just continued to smile.

Bali is a small island, and it took me only two hours by air-con tourist bus and no-air-con bemo (a van with two benches in back, jammed full of about twenty people, their luggage, their pets, and their families) to get to the town of Penelokan, on the edge of Gunung Batur's volcanic crater. Indonesia was ridiculously green. I have been to many lush tropical places, but Indonesia's green was so deep and pure it seemed surreal, as if a drug had heightened my senses. Statues of Hindu gods in stone and wood marked every crossroad, each one a little artistic gem, perfectly rendered. Metallic crooning *gamelan* music wafted through the air at every other turn. The men wore white and gold, and the women wore sarongs so brightly colored they nearly burned my retinas.

The view from Penelokan was stunning. The crater was a perfect circle maybe ten miles in diameter and four hundred feet deep, and Gunung Batur rose, red lava over green forest, from the exact center. A crescent-shaped lake took up the eastern third of the crater. The remaining floor was scarred by previous volcanic flows, some of which had overrun whole towns. Not far from Gunung Batur was a sea of black lava from which rose a verdantly green cone-shaped hill. The black lava reminded me of Mile Six Beach near Limbe. And of Laura's naked corpse splayed on its fine black volcanic sand.

I hitched a ride on a pickup truck down the steep switchbacking ribbon of road that led through a volcano-destroyed ghost town to the settlement of Toyah Bungkah at the foot of the mountain. More of a hill, really, maybe two thousand meters high, and that in heels. But nobody ever shelled out fifty U.S. dollars for a guide to lead him up a hill.

Toyah Bungkah was pleasant enough. Scenically located between the mountain and the lake. More lodges than you could shake a stick at, and stores selling Cokes and Marlboros and Snickers and the other American logos you could find anywhere in the world these days, but the people seemed a lot more friendly than those of Kuta Beach. Lots of would-be guides, but they didn't hassle me too much. I didn't intend to climb Gunung Batur. I was just here to check the lodges. I had noticed in Kuta Beach that I had had to sign in to my bungalow, and was hoping that was a universal government mandate.

It was; by government decree every lodge had a thick black binder at their front desk in which resident foreigners had to enter name, country, and passport number. What luck.

I pretended to consider staying at each lodge in turn, actually pretty typical shoestring backpacker behavior, except I wasn't seeking the lowest price and trying to bargain it down, I was looking through all the registers. No joy. No Lawrence Carlin, no Michael Smith, no Morgan Jackson. And no Stanley Goebel, although I doubted The Bull II was still traveling under that passport.

By the time I had exhausted the possibilities, it was still midafternoon, and I was depressed and disappointed. If I rushed, I could still make it back to Kuta Beach tonight, but what was the rush? I had struck out there just as I had here. My whole flight to Indonesia was beginning to feel like an embarrassing moment of madness. It was nice of Talena to have been concerned, but I should be so lucky as to be endangered. I decided to stay the night and in the morning climb Gunung Batur. Since I'd apparently come to Indonesia to exercise futility, I might as well try to enjoy myself.

I didn't hire a guide. How hard could it be? You just went up until you could go up no more. Admittedly there were a few false starts in the forested trails, and a couple more past the tree line on the barren lava crags that rose to the top, but I made it. Two weeks on the Annapurna Circuit had toughened my legs so much that this low-altitude ascent felt like a walk in Golden Gate Park. The lava was razor-sharp, but that just meant my boots gripped it more firmly.

The top was a U-shaped wall around the central crater, like a castle wall surrounding the treasures within. The interior of the crater was lushly green. There was a distinct smell of rotten eggs, and at one point I smelled burning rubber and looked down to see my boots bubbling on one of the hot rocks. Only a few meters separated me from magma, I reckoned, quickly stepping away.

The last eruption had been some twenty years previous, and historically speaking, Gunung Batur was about due for another, saith the Lonely Planet. Looking down I could see a half-dozen black frozen-lava rivers running all the way to the lake. I wondered how it felt to live in Toyah Bungkah, knowing that any day you might be immolated by a river of searing lava. I guess not that different from living in San Francisco, knowing that you're next-door neighbor to the San Andreas Fault.

I climbed back down and hitched a ride back up to Penelokan with a friendly French cyclist named Marc. Three bemos and three hours later, at nightfall, I was back in Kuta Beach, at the Internet World Cafe, reading the latest addition to the Thorn Tree conversation.

```
BC088269      Green.
11/10 04:07   And a ski mask.
              How you been, Paul?
```

It was him all right. It was the last line that gave me shivers. That friendly how-you-been. As if he knew me. As if my copycat The Bull II theory was correct. I should have felt triumphant, but I felt frightened, and looked around in the cafe as I read it, as if he was right there, watching me.

Then I checked my e-mail. Talena reported that the latest message was from a different IP number and that I should come home. I reread it. She did not mention what the new IP number was.

It was 8 P.M. Indonesia time. I couldn't remember if that made it 8 A.M. or 6 A.M. or 10 A.M. or what in California. Also I was too pissed off to care. I found a Home Country Direct phone, gave the AT&T operator my credit-card number, and called Talena at home. It rang three times and went to the machine. I pushed NEXT CALL and dialed it again. And again. The third time, she picked up.

"Whosit?" she croaked.

"It's Paul, how's it going, what's the new IP number?"

"What?"

"You said there was a new IP number but you didn't tell me what it was."

"Paul . . . fucking . . . *fuck*. Do you know what time it is here?"

"No."

"It's four in the fucking morning."

"Well, I'm sorry. Now what's the number?"

"Fuck you, you obsessive shit! I was trying to sleep!"

I swallowed and admitted to myself that I was arguably being a little rude. "I'm sorry. But, look, I flew halfway around the planet for this, and I need your help."

"Aw, fuck. Call me back in five minutes." And the line went dead.

I went and got a green Fanta. My favorite soft drink, tragically unavailable anywhere in the world outside of Southeast Asia. Africa had had a whole rainbow of various Fanta colors . . . except for green. I gave her seven minutes and called Talena back.

"Hi, you annoying rude little shit wake-up caller," she said, but she sounded grumpy rather than angry. Her voice sounded tinny.

"And a top of the morning to you too."

"You having any luck over there?"

"No," I said.

"Good. Come home."

"Talena, just give me the new number. I'm sure you have it already."

"Yes, I do," she said. "But I'm not going to give it to you. You're just going to use it to get in trouble."

"Talena . . ." I hesitated. "Look. There were actually a couple of things I never told you, because they just sounded totally crazy."

"Well. You sure pick a good time to fess up."

"I think I may already know this guy. And I think he might have already come after me on the trail in Nepal."

There was a pause, then she said, "You better unpack that a *lot*."

I told her about my copycat truck-killer theory, and about how the man in the ski mask had pursued me on the trail, which I hadn't mentioned before for fear of sounding paranoid.

When I was finished, she said, "So your pet madman has *already tried to kill you* and you're going after him *again*?"

"Yeah," I said. "But, listen, I know what I'm going to do when I find him."

"Yeah? What's that?"

"Nothing," I said. "If I see a face I recognize, I'm going to turn right the fuck around and come straight back to California that same day. Do not pass Go, do not collect two hundred thousand rupiah."

"Well, I'm glad to hear your sanity is leaking back to you in dribs and drabs."

"But I need to know if I'm right," I said. "And if I'm right, I need to know who it is. And to have even a chance of that, I need you to give me the new IP number. Please."

"He might have left Indonesia, you know. What if the new number's in China? You going to follow him there?"

"No. Then I'm going to sit on the beach for a week and come home."

She thought it over. Then she thought it over some more. As I opened my mouth to plead my case again, she said, "All right. On one condition."

"What's that?"

"That you e-mail me every single day like you promised to do. There was no e-mail yesterday."

"I'm calling you now," I protested.

"That's not yesterday."

"It is my time."

"Okay. Listen up. You are to call or e-mail me every single day, my time, with any and all information that you have. Or there will be hell to pay, believe you me. Oh, and you are also to tell me, right this very second, absolutely anything else that you have left out of the story."

"E-mail every day," I promised. "And I haven't left anything else out."

"If you have, you better hope The Bull gets you before I do," she warned. And then she gave me the number.

"Good-bye," she said.

"Wait," I said.

"What now?"

"I just realized. I guess I have left something else out."

"Tell me," she said.

"It's just . . . you know how I said that a friend of mine was murdered two years ago?"

"Yes?"

"She wasn't just a friend," I said. "She was my girlfriend."

"Your girlfriend."

"Yeah."

"Paul?" she asked, and her voice was husky.

"Yes?"

"Please, please, please don't do anything stupid. Please. Try to come back in one piece."

"That's what I'm best at," I said, trying to be jaunty.

"Don't you make a fucking joke out of it," she said sharply. "Don't you fucking joke. Promise me you won't do anything stupid. Promise me when you see him you'll turn around and walk away."

"I promise," I said.

"You better take care of yourself."

"I will. Bye."

"Bye."

I hung up and stared at the IP number I had written on my hand. I didn't know if I could keep my promise. If the number did lead me to the killer, I didn't know what I would do. What I had told her was the truth, my plan really was just to get a name and get the hell out. But that was only a plan. I didn't know what I would actually do. I wouldn't know until it happened.

The new number led me to the Sukarnoputri Cafe, Mataran, Lombok, Indonesia.

14

TETEBATU BLUES

The 10 A.M. ferry eventually left at 2:30 P.M. But it was worth the wait. The ocean was the purest blue imaginable. Like the green of the islands. It was as if only Indonesia used the real colors, and everywhere else had washed-out imitations. It took only four hours to reach Lombok, the next island over in Indonesia's endless chain, roughly the same size as Bali but according to Lonely Planet very different, Muslim, not Hindu, poorer, more rural, not near as heavily traveled. My kind of place. The ferry was stuffed to the gills with about three hundred people, two-thirds of whom were backpackers. There were only four lifeboats, and I thought uneasily about the occasional reports from Indonesia of Hundreds Dead in Ferry Disaster. But there was no disaster. We got into Lembar port in the middle of an astonishingly beautiful sunset, the sun enormous and crimson, the sky littered with pink cotton-candy cloud-dragons, the ocean so blue it was nearly purple.

A gaggle of bemos awaited us, and their drivers herded us to Mataran, the biggest city in Lombok, maybe half a million people spread out over a long narrow snake of a city. We passed department stores, vegetable markets, men welding with cheap sunglasses as goggles in open lots that had been turned into mechanic's shops and decorated with a thousand dying machines. We overtook donkey carts and other bemos and Cadillacs. We were just in time to hear the sunset call to prayers from the mosques in town, that haunting atonal call that sounds like a terrible lamentation.

Our bemo driver took us to the Hotel Zahir, which presumably gave him a kickback for everyone he brought who stayed there. Normally this arrangement irritates me, but I wasn't in a mood to pigheadedly find somewhere else. The room had a fan and a mosquito net, and while there was no hot water, who wanted it in the sweltering hundred-degree heat? There were no names I recognized on the ledger. I got onto the hotel's computer to send an update to Talena, my eyes watering with sleepiness. I was nearly dead with exhaustion even though it wasn't that late. Bushwhacked by jet lag, I curled up in my mosquito net and fell asleep to the crooning of gecko lizards, crying out their name: *geck-ooh, geck-ooh, geck-ooh.*

In the morning I took one of the local-transit bemos, which acted like buses, to the central market, where Lonely Planet told me I would find the Sukarnoputri Cafe. I politely declined several offers to show me around the market, which did have an impressive array of carpets and sarongs and sculpture and extraordinary wooden masks, and checked out the Sukarnoputri. It was low-ceilinged, dark, and refreshingly cool, with dirt floors and a Bob Marley poster in the corner. Eight computers. Six people. Nobody I recognized. But again, what had I expected? That I would wander in just as The Bull II was there, and he would be so overcome by guilt that he would e-mail me a full confession right then and there?

I went round the lodges. Mataran probably had hundreds of hotels, but most of them were for Indonesians, and only a dozen or so were mentioned in Lonely Planet. It took me a few hours to get around to them all. None had had any familiar names staying there recently. Another strikeout.

I sat in a pleasant open-air park, concrete walkways around and over a gleaming blue pool, and reread my Lonely Planet to see what there was to do in Lombok. Hang out and get high on the Gili Archipelago — okay, they didn't explicitly say "get high," but the meaning was clear. Hang out and surf at Kuta Beach, which was apparently very different from the Kuta Beach in Bali, nearly deserted. Go east and take a ferry to the next island over. Or climb Gunung Rinjani, a real mountain more than three thousand meters high, in the center of the island. A three-day climb requiring tents and food and the works.

If The Bull II existed, if he was still on the island, and if he was an adventure traveler, all of which I was seriously beginning to doubt, then he was probably on Gunung Rinjani. But even if he existed, I thought he was probably moving on, island-hopping to the east, going to the real adventure, the real wilderness, of Irian Jaya. And I was beginning to feel that there was no point in following him. This was a very big country, and he had a two-day lead.

I found a compromise. Lonely Planet said that generally you climbed Gunung Rinjani up from the north and then down to the south, coming down to the village of Tetebatu in the middle of the island. Tetebatu was easily accessible by road, high enough at 1000m that it was noticeably cooler than the rest of the island, and a pleasant place to stay. I could wander around the verdant jungle and watch waterfalls and monkeys. That sounded fine to me. I felt more than a little like a monkey already for coming here at all. Maybe I could pick up some tips on appropriate primate behavior.

"Easily accessible" turned out to be a wee bit of an exaggeration. It was a small island, but the trip took six hours. A bemo to the transit center in Pao Montong, and an hour-and-a-half wait as the next bemo driver negotiated with the authorities there. I quenched my thirst by eating a bushelful of tasty *rambutan* fruit, familiar to me from Thailand. Then a bemo up to Kotoraya. Then a horse cart up a slow, muddy road. To top it all off the rainy season decided to make its first official appearance, and a monsoon poured down on me as I sat in the back of the rickety horse cart, as if God had picked up Lake Superior and decided to dump it on my head. After a few minutes of this my wizened driver looked back at my drenched condition, stopped his horse, went to the side of the trail, and cut a huge banana leaf free with one of the *parangs* all rural Indonesians carry. He gave it to me and when I draped it over my head I found it made for a remarkably effective umbrella.

When we finally got to Tetebatu I ate a very tasty meal of *nasi goreng* at the first bamboo-walled cafe I found and watched the rain hammer down all around, wishing I had brought more reading material. An hour later the torrent abruptly turned into a trickle and vanished, the transition taking maybe three minutes. The sun was already breaking through the crowds as I gathered my pack and squelched toward the second LP-recommended lodge. The second, because the first one mentioned in The Book tends to be overcrowded.

Tetebatu was indeed very green. It consisted of a couple hundred wooden buildings spread along a single steep, wide, winding dirt road, plus one stone mosque, surrounded by miles of rice paddies. The whole town was patrolled by wandering packs of mangy dogs, and goats and chickens picked their way along the road. Rural bliss. If I was Indonesian, I'd rather live here than in the crumbling, filthy, crowded shantytowns that I had seen on the way out of Mataran. I knew that growing rice was literally backbreaking work, but it had to be better than the shantytowns.

The Mekar Sari lodge was about a hundred feet off the main road. It was run by a very pleasant Dutch woman named Femke, who gave me a room and showed me where I could dry out the soaking-wet contents of my pack. My room was a tiny freestanding wooden cabin, and when I opened the windows I could see Gunung Rinjani rising above miles of rice paddies, with the dark shadow of jungle barely visible at the end of the cultivated area.

I spent a day in Tetebatu doing virtually nothing. I was woken early by the keening dawn call to prayers, which cued a hoarse symphony of shrieking dogs that lasted for half an hour; by the time it had ended, I was firmly and irritably awake. I had a shivery-cold *mandi* bath. I halfheartedly checked the lodge registers, but I knew before I did so that there was no point. I had drinks with two very nice French girls before they left town, on their way to Flores to see the Komodo dragons, and we practiced each other's language. I played chess against one of the village elders, our every move watched and criticized by a crowd of a dozen children, with the sound track provided by the ever-present duo of Bob Marley and Tracy Chapman. I eked out two wins and a draw after losing the first game. I ate *satays* and pineapple and fresh coconut. I sent Talena the depressing lack of news from Mekar Sari's shiny new computer. I wandered through the madman's checkerboard of rice paddies that surrounded the town, walking on the muddy ridges that separated the paddies from one another. At two o'clock the monsoon hit. At four o'clock it cleared away. I ate with a Dutch couple,

Johann and Suzanne, and we chatted and showed each other matchstick tricks. I fell asleep feeling deeply frustrated. I had come here for nothing. But I didn't know what to do.

The next day Johann and Suzanne and I hired a twelve-year-old boy to lead us into the jungle to one of the waterfalls. We passed fields of sunflowers and clouds of butterflies. We saw black howler monkeys dancing from branch to branch, ooking and whooping at one another. We descended steep, slippery wooden steps and swam in the waterfall, which plummeted sixty feet down a cliff, beautiful and so strong that Suzanne could not stand directly beneath it, and even Johann and I were nearly knocked over. The boy led us back to town for noon. Johann and Suzanne left for Kuta Beach, the Lombok one, and invited me to come along. I almost accepted but decided to wait a couple of days. I was beginning to accept that my mission had failed, and I was growing to like it here. My kind of place. My kind of pace.

Around two o'clock I walked from Mekar Sari toward the elder's house, intending to see if he was up for another afternoon chess game. I passed the Harmony Cafe, where four people sat on the patio; two remarkably pretty blond girls in sarongs and bikini tops, and two men wearing only shorts, one with red hair, the other with a shaved head and a gallery of tattoos. Pretty risqué for Muslim Lombok, I thought, without really paying attention to them. But then the Indonesians were used to tourists behaving outrageously. Most of them didn't really mind. Or, they minded, but didn't really care to make an issue of it so long as we brought them money. Picking white coconuts, that was what they called the tourist trade.

As I passed, the man with the shaved head and tattoos cried out: "Paul! Paul Wood!"

I turned, and recognition hit me like a lightning bolt. Morgan Jackson. Wearing the world's biggest shit-eating grin.

I froze and just stared at him. He turned to his companions. "Paul's an old mate of mine. He was on that Africa truck
I was telling you about." He turned back to me. "Come join
us for a beer!"

And I did too. I don't really know why. Maybe habit. God
knows how many times I'd sat down and had a beer with
Morgan Jackson in Africa. Maybe I was surprised that he
was with friends. I'd never imagined The Bull not traveling
alone. Maybe it was just the social pressure of the situation,
stupid as that sounds. Whatever it was, I broke my promise
to Talena, and I didn't turn and collect my things and head
straight back to California. Instead I sat down next to Morgan. I even shook his hand and smiled.

"This is Kerri and Ulrika, they're Swedish," he said,
pointing to the girls, "and my mate Peter, he's Dutch. We just
came down from the mountain." He gestured to Gunung
Rinjani. His three friends smiled and said hi.

"So how you been?" he asked. "What are you doing
here?" There was an edge to his voice. His body language
told me he was uncomfortable: hunched up, defensive. He
was one of those rare big men—and he was *big*, I'm not small,
but he had three inches and probably forty pounds of muscle
on me—who usually seem totally comfortable in their skin. I
looked into his eyes and realized he was as surprised and
alarmed to see me as I was to see him.

"Just traveling," I heard myself say. My mouth seemed to
be speaking without any direction from my brain. My brain
was still in shock. "I got laid off a few days ago and figured,
you know, why not the road?"

"Damn straight," he said, and took a long swig from his
Bintang as mine arrived. I studied him for a moment. He was
even more heavily muscled than he had been in Africa. The

shaved head was new. So were the tattoos: a sinuous dragon around each bulging bicep, a complicated pattern of what looked like razor wire across much of his back, and a chain of Chinese characters down the front of his chest.

"You staying here too?" he asked, motioning at the lodge behind the cafe.

"No, Mekar Sari, up the road a bit," I said automatically. There was a pause.

"How long have you been on the road?" I asked.

"Couple months," he said. "I was in Nepal for a while, then a few days in Bangkok, then down here. Where are you staying?"

"No kidding?" I said. "I was in Nepal last month. Did the Annapurna Circuit." Again, I can't imagine why I said this.

"Is that so," he said. "Why, I was there myself. Surprised we didn't run into one another." We glanced briefly into each other's eyes, then both of us flinched away. What felt like a long silence followed. I think his friends could tell there was tension between us and didn't know what to say.

"How about the rest of the usual suspects?" I eventually came up with after desperately searching for a way to break the silence. "Still in touch?"

"I am," he said. "I'm based in Leeds these days, and they're mostly in London, but we stay in touch. Saw Lawrence a few months ago. How about yourself?"

"Most of them, yeah," I said. "E-mail and so on."

"You still working in IT?" he asked.

"Was till they laid me off," I said.

"How long are you staying in country?"

"Don't know," I said. "Few weeks. You?"

"Not too long," he said. "Another week or two. Long as the money holds out. Don't start work up till January, but I'm pretty near dead skint as is."

Silence fell. We drank from our Bintangs. I tried to tell

myself that I was sitting next to a serial killer, to the man who had murdered Laura, and I couldn't really believe it. That wasn't the sort of thing that really happened.

I realized that though it was only midafternoon it had grown much darker since I had sat down. When I looked up I saw that storm clouds were beginning to gather. The afternoon's monsoon was en route.

"I should get back to my lodge," I said, hastily rising as the wind picked up and the first few fat raindrops smacked into the ground. "Don't want to get rained out."

"Well," Morgan said. "I'll see you around." His expression could have been a big smile. Or an animal baring its teeth.

My wooden hut's door and window could both be barred from the inside. I was grateful for it. I locked myself in, mind working furiously. It had to be him, absolutely had to be. Morgan was The Bull II. Morgan had gutted Laura on Mile Six Beach and crushed Stanley Goebel's skull in Gunsang. Morgan Jackson. Larger than life.

When the truck had first met, on the ferry to Gibraltar, Morgan had been an overwhelming presence, a big Australian who wore a Tilley hat decorated with shark teeth, "tiger shark, caught him myself fishing offa Darwin," he'd explained. At first he was almost universally disliked. He was ridiculously competitive, and full of boast and bluster. "He's just so OTT," Emma had sniffed, as only aristocratic British women can sniff, meaning Over The Top, Brit slang for loud and obnoxious and in-your-face.

But he'd gradually won us over. He worked hard, and he was a terrific cook, and after a while his arrogance and inability to laugh at himself seemed quirks instead of flaws. He told us later in the trip that he felt he was born in the wrong century, that he should have lived in the colonial era. We agreed.

We took to calling him the Great White Hunter, and he accepted the nickname proudly.

I had a million memories of Morgan. Morgan next to the campfire with a can of San Miguel in each hand, one still full of beer, the other converted into a bong. Morgan losing his temper while we dug ourselves out in the Mauritanian thorn forest for the umpteenth time, withdrawing the ax from its sheath and taking out his frustration by single-handledly hacking down a thorn tree in three minutes, chanting "mother*fucker* mother*fucker* mother*fucker*," as the rest of us stared in awe, then giving us a toothy aw-shucks grin when it crashed to the ground. Morgan negotiating at the top of his lungs in a Mali village market, giving the man a belligerent shove to make him drop the price of green peppers by fifty CFA per kilo. Morgan constantly leering at the pretty girls on the truck—Emma, Laura, Carmel, Kristin, Michelle—in a manner so cartoonish it was somehow inoffensive. Morgan working the winch single-handedly to pull the truck out of one of the craters on the Ekok-Mamfe road, stripped to his waist, every vein on his neck standing out with the effort. Morgan hunting for his misplaced hat on the beach at Big Milly's in Ghana, furious, biting everyone's head off until it turned up behind the bar. Morgan sick with malaria, crumpled into a fetal position at the back of the truck, groaning with every bump that we hit, until he raised a feeble arm to indicate that he needed a toilet stop, and Steve and Lawrence half carried him behind a stand of trees by the side of the road. Morgan dragging himself up Mount Cameroon on sheer willpower, dripping sweat, just one week after that.

He was a good guy, the Great White Hunter. And yet. There was a reason why he'd made it onto my short list of three. He had that explosive temper. He had zero sympathy and zero empathy for anyone's weaknesses or shortcomings. He got along, he was friendly, he was socially adept . . . but you never felt any *warmth* talking to Morgan. Always the sense that he was perfectly capable of forgetting the rest of us and walking away at any moment, without so much as a glance over his shoulder. He'd left the truck a couple of times, in Burkina Faso and again in Ghana, for a few days. Mind you, a lot of us had done that, when we needed a break from truck life . . . but he was the only one to leave *alone*.

But while I'd thought in the abstract that he was a potential killer, it was a total stomach-churning shock to realize that it was actually true. That he had killed people, friends and strangers alike . . . and mutilated their bodies . . . It was so hard to reconcile this fact with the garrulous, gregarious Morgan we knew and loved despite his many faults. I tried to come up with reasons why I could be wrong, why it might not be him, how I could have misinterpreted everything. There weren't any. There was no other possibility. It was Morgan. He had hid it well, but he was sick in the head, like a rabid dog.

I wished some of the other truckers were with me. Seeing Morgan again gave me the irrational feeling that all the rest of them were just around the corner, camping next to the Big Yellow Truck. Maybe I should have contacted Hallam and Nicole and Steve after all, should have told them what I suspected. They might have come to Indonesia with me. They would have known what to do. They were good at that. But there would be no help, no advice. In some ways I was more alone than I had ever been. The nearest person who knew me was Carmel in Sydney, a good two thousand miles away. Unless you counted Morgan Jackson himself.

The rain fell so fast and strong that it sounded different from rain back home, not a pattering but a load roar on the roof. I decided to go e-mail the news to Talena. I rolled out of my bed and approached the door. Then I froze. It occurred to me for the first time in a way that actually meant something that I was in great personal danger. That Morgan had already come after me up on the Himalayan trail, and that it would be no great matter to find out what cabin I was staying in. And that midmonsoon would be the perfect time to kill me, with zero visibility, everyone staying inside, another hour to hide my body before the monsoon ended. He could have followed me to my cabin, he could be standing outside right now, armed with a machetelike *parang*, patiently waiting in the rain for me like the Great White Hunter he was.

I stood there, my hand outstretched toward the bar that guarded the door, sweating heavily, and not from the humidity. Maybe he wouldn't try anything. He was with friends. That helped. But then he was with friends, a truckful of them, when he had killed Laura.

I thought of Laura, dying on the beach trying to hold her belly together, and I began to grow angry. I had a name and a target for my fury, and it grew inside me like a fire that has found dry wood, physically warming me, blotting out the cold icy fear. She was the only woman I had ever loved, and he had gagged her and probably raped her and gutted her like an animal.

What am I supposed to do, stay in here all day? I thought, and I yanked the bar off the door and pulled it open with unnecessary violence. The rain poured into my cabin in what felt like sheets of solid water. I stepped outside, looking quickly around, ready for a fight, *parang* or no *parang*. There was no one there.

It was only twenty steps to Mekar Sari's covered patio, but by the time I got there I looked as if I had swum the distance. Femke was sitting on her hammock chair, breast-feeding her baby. Through the window I could see her Indonesian husband working to repair a broken chair.

"Hello, Mr. Wood, are you enjoying our rainy season?"

"Very much," I said. "I need to use the computer . . . ?"

"Sure thing." She stood up gracefully, without interfering with her baby's meal, led me over to the corner of the patio where the computer stood, clicked on the connection icon on the desktop. I watched the connection window open, with the little icon of the telephone and wires. But instead of disappearing after a little while, a tiny red X appeared at the end of the wire.

"*Scheisser*," she said. "Sorry, Mr. Wood. The storm has damaged the phone lines."

"Oh," I said. "Shit."

"Maybe tomorrow," she said, "it usually takes them a day or two . . ."

"All right. Thank you anyways," I said.

"Wait," I said as she stood up, "could I write an e-mail and put it in your out-box? So it would go out the next time you connected?"

"Certainly," she said, and opened up Outlook for me. "Just close it when you're finished."

"Thank you," I said, and sent a quick message to Talena:

```
Subject: To be opened in the event of my
     death or disappearance
His name is Morgan Jackson. He was on the
     Africa truck.
```

I thought the subject line was kind of funny. I was in that kind of mood.

When I was finished I saw that Femke had gone inside to check on her husband instead of returning to her hammock chair. I padded back across the wooden patio, dripping with every step.

Just inside the patio screen I saw one of her husband's *parangs*, protruding from a wooden block. I stopped and looked over my shoulder. Neither of them was looking. I reached down, took the cold wooden handle of the *parang*, and pulled it free. It took a surprising amount of force. Her husband was much smaller than I but apparently very strong.

But I worked it free with a second violent jerk and walked back to my cabin.

Once inside I quickly dried the iron blade with a T-shirt and examined it carefully. Like a machete, but curved like a scimitar. A blade maybe two feet long. The handle was well-worn hardwood. It felt good to have a weapon. A sword. I imagined swinging it at Morgan Jackson. It was a pleasing image.

The rain lasted longer that day, three and a half hours instead of two, and the sun was already sinking into the horizon when it let up, sudden as a thunderclap. I knew what I should do. What I should do was pack up and find a horse cart (*cedak* in local parlance) willing to drag my sorry ass down the muddy smear that was the road to Kotoraya. Then I should take a bemo back to Mataran and e-mail Talena. And the next day I should ferry it back to Bali, head for Denpasar airport, and fly back to the good old U S of A, mission complete, Laura and Stanley Goebel's murderer identified.

But that is not what I did.

15

RUN THROUGH THE JUNGLE

I had an early dinner at Mekar Sari.

"Mr. Wood," Femke asked me, after serving a superb dish of *gado-gado*, cooked mixed vegetables with peanut sauce over rice, "have you by any chance seen a *parang* anywhere near here today?"

"No," I said, affecting surprise.

She shook her head. "These people. They're terribly racist, did you know that? Because I am white, they think it is perfectly all right to steal from us anything that they can."

I made sympathetic sounds, feeling a little guilty, and went to bed before the sun had sunk into darkness.

Hypothetical question. Suppose you have identified to your own satisfaction, beyond any reasonable doubt, a serial killer who has murdered at least two people for sure, one of them a woman you loved, and who will probably kill again. Suppose you know that there is no chance of the authorities ever catching up with him, because you have no hard evidence, and furthermore he was smart enough to commit his murders beyond the jurisdiction of competent authorities. Suppose further that you and the killer know each other well. Suppose even further that he must also know that you know, or at least be very deeply suspicious. And finally suppose that you encounter one another in a remote Third World village.

The question is . . . no. There are three questions. One, what is the right thing to do? Two, what is the smart thing to do? And three, what do you actually do? Those were the questions that ached in my brain that night as I lay behind a locked door and window and stared at the ceiling, listening to an unnerving keening noise, just at the edge of hearing, that radiated from the rice paddies. Some local critter, I guessed, like a cricket but more disturbing.

The smart thing to do, that was easy. Run like hell.

The right thing to do—well, never mind *right* in the moral sense. We were way past morals. Try *right* as in what I wanted to happen. I wanted Morgan Jackson dead. Of that I was certain. I was as opposed to capital punishment as the next guy. Amnesty International was my favorite charity. But I wanted him dead. It wasn't even the threat he posed to future victims. I wanted him dead for what he had done to Laura.

Could I kill him? Almost certainly not. He was the Great White Hunter, he was bigger and stronger than I, and he had killed before, and overall was about a hundred times as dangerous as yours truly. But aside from practical considerations, could I, as in could I bring myself to do it? *Would* I kill him? I didn't know. In the heat of action, maybe, but in cold blood . . . I didn't know. Talena had said I wasn't a killer. But she barely knew me.

Let me stress that I had no crazy plans about breaking into his room and running amok with the *parang*. I wasn't going to try to exact revenge all by my lonesome. My self-preservation instinct remained strong. So why didn't I leave? Why wasn't I already in Mataran? I didn't know. I don't know. It wasn't mental paralysis, though the effect was much the same. It was just a deep-rooted feeling that I shouldn't go. That somehow my work there was not done.

Maybe, looking back, I was just waiting for him to come to me. I wasn't afraid anymore. My anger didn't leave any room for fear. I understood, for the first time in my life, what people were talking about when they talked about *cold fury*. I understood how it could last for years.

So when it was well past dark I unbarred the door and stepped outside into the warm damp night, Maglite in one hand, *parang* in the other.

He wasn't there. Nobody was there. I shined the Maglite around. Its beam was swallowed up by the darkness. The moon was not yet up. Last night the starlight had been bright enough to navigate by, but tonight a thick tapestry of cloud hung overhead, and the darkness was absolute.

I closed the door behind me and began my trek to the Harmony Cafe. I had to walk a zigzag rice-paddy-ridge path for five minutes and then go down the muddy road about half a kilometer. There was nobody else on it. A donkey whinnied somewhere, and something splashed in one of the rice paddies. A cool wind blew in fits and gusts. The air was fragrant with the clean sweet smell of recent rain. I was nervous but not frightened. The *parang* was comforting in my hand. I didn't know what I was doing.

Like many Indonesian lodges the Harmony was built as a U-shaped bungalow around a flagstoned patio. I crept around the edge of the building, looking in windows. There were still three rooms that flickered with candlelight.

In the first, an old Indonesian man lay back on a moth-eaten bed, smoking ganja. I glanced in the second window, and past a curtain that covered it incompletely I got an eyeful of two topless Swedish beauties giggling and comparing their tan lines by candlelight. They seemed so completely incongruous to the pervasive sense of menace I felt that I nearly broke out laughing. After a moment's ogling I tore my attention away from the walking male fantasy and went to the third room, where Morgan and his redheaded friend Peter were lazily playing cards while Peter smoked a joint. I noticed that Morgan waved off Peter's offer to share. Very unlike him. Unless he was planning some kind of activity for which he did not want to be stoned.

I stood there for a while, indecisive, and then I walked back across the road and found a big rock to sit on, close enough that I could still make out shapes at the Harmony Cafe, far enough away that I wouldn't be noticed. I sat there for a long time. I placed the *parang* and Maglite between my feet. I think I fell asleep.

Something brought me back to consciousness. At first I couldn't tell what. I looked around. The moon had risen. I suddenly realized that in the moonlight I might well be visible from the Harmony, so I backed away another twenty feet.

And only just in time. A shape detached itself from shadow and set off up the road. It moved away from the Harmony, toward Mekar Sari. A tiny circle of light led its way on the ground. Someone carrying a flashlight, I saw, as my eyes focused. And carrying something else. A *parang*, like mine. Morgan Jackson come to kill me. I must have heard him leaving his room. I hesitated for a moment. Then I followed him, flushed with adrenaline, like when I had found Stanley Goebel's body. Every sense on high alert, every muscle ready for action.

The wind had picked up, for which I was grateful. Its soft whoosh helped to conceal the squelch of my boots in the mud. It was hard to follow him without using my Maglite, but I managed. It helped that I knew where he was going. Once I almost overbalanced and plunged into a rice paddy, but after a vertiginous moment I recovered my footing. He was moving much faster than I, armed with a flashlight and less concerned about noise, and when Mekar Sari loomed out of the darkness I could no longer see him. For a moment a wild panic rose in me, thinking that he'd seen me following, that he waited in ambush. But then I saw movement right next to my cabin. He was there, underneath the window that faced Gunung Rinjani.

I came as close as I dared, up to the *mandi* shack about twenty feet from my cabin, and peeked around the corner at him. I could see him clearly, silhouetted against the pale wood of the cabin. He waited patiently for a good five minutes, sitting on the chair beneath my window where I ate my breakfast, his head cocked, listening carefully. I focused on breathing silently. I slowly tensed and relaxed each of my muscles so that they did not cramp. I couldn't remember where I'd read about that trick. Some trashy fantasy novel. The *parang* felt very heavy, but I did not dare put it down and risk a noise.

After the five minutes had passed he stood up, calmly walked up the three steps that led to the door, and pushed it open. He stood still for a second, as if surprised that it had not been locked. That was my chance. I knew it as it passed. In that moment of surprise I could have charged him from behind with my *parang*, could have had a better-than-even chance of getting the first swing in. I didn't try it. I didn't really even consider trying it.

He turned on his Maglite and inspected the room. I heard him grunt in surprise. Then he turned around and played the light around, and I ducked behind the corner of the *mandi* stall. I heard him laugh, quietly but perfectly audible at my distance, as if he'd just gotten a joke.

"You out there, Balthazar?" he asked, his voice low but carrying, his Australian accent harsher than usual. "You been keeping an eye on your old mate Morgan? I reckon you are. I reckon you're right behind that *mandi* there, aren't you?"

I focused on breathing absolutely silently.

"I think we should have a bit of chat, mate," Morgan said.

"Just a full and frank exchange of views. That's all I came here for." I heard the creak of wood as he stepped down from the doorway.

"Of course if you prefer," he continued, "we could settle this the old-fashioned way. *Mano a mano*. Deeds not words, eh? Step right out, Mr. Wood . . . if you think you're hard enough."

I didn't move. I couldn't decide how to hold the *parang*. Low, to slash upward when he turned the corner? Or up, like a sword, to defend myself?

"Fair enough," he said. "No need to make this a dialogue now. I always preferred the monologues myself. I reckon you've been doing some snooping, haven't you? Been thinking, what's my old mate Morgan been up to? What kind of shenanigans? And by now you've got a pretty good idea, I reckon. Right now you're deeply concerned about your own fair skin, aren't you, Woodsie? Anxious about the future of your own ocular capabilities, if you take my meaning?"

I listened desperately, for the sound of his boots, and to the sound of his voice, trying to work out how close he was. I didn't think he was coming any closer. But I knew the Great White Hunter could move like a cat when he wanted to.

"Well, I didn't come here for that. I'm on holiday, don't you know?" His laugh rippled through the darkness. "And the truth is I like you, Paul. Always have. And I'm not too fussed about any snooping you may have done. Anything you dredge up, it's not going to do me any harm, I think we both know that. Fact is I'm impressed. You were always the Internet wizard, weren't you? Presume that's what led you here. I'll have to take more care in the future. Point taken. And as for you, you'd best take *my* point. Take it to heart."

And here his voice became edgier, angrier. Became the voice of a murderer.

"My point is, *fuck off*. This is your only warning. Sod off back to America and stay there. I'm a patient man but my patience has its limits. Don't make me work my magic on you, old boy. Don't wave a red flag in front of The Bull. You hear me?"

He waited, as if I was going to answer. Finally he laughed again.

"Silence is golden, isn't it, mate? Ain't that the truth. Well, that's *precisely* the lesson I wanted to drill into you, so I suppose I can't complain . . . You take care now, Paul. Me and my little band are off tomorrow. I recommend you stay here. In fact I insist, and I warn you, I'll make it my business to stay informed of your activities. And I recommend you avoid seeing me *ever again*. Now piss off and fare thee well."

And then he walked away, deliberately noisy, whistling loudly—that British Army tune from *Bridge on the River Kwai*—his boots crunching away from me, taking the long way back to the Harmony around Mekar Sari. I found I could breathe again. As the whistles diminished into the distance I scrambled back into my room and barred the door. I was very glad to be alive.

Don't wave a red flag in front of The Bull. Words to live and die by.

I dreamed of Swiss Army knives and of *parangs*. But I woke alive and whole and unimpaled, and I was grateful for it. I lay in bed a long time, luxuriating in each breath, full of wonder at my own existence, that I could draw in the air and expel it again, could with a twitch of my mind cause that heavy lump of flesh called my left leg to rise into the air and let it fall again, could experience the world around me with so many different senses.

I flung the window open and stared out at the glorious sight of Gunung Rinjani above the rice paddies for some time. Even the thickly overcast day could not dim my joy. After a little while I arose and dressed and went to the Mekar

Sari patio to collect banana pancakes and rose tea from Femke. I took them back and breakfasted, sitting in the chair under my window. The same chair in which Morgan Jackson had sat not twelve hours ago, a *parang* in his hand, hunting me. It seemed like a bad dream, like a scene from a childhood TV show.

Had he meant to kill me? Had he decided not to only because I was awake and alert? I didn't think so. I thought he had been telling the truth, that he had only meant to warn me, and had brought the *parang* to keep me from going after him. *I've always liked you, Paul.* Which was true. I'd always gotten along well with him. Better than most on the truck.

Funny that he had called himself The Bull though. He knew that I knew that he wasn't, that he couldn't have killed any of the people in Southern Africa, because he was with me on the truck during that time. Maybe somewhere in the twisted pathways of his mind he had decided that he was The Bull, and the other killer was the copycat. It made no difference.

I should have felt terrible fear or terrible fury. I felt neither. Somehow they had canceled each other out. Instead I felt immensely relieved. Last night's confrontation had somehow provided the closure I had stayed for. I would do as he said. I would stay in Tetebatu another day, and tomorrow I would go to Mataran, let Talena know what happened, and leave the country. But I certainly wasn't going to leave him be. I would find some way to get him. Not here, not in Indonesia, not *mano a mano*, not without a plan. That would be little more than suicide. But I had his name now, and I knew where he lived. Mission accomplished. I had not merely identified The Bull, I had faced him and taken him by the horns. Well, maybe not *quite* . . . let's just say I had run with The Bull. Anyway, I felt I could leave with my head held high. I knew it was a stupid macho thing to want to feel that way in the first place. But it still made me feel good.

I anticipated telling my story to Talena, sitting in the Horseshoe across from her, looking into those blue eyes as she looked back at me with . . . well, quite possibly with disgust at my violation of my promise to her, and the reckless stupidity of following Morgan through the night. But I felt good about the image all the same. Surely she would be impressed, on some level, at what I had done. I was eager to go home and tell her all about it.

First, though, I wanted to accentuate my stupid macho feeling of accomplishment. I wanted to go fuck with Morgan's mind just a little.

I stepped into the Harmony Cafe. He wasn't

around, but the Swedish girls Kerri and Ulrika were there, and we said hi and smiled at each other. They sat next to their Karrimor packs, obviously waiting for Morgan and Peter. I bought a Coke, thinking wistfully of the two pairs of perfect breasts I'd seen last night, and asked them where Morgan was. They pointed me to a dark room just off the patio.

I had to duck my head to get in the doorway. It was the computer room, dirt-floored, furnished with a single desk. Morgan sat behind the computer. He was wearing his much-battered Tilley hat with shark teeth. When he looked up and recognized me he looked alarmed. I felt alarmed too. Suddenly coming over here and pulling a hair from The Bull didn't seem like such a smart idea.

I recognized the pattern his fingers made on the keyboard—Alt-F4, closing down whatever window he had had open—then he relaxed back, cool as the proverbial cucumber, and said, "And what can I do for you, Mr. Wood?"

My idea had been to leave him with the notion that maybe I hadn't been behind that *mandi* last night, that I hadn't heard his soliloquy. Just to seed a little uncertainty in his life, keep it interesting. I suddenly wasn't sure if that was such a good idea. I cleared my throat and said in a worryingly quavery voice, "Just came by to say good-bye. You off today?"

"We are indeed. Kuta Beach. The Lombok version. And yourself?"

"Thought I'd stay here for the day," I said, "maybe go back to Mataran tomorrow, Bali the next day."

"That sounds very sensible," Morgan said.

We looked at each other for a while.

"Well," Morgan said. "You take care of yourself."

"I'll try," I said. And I turned to walk away, kicking myself for having come at all.

I walked back to Mekar Sari. The air was so thick with humidity that I felt as if I was swimming, not walking. The phone lines were not yet back up. I felt bad about breaking my e-mail-every-day promise to Talena, but I figured I would feel even worse if I broke my staying-here-until-tomorrow promise to Morgan. And it wasn't really my fault. What could I do about the monsoons knocking out the phones?

I spent the day playing chess, eating, and reading through my Lonely Planet. Indonesia actually sounded like quite a cool country and I would have to come back sometime. But I wasn't going to stay for my whole three weeks. I had plans already forming. I wasn't going to go after Morgan Jackson here, but if he thought I was going to leave him alone, he was terribly mistaken.

Something nagged at me all day long, the feeling that I'd forgotten something important. I ignored it in the hopes my subconscious would throw it up when least expected; but the hopes went unfulfilled. I fell asleep trying to make myself remember it. The next morning I went to the patio for my banana pancakes and rose tea, and Femke added one more ingredient to the breakfast; a folded piece of paper, taped shut. I looked at her quizzically.

"Your friend Mr. Jackson gave it to me before he left," she said. "To give to you this morning."

"Oh," I said. I managed to get to the relative privacy of the chair below my window before tearing it open and reading it. The words were scrawled so clumsily they were nearly illegible, but I managed to decipher it:

WOODSIE OLD BOY
AREN'T KERRI & ULRIKA A TREAT?
NEVER DONE TWO AT THE SAME TIME BEFORE
BUT DOWN IN KUTA
THEY'RE GOING TO MEET THE BULL
JUST THOUGHT I'D LET YOU KNOW . . .
HA HA HA & TA

I read it again. I felt very cold.

I was sure they were already dead. That was why he had me wait a day.

Even if they weren't, I knew I shouldn't go after him. Here in Indonesia, without some kind of a plan, I wouldn't have a chance. He would kill me. I should leave him be, follow yesterday's plan, go home and there work out some way to get him. Rushing after him to save two perfect strangers was the worst kind of foolishness. *This changes nothing,* I told myself. *Go with yesterday's plan. Yesterday's plan was sound.*

Yesterday's plan was sound, and sensible, and utterly cowardly. It was very convenient how my elegant plan for revenging myself on the man who had murdered Laura involved letting him walk away and kill two more girls. Very convenient how it got me the hell out of danger as soon as was humanly possible. Abandoning the two Swedish girls, perfect strangers or no, was the act of a contemptible coward, and I knew it. Even if I was sure that they were probably already dead.

What if they weren't? He couldn't plan for everything.

Maybe something had gone wrong. Maybe he'd gotten sick. They might still be alive. And even if they weren't, the sooner I got there, the better chance of getting the authorities to catch him before he left Indonesia.

Even as I contemplated this, a raindrop the size of a marble smacked into the sheet of paper, smearing the cheap ink. I looked up. Dark clouds roiled the sky. I could see flickers of lightning on the horizon. The monsoon was back, and this time, I could tell, it wasn't going to fuck around.

No time to lose, I thought, and five minutes later I was packed and paid up. Femke looked at me as if I was crazy when I told her I had to go to Kuta Beach right away. I guess I could understand why. It was already pouring as I began to slog along the rice paddies toward the road. Not quite running, but close.

I left the *parang* behind. I was through with that particular madness.

16

MEET ME ON THE BEACH

It cost me a lot of money to get to Kuta that day. I can't blame the drivers. I wouldn't have wanted to go any-where in that weather either. The storms of the previous few days had been mere warm-ups for the main event. The rain hit so hard I thought it might leave bruises. Visibility was approximately three feet. The *cedak* driver who took me from Tetebatu to Kotoraya wore his arm out whipping the horse with his bamboo switch. The bemo drivers were only a little better off. At one point on the leg from Kopang to Praya the driver slammed on the brakes and swerved so hard that two wheels briefly left the road. The road was too slippery for the brakes to have much effect, and I thought for a second that I was going to be roadkill, but the driver weaved with super-human skill through a herd of water buffalo that appeared suddenly out of the monsoon like dark omens.

In the end I made it. My watch told me it was five o'clock. This Kuta Beach was nothing like the one on Bali. It was simply a road that ran along the coast, with jungle on one side and beach on the other, and eight hotels clustered near the T-junction that connected to the rest of the island. I walked along the road to the nearest hotel. I didn't hurry. I didn't mind being soaked any more. I and all of my possessions had been soaked all day.

I checked into the Anda Cottages, which had no Morgan/Peter/Kerri/Ulrika in the register, went into my cottage, changed into my swimsuit, and hung the rest of my clothes out to dry. I didn't feel the desperate need for speed that I had felt when the day had begun. After seven hours of travel, there didn't seem any point in worrying about another fifteen minutes. And nobody was killing anybody in this downpour, of that I was pretty sure, not unless Morgan was going to break into their room and start swinging a *parang* wildly, and that seemed unlikely. His modus operandi was the ambush.

And besides, the most likely scenario was that they were dead already.

I went to the common room to find out what was going on. I wasn't sure how I would bring up the subject. "So, anybody find a couple of murdered Swedish girls around here?" didn't seem like a winning conversation starter. But then I saw faces that I recognized, Johann and Suzanne, the Dutch couple from Tetebatu, drinking Bintang-and-Sprite shandies. They waved at me, and I joined them.

"When did you get here?" Suzanne asked.

"Today," I said. The waiter came by, and I asked him for a beer, and then, as I realized I hadn't eaten since the banana pancakes except for half a pineapple in Pao Montong, a dish of *nasi goreng*, spicy vegetable fried rice.

"You came here through the rain?" she asked.

I nodded and smiled sheepishly.

"We didn't think the roads were open," Johann said. "We were supposed to take a Perama bus back to the ferry today, but they said they could not go because of the monsoon." Perama was the Indonesian tourist authority, which provided air-con buses between major tourist destinations. A little more expensive than bemos, and without their gritty authenticity, but a whole lot more comfortable.

"The roads were pretty bad," I admitted. "I'm surprised I got here."

"Have you been in Tetebatu?" Suzanne asked.

I nodded and drank greedily from my Bintang, which tasted wonderful and felt much deserved. "How are things around here?"

"They're good," Johann said, and Suzanne nodded her agreement. "Very peaceful. You can rent mopeds and bicycles and go up and down the road. An excellent road with nothing on it. The beach right here"—he motioned toward the sea—"is not so good . . ."

"Coral pebbles, not sand," Suzanne clarified. "Difficult to walk on or lie down on."

"The surfers like it though," Johann said, and he and Suzanne exchanged looks and laughed at some private joke.

"Lots of surfers here," Suzanne said.

"But down the road to the east, maybe two miles . . ."

"Oh, yes, there's a *perfect* beach," Suzanne said. "Wonderful. A big white . . ." She made an arc with her hands, searching for the right English word.

"Crescent," Johann filled in. "It must be nearly a kilometer long."

"But it's dangerous," Suzanne said. "You must remember, if you go there. The owner here, he says there's a terrible riptide in the middle of the beach, and people die there every year. Swept out into the ocean and drowned."

"There are no signs there, can you imagine?" Johann said. He sounded a little outraged. "No signs at all. It's disgraceful. But as long as you're careful, it's a perfect beach. And there's nobody there."

"A few locals with coolers on their heads, selling Cokes and pineapples, and that's it. No buildings, no stores, no hotels," Suzanne added.

"Sounds like paradise," I said. My *nasi goreng* had arrived, and I attacked it as they chatted to each other, nostalgically, in Dutch.

Five minutes later I felt a thousand times stronger. "Listen," I said, "I ran into an old friend of mine in Tetebatu, I think he was coming here, have you seen him?" I described Morgan and company.

"Oh, yes," Suzanne said. "The big man with all the tattoos. We had lunch with them yesterday. The girls seemed very nice. There was no Dutch man with them though. I think he went east to Flores instead of coming down here. Just your friend and the Swedish girls."

"They went out to that beach, didn't they?" Johann asked her.

"They did," Suzanne said. "During the rain. When everyone else was staying in they went out to the beach. Your friend said that it was best then, that swimming in the rain was better because you didn't get so hot."

"And nobody follows you around trying to sell you a sarong," Johann added, and they both laughed. Sarong salesgirls were the bane of Indonesian travelers. I didn't laugh.

"Did you see them afterward?" I asked.

"Let's see . . . did we?" Suzanne said, thinking about it. "I think we saw your friend last night, on the road."

"Yes, we did," Johann said. "But not the Swedish girls."

"That's right," Suzanne said. "Just your friend Morgan."

I sipped from my beer to cover my consternation. I felt so cold I nearly shivered. Morgan had taken Kerri and Ulrika to a deserted beach yesterday, a beach already known for death by drowning, with the monsoon thundering down and nobody else around. And he had been seen again, but they had not.

"I have to go," I said, putting my beer down half-finished. I was sure it was too late but that was no reason to delay. "I forgot something. I'll see you later."

I fled from their startled okays and went back out into the

rain. It had not let up, which seemed amazing to me. Surely all the fresh water in the world had poured down on Indonesia in the last eight hours, and there could be no more to dump on us. I went to the roofed area I had caught out of the corner of my eye when I had entered the Anda Cottages compound, where the mopeds and bicycles were stored, along with a crudely lettered "For Rent" sign.

An Indonesian boy who couldn't have been more than twelve years old sat watching the bikes. I told him that I wanted to rent, and he looked at me as if I was crazy, but only for a moment. Every Indonesian knows that all white people are crazy; taking a bike during the height of a monsoon was not insane enough to be noteworthy. Mad dogs and Englishmen and all that.

"You want bike or motorbike?" he asked. His English was passable. For a moment I wondered how many languages he spoke. Most of the Indonesians in the picking-white-coconuts business could conduct business in English, German, Dutch, and Japanese, at a minimum.

"Bike," I said. I wanted to get there fast but I'd never driven a motorbike before and figured these were not ideal conditions to learn in. He gave me a battered old iron thing which was a little too short and reminded me of the bike I once rented in China that lost its pedals five miles from town. But better than nothing. I wheeled out of the Anda Cottages and headed off down the road, in the direction Johann had indicated, looking for the beach.

The road was superb, no cracks or potholes, and nobody else on it. Jungle to my left, coral beach to my right, rain absolutely everywhere. I could barely hear the roar of the surf over the machine-gun noise of rain on the road. Once I built up a good head of steam the bike moved like a racing machine, carried along by its own massive inertia. The road inclined slightly upward, which was good. I didn't like my chances going downhill at that speed in that rain with those brakes. The beach began to slope downward to my right, steeper and steeper, until there was a wedge of vegetation between me and the coral gravel, a wedge that widened and widened until I had jungle on both sides. It was getting darker; either the clouds were growing even thicker or the sun was setting. The jungle was thick as a wall, and the clouds were so low I seemed to be riding through a tunnel.

Suddenly the jungle to my right vanished, replaced by a steep rocky slope that dropped to a beach so white it seemed to glow. Crescent-shaped, like the blade of a *parang*, the beach ran almost perpendicular to the road and was framed by a high wall of jumbled rock too steep to be navigable anywhere but where it met the road. It was a good half mile long, and I could only just make out the other end through the rain.

The opening in the wall of jungle to my right was only about a hundred feet long, and by the time I'd reacted and the brakes had stopped the bike, the beach was once again hidden behind vegetation. I walked the bike back to the rocky slope above the beach, leaned it against a tree, and began to descend. My Teva sandals were soaking wet, the rocks were slippery with rain, and I had to use my hands to brace myself on several occasions.

Then I was on the beach. It was amazing how white the sand was even though it must have been darkened by the rain. Fine sand, damply solid, easy to walk on. It was about a hundred feet wide at its thickest. The storm was intensifying, and I had to shield my eyes with a hand to see anything. The whitecapped waves roared and plunged into the beach again and again, as if they wanted to pillage it, carry every grain back to Davy Jones's locker. Even in the bay they were at least six feet high. The open sea was twice that size, a churning maelstrom of whitecaps.

I couldn't see anything but sand, sea, rocks, and jungle

high above. It didn't seem likely that he'd hide bodies here. They would have stood out like crazy against the sand. Maybe he'd hidden them under cairns of rocks? Hard work, but he was a big strong guy. I began to follow the line of the rocky slope, looking carefully under the rocks. The sky had grown darker still, and I had to squint against the rain.

After maybe five minutes I heard a shout and nearly jumped out of my skin. I looked up. And nearly jumped out of my skin again.

"Balthazar Wood!" Morgan shouted. I could barely hear him through the rain and the sea. "As I live and breathe!"

I was about halfway along the beach. He was a little farther along, maybe thirty feet away from me, between me and the ocean. I could see footprints leading back toward the ocean. He wore a blue swimsuit and carried a *parang* in his right hand like he knew how to use it. I was sure he did. He was the Great White Hunter after all. He seemed an unreal figure, something out of a bad dream, looming out of the rain with his shaved head and that blade in his hand and those Chinese-dragon tattoos on his arms, as heavily muscled as a Marvel Comics superhero. His eyes shone with anticipation and his face was stretched into a giant carnivorous grin.

I backed away toward the road along the slope, moving slowly, thinking furiously. He followed, equally slowly. There was no rush after all. He had me at his mercy. There was no way I could scramble to safety up this steep slippery slope, and there was nowhere else to go. He must have been waiting for me. He must have seen me from up high, come down, and swum along the beach in order to catch me by surprise.

"I gave you a little examination, Woodsie!" he cried. "I put you to the test, and I'm sorry to say that you've failed!"

No, there *was* someplace to go. There was the ocean. He was a stronger swimmer than I was, but could he swim fast carrying that *parang*? I very much doubted it. But he'd already thought of that, he was moving to cut me off, staying between me and the surf.

"I warned you, Paul! I told you to fuck off and leave me alone! But you just couldn't do that, could you?"

My anger had abandoned me when I needed it most. My limbs were weak with terror. I was shaking so badly I could barely focus my eyes. "You sick fuck!" I hurled back at him, or tried to, but I had no breath in my lungs. He must have read my lips; he laughed.

"Don't you go worrying about those beautiful Swedish ladies you came down here to rescue now," he said. He was close enough that despite the drumming rain I could hear him without shouting. "Were you dreaming of saving their lives and receiving a few grateful blow jobs? They've landed you in a world of trouble, my boy. But they're still compos mentis, they're just fine. They went off back to Bali last night. Not without giving me a fond farewell though. That Ulrika is a wildcat in bed. You think I'm going to rid the world of a piece of ass like that? Now, *that* would be a *real* sin."

"How?" I asked, still breathless. "How could you kill Laura? Why?"

His lips thinned and he spat. "That whore Mason? Fuck her. That cunt got exactly what she deserved."

I would make him pay, I told myself. If I somehow got out of this, I would make him pay. "And Stanley Goebel? Did he get what he deserved?"

"Ah, him. Woodsie, I swear, I didn't even know his name when I did him. He was an act of pure opportunism. Just one more for The Bull. One more just like you."

He raised the *parang* high, to slash downward, and stepped toward me. I wish I could say I tensed myself for a furious never-say-die battle, ready to fight like a cornered wolverine. But the truth is, when I saw that blade gleaming above me in the rain all my rage and courage melted away, and I cringed away from him, arms over my head, whimpering.

He could have swung the *parang* and ended my life. Instead he kicked me behind the left knee and I crumpled forward onto my hands and knees. I closed my eyes and waited for the fatal blow. But it still didn't come.

"You never know, Woodsie," he said. "Maybe if you try very, very hard you could convince your old mate Morgan that you really would leave him alone if you lived. Maybe if you sound just pitiful enough. Maybe if you show him what a truly pathetic fuck you really are."

He was only toying with me. I knew that. He wouldn't let me go, not now, no matter what I said or did. He just wanted to humiliate me before killing me. I scrabbled backward on my hands and knees toward the rocky slope. One possible chance. But I felt too weak with fear for it to work. He followed.

I was going to die here. I felt a terrible cold certainty. These were my last moments on this earth. I tried to say something, to beg and plead like he wanted me to, to play for time, but I was so frightened I couldn't even speak. Not in words. I tried, but all that came out of my mouth were meaningless moaning noises.

My right foot came into contact with solid rock. I stopped backing up.

"Very disappointing, Woodsie," he said, as I crouched at his feet. "I thought you'd put up more of a fight. But you're just a sniveling little worm, aren't you? You and your woman both. That cunt Mason. She begged and sobbed and pleaded and sucked and licked, she did. But it didn't do her any good in the end. You'll have to try a little harder than—"

Maybe it was the mention of Laura that gave me strength. Maybe it was just raw animal instinct, fight or flight, a last desperate convulsion of muscles. He hadn't noticed that I had backed into the rocks behind me like a sprinter backs into starting blocks. I lunged forward with all the strength I had, not at him but past him, and I ran for the sea. I don't know if he swung at me or not, but if he did, he missed. After a few steps I stumbled, tripped up by the combination of forward momentum and rain-soaked sandals, but somehow righted myself midstride and continued into the surf.

When the water was thigh high, and I could no longer run, I paused to tear my sandals off and dared a glance over my shoulder. One of the six-foot waves nearly knocked me off my feet but I managed to keep my balance. Morgan followed me into the water, moving at an unhurried jog. He had discarded the *parang* on the beach.

He looked amused rather than concerned. I knew why. I had no hope of outdistancing or outwrestling him. I was a comfortable swimmer, I had spent most of my teenage summers on the shores of Lake Muskoka in Canada, but Morgan had grown up on the Australian beach. He swam like a shark. And he was at full strength, where I was sick and weak with fear and couldn't fully extend the knee he had kicked. All things being equal, he would easily reach me, and when he did, he was much too strong for me to have any hope of survival.

But all things were not quite equal.

I dived into the water and started to swim, controlling my motions, trying to keep my stroke smoothly powerful instead of frantic. After a few dozen strokes I allowed my feet to dangle downward for a moment, and I felt it.

The riptide. My salvation. It grabbed at my ankles and pulled, and in moments I had been sucked right in. Johann had been right, it was a monster, two or three hundred feet a minute. I swam straight into the center of the flow, allowing the current to carry me straight out, then I turned, treading water, and looked for Morgan.

He was behind me, not far, maybe forty feet away. We were still in the bay but the sea was already so rough I could only glimpse him from wave-tops. The gap between us widened. Then he reached the riptide, and he abruptly stopped swimming, started treading water, and looked out to the fearsome waves of the open sea, only a hundred feet away.

I knew what he was thinking. I had nothing to lose. I was obviously better off taking my chances in the open ocean and hoping that a stray boat picked me up or the tides happened to wash me back to dry land. Better some chance than none. But he had to work out whether it was worth risking his own life here in the water by expending the time and energy required to find me, catch me, and kill me. Not easy when we got out to the open water with its high waves, not on a day like today, not with the sun plummeting toward the horizon.

He turned and swam away, parallel to the beach, out of the riptide, away from me.

I had no time to feel relief. The current dragged me out of the bay and into the full, colossal, relentless force of the sea. I nearly drowned in those first few minutes. The churning waves threw me around like a rag doll, like a twig in a flood. I tried to float faceup, but they immediately drove me under. I went back to treading water, but I had to work so hard to keep my head in the air that I knew I could not last long. Even when I did manage to breathe I had to keep my mouth pursed in a narrow slit to filter out the thick rain. When I breathed in just as an errant wave hit, and choked on a mouthful of salt water instead of a lungful of air, I panicked and only just managed to keep afloat with a frenzied dog paddle before getting hold of myself again.

I gave up on keeping my head above water all the time. I tried to conserve my energy, letting myself drift beneath the surface, coming up just long enough to breathe. That worked better than all-out struggle, but I could still feel myself growing slowly weaker. And I could no longer see land or even guess in which direction it lay. Downwind, probably. I could barely work out which way the wind blew, much less make any progress in that or any other direction. But I got the

vague impression that the current was carrying me exactly
the wrong way.

Looking back it's amazing how calm I felt. I guess fear is
all about imagining the future, and while I was in the water I
was much too busy staying alive to imagine anything at all.

Time passed, quite a long time, but I had no sense of it. After
a while it seemed as if I had always been in this ocean, struggling for my life, that my other memories were nothing more
than a momentary daydream. I was dimly aware that night was
falling, the storm was abating, the rain slacking off and the
waves growing calmer. But my muscles too were weakening,
and I had to expend every iota of energy I could muster just to
keep my head above water long enough to breathe.

When the silence was broken by the violent yodel of a
horn I was so startled that I lost the rhythm of my movements
and nearly drowned again. But I clawed my way back to the
surface with desperate spasmodic movements, woken from
semiconsciousness, perceiving the meaning of that horn
through the thick fog of total physical exhaustion. A boat.
There was a boat nearby.

I tried to shout, but between exhaustion and my brine-
burned throat, only a wheezy rasp emerged. The horn
sounded again, even louder this time, so loud it was actually
painful. When my head submerged I could hear the thick
churning sound of the boat engine through the water. A few
moments later I saw lights and heard human voices, and I
found some untapped reservoir of strength and began to
swim toward the light.

When I next looked up I was blinded by one of the lights.
I waved my hands high in the air and tried to shout. Again I
failed. But it didn't matter. They had seen me. "Over there!"
a woman shouted. "There's someone over there!" I treaded
water, forcing my limp arms to wave, until the boat loomed
up next to me and strong hands pulled me on board.

I grabbed a railing to stay upright, my legs too weak to stand unsupported, and looked at my saviors. Four Indonesians and three white people. I recognized the whites. Johann and Suzanne. And Talena Radovich.

"You stupid fucking idiot," Talena said, and gave me a big hug.

17

ENDS, TIGHTENED

By the time we docked I had started to recover. I had drunk about a liter of fresh water, my legs were strong enough to walk or at least stagger, and my mind had more or less fallen back into place. The memories of my encounter on the beach, and my ninety minutes in the water, already seemed completely unreal. I felt very much like I had woken from a nightmare.

Before getting off the boat that had saved me—a fair-sized boat, about forty feet, from the look of things a dive boat when not being used to rescue stupid tourists who went to the beach alone and got caught in the riptide—I thanked the Indonesian boatmen profusely and gave them most of the soggy wad of Indonesian cash in my travel wallet. Johann, Suzanne, Talena, and I walked back to the Anda Cottages, only a few minutes from the dock. They led me into the common room, sat me down, and bought me a richly deserved bottle of Bintang.

"You are very lucky," Johann said, "We warned you about the riptide."

"If your friend hadn't come looking for you . . ." Suzanne shook her head.

"Yeah," I said. "Well." I stared at Talena. I couldn't get over her presence.

"We're glad you're all right," Suzanne said. "You must be very tired. So are we. See you in the morning?"

"Sure," I said. I hugged them good night, as did Talena. I felt a brief and entirely unjustifiable spurt of jealousy when she hugged Johann.

Talena and I sat back down and stared at one another for a moment.

"What are you doing here?" I finally asked.

"Saving your stupid, ignorant, pathetic, moronic, stubborn, bullheaded, perverse, idiotic, shit-for-brains, skinny little ass," she said. "What does it look like I'm doing?"

"Oh." I considered what she had said, and added, "Thank you."

"Since you so promptly broke your promise to e-mail me every day—"

"The rain knocked the phone lines out," I protested. "I couldn't."

She gave me a skeptical look. "Yeah, and I'm sure you tried as hard as you possibly could. Anyway, I took a couple days off and burned some frequent-flier miles to see what kind of trouble you'd gotten yourself into. And then this morning I get this e-mail from some freaky-ass address telling me that you've found the guy and you know his name. So then I figure you're really in trouble. And I have had the day from hell, believe you me. I got to Tetebatu about an hour and a half after you left, and it was hard enough getting there, never mind here. Lucky for you I bumped into your Dutch friends. We went down to the beach and found your sandals in the water. So we came back here and got the boat. Seems like it happens a lot. You're lucky they know exactly where the current takes people after the riptide gets them."

"Yeah."

"It wasn't just the riptide, was it."

"No."

"What happened?"

I told her the whole story, omitting none of my stupidities.

"Well," she said, when I had finished. "Well. Well, you're just very lucky to be alive, aren't you now?"

"Yeah," I said. "I think you saved my life."

She barked a laugh. "No shit, Sherlock."

"Well. Jeez. No one's ever saved my life before. I guess —"

"Stop," she said. "Don't get all maudlin on me. I hate that."

"Oh. Okay."

She finished her beer. "Also there's a theory that when you save someone's life you are then karmically responsible for everything that they do for the rest of their life. And no offense, but considering your recent errors of judgment, that sounds like a real Atlas-esque weight on my shoulders so I'd really rather be reminded of the whole subject as infrequently as possible if you're okay with that."

"Fine," I said.

She stood up. "I think it's time for us to get the hell out of Dodge. Let's go."

"Go? Where are we going?" I asked.

"We're going to pack your things and leave town."

"It's too late for the bus."

"Bus?" She shook her head, amused. "You've been traveling on a shoestring too long. I hired a taxi for the day. Only twenty bucks, you know."

"Oh," I said. She was right. That alternative had never even occurred to me.

I packed quickly, thinking of Morgan following us to the Anda Cottages for a bloody denouement. Then we were in her taxi and she was talking to the driver in Indonesian as we pulled away.

"You speak the language?" I asked, surprised.

"I spent a couple months here researching the last-but-one edition," she said. "And it's the world's easiest language. No grammar, no tenses, no verb forms, no nothing. You wouldn't want to write poetry in it but it takes about two weeks to learn."

"Oh," I said, feeling hopelessly incompetent next to her.

About twenty minutes later, I said, "We have to go to Tetebatu."

"What?"

"Tetebatu."

"What for?" she asked suspiciously.

I had realized what had nagged at me all day yesterday was what for. "There might be a clue there. An important one."

"Paul, listen to me," she said slowly, as if speaking to a child. "You almost died today. There is a bad man out there who wants you dead. We're getting you out of the country as soon as we can without making any detours."

"I'm going to Tetebatu," I said. "You can come or not."

"You ungrateful little shit!" she exclaimed, amazed. "What happened to 'thank you for saving my life'?"

"What happened to not reminding you about that? . . . Okay, sorry, that was uncalled for. But I just need to go to Tetebatu for thirty minutes. To look at the computer he used there, that's it. Then we can leave."

She gave me a long, level, unimpressed look. But then she leaned toward the driver and gave him new instructions, and soon enough—taxis really were a lot faster than traveling via bemo—we were back in Kotoraya.

The taxi couldn't make it up the muddy road to Tetebatu, but I paid a small boy to go roust a *cedak* driver out of bed, and a hundred thousand rupiah convinced him to take us up there. Us because Talena wasn't letting me out of her sight. Several times the *cedak* got stuck and we had to get out and push, and we both slipped and fell more than once, and by the time we got to Tetebatu we were both covered with mud and Talena was furiously not speaking to me.

I went straight for the Harmony Cafe. What had nagged at me was that when I had gone to see Morgan the morning before last, before he left for Kuta, he had been at the computer—even though the phone lines were down. What was he doing? My guess, considering the comment he'd made the previous night about being more careful on the Internet, was that he was trying to wipe out traces of what he'd done on that computer. I wanted to check in case he'd left any trail. I sure hoped he had. I didn't want to tell Talena I'd brought her here and caked her in mud for the sake of a wild-goose chase.

I bought a Coke and sat down at the Harmony Cafe's computer, Talena at my shoulder. First of all I checked the browser history, then the Temporary Internet Files directory. As I'd suspected, all the files there had appeared within the last two and a half days. He had wiped the directory and browser history clean before he left.

"So we're here for nothing?" Talena said, ready to erupt.

"Not necessarily," I said. "He got rid of the obvious things, that's all."

"So what's not obvious?"

"Cookies," I said, navigating through the Windows directory tree.

"Come again?"

"Cookies," I repeated. "I don't know who named them that. Some developer who watched too much *Sesame Street* I guess. They're files that your browser writes to your machine if sites request it."

"Wait a minute. When you go to a website it can put files on your computer?"

"Not exactly. It asks your browser to store certain information in a safe location on your drive. It can't put a virus on your machine or anything. You can tell your browser not to save them, but that's generally a bad idea."

"Sounds like a pretty good idea to me," she said. "What's the point of these . . . cookies?"

"Basically they get around the problem that HTTP is a stateless protocol."

"Paul. English."

"Well. Basically there's no way of telling when you look at a page if you've looked at it, or other pages on the same site, anytime recently, without using cookies. For example if you've already logged in or not. There's ways around this by messing with the URL . . . sorry, the page address . . . but cookies are basically easier."

"Easier for who?"

"Easier for people like me who build websites."

"And of course they're the ones who really matter," she said with heavy sarcasm. "So did Mr. Jackson leave any interesting cookies on this machine?"

"Can't tell from here," I said, examining the cookies directory. "There're some that were modified while he was here, but I'll need time and a real connection to see if they're anything interesting." The phone lines were back up, so I didn't have to write all the information down, I just zipped up the relevant cookie files and uploaded them to my Yahoo! Briefcase repository.

"We're done," I said.

"That's it? That's what we came for?"

"That's it."

"Paul," she said, "I would just like to remind you that thanks to that ride up here I have taken not one, not two, but three mud baths, and my entire ass feels like a giant oozing blister, and now we are about to ride back down that same road. My point being that if you don't find something useful in those, I will punish you severely."

"Is that a promise?" I asked mock-eagerly, and she cracked a smile despite herself.

"I'd be happy to put it in writing. Now let's get moving. There's a warm bed waiting for me in Mataran, and if you're very good, I'll let you sleep in the gutter outside."

It was the Hotel Zihar, same one I had stayed in what felt like ages ago. We slept there, and in the morning we went to the port and hired a speedboat that took us back to Bali. It was a glorious morning ride. The sun had replaced yesterday's storm, and the sea was surprisingly calm, and the salt air made me feel alive. Everything made me feel alive after the last few days of dancing with death. Overcome with good feeling I turned to Talena when we were halfway there and gave her a bear hug and kissed her on the cheek. She laughed and pulled away . . . but not, I was pleased to notice, until after a few moments of returning the embrace, and not without pink cheeks.

"Thanks," I said, almost shouting over the speedboat's howling engine.

"I told you not to mention it," she said, but she was smiling.

"Right. Well, thanks just for being here. You sure came a long way to help me out."

"I guess I did."

I wanted to ask her why. I guessed she liked me a lot. Maybe even as much as I liked her. But on the other hand we had only met a few times, and she had just flown halfway around the planet, potentially into danger, to find out why I had suddenly gone silent on her. I couldn't quite convince myself that this was just a side effect of my natural charm.

Maybe she had just been propelled by an overpowering whim, like the one that brought me to Indonesia in the first place. Or maybe there had been some other factor. I wanted to ask, but I could tell by her body language that she didn't want to talk anymore, so we just smiled at each other for the rest of the journey.

In Denpasar we both managed to change our flights to that day, but I was flying Garuda Airlines, and she was flying Cathay Pacific. My flight left first. We hugged quick good-byes and promised each other we'd meet the next night at the Horseshoe, and I boarded the plane. While Indonesia is a wonderful place, I have never been quite so relieved to leave a country.

FOUR

CALIFORNIA
REDUX

18

A LETTER FROM THE MAN

My second homecoming in the space of two weeks, and this one felt a lot better. I was unemployed, but that made me happy. It helped that I was financially secure for a good six months at least. I had a woman in my life again. Okay, nothing had happened between us, and realistically probably nothing was going to happen, but the thought of soon seeing Talena again put a spring in my step. Most importantly, I had nearly died on this most recent trip, and every sight, sound, smell, and experience resonated with a new you're-so-lucky-to-be-here-for-this sweetness. I wanted to skip down Haight Street telling everyone I passed, "You're lucky to be alive! We're all *so fucking lucky*!" I highly recommend the feeling. Though I can't recommend what I went through in order to feel it.

I ought to market this, I thought to myself. Near-death experiences, preferably in an exotic location and at the hands of a violent madman, culminating in a rescue by a beautiful woman, as a cure for depression. Form a company that specialized in setting this all up, like that Michael Douglas movie *The Game*.

Physically I was fine. The bruise behind my knee where

Morgan had kicked me was an ugly purple color but no longer hampered my mobility. Fighting the ocean had been exhausting, but marathon runners go through worse. The Annapurna Circuit had left me in the best shape of my life, and I was recovering in a hurry.

The only fly in my ointment was my memory of what I had thought was my last moment. When I had cringed and whimpered like a whipped dog, instead of fighting, or at least standing coolly up to what I had thought would be the final stroke of Morgan's *parang*, using my last breath to spit in his face. All my life I'd thought of myself as—well, maybe not a hero, but at least somebody with backbone, with courage. I'd seen a lot of the world, gotten into a lot of dicey situations, and until then I'd felt I'd handled them with sangfroid. But that moment, when for the first time I had thought I wasn't just going to die, I was going to be killed, slaughtered like an animal . . . I'd crumbled. There was no other way to put it. I had been tested, and I was a coward. In a way it was that that had saved me, and that was something; I had recovered and escaped, and that was something; but still, every time I thought about that moment, I grunted and twitched with shame.

Fortunately, it was pretty easy not to think about it. Or to treat it like a bad dream. My week in Indonesia had been so sudden and brief and hyperintense, it seemed to exist on a whole different level than all my other memories, to have been detached from the rest of my life, as if it somehow didn't really count.

From Denpasar to Los Angeles I traveled not merely in space but also in time; I left Denpasar at 2:30 P.M. and got to L.A. at 12:45 P.M. on the same day. The miracle of time zones and the International Date Line. When I got back to my apartment it was only three, and I felt drained. My sys-

tem still hadn't adjusted to Indonesia time when I left, and
here I was messing it up again. But I had a crepe and a double espresso at Crepes on Cole and went up to my apartment
surfing on a caffeine high.

My reflexive desire upon walking in was to check my
e-mail, but my employers had repossessed my laptop, so I
went to the Cole Valley Copy Shop to use their public termi-
nals instead. Lots of e-mail, most of it spam. I filtered it down
to five messages I actually wanted to read; a FuckedCom-
pany sporadic update, chatty e-mail updates from Rick and
Michelle, news of a contract job from the only recruiter I
trusted, and most interesting of all:

```
Date: 11/15 14:03 EDT
From: aturner@interpol.org
To: PaulWood@yahoo.com
Subject: Case file opened
```

Mr. Wood,

Your e-mail of 11/07 was forwarded to me as
of 11/09 and I found it credible and deserving
of further investigation. On 11/11 while
researching our internal infobase I discovered
a recently opened South African case file
related to the same subject. I have been in
contact with Renier de Vries of the Cape Town
police, who is heading that investigation,
and I understand that you indirectly prompted
the opening of that case file as well.

We intend to actively pursue this case. I
will be in California as of 11/17 and would

very much like to interview you. Please
advise me how to contact you and when/where
would be convenient for an interview.

Thank you for your time and information.

Anita Turner
Special Agent, Federal Bureau of Investigation
Interpol Liaison Officer
NOT PGP SIGNED
Because unencrypted electronic mail is an
insecure medium, the integrity of this
message cannot be guaranteed. Never e-mail
classified or privileged information.

"Hot damn," I breathed, rereading. It seemed that if you whacked at a hornet's nest hard enough and often enough, they would eventually come out to see what it was that you were after. I sent back my phone number and let her know that I was available at her earliest convenience.

I thought about investigating those cookie files, but I was tired, and to be honest I didn't really think they'd contain anything valuable, and without an income I didn't want to be paying eight bucks an hour to do research at the copy center. Instead I went home to sleep.

My daytime exuberance counted for nothing. It was a long night, full of nightmares.

I woke sometime around dawn, visions of Morgan Jackson's torture chamber dancing in my head. I felt far more tired than I had when I had gone to bed ten hours earlier. My whole body was encrusted with stale sweat, and I had a headache. A jet-lag hangover. One thing that didn't get better with experience.

I looked out the window to a San Francisco streetscape so foggy it mighty have been part of a dream. I considered making myself coffee but decided shock treatment was necessary so I swigged a triple Glenfiddich. It ran down my throat like molten lava, and after I successfully fought a powerful wave of nausea, I started to feel better almost immediately. Kill or cure, that's my motto.

I didn't want to stay in. Nor did I want to go out. There wasn't much open at that hour anyway. For all its Sin City Extraordinaire reputation, San Francisco had a shocking dearth of twenty-four-hour establishments. The reputation wasn't totally unwarranted, there were probably drug-fueled S&M avocado raves going on all over as I slouched on my couch, but as for a decent breakfast at an indecent hour, forget it. There was a diner down at Market and Castro, but that was some distance away, and I didn't relish the thought of the steep walk back up to Cole Valley.

I wished I had a computer. Nothing like a dose of the Net to make an hour or two vanish away. But my damn company had taken my laptop away. At least they had done me the courtesy of laying me off while they were at it. I wondered how Rob McNeil was doing. I should give him a call. Though I expected he was as pleased as I by the development.

Then I realized, I did have a computer. An old 250 MHz Pentium with 96 meg of RAM. Big box, not a laptop, tower configuration. Seemed like a screaming monster when I had bought it three and a half years ago, before I became such a hotshot coder that my employers supplied me with a new laptop twice yearly. Now it was so obsolete I had forgotten that I had it. Stored in the back of my closet.

I unearthed it, reconstructed it on my desk, turned it on, watched the Windows 95 start-up screen with something like fond nostalgia, and logged in. Beautiful. Now all I had to do was connect to the Net. Unfortunately, I realized, I couldn't do that. I had long ago cut the phone company out of my life, as befitted a dinosaur monopoly of the previous century, and now had only a cable modem and a cell phone. Unfortunately I didn't have the drivers that would allow the computer to talk to the modem. I could get the drivers off the Internet . . . a nice Catch-22. Maybe I should just go buy a real computer. But no, when income is zero, expenditures must be minimized.

The phone rang. I looked up with genuine shock. It was just past 7:00 A.M. Nobody calls anybody at that hour, not even telemarketers stoop that low, not yet. I picked it up and said, "Hello?" Dire thoughts of Morgan Jackson outside, of the first scene of *Scream*.

"Balthazar Wood?" a female voice asked.

"Who wants to know?"

"This is Special Agent Turner. I'm a federal agent currently seconded to Interpol's NCB for the United States."

"Oh." I shook my head to clear it and regretted my first response. Way to go, Paul, act in a suspicious manner when the FBI agent calls. "Yes. I received your e-mail."

"I hope I didn't wake you up?"

"No, I was up. What is it, ten o'clock on the East Coast?"

"I'm presently located in San Francisco," she said. Her voice ought to have been taped so that future generations would have a perfect definition of *no-nonsense*.

So that's who calls at seven in the morning. Federal agents. "I see," I lied.

"You said you'd be available for an interview at my convenience. Would that include oh-nine-hundred hours today?"

I blinked, my mind briefly boggling at the thought that I was talking to a woman who actually used *oh-nine-hundred* in a nonironic way, then I said, "Sure."

"Excellent. I'll be waiting in a room in City Hall." She

gave a number, and added, "You should probably get there early. The building can be hard to navigate."

"I'll see what I can do," I said. "See you there."

"Excellent," she said again, and hung up.

I hurriedly showered and shaved and dressed in my job-interview suit, and caught the downtown-bound N-Judah at just the right time to be crushed by approximately nine hundred similarly dressed men and women who had managed to pack themselves into a streetcar that on paper fit sixty. When we stopped at Civic Center I realized at the last moment that this was my stop, that I no longer went to my job at Montgomery. I made a few enemies getting out.

City Hall was a labyrinth and I had forgotten my ball of twine. By the time I found the room it was ten past nine and I was sweating with frustration. I wished I had gotten my folder of evidence back from Talena to show this Turner woman. I was also very nervous. Contact with authority figures of any kind—the real authority figures, not bosses or tour guides, but the kind who carry guns—always makes me nervous. Even when I'm innocent, or even, as in this case, when it's my complaint that brought them.

Anita Turner was not the Scully-esque babe I had secretly been hoping for in the most juvenile corner of my mind. Forty-something, fit but weathered, her face as wrinkled as crumpled newspaper. She sat on one side of a metal desk, facing the door. Two folding chairs faced her. One of them was occupied by Talena. I was surprised but pleased. I was extra pleased by the familiar-looking folder of papers that adorned the desk. There were two other things on the desk. One was one of those matte black speakerphones that look like some kind of cross between a marine subspecies and the face-hugger from *Alien*. The other was an expensive digital audio recorder.

"Mr. Wood," Agent Turner said. "Better late than never."

"Sorry," I said, taking a seat as she leaned over and pressed RECORD. My nervousness doubled. It hadn't occurred to me that every stammer would be recorded for posterity.

"My name is Anita Turner, special agent for the Federal Bureau of Investigation, presently seconded to the Interpol liaison office," she said, and motioned to us.

"Talena Radovich," Talena said without hesitation. "Web editor and roving reporter for Lonely Planet Publications."

"Balthazar Wood," I said. I barely but successfully fought the urge to crack a joke such as "No-good bum with no fixed address," and instead added nothing at all.

"In a little while I'm going to conference in Renier de Vries of the Cape Town Police Force," Agent Turner said. "Who I believe you have already met, Miss Radovich." Talena nodded. "But first I just want to establish the bare bones of the case. First of all, before we begin, would either of you like a beverage?"

We shook our heads, although I rather wanted to ask for one. I'd already had a gargantuan coffee but liked the idea of Special Agent Anita Turner asking me whether I took milk or sugar while a recorder caught it all.

"Excellent. We will be pleased to serve you lunch in a few hours."

I thought: *A few hours?* Talena looked equally taken aback.

"Now," Special Agent Turner began, "let us establish the background material . . ."

And the inquisition began.

When the inquisition ended four hours later it left me with a profound new respect for the FBI. I understood for the first time why interrogation was classified by many as a science. She had systematically drained me of every scrap of information I had, including many I had forgotten. She had methodically classified everything I said as corroborated fact, eyewitness evidence, extrapolation, or speculation (or, presumably, lies, although I hadn't told any of those, at least not knowingly). She took names and contact details when available of everyone I knew even remotely connected with the case, and everywhere I had stayed in Nepal and Indonesia. She zeroed in on the slightest hesitation, the merest chink of guesswork or assumption, in anything Talena or I had said, and attacked until all it concealed was revealed to her searchlight mind. Even Renier de Vries had sounded impressed over the phone. For the most part he too had just answered Special Agent Turner's questions.

When it was all over she gave us a curt thank-you and began packing her notes and recorder into a briefcase. Talena and I looked at one another and I said, "Can you give us some idea of what happens next?"

She looked at me as if amazed by my temerity, but she answered. "Eventually, if everything goes well, you will be called upon to repeat some of this in a court of law."

"But . . . I mean, what are the chances of everything going well? Are you going to go out and arrest Morgan Jackson tomorrow, or is Scotland Yard going to get him when he gets back to Leeds, or . . . what?"

"Frankly, Mr. Wood, I'm very reluctant to tell you anything at all about our investigatory process, given your well-documented history of running off half-cocked and nearly getting yourself killed."

She looked at me, and she had a scary intense look, but I think I had one too.

"Paul," Talena said, putting her hand on my arm, "I think we should go."

I shrugged her hand away and leaned forward. "Because I don't think anyone's going to arrest him at all," I said. "I think all this information is going to go into your infobase, and Mr. de Vries is going to try to go after the other killer, the one who killed the South Africans. But I think we all know he's not going to get anywhere. And I think we all know that nobody's going to arrest Morgan Jackson."

"Mr. Wood," Agent Turner said sharply, "your cynicism does you no credit."

"So you think he's going to be arrested?"

"I guarantee you that this case will be pursued with as much vigor as any other Interpol case I have ever seen."

I laughed, putting as much contempt into my voice as I could, and sat back in my chair. "Now that is a very revealing answer."

"Look, Mr. Wood," Agent Turner said, and she sounded almost conciliatory, "I want to stress that you have done the right thing. You've gone to the appropriate authorities, and I will be opening a real live wire of an investigation on this case. You can sit back. Morgan Jackson is no longer your problem and you should leave him alone."

"You mean you can envision Morgan Jackson being arrested?"

"I certainly can."

"All right. Then I have two questions. In this pretty little vision you have, *who* is arresting him and *on what charge*?"

She didn't answer me, just looked back at me and gave a little shake of her head.

"That's what I thought," I said. "This doesn't change anything. I don't know shit about international law, but I do know it's basically toothless."

"I do know something about international law," Talena said suddenly, and I thought she was going to contradict me, "and you're so right. There are men walking around scot-free right now in the Balkans who are guilty of genocide and ordering mass rapes and the worst crimes imaginable, and the West could get a hundred people to testify against each one . . . and there they are. Walking around. Or, more likely, driving around, in their big fucking bulletproof Mercedes between their big fucking mansions."

I sensed I had hit a hot button.

"All right," Agent Turner said wearily. "All right. Mr. Wood, Miss Radovich, I hear your concerns, and I'd be lying if I said I didn't share some of them. No. We're not going after Morgan Jackson for the crimes he has committed. What we are going to do is keep a very close eye on him. One thing about serial killers is that you can be confident they will kill again. The next time he strikes, particularly if it's in a First World nation, I will do my best to ensure that somebody is waiting for him."

Talena and I shouted at the same time:

"The next time — !" from her.

"First World nation — !" from me.

We stopped when we heard we were interrupting each other and motioned to each other to go ahead. Eventually I convinced Talena to begin.

"You're saying you're going to sit around and hope you catch him next time? That's your big fucking plan? We've told you that there's a madman wandering around the world killing people at random and all you can say is wait until we get lucky?" she demanded.

"Miss Radovich, please be realistic —" Agent Turner said defensively.

I interrupted. "Do you *not fucking get it*? He's not going to kill anybody in a First World nation! He's not going to do it because he's *too fucking smart*! He can kill all the victims he likes when he goes traveling, any shape or size or color or creed he's in the fucking mood for! It's a fucking buffet out there! You wait for him to go after someone in New York or London and you'll be waiting *forever*!"

"All right!" Agent Turner snapped. "All right! Shut the fuck up!"

We shut the fuck up. It was like hearing a nun swear.

"Okay," she said. She looked at the recorder and the phone, presumably to be sure that they were off. "Yeah. The truth is he's outsmarted the world. The truth is that unless he fucks up at a kill site there is shit-all we can do in terms of actually arresting him. What we could do is try to keep track of his movement between borders and inform the relevant authorities in his destinations."

"Now you're talking," I said. "Why didn't you say so? That would make for some nice frontier justice. If he goes to Kenya, just leak to Moi's Boys that he might be big trouble, and that nobody would make a big fuss if his remains turned up sealed in a forty-gallon oil drum, and they'll take care of the rest for us."

"We could do that, but we're *not going to*," Agent Turner said.

"What? Why?" Talena asked.

"Because we're talking about *Interpol*, not some kind of Wild West sheriff," she said scathingly. "It's not something we do. It's not something we have the authority to do unless one of our member states has prima facie evidence to arrest the suspect on a charge, and even then only under certain very tightly restricted conditions that make it basically useless in this case, even if we did have evidence, which we do not. You're right, he's not going to be arrested. Not on what we have. We have no real evidence."

"What do you want, a signed confession?" Talena asked. "And if we had one, would it make any real difference?"

"Honestly?" she asked.

"Honestly."

"Probably not," she said. She gave us a defeated shrug. "But you never know. We still might get lucky."

19

COOKIE MONSTERS

We went for a coffee afterward, Talena and I, at a little cafe on Market Street.

"Shouldn't you be at work?" I asked her.

"I go back tomorrow."

"Hmm."

We sipped coffee at each other.

"You look nice in a suit," she said.

"Enjoy it while it lasts," I said. "I wear ties for interviews, weddings, and funerals. And court appearances and depositions, as of today. That's it."

"Men," she said. "You pay them a compliment and they tell you that they hate it."

"There's not a whole lot that justifies my whole gender's existence, is there?" I teased.

"Don't get me started," she said. "Especially don't get me started on stubborn idiots who go endanger themselves for no good reason."

"No good reason? I found him, didn't I?"

"Yes, you found him." She sighed. "And you were very brave and resourceful. Pity about you being so stupid or you'd almost be admirable. But honestly, what good does the name do? You heard the lady. Even if he'd given you a signed confession it probably wouldn't change a thing. He's going to go on doing what he does until he fucks up and picks on somebody one size too big."

"Maybe," I said.

"What I don't understand is why. I mean, I have a degree in psychology, I'm supposed to have some understanding why people do the things they do, but not this guy. Most Western serial killers are totally fucked up, especially sexually, with the worst childhoods imaginable, and they're really sublimating their sexual urges into murder, but from what you say, Morgan Jackson wasn't—what's so funny?"

"Nothing," I said hastily. I had thought to myself: *Well, she's talking about sexual urges at last, Paul, that's a heck of a start*. "No, he wasn't like that. He seems stable enough. Actually he seems more stable than just about anyone else I know. It's just that he's a total sociopath. It's all just a game to him. On the truck we called him the Great White Hunter."

"The world is full of sociopaths," Talena said. "Half the really successful businessmen you'll meet are textbook cases. Most of them don't go around killing people."

"Maybe because they don't realize how easy it is," I said.

"Yeah. That's what's scary. You see what he does and you wonder why there aren't hundreds of people doing it. They would, you know. In the West people think that anyone who goes around killing people for fun, they have to be sick, deranged, brain chemistry problems. It's nice that they can think that. But it's not true. It happened all the time in Bosnia. Normal people, middle-class, stable homes, good jobs, turned into monsters. Sometimes overnight. One of them was someone I knew. Not close, but still. He always said it was for his people, for his country, but really, I think he was just like Morgan. Just because he could. Just to show he had the power. And it's not just Bosnia. You know that. Rwanda. Cambodia. Same thing."

"Huh," I said.

We looked at each other.

"That's awful too," I said. "But I don't think it's really Morgan's trip, not exactly. I don't know, I'm just guessing, but I think I knew him pretty well. I don't think it's all about power, for him. It's the thrill of the hunt. Murder as some kind of extreme sport. I guess it's crazy, but so is BASE jumping, you know?"

"It's not really all that different," she said. "Different excuse for the same thing, is all."

After a pause I swallowed, and said, "Hey. There's something I've been meaning to ask you."

She looked at me cautiously. "What?"

"Why did you come find me?" I asked. "You . . . I mean, I know we were kind of instant friends, or whatever, but we really didn't know each other, and it wasn't like you knew for sure I was in trouble, and . . ."

"I knew," she said, "believe me."

"Okay, you knew, but you didn't know for *sure*, and you didn't really know me, and you suddenly took a vacation and flew to Indonesia for me. And don't get me wrong, I'm really glad you did, and—it's just that I'd like to think I would have done the same thing for you, and maybe I would have, I hope I would have"—she was looking at me with a flat hard-to-read expression, and I began to flounder—"and, it's just, I don't know. Just it seems like it was a fairly big thing you did for me, so thank you again, and I just wondered, you know, why, what motivated you, that's all, though I don't know, maybe . . ." My mental censor finally kicked in and told me to shut the hell up. I came up with the elegant finish of, "Whatever. I don't know."

She looked at me for a moment, and I realized she was thoughtful rather than amused or contemptuous, for which I was very grateful.

"I lost a lot of friends in Sarajevo," she said. "And a boyfriend. They'd go off and do brave things, trying to help friends of theirs, or stupid things. Trying to get a little girl's doll, one time. Anyways, they wouldn't come back. Not alive. I wasn't able to save any of them. I tried, a couple of times, but I was too late, or I didn't do enough." She shrugged. "Anyway. That was a long time ago. But you going there—it felt like it was happening all over again. So I decided that this time, fuck it. This time I was going to stop it."

"Oh," I said inadequately.

"And it worked!" she said brightly. "I actually saved someone. First time. So now you have to stay out of trouble. No more jaywalking for you. You're going to be a very safe and cautious boy now, right?"

"Well, you know," I said, trying to make a joke out of it, "I can try, but trouble is my middle name, and when I see the Bat-signal, it is my duty to respond. How else can our fair city be kept free of crime?"

I was dodging the question and hoping she wouldn't notice. She looked at me for a long, suspicious moment. Then a thought hit her, and she sat straight up, alert.

"What did you mean, 'maybe'?" she asked.

"Eh?" I said, avoiding her suddenly icy blue gaze.

"When I said Morgan is going to go on doing what he does until he fucks up, you didn't say 'yes,' you said 'maybe.' Why is that?"

I shrugged.

"Paul. Don't go clamming up on me now."

"I don't know," I lied, "I just said it."

"Oh, no." She slammed her coffee down so hard that although it was half empty some of it splashed out on her hand. It must have scalded, but she didn't react. "Oh, you totally stupid *asshole*. Don't tell me you still have some kind of *plan*. Don't tell me you're still not going to leave well the fuck enough alone."

"I don't have any kind of concrete plan," I said. "But if the opportunity presents itself, I'm going to do something about Morgan Jackson."

"Like what? Become Victim Number Three? That'll sure show him. You were five seconds away just a couple days ago, in case you've forgotten already. Do you have some kind of fucking death wish?"

"Relax," I said. "It's a moot point. I said if the opportunity presents itself. Doesn't seem likely that it will anytime soon." I was prevaricating a little but didn't want to provoke her any further.

"I see," she said.

Clearly she could tell I was not telling her the whole truth. We sipped coffee at each other again. This time the air was hostile.

"Well," she said, standing up. "I'm going home. Give me a call if you ever get that much-needed lobotomy."

I went home too, after a period of kicking myself and imagining the countless different ways I could have handled that conversation better. I decided to kill time by getting my old computer hooked up. I went down to the copy center, bought some floppy disks, downloaded the cable modem drivers onto them, came home, installed the drivers, played around with the configuration until it finally started working. I was back on the Net. This computer was a little slow but not too bad. I considered replacing Windows 95 with Linux but decided to delay a while.

First I went back to the Thorn Tree. There was, as I had half expected, one final message tacked on to the conversation I had started.

```
BC088269      Consider that your final final
11/17 04:07   warning.
```

```
           Live long and prosper, Paul. And
           don't ever fuck with me again.
```

"Fuck you," I muttered under my breath. An easy thing to say from the safety of my Cole Valley apartment.

I went to my Yahoo! Briefcase account and downloaded the zip files with the cookies from that machine in Tetebatu. I examined the list of files:

```
aol.com
canoe.ca
excite.com
footballunlimited.co.uk
hotmail.com
lonelyplanet.com
lycos.com
microsoft.com
msn.com
netscape.com
nytimes.com
rocketmail.com
roughguides.com
times.co.uk
yahoo.com
216.168.224.70
```

The file names indicated the site that the cookie referred to. Most of the sites were pretty well known and pretty much what you'd expect on a backpacker machine. But that last one, 216.168.224.70, was an IP number instead of a DNS name. That was unusual. I examined the cookie:

```
server=Microsoft Active Server Pages Version
3.0
session=HX8338947MUT7G-KXFWJ38
```

Nothing useful there. Sites that run on Microsoft ASP are automatically configured to leave cookies so that they can track user access over a period of time. It didn't tell me anything about what was on that site. But that was easy enough to find out. I typed *http://216.168.224.70/* into my browser address window.

A pop-up window appeared asking for my username and password. The browser contents did not change. No welcome page, no nothing. Whatever this site was, its owner didn't want anyone looking at *anything* unless they had a name and password. Pretty unusual in a medium where page views were the measure of success. Pretty unusual for a vanity site too. Pretty unusual full stop.

I tried a whois:

```
whois: 216.168.224.70

Administrative Contact, Technical Contact,
Zone Contact:
Merkin Muffley
P.O. Box 19146
Cayman Islands
mm9139@hotmail.com
```

Well, that gave me a contact name, but . . . "Merkin Muffley"? I didn't think so. That was the president's name from *Dr. Strangelove*. Somebody had pulled a fast one on Cayman-Domain and Network Solutions.

So what we had here was a site with a moderately paranoid level of security registered under a false name and presumably hosted in the Cayman Islands. Could have been a lot of things. An offshore bank, say, or one of those buy-a-second-passport offers you see in the back pages of *The Economist*, or some kind of connection to money launderers or drug runners or God only knows what sort of illicit activity.

But probably not. First of all because it's unlikely anyone would have connected to one of those from a hovel in Tetebatu. But second of all because it really wasn't that secure. That pop-up login window wasn't encrypted; anyone with a packet sniffer on the network could read what the user typed in. Anyone with serious resources would have done a far better job. It looked more like a site thrown together by some amateur who wanted to make it as secure as possible without actually understanding the myriad problems of security.

It was still going to be problematic. I wasn't really a hacker. I was probably enough of a programmer to become one in the space of a few days, I could go out and get some Cult of the Dead Cow software or hacker scripts, but realistically, it wasn't my forte, and most hacking isn't near as easy as newspapers and movies make it seem.

For fun I typed "thebull" into both the username and password fields and clicked on OK. "Invalid username" said the computer. So I tried "taurus" instead of "thebull," thinking of that five-year-old Usenet conversation I had dug up. And the pop-up window responded: "Invalid password."

I paused. That was interesting. The changed response indicated that "taurus" was in fact a valid login name. I still didn't have the password, but finding a username was a lucky beginning. And what a username. Taurus. The sign of the bull. I couldn't imagine what might be lurking behind that username/password window, but I definitely wanted to find out.

All I needed was a password.

I pondered the problem, but only for a little while, because it was the most common and well-understood problem in the field of computer security. Password protection, when combined with well-chosen passwords, is a highly

secure way to ward off intruders. A good password can easily
take a thousand years to crack. But most people choose terrible passwords. Their dog's name, or their four-digit PIN
number, or the word "password." And that makes them vul-
nerable to a dictionary attack.

A dictionary attack is the simplest, crudest, most brute-
force type of hacking there is. You write a program that automatically connects to the computer you want to break into
and, one after the other, methodically tries every word in the
English language and every possible four-digit combination.
A good password, eight random numbers and letters, is one
of three trillion possible combinations, so many that it would
take a dozen life spans to go through all the permutations. A
dictionary attack looks at only forty thousand or so of those.
But thanks to the hacker's best friend, human nature, those
forty thousand probably include about 90 percent of all the
world's passwords.

It was well within my capabilities to write a dictionary
attack from scratch. It's very easy to get a list of all English
words from the Internet, then to write code that simulates a
Web browser and goes through every word in the language,
trying each as a password. It probably wouldn't have taken
me more than half a day. But my attitude toward code has
always been: Why write it when you can steal it?

I called up Google, typed "Java dictionary attack"—Java
being my programming language of choice—and ten minutes
later I was tweaking someone else's attack code. It was good
code, with some extras I hadn't thought of, such as including
a long list of fictional character names as part of the attack
dictionary. I had to make only a few small changes to aim the
attack code at my target site.

Half an hour of tweaking and testing later, I launched the
dictionary attack. Then I waited for it to report its access
speed. This was key. The simplest way to disable a dictionary

attack is to periodically slow down the server's response time to a login attempt. Microsoft, for example, ensures that after every five failed Windows logins, it pauses for a full ten seconds before allowing another attempt. This slows down a dictionary attack enough that it becomes nearly useless. I was relieved to find out that the "taurus" site's homegrown security did no such thing, and my dictionary attack was cycling through ten attempted passwords every second. The attack would take less than an hour and a half.

I was impatient for a response, but you know what they say, a watched site never cracks. I went out for a long walk through Golden Gate Park, reminding myself that there was still a good chance that the attack would fail, that the password would be complex enough to fall outside my list of words and names and numbers. I tried to imagine what the right password might reveal. Morgan Jackson's online diary? I didn't think so. Not at all his style. I told myself to dial down my expectations. Maybe it wasn't even related to the killings. Maybe it was just some kind of particularly sick porn site.

I walked all the way to the beach and back, trying to pretend that I wasn't itching for every second to pass faster. When I got home I rushed through the door and to the computer. And the computer screen reported:

```
Password found. A valid password is:
"dilemma."
```

With slightly shaky hands I called up the site in my web browser and logged in as "taurus," password "dilemma."

And the browser filled with data. Not very much data. The simplest arrangement imaginable, black text on a white background. There were only thirteen words, but they were enough to set my heart racing.

The Bull
Add Entry
Bulletin Board
Leader Board
Current Log
FAQ
Register
Archives

Being a longtime Webhead, I went straight for the FAQ.

Frequently Asked Questions

What is The Bull?

The Bull is an online dead pool with two
unique qualities. In other online dead
pools, players guess who will die and are
awarded points for being correct. As a
player of The Bull you choose who dies and
you are awarded points for both quantity and
quality.

What do you mean, I choose who dies?

I mean you commit murder. If you have somehow
found this site and you're not okay with
that, don't worry. Participation is optional
as of this writing.

*I'm okay with killing people. How do I get
points?*

First of all, you have to register.

How do I register?

Just go to the registration page *here*, and
enter a password. You will be given a
username (of the form "NumberOne,"
"NumberTwo," etc for purposes of anonymity
and security). Users are strongly discouraged
from having multiple usernames.

What happens after I register?

Then you go out and kill someone, and post
evidence to the site. Then you keep doing it.

What kind of evidence?

Photographs are a start, but they are not
sufficient as they are too easy to fake. Videos
are better, particularly if they have audio
tracks as well. Pointers to corroboratory
evidence, such as news articles, are often
your best bet if available. And every victim
must have the mark of The Bull.

What is the mark of The Bull?

Two matching red Swiss Army knives driven
into the victim's eye sockets.

Isn't that a pretty weird mark?

Yes. That's the point.

Are there any rules about who I kill?

We don't have any rules. However we have some
very strong recommendations, such as:

-only perform kills where you are beyond the
 jurisdiction of competent police forces, eg
 Third World countries
-don't kill anyone you know socially
-don't kill anyone if the situation is
 anything but perfect
-don't ever get fancy
-after the deed is done, get out of the
 country

In general we recommend that new users
examine the log carefully to get an idea
of techniques that have been used
successfully.

*Isn't it dangerous posting evidence of my
kills to a website?*

You bet your sweet ass. Don't **ever** access
this site except from some public location
such as a Web cafe, and when you're through,
clear all traces of your access by deleting
the browser history and Temporary Internet
Files (click *here* for details.)

How do I get points?

There are two types of points: substance, and
style.

How do I get substance points?

After you add an entry (via the Add Entry page *here*) each qualified user may award you 5 substance points if the evidence you posted convinces them that you actually performed a kill.

How do I get style points?

Each qualified user may also award you 1–5 style points, and may also comment on your kill.

What is a qualified user?

You become a qualified user the first time at least half of the existing qualified users grant substance points to one of your kill entries. You can only award points to kills which occur subsequent to your achieving qualified-user status.

Doesn't that mean that as the number of users increases, the number of potential points you can get for a kill increases as well?

Yes. This is deliberate and ensures that the leaderboard is not necessarily monopolized by the users who have been here the longest.

What are style points awarded for?

It's hard to say, and we like to be surprised, but in general kills are considered stylish that involve:

-a high-profile target (eg a fellow traveler
 rather than a local)
-multiple simultaneous victims
-subsequent media coverage
-a difficult location (eg a crowded lodge)
-pleasing aesthetics

*Aren't you concerned that the authorities
will discover this website?*

Not really.

First of all, the information on this site
cannot be tracked back to its contributors.
The site itself is registered to a false
name and administrated anonymously by
NumberOne, thousands of miles away from the
actual computer that hosts it. Everyone who
uses the site is anonymous. So its discovery
would be a mild annoyance, not at all a
disaster.

Second, we don't think that anyone is
going to find out. No search engines have The
Bull's address. Nobody knows to look for
it. We very nearly don't exist. The only
way we could be discovered is if the attempt
to recruit new players goes awry—so please
be very very careful about that, and only
use the appropriate recruitment technique—
or if one of you tells the rest of the
world. But we think that's doubtful.
After all, considering our raison d'etre,
who wants to have us on their bad
side . . . ?

But if our location ever is discovered, we
will move the site to one of our fallback
locations.

What is the primary fallback location?

Sorry: qualified players only.

*What is the appropriate recruitment technique
for new players?*

Sorry: qualified players only.

I leaned back from my computer and stared at it as if I
saw aliens breeding in its innards. Which in a sense I did.

"Holy fuck," I said, and then, more eloquently, "Holy
fucking *fuck*."

20

BULLSITE

I saved the FAQ to my drive and looked next at the Current Log.

```
Entry #: 57
Points to date: 21
Entered by: NumberThree
Entry date: 13 Nov 2000
Kill date: 9 Nov 2000
Kill location: Rio de Janiero, Brazil
Victim specifications: 2 street children in
    Brazilian slums
Kill description: Strangulations in a back
    alley.
Media files and URLs:
  Photographs here, here and here.
    Copy of police report by People for
    Children here.
Scores:
  NumberOne
      5 substance, 2 style. "Multiple but
      otherwise unremarkable."
```

NumberTwo
  5 substance, 3 style. No comment made.
NumberFour
  5 substance, 1 style. "Not up to
  NumberThree's high standards."
NumberFive
  No score yet.

Entry #: 56
Points awarded: 27
Entered by: NumberFour
Entry date: 5 Nov 2000
Kill date: 18 Oct 2000
Kill location: Gunsang, Nepal
Victim specifications: Stanley Goebel,
  Canadian backpacker
Kill description: Ambush in an abandoned
  village near the trekking trail.
Media files and URLs:
  Pictures available *here* and *here*.
  The Nepali police called it a suicide(!),
  but the kill was corroborated on the Lonely
  Planet Thorn Tree *here* by its discoverers.
Scores & Comments:
NumberOne
  5 substance, 4 style. "Neatly done.
  Aesthetically pleasing."
NumberTwo
  5 substance, 4 style. "Pretty lucky you
  got that corroboration."
NumberThree
  5 substance, 4 style. "I've been on the
  Circuit, I have some idea how difficult
  it would have been to find the right
  moment. Good work."

NumberFive
   No score yet.

Entry #: 55
Points awarded: 18
Entered by: NumberFive
Entry date: 21 September 2000
Kill date: 19 September 2000
Kill location: Bangkok, Thailand
Victim specifications: Thai prostitute, name
   unknown
Kill description: Lured victim to hotel room
   for assignation, strangled.
Media files and URLs:
   Digital video with audio is located *here*.
   Corroboration from the Bangkok Post's
   "Nite Owl" column *here*.
Scores:
NumberOne
   5 substance, 1 style. "Thai prostitutes
   are exceedingly banal."
NumberTwo
   5 substance, 1 style. "Boring and
   frankly I find the sexual aspect
   disgusting."
NumberThree
   0 substance, 0 style. "I'm not
   convinced. The video is blurry, the
   audio could be faked, and lots of
   Bangkok prostitutes turn up dead."
NumberFour
   5 substance, 1 style. "Real, but
   that's the only good thing to say
   about it."

Entry #: 54
Points awarded: 35
Entered by: NumberOne
Entry date: 9 August 2000
Kill date: 30 July 2000
Kill location: Luxor, Egypt
Victim specifications: Eric & Lucy Hauptmann,
    middle-aged American tourists.
Kill description: Gunfire ambush during a
    camelback safari in the desert.
Media files and URLs:
    Photographs and audio *here*, *here* and *here*.
    Lengthy article in The Times of London
    which suggests that the attack is that of
    a terrorist faction *here*.
    Other related articles *here*, *here*, *here*
    and *here*.
Scores:
    NumberTwo
        5 substance, 5 style. "Again the
        standard we strive to meet."
    NumberThree
        5 substance, 4 style. "Very impressive."
    NumberFour
        5 substance, 5 style. "Well worth the
        wait."
    NumberFive
    5 substance, 3 style. "Pretty good."

Entry #: 53
Points awarded: 32
Entered by: NumberThree
Entry date: 14 April 2000
Kill date: 11 April 2000
Kill location: Jungle, Suriname

```
Victim specifications: Thomas Harrison,
    British backpacker
Kill description: Multiple stab wounds.
    Nighttime ambush.
Media files and URLs:
    Digital video with audio here.
    Corroboration from London's Guardian
    newspaper here.
Scores:
    NumberOne
        5 substance, 3 style. "Neatly done, a
        worthy target."
    NumberTwo
        5 substance, 3 style. No comment made.
    NumberFour
        5 substance, 4 style. "Often,
        paradoxically, kills are more difficult
        at night."
    NumberFive
        5 substance, 2 style. "It's okay. Not
        real memorable."
```

View archive of previous entries

"Aw, shit," I said aloud, when I was finished. I felt sick.

I didn't want to read any more, but I had to see one more thing. I saved the Current Log file and went to the archives. Fifty-two more entries, dating back to May 1996, when NumberOne initiated the whole thing. NumberTwo had joined in July 1996. NumberThree had shown up in 1998 — he was Southern Africa's The Bull. NumberFive was a recent recruit, less than a year on The Bull.

And NumberFour, Morgan Jackson, had begun his career with this:

Entry #: 28
Points awarded: 27
Entered by: NumberFour
Entry date: 9 July 1998
Kill date: 15 June 1998
Kill location: Limbe, Cameroon
Victim specifications: Laura Mason, British
   traveler
Kill description: Ambushed on the beach at
   night, eviscerated.
Media files and URLs:
   Photographs *here* and *here*.
   Corroboration from various British papers
   here, *here* and *here*.
Scores:
  NumberOne
       5 substance, 4 style. "Well done.
       Welcome. An impressive debut."
  NumberTwo
       5 substance, 4 style. "Central Africa?
       You've got more guts than me. (sorry)."
  NumberThree
       5 substance, 4 style. "Bienvenue. I wish
       you a prosperous career."

I didn't want to look at the photographs, but I did. Laura
on the beach. I'd seen her there, but it was far more horrific
seeing this picture now than it was discovering her then. My
hands shook so badly I couldn't shut down the window and I
had to stab at the computer's OFF button instead. I was making grunting noises with every breath. I felt as if someone had
kicked me hard in the stomach.

The Bull was a fucking *game*. And Morgan was only one
of *five*.

21

DEMON PRINCES

I didn't know what to do. I wanted to call Talena and talk to her. At the same time I didn't want to talk to anyone, didn't want to ever have any contact with that repugnant animal called *Homo sapiens* ever again. Move to Tibet and find a cave in the Himalaya and sit there forever. That was what I really wanted.

I went out to get a very late breakfast. I got to the Pork Store half an hour before it closed. Best breakfast in the city, but that day it might as well have been cardboard. I must have looked like hell, and I was muttering to myself, and the waitress gave me a wide berth and rushed to give me the check. I must have looked pretty weird and disturbing even for the Upper Haight, and that's saying something.

The food helped me pull myself together. I went back to my apartment and turned the computer back on and went back to The Bull. Forcing myself to be analytical, investigative. To save every speck of data I could find on the site, and then hunt through it to find out whatever I could.

The bulletin board was only available to qualified users. I didn't try to register or add an entry. That left me with just the FAQ and the logs. I read through every single entry, starting in chronological order, making notes in a Notepad file as I went through.

NumberOne was responsible for thirteen entries. NumberTwo was responsible for twenty-one, but hadn't made an entry in the last six months. NumberThree had done ten. NumberFour, Morgan, was responsible for seven. NumberFive had six entries, all Thai prostitutes.

The total number of reported deaths was sixty-seven, although several entries, particularly from NumberTwo, were considered questionable and got few if any substance points. Sixty-seven murders. These five madmen had killed sixty-seven people over the last five years, and it looked like I was the first person to discover them.

They had begun by killing locals. For the first couple of years they went to Third World countries and murdered poor helpless poverty-stricken natives. The majority of victims were still locals. But in the last couple of years they had moved to killing travelers in a big way. Partly for style points and partly because they were easier to corroborate. NumberTwo, in particular, lamented how difficult it was to get outside media to verify that you had murdered some street kid in Calcutta. But travelers were still a minority; a mere eighteen of the sixty-seven victims were citizens of First World countries.

I tried to extrapolate personalities from comments. NumberOne, presumably the original Bull, that Usenet "Taurus," was patronizing, full of himself, and used flowery words. NumberThree was much the same. NumberTwo didn't make comments very often, and when he did, used slang. NumberFour, Morgan, stuck to commenting on the difficulty of each entry. NumberFive appeared to be the odd one out, a sexual sadist who didn't have the command of the language that the others did, who often seemed a little defensive and didn't get along with the others. I got the sense they regretted that they had recruited him.

Details of the *appropriate* recruitment technique were restricted to qualified users only. I wondered how it worked. Had any of these five ever met face-to-face? I doubted it. At least not until they were very confident in one another. Far too dangerous. So what was this technique? How did you safely bring a new member to The Bull?

I guessed it worked the same way online child-porn rings worked. As repulsive as The Bull, but far more common if the newspapers were any guide. Your target market consists of the people hunting in the deepest, darkest, ugliest, most disturbing corners of the Net, the most loathsome hard-core porn sites, most unspeakable Usenet rape fantasies, the sick underworld of faked snuff films and elaborately documented torture fiction. They looked for users who contributed — anonymously, of course — to these sites. I guessed they wanted people who seemed homicidally fucked up but in a cold, con-trolled way, although it looked like they had misjudged with NumberFive at least. Then they talked to them on an anony-mous IRC chat line or a secure instant messaging connection, talked to them regularly until they thought they knew and understood the potential recruit, and if they passed muster, then they popped the question — invited the recruit to join The Bull.

That IRC fragment I had dug up weeks ago, with its weird talk of being a "sequential homicide artist," that must have been from one of those recruiting sessions, there must have been someone else online that NumberTwo and Num-berThree were talking to. Maybe it was Morgan Jackson.

I went back to the site and looked at it more carefully, doing a technical analysis. It was a Microsoft FrontPage/ASP-powered site; the .asp filenames and HTML source for the pages confirmed that. The media files were stored on the site, but the links to corroborating data were URLs to the newspaper or other sites in question.

It was the work of a developer who knew a lot less than he thought he did. A semicompetent ASP programmer who thought that he understood how the Web worked and he had guaranteed security and anonymity on his site. Very wrong. First of all, he had neglected to warn his users to wipe the cookie files on client machines. Second, he was using an unencrypted login. Third, they had that simple "taurus" username/password combination for guests, where they should have an unintelligible mix of numbers and mixed-case letters.

Fourth, and potentially most dangerous to them, were the links to corroborating data. Every time you click on a link in the Web, the site you go to may log not just the IP number of your machine, aka the client address, but the IP number of the site whose link you clicked on, aka the referring address. Which meant that there were Web logs out there with entries that had The Bull's IP number as the referring address, one entry for each time that a user of The Bull had clicked on that link—and each of those entries also held the client address, the IP number of the machine utilized by The Bull's user at the time.

In fact one of those Web logs was the Lonely Planet Thorn Tree. My own account of Stanley Goebel's death had been used as corroborating evidence so Morgan could get his precious dead-pool points. I couldn't remember if Lonely Planet logged the referring address or not. If they did, I could look them up, find out what computers the other users of The Bull had used to read that corroborating evidence.

But the rule that The Bull should only be accessed from a public terminal was sound and alleviated a lot of their risk. If they had followed it. Rules are meant to be broken. Morgan had broken one of The Bull's rules, he had gotten fancy, he had had a conversation with me on The Thorn Tree. And he had begun his career by breaking another, by killing someone he knew socially. I wondered how he could have hated Laura so much. I wondered how anyone could have hated Laura.

It occurred to me as I logged off that I had just left my traces on The Bull. Like Heisenberg said, the observer affects the observed. I had not gone through Anonymizer or SafeWeb or Zero-Knowledge; so I might have left my own IP number in The Bull's Web logs several thousand times over, once for each login attempt. If The Bull was set up to log user accesses, and if the site administrator actually paid attention to its Web logs, my dictionary attack would stick out like the proverbial sore thumb. And cable modems have fixed IP numbers. It was possible—difficult, unlikely, but possible—to determine my name and address once given that IP number. I might have just opened a path for The Bull to get to me.

For a moment I felt frightened. Then I realized that Morgan already knew my address. Last year when I moved in I had sent out a mass e-mail to all my friends and relatives and fellow Africa truckers. If he wanted to come get me, he knew where I lived. But I didn't think he was going to. I thought he was certain I was harmless.

I intended to show him he was dead wrong.

I went for a walk because my apartment seemed claustrophobic again. Maybe I shouldn't renew the lease after all. I was beginning to associate it with horrific discoveries. I walked all the way down Haight Street to Market and then I turned around and walked back again, chewing the facts I had discovered, trying to smooth them into a digestible mass.

Then I called Talena.

"Hello?" she answered.

"Hi. It's Paul."

"Oh. Hi." She waited expectantly. I think she thought I had called to apologize.

"Listen. There's something you should see."

"What's that?"

"Do you have two phone lines?"

"What? No."

"Okay. I'm going to give you an IP number, a login, and a password, and you should go there and read what you find."

"Paul," she said, "does this have anything to do with The Bull?"

"This has everything to do with The Bull."

"Paul, *stop*. I mean it. Get it out of your head. I'm not getting involved any more."

I almost started arguing furiously, but I thought of a more cunning tactic. "Okay. I understand that. And to be honest you probably don't want to read this. It's the most disturbing thing I've ever seen. But I felt, you know, I should at least call you and try to tell you about it."

There was a silence. Then she sighed, long and loud, and said, "Tell me."

"I will. But first of all, and this is the important thing, is you want to go through SafeWeb. SafeWeb-dot-com. Enter the IP number into the address field on its home page."

"Or the Men in Black will find me and kill me?" she asked sarcastically.

"It's a distant but distinct possibility."

"Uh-huh. All righty then. What's the number?"

I told her, and added the login and password.

"Taurus? The sign of the bull? . . . what is this?"

"You wouldn't believe me if I told you," I said. "You'll have to look at it yourself. Call me back after you've had a look."

"I'll call you back," she said, and she sounded worried.

We said good-byes and hung up. I thought about calling Agent Turner, she'd given me a business card before we left, but I decided to wait to talk to Talena. Maybe it was best not to talk to Agent Turner. If we were going to talk to anyone at this point, it should be the media. CNN and MSNBC and the *New York Times* and England's *Guardian* and France's *Le Monde* and all the big international papers. Let them break this story.

But what would that do? What would that really accomplish? Probably nothing. Which of those five would be put beyond harming anyone again? Probably none of them. It might scare them a little, might make them cool down for a few months. But the media had the collective memory of a gnat. Another year and stories about The Bull would be in the Whatever Happened To . . . ? category.

The harsh truth was that nobody would do anything unless I did something.

I went back to my computer and returned to The Bull's site. I wanted to get all the data off it. I had all the text, but I wanted all the pictures, all the digital media, all the grotesque unwatchable stuff, as evidence. Thankfully cable modems are fast as hell. It only took half an hour to get the hundred or so files. I zipped them into a single file, but they wouldn't fit in my Yahoo! Briefcase, so I bought one year of a five-hundred-meg XDrive.com partition on the spot and put it there. Pricey but I wanted offsite backup. This was critical evidence.

I thought about registering The Bull's site with Yahoo! or Google, flooding them with traffic from every headcase who searched for words like "evisceration" on the Net, but while this would be a petty form of justice, it would probably just make them move to a fallback location and alert them that their cover had been at least partially blown.

I was composing my dead-man-switch letter to the world's media organizations when Talena called me back.

"Paul?" She was almost whispering.

"Yeah."

"This is some sick shit."

"Yeah."

"What are you going to do?"

"What makes you think I'm going to do anything?" I asked, trying for an innocent tone.

"Paul."

"Okay," I said. And I told her my plan.

She didn't seem impressed. But I was past caring. While writing my To Whom It May Concern letter, documenting all the facts of the situation in cold impersonal prose, I had felt that cold fury well up inside me again, twice as intense as before. It made me feel strong, and I didn't think it was going to go away this time. I promised myself it wouldn't. I promised myself there would be no repeat of that moment I had whimpered and cringed before Morgan Jackson.

I wrote the letter as simply and clearly as possible, the way I'd written my Thorn Tree post, but this time I left nothing out. I included a pointer to the complete contents of The Bull's site on my XDrive account, and the login and password required to access those contents. I cc'd the major newspapers in as many First World countries as I could find, and added Agent Turner's contact details. No doubt she would thank me for that.

Then I configured my Yahoo! Calendar account to send that e-mail one month from today, and again two months from today. That way even if my plan went utterly wrong, in the worst way, and even if Talena walked in front of a bus, everything I had found out would still get out. I was being unnecessarily paranoid, I knew. After all, the first step in my plan was to tell every detail to several more people. But I didn't want to take any chances that might benefit those five fuckers who played at the game they called The Bull.

Five serial killers, awarding one another style plaudits over the Internet. It was like hotornot.com for murderers. I mentally christened them the Demon Princes, after a surprisingly memorable sci-fi series I had once read about a man who hunts down the five archcriminals who killed his parents. I wasn't going to be as obsessive and ruthless as Kirth Gersen, the protagonist of those books, who had lived for nothing else except hunting down and killing each of the five in turn. Not quite as obsessive. I was only after one of them.

By now it was a blood oath. One way or another Morgan Jackson was going down. And now I thought I knew the way. I had a plan. It felt like a good plan. It felt right. It felt appropriate that this ended where it began.

Africa.

22

DARK CONTINENT
DREAMING

There were twenty of us in Africa. Hallam Chevalier, our laconic and casually competent Zimbabwean driver. His gregarious Kiwi wife, Nicole Seams, radiator of good cheer. Steven McPhee, a St. Bernard of a man, a brilliant mechanic, a big friendly Aussie a lot smarter than he looked. Those three were in theory the official representatives of Truck Africa, the company that owned the truck and sent it across the continent every so often. But after a couple of weeks there was no distinction between them and us.

The passengers came from around the world. Claude, a French teenager who had come on the truck barely speaking any English, a wildlife expert, a proudly lazy good-for-nothing loved by everyone. Mischtel, a lanky Namibian/German girl with an inimitable deadpan sense of humor. Jose, a phlegmatic Mexican with a razor-sharp mind, easily the smartest of us. Lawrence, a hard-drinking, hard-nosed Kiwi who somehow always got his mitts on the last beer. Aoife, an Irishwoman who could cook like Julia Child and find music anywhere in the world. Carmel, a garrulous Australian computer guru who liked everything about Africa except the chocolate deprivation. Melanie, a Scottish chiropractor and oceangoing sailor who simply refused to be fazed by anything.

And a crowd of Brits. Chong, nicknamed "Chong the Indestructible," a ferociously fit marathon man, the most British person on the truck despite his name. Emma, aristocratic and model-pretty, who was ready for absolutely anything so long as her moisturizer supplies were adequate. Her "slightly less evil twin" Kristin, a movie producer back in Real Life, who had the rare gift of making people who assisted her with anything feel afterward as if they were the ones who had been done a favor. Michael, the most charming man alive, taking every disaster in stride as if it was the day's entertainment, with an amazing knack for finding hashish in even the most remote corners of the globe. Robbie, a good-natured London club kid with a first-rate mind on the rare occasions that he chose to use it. Rick, a social animal armed with sandpaper wit that stripped the slightest hint of pomposity from anyone within twenty paces, and a heart of gold beneath. Michelle, everyone's little sister, a slightly dazed and comic-book-pretty little blond girl who seemed incredibly out of place in Africa but handled it with surprising aplomb.

And Laura Mason, everyone's sweetheart. And Morgan Jackson, the Great White Hunter. And me.

Aside from Hallam and Nicole, none of us knew each other before the day we met. From a certain perspective the whole trip sounds like either a *Survivor*-esque reality show or some kind of ethically questionable psychological experiment: Take a large group of perfect strangers, force them together nearly twenty-four hours a day and seven days a week for four months, give them an extreme task such as driving across West Africa, make them work for the bare necessities of life such as food and shelter, and see how they cope. We coped all right. It turns out that people are good at coping when they have no other choice.

In chemistry, when chemicals are brought together in conditions of extreme heat and pressure, certain combinations are apt to violently explode. Other combinations repel one another and simply will not mix under any circumstances. However, there are some rare chemicals that will *only* bond under those conditions—and will form stronger bonds than those found anywhere else in nature.

I think people are the same way. I think groups of people in intense situations will explode, fragment, or gel. Our truck group didn't go to war together, we didn't survive a plane crash together, but compared to the plastic existences led by most people in the First World at the end of the twentieth century, our time together was unspeakably raw and intense. And we had the right combination. There were other overland trucks who attempted to cross the continent at roughly the same time, and we heard of some that fragmented, where the driver and passengers battled daily, where half the group fled the truck for weeks on end to travel independently and returned only reluctantly if at all. But we had just the right combination.

In chemistry they call it *sublimation* when a substance moves from a solid to a gas without ever becoming a liquid. Something similar happened to us. We started as strangers and somehow became a tightly knit tribe without ever really passing through the stages of acquaintancehood and friendship. Many of us would never have become friends. It wasn't in us. But members of your tribe do not have to be friends. Sometimes it is better that they are not. That was the most important lesson that Africa taught me.

This was my plan:

I wanted Morgan Jackson dead. I was willing to kill him myself. I was sure of that now. I wanted to turn the tables on him, track him down in some desolate corner of the Third World, and do unto him as he had intended to do unto me.

But. I doubted I could find him when next he traveled, and he certainly wasn't going to respond to any invitation I sent him. Also he was still bigger, stronger, faster, more dangerous. Even if I could find him again, I didn't have a chance. Not alone.

And who would help me? Certainly not Talena, and I couldn't fault her for that, not for a second. It wasn't a blood oath for her. It wasn't *personal*.

Morgan Jackson was a psychopath, a murderer, a serial killer; he had violated the laws of God and man; but he had found a loophole, he performed his atrocities outside the range of those who steadfastly enforce those laws. He would never be brought to justice by them. Nor by the ruthless, impersonal law of the jungle. But there is another kind of justice, and another kind of law. When he killed Laura Mason he had killed one of his own tribe. Nations and governments might be powerless, hamstrung by their own rules, but tribes have no such limitations. They do not do what is written; they do what they think is right.

I flew to London.

FIVE

THE
OLD WORLD

23

TRIBAL COUNCIL

When the plane lifted off, my plan consisted of a vague image of myself and the sixteen other truckers sitting around a green baize table, where I told them what had happened and gave a fiery speech in Laura's memory, and we got up and went en masse to the door, shoulder to shoulder, ready to revenge ourselves on Morgan. Fortunately by the time I landed in Heathrow I had thought things through with greater clarity. For one thing some of us did not live in London. For another I remembered well how impossible it was to get the group of us to agree on something as small as a lunch hour. We were a tribe, not a hive mind. And when you want a tribe to take military action, you don't convene a meeting of every single member. You talk to the hunters.

I decided on Hallam, Nicole, Steve, and Lawrence. I knew that Hallam and Nicole, as the driver-and-courier couple, had felt responsible for Laura's death. They wouldn't want to be left out. They were also two of the most all-around capable people I knew. Steve was a lovable Australian, but he had a very checkered background: He'd learned his mechanics in prison. He was big and tough and useful, and no stranger to violence, and he and Laura had been great pals.

As for Lawrence—well, we'd never been the best of friends, but that was primarily because he and Laura had had that fling early on in the trip. It had ended amicably enough, but I think inside he had taken her death nearly as hard as I had. And while a great guy, he could be a mean, intimidating, vengeful son of a bitch when it suited him. We had called him "The Terminator" on the truck. Just the man you want on your side.

None of them got any advance warning. I was in sporadic e-mail contact with all of them, I knew they were all working in London, but I didn't call them in advance to tell them what was going on, or even to tell them that I was coming. It would have felt inappropriate. Something like this had to be told face-to-face. And I didn't want to make up some reason for visiting when the truth was that I wanted to recruit them into hunting down Morgan.

I got to Heathrow at 9 A.M. I'd slept just enough to be dazed and confused and irritable. I took the Tube in to Earl's Court and read the *Guardian* on the way. Thankfully it was Saturday and therefore not too crowded. After checking into the nearest hostel I called Hallam and Nicole. It took me three tries, as London had once again changed its entire telephone numbering system.

"Hello," Nicole answered.

"Nicole," I said. "Hi. It's Paul Wood."

"Paul! How are you! Where are you? It must be five in the morning over there."

"I'm in London. Earl's Court tube."

"Oh, fabulous! When did you get in?"

"An hour ago."

"What are you doing here?" She must have heard something in my voice, her tone had dropped from excited to worried.

"I need to talk to you and Hallam. I was hoping I could come over."

"Of course. When?"

"Now. And I'd like you to call Steve and Lawrence and have them come over to your flat today too. Tell them it's important."

"Steve and Lawrence. All right, I'll sort them out. Can you tell me what this is about over the phone?"

That was Nicole; no surprise, no demurral, just calm acceptance moving straight into action. Her husband was the same way. They were one of those perfect couples who must never break up because they give hope to the rest of us in this imperfect world.

"It's about Laura," I said.

"Laura," she repeated. "I see. I'll see to it that they're here as soon as they're able. Do you have our address?"

"I do. I'll be there soon."

When I arrived, Nicole kissed me hello and sat me down in their living room with a cup of tea and a plate of toast and scrambled eggs. She was petite but ferociously fit, with a runner's build and one of the world's warmest smiles.

"Get you anything else?" she asked.

"That's fine, Nic, thanks."

"Good flight?"

"All right."

She nodded, sat down across from me, and scanned through the morning's *Times* as I ate and drank. Hallam was in the shower. I looked around their apartment. Decorated with attractive bric-a-brac from around the world, and postered with countless shots of The World's Most Beautiful Places, many of which had Hallam or Nicole or both in the foreground. I recognized some of the backdrops. Hallam playing Spider-Man halfway up an overhanging karst spire that jutted from the ocean somewhere near Krabi on the west coast of Thailand. Hallam and Nicole at Tilicho Tal, the world's highest lake, a side trip from the Annapurna Circuit.

Nicole in front of the grave of Cecil Rhodes, in Zimbabwe's Matopos Park.

Hallam came out of the shower with a towel wrapped around him, a bulldog of a man, and he grinned ear to ear when he saw me. "Paul, mate. Been too long." We shook hands, our tribe's secret handshake, ending with a finger snap the way the Ghanaians do it.

"I rang Steve and Lawrence," Nicole said. "They should be here in about an hour. Do you want to wait until we're all assembled?"

"Probably easier that way," I said.

"Fair enough," Hallam said. "Watch the telly then? Should be some Champions League highlights from last night."

I turned on the television as he disappeared into their bedroom to get dressed. Nic and I made small talk to pass the time. I told her about my layoff and she made sympathetic noises. She was working as a travel agent and enjoying it, and she and Hallam were planning their next trip already, rock climbing in Tunisia. Hallam's contract ended in a couple of months. He had served two years in the Paratroopers before a medical discharge for a detached retina that couldn't be trusted to take the shock of another opened parachute, then a year driving for Truck Africa, and now he made a good living as a contract security consultant.

One of the strong impressions Africa had made on me was that I was completely useless. As were most of the people I knew. Computer programmers, lawyers, accountants, publicists, graphic designers, copywriters—these abstract jobs counted for absolutely nothing in a place where you actually had to fight for your existence. Hallam was quite the opposite. Driver, soldier, mechanic, carpenter, welder, ditchdigger, bridge builder, expert rock climber, you name it, he was Mr. Useful. Nicole was more of an abstract thinker and people person, but I remembered days she'd spent covered with grease, helping Steve and Hallam fix the old, fragile truck engine for the umpteenth time.

We watched Manchester United rout Anderlecht until finally the doorbell rang, and Steve and Lawrence came in together.

"Bastard found me on the Tube," Lawrence explained. "I'm standing next to this drop-dead blonde, just about to chat her up, and all of a sudden there's this great human mountain in front of me, saying"—and he gave us a sarcastic rendition of Steve's thick country Australian accent— "'Lawrence, you bloody auld cunt, how are yae?' She couldn't get away from us fast enough."

Human mountain was a pretty good description. Big, blond, and thickly muscled, with a cheerful grin perpetually spray painted on his face, Steve McPhee looked like the walking model for some neo-Nazi definition of the Master Race. He was the lead mechanic for some type of car-racing team a few notches below Formula One. Lawrence, thin and wiry, with twitchy mannerisms, disapprovingly pursed lips, and the look of a bird of prey, seemed a scrawny refugee next to Steve. He was a loans officer for a bank and claimed to take great pleasure in turning down mortgage applications.

"And how are *you*, you bloody old cunt?" Steve asked, shaking my hand, Ghana-style. He kissed Nicole on the cheek and waved hello to Hallam and sat down. Lawrence followed, performing the same greetings.

"Now what's this all about, a reunion of the Old Colonials Brigade?" Lawrence asked, sitting down. "This room is like a bad joke. Two Kiwis, an Aussie, a Zimbabwean, and a Canadian walk into a pub . . ."

"It's about Laura," Nicole said quietly, and all the good cheer and bonhomie fled from the room like somebody had turned off a light. They all turned to me.

———————

"Right," I said, and I felt nervous. Not about what I was going to say, or about talking to them—this didn't count as public speaking, these were my homeys I was talking to—but about what I was going to start. I wished I could feel more confident that there would be a happy ending.

"Right," I repeated. "Well, there's a long version and a short version. I'll give you the long version in a moment, I've got papers and pictures and, do you have a Net connection here?" I asked, and Nicole nodded yes, "but the short version is this: I found out who murdered Laura. I found out for a fact. It wasn't any Cameroonian. It was Morgan."

They didn't say anything. I studied their faces. They looked worried, surprised, appalled . . . but not *shocked*. No, none of them was shocked to hear the proposition that Morgan Jackson was her killer. I guessed he'd been in the back of everyone's mind all along.

"You better give us the long version of that now," Hallam said gently.

"This all started not even a month ago," I said, and didn't really believe it. It felt as if a lifetime had passed since that day. "I was off trekking in Nepal, on the Annapurna Circuit, with this South African guy named Gavin, and we were exploring this abandoned village called Gunsang . . ."

After I finished there was a long silence. My folderful of evidence—pictures and Web printouts and my time line—was scattered around the table, much thumbed and read. My audience of four wore stone-serious faces. Only a couple of hours had passed, but I felt as if I had gone on all day, felt as if night had fallen despite the most un-London-esque sunshine that streamed in through the windows.

"Just a moment," Nicole said, and disappeared into the bedroom.

"He's back in Leeds," Hallam said thoughtfully. "Morgan is. Got an e-mail from him just yesterday, saying he was back from the trail."

"I can't believe it," Steve said. "I mean, I believe every word, Paul, never you worry about that, but I just can't believe it, if you get me. He always seemed like a bit of a hard lad, bit of a harder-than-thou chip on his shoulder, eh, but all this shite? He's bloody mentally demented, is what he is."

Nicole reappeared, a postcard in her hand.

"Sent us a card from Nepal," she explained. "Where's that picture of that ledger entry . . . ? Here we go." She compared the two, nodded sadly, passed them around. It didn't take a handwriting expert to see that the same person had written both. I was glad of that extra bit of evidence.

Nobody said anything for some time.

"Feel like I'm at a funeral," Hallam said. "What say we continue this conversation down the pub? Don't know about the rest of you, but I could do with a pint, and our local just opened."

Lawrence, who normally loudly seconded any motion that involved beer, didn't say a thing. His face was as set as an iron sculpture.

"Sensible plan," Steven said.

We went down the pub. The Pig & Whistle, a genuine old English pub, none of your new well-lit chain pubs serving Thai lunches for this crowd, thank you very much. Hallam bought a packet of Marlboro Lights along with the round and all of us lit up except for Lawrence.

"Don't usually smoke in England," Nicole said. "Only when we travel."

"Same," I said.

"That so? Same for me," Steven said. "Birds of a feather, hey?"

Hallam cut through the banter and said to me: "What do you have in mind?"

I didn't want to say it. It sounded so melodramatic, so over-the-top. I hesitated, trying to find the right phrasing.

Lawrence made it easy for me. "I say we find the bastard and kill him."

"Easy there," Nicole said, "let's not jump to any conclusions just yet . . ."

"Fuck that," Lawrence said. "Sorry, Nic, but no one else is going to do fuck-all, and that son of a whore needs killing. Wish there was something worse. Killing's too good for him."

"What did you have in mind?" Hallam asked me.

"Pretty much that," I said quietly.

"Vigilante justice," Nicole said, skeptically.

"Tribal justice," I said. "Only kind of justice he might get."

"Bloody dangerous game to play," Steven said.

"The most dangerous game," Hallam said, and I half smiled at the joke.

"It's no fucking *game*," Nicole objected. "Let's try and keep a fifty-fifty mix of brains and testosterone here. I don't want to see you lot downing a few too many and going off on some mad mission to Leeds tonight."

"And what do you want to do, Nic?" Lawrence demanded. "Cut him off your Christmas card list and wait for Interpol to grow itself some testicles? You want to fucking sit back and do nothing?"

"Easy, Lawrence," Hallam said gently.

"It's okay, Hal," Nicole said. "Lawrence. That's not what I'm saying. She was my friend too. I was there when we found her. I'm just saying, whatever we do, we have to be careful, and we have to be patient."

"But the long and the short of it is that he needs killing," Lawrence said. "Do you agree or not?"

"Lawrence . . ." Hallam said.

He had a warning note in his voice that normally would have shut any of the rest of us up in a microsecond, but this time Lawrence kept on. "Just let her answer, Hallam. Do you agree he needs killing?"

"You worried I've turned into some kind of vegetarian pacifist, Lawrence?" She sounded darkly amused. "You needn't worry. But what's done is done and we're not going to get her back. I don't want revenge so much as I want to make sure he doesn't ever do it to anyone else. And if the only way to do that is what you're suggesting . . ." She shrugged casually. "Then so be it."

"I can't think of any other way," I said. "And I've tried hard. I've talked to the FBI, and Interpol, and governments . . . they can't touch him."

"It's not an easy thing you're proposing," Steven said. "A man like Morgan, he'll be hard to hunt down. Nic's right, we daren't go off half-cocked here. I'm as bloody maddened as you, Lawrence, I reckon we all are. But keep yourself on a leash."

"I'm doing just that," Lawrence said. "I'm not halfway to Leeds already, am I? I just want to make sure we don't satisfy ourselves with some mealymouthed can't-be-arsed compromise like 'let's just alert the media' or some such."

"Hallam?" I asked. "What do you think?"

Our de facto leader, always. Would have been from day one even if he wasn't the driver.

"I'd like to know how we're supposed to get at him," he said. "It's not worth getting one or all of us killed or locked up."

Nicole nodded her agreement.

"I reckon Mr. Wood here came with a plan," Steve said. "Didn't you, Woodsie?"

They all looked at me.

"As a matter of fact I did," I said. "It's a pretty basic one. Bring him to us. Lure him to Africa. Hoist him on his own modus operandi."

"Africa?" Nicole asked. "And what makes you think he'll want to go there?"

"He's a traveler, isn't he?" I asked. "He's gone home because he's out of money, but he doesn't start work up until January. My idea is that we get someone to give him a call and tell him they've got a last-minute cancellation for a week in Morocco, and the whole shebang is prepaid, and it's all his for fifty pounds but he has to leave in three days' time or something. Tell him that they got his name off the Truck Africa mailing list or some such. Only room for one person, so he can't bring a friend. If he has any."

"That'd work," Steve said. "He'd be on that like bloody flies on Marmite. He'd take out an overdraft if he had to. He loved Morocco."

"We all did," Nicole said.

"Laura especially," Lawrence added quietly.

"Of course I'll pay for his trip," I said. "I've got the almighty American dollar on my side."

"The mighty British pound is no weak sister," Lawrence said. "I'll split it with you."

"If we decide to do this," Nicole said, "we'll all split the cost."

"If?" Lawrence asked, with an edge in his voice again.

"I'm no weak sister either, Lawrence," she said. "But I'm suggesting, no, I'm telling you that we'll all sleep on this. We'll all go home, get some sleep, and give it some hard fucking thought. And if I sleep on it, and the answer is yes, I'll arrange all the travel plans and get a mate of mine at the agency to make the call. That satisfy you?"

"It does," Lawrence said, apologetic.

We all drank deeply from our pints and, except for Lawrence, lit up new cigarettes.

"Tomorrow?" I suggested. "Right here in the pub? Six o'clock?"

It was agreed.

The conversation died down to nothing after that. Hallam and Nicole and Lawrence looked grim. Steve looked his usual cherubic self, but even he was staring off into space, thinking hard. We emptied our pints in silence.

"Do you want to stay at our place?" Nicole asked me, as we got up to leave. "That couch is more comfortable than it looks."

"That's all right," I said. "I've already checked into a hostel."

I didn't want my presence to disturb their deliberations. It would be easier for them to think and talk about it if I wasn't there. I didn't want to push them into joining me. On the contrary, I was already beginning to wonder if I had done the right thing by dragging my friends into my vendetta. Steve was right, it was a bloody dangerous game, and any of those who decided to join me could very easily wind up hurt or dead.

Laura and I had our first and only fight in the Mount Afi monkey sanctuary near the Nigerian border. And if I'd handled it a little better, if I hadn't kept picking at it like a scab, it all would have been different. She wouldn't have been murdered. People tell you not to blame yourself, but what do you do when it actually was your fault? When you know for a fact that if you had acted a little bit better, if you had been a little less petty and self-righteous, then a terrible thing would never have happened?

The monkey sanctuary was a wonderful place. A good thing too, because the one-hour journey we were promised turned into an all-day marathon. Typical for Africa, and especially Nigeria, which at the time would have made anyone's short list of the ten worst countries in the world. Ruled by a brutal kleptocracy, unanimously voted the most corrupt place on earth, hot, dusty, polluted, ugly, overcrowded, a place where nothing worked, where nobody wanted to help anyone else, where even the food was bad. At that time, in Nigeria, one of the world's largest oil producers, you could only buy gasoline on the black market, because the country's entire domestic gasoline output was stolen on its way out of the refineries. It was potentially a rich country, but it had been systematically looted for decades and was rotten to the core.

The only point in its defense was that most of the roads were marvelous by African standards—other than the check-points every few miles where ragged men with guns requested a "dash" before allowing vehicles to pass—but the road to Mount Afi was an exception, a muddy track that forded several thigh-deep rivers on its way up. This was a good thing; it was only because the road was nearly impassable that the Mount Afi rain forest had not yet been destroyed; but it made for a long and difficult day.

The truck punctured a tire and bogged down on the muddy approach to the second river. At first we weren't too concerned. During our three months of travel, the truck had lost a half-dozen tires and gotten stuck at least fifty times, and we had become experts at getting it on its way again. Dig the tires free, fix the one that was punctured, unhook the sand mats—imagine a pair of flat cheese graters about ten feet long, twice as wide as a truck tire, with holes two inches in diameter—thrust them under the tires to give them traction, and stand back as Steve or Hallam coaxed the truck forward along the sand mats to stability. By now our group formed a well-oiled excavating machine, and we could usually get ourselves out of a quagmire within half an hour. But not this time.

It was fun at first. We had at least gotten stuck at a picturesque site. The river, maybe twenty feet wide and four deep, burbled through thick jungle rich with butterflies, flowers, and brightly colored birds, where if you stopped and listened you could hear animals rustle through the distant bush. A little trail ran into the jungle, and Claude found a pineapple bush just two minutes' walk away. It was rainy season, but the sky was blue, flecked with harmless little clouds. The best day we'd had in weeks.

While Lawrence and Morgan and I dug, Michelle slipped and acrobatically fell face-first into the mud while bringing us water, and everyone burst into laughter at her horrified mud-masked expression when she realized Nicole had videotaped the moment. When Rick and Michael and Robbie took over, Chong and Mischtel started an impromptu mud-wrestling match that grew to include a half dozen of us. Emma and Carmel and Kristin went swimming in the river after their stint of digging. We were relaxed, joking, glad to be out of the thick cloud of smog that chokes every Nigerian city.

But the deeper we dug, the softer and stickier the mud got. We lowered the tire pressure and tried sand-matting out, but the wheels spun uselessly, serving only to drive the sand mats deeper. It took another ten minutes of digging to extricate them. Morgan and Lawrence and I took over from Chong and Steve and Hallam. Tempers began to fray. A mud fight had developed among the nondiggers, and when Michelle ran from Claude to hide behind Morgan, she got in his way, and he snarled, "Will you just fuck off and die?"

"We're trying to fucking work here," Lawrence added, "in case you hadn't fucking noticed."

Michelle fled. I wanted to say something too. My mood was growing increasingly foul. The people who weren't digging didn't realize how badly the truck was bogged down. My guess was that we would have to winch the truck across the river, which would take all day and leave us groaning with exhaustion, and then on the way back we would somehow have to cross this swamp again.

Michelle and Claude apologized. We paid them no notice and kept digging. I began to wonder if we were doing any good at all or just helping the truck sink into the mud. The mud fight continued, and Laura threw a big handful that hit me right in the face. A little got into my eye, which began to tear up painfully, and I would only worsen it by rubbing with my mud-soaked hands, so I dropped the shovel and staggered toward the river to wash my eye out. Laura rushed toward me, wearing an expression of abject guilt, apologizing.

"You want to look where you're fucking throwing?" I said angrily. The first harsh words I had ever sent her way. She reached for my eye, but I shrugged her aside and ducked into the river. The water was thick with dirt, and it took me some time before I could blink my eye clear of grit.

"I'm sorry," Laura said. "I'm really sorry. I wasn't aiming at you. I slipped."

"How about you guys try not throwing mud around at all?" I asked, directing my anger at everyone. I was going to storm back to continue digging, burn my angry energy that way, but Chong had already taken up the shovel I discarded.

"Relax," Laura soothed. "We'll make lunch. You'll feel better when you eat."

"I'm sick of this fucking truck," I said. It was a common sentiment. Truck life was draining and often difficult. But I had never meant it more.

"Come on," Laura said. "Help me get the table out."

"I'm serious," I said. "I'm not just saying it. I've had enough of this shit."

I was serious, and she realized it. She looked at me, concerned, obviously trying to work out what to say, how to improve my mood and change my mind back.

I wasn't in the mood to be placated. I approached Hallam, Nicole, and Steve, who had just finished repairing the perforated tire. "This is bullshit," I complained. "We're just digging ourselves deeper. We'll have to fucking winch our way out."

"It's not looking good," Hallam admitted. "I'm going to give it one more try, then we'll break out the winch."

"This poor old sheila wasn't meant for hard living," Steve said fondly, patting the side of the truck.

"We should have traded this piece of shit in for a few Land Rovers three months ago," I muttered.

Nicole opened her mouth to say something, closed it, then looked at Laura. "Shall we get lunch going?" she suggested brightly.

Laura nodded, and they began the routine: unlocking the cages that held fresh water beneath the sides of the truck, extricating canned foods and bread and vegetables from the stores beneath the floorboards, easing the table out from its slot between the cab and body of the truck, and constructing lunch for twenty, in this case tuna salad and leftover rice from the night before. After a little while I started to help. My anger had faded. But my resolve to leave the truck remained strong.

Rescue came a little later, in the form of the monkey sanctuary's Land Rover followed by a gaggle of Nigerians on "machines," or motorcycle taxis. We decided to leave the truck where it was, guarded by Hallam and Steve and Nicole, and negotiated rides up the road with our saviors. Half of us got rides on the Land Rover. I got stuck on the back of a "machine." My driver was all of seventeen years old, and first he crossed the river on a bridge made of a single four-by-four, then revved the engine and attacked the steep, rutted, uneven, stony road at terrifying speed. For parts of the journey I had my eyes closed, but in the end we made it alive. And the monkey sanctuary, run by an American woman who had come to Nigeria on a ten-day visa fourteen years ago and had not yet left, was a fantastic place, a verdant paradise beneath a deep canopy of rain forest, shockingly and wonderfully green after the crumbling gray concrete and smog of the rest of the country.

The next morning, after breakfast, I sat in the tent watching Laura pack her toothbrush away, and said, "I meant what I said yesterday."

"Which thing was that?" she asked without turning around.

"I want to leave the truck."

She stopped and turned around. "Paul. I know you were upset. But let it go."

"It wasn't yesterday's digging," I said. "I'm just sick of it. I'm sick of our lives revolving around food. I'm sick of being the circus everywhere we go. I'm sick of sleeping in tents, I'm sick of cooking for twenty people every five days, I'm sick of having zero privacy, and I'm sick of having to keep going whenever we go someplace I want to stay and having to stay every time we go somewhere I want to leave. And yeah, I'm sick of digging that fucking truck out of the mud too."

"I thought you wanted to cross the Congo. The truck's the only way."

"I don't think we'll make it. But even if we could . . . I'd love to cross the Congo, but not on this truck."

After a pause she said, "Are you talking about leaving alone?"

"What?" I asked, shocked. "No! Definitely not. Together. I want us both to leave. We can fly to Zimbabwe and visit my aunt and uncle. Or to Kenya if you'd rather go there."

"I'm not going."

I hadn't expected so flat a rejection.

After a moment, I asked, "As simple as that?"

She looked at me defiantly. "These are our people. You know that. And I'm not leaving them. If you want to go, you can go on your own. But I'm staying. And if you want to stay with me, you're staying too."

"That's . . . that's . . . this is . . ." I spluttered.

"What?"

I didn't know what I was trying to say, so I just looked at her.

"Is it the lifestyle you hate?" she asked. "Or the people? I know you're not a people person. But I thought you liked everyone."

"I do," I said. "I know. I mean, you're right, I agree, these are our people. I just can't handle truck life anymore."

"You're going to have to."

I finally worked out what I wanted to say. "I thought our being together was more important than staying with the people around us."

"They're just as important," she said, very seriously, looking me straight in the eyes. "I'm not saying you're unimportant. You're not. That should be obvious. You're the world to me, Paul. You know that. But these are our people. They matter just as much. To both of us. I just wish you could see that. But until you can, I'm not going to let you make this mistake."

I wish I had listened to her, really listened to her, to what she was trying to say. But I was angry, and I was upset, and I was eager to wallow in self-pity, and what I heard instead was: *They're more important to me than you are; and I know you won't leave me; and I'm going to use that to get my way and make you stay.*

"Fuck this," I said. "I'm going for a walk."

I stalked out of the tent before she could stop me.

I was so upset, replaying our conversation over and over again in my mind, layering the worst connotations imaginable on everything Laura had said, that I walked for a good half hour before looking up and realizing that I was completely lost. For a while I had walked through a little community of farming huts that adjoined the sanctuary, neatly kept wooden huts alongside a stream and surrounded by fields of vegetables, fields where the locals had wisely retained a few big trees in order to protect themselves from the crippling midday sun. From there I had taken a wide dirt path into the forest. But the path had shrunk and forked and subdivided, and I wasn't sure where I stood could even be called part of a trail at all. I was, however, sure that I could not retrace my tracks.

"Shit," I muttered. I looked around. At least I could see. This was not like the dense mangrove jungles of the south; this was rain forest, where the trees rose a hundred feet into the sky before their branches jutted out, their canopy swallowing so much light that the underbrush was relatively thin. I could see a fair distance in most directions. But it all looked the same. Waist-high bushes, young trees, fallen branches, enormous vines coiled like snakes around mossy fallen tree trunks, all carpeted by golden petals of some flower that must grow high in the canopy.

"Shit," I said again. Lost in African rain forest. A glorious and wonderful place to be lost, but still embarrassingly stupid and potentially dangerous. The vines reminded me uncomfortably of the pythons that lived in the jungle. And there were leopards. I heard something rustle in the distance and twitched nervously before getting hold of myself. Carnivores were extremely rare and not likely to attack something my size. The only real danger was not being found. If I stayed where I was, they would come and find me. Somehow. The people at the sanctuary would send out locals who would work their local magic and track me down.

I shook my head. Maybe Laura was right for an entirely different reason. Maybe I shouldn't leave the truck because on my own I was too stupid to live.

I decided to look around to see if I could find a more obvious trail. I didn't want to be like Robbie in the desert, walking when he should have stayed put, but ten minutes of casting around for landmarks couldn't hurt. I had a vague idea that I had been going east and downhill. The sun was too high for me to judge directions, so I just went uphill.

After five minutes of walking I paused to silently appreciate the rain forest's majesty and perceived, just barely, at the edge of my hearing, the welcome sound of burbling water.

After a couple of false starts I worked out where it was coming from and found the stream that was its source. Some animal had been drinking at the stream but fled before I could see what it was. I wished I had, but it didn't matter. The important thing was I was no longer lost. Triumphant, feeling very intrepid indeed, I followed the water upstream until I found the village near the sanctuary.

I wasn't really relieved, because I had never really been nervous. The rain forest was too beautiful for me to be frightened. I was glad that I had been lost. How many chances would I ever get to know what it is like to be alone in the African rain forest? If I had been with anyone else, I would have talked to them, would not have had the chance to understand how pure, how peaceful it was. I wished Laura had come. We could have sat quietly together and appreciated it. That would have been better than being alone. But anyone else would have spoiled it.

Which, in a nutshell, was my problem with the truck.

When I got back, our group was just saddling up for an expedition to visit the chimpanzees. It was an interesting place, I suppose. Laura and I maintained a cold silence during the expedition. For once I wasn't annoyed by the presence of the usual crowd. It made it easy to keep my distance from her.

When we got back to the tent we shared she looked at me expectantly. I knew what she was waiting for. An apology and an admission that she was right.

"I'm tired," I lied, and closed my eyes.

We would have been fine. Things were tense and distant between us for the next week, but I think we were just a day or two from an emotional outpouring of apology and understanding and warmth. The fact it was our first fight made it a little more difficult to kiss and make up, that was all, because we didn't yet quite know how.

The backbreaking toil of the Ekok-Mamfe road just inside Cameroon, where we worked eight hours a day for three days to travel twenty-five miles, didn't help anyone's mood and certainly didn't make me want to stay with the truck a moment longer than necessary. It was the worst road in the world, featuring muddy potholes bigger than our truck, and numerous detours that gave up on the road and went through raw jungle instead, but each day little Toyotas and Peugeots passed us with relative ease. When they got stuck, the eight or ten passengers jammed into each car had enough strength to simply get out and push their vehicle out of the mud. We had to dig and winch every time. It didn't help that both Steve and Morgan, our two strongest workers, had come down with malaria. Only Hallam and Nicole maintained anything like a good mood, and I suspected it was forced for the sake of the rest of us.

Laura and I maintained a cordial but cold détente throughout the Ekok-Mamfe ordeal. Then she twisted her ankle and couldn't climb Mount Cameroon. She gave me the blessing to go without her. I took it. The conversation was polite, but not warm.

The night I came back we shared a quick kiss and told each other our stories, but that was all. A slow thaw had already begun. I knew that she was just waiting for me to apologize to her and agree to stay with the truck as far as it went. I even knew by then that I would do just that. But, as stupid and petty and childish and sulky and self-centered as it was, I felt like I had been unfairly manipulated, and so I would hold out a little longer. Just a few more days.

The next day the truck went to Limbe, Cameroon, where we camped on the black volcanic sand of Mile Six Beach. Morgan, by now recovered from malaria, hitched down the road along with Lawrence, Claude, and Michelle, to stay in hotels in town. But later, after dark, he came back. He came back and found Laura alone on the beach. Alone because I wasn't with her. Alone because I was still pettily angry enough to decline her offer to come swimming. Because of that, because of me, Morgan found Laura alone, and killed her.

After the meeting with Hallam, Nicole, Steve, and Lawrence, I roved around a few of my favorite London haunts: watched some Covent Garden buskers, browsed idly through some Charing Cross Road bookstores, walked along some of the Embankment, saw a forgettable movie at the Roxy in Brixton, and took the Tube back to Earl's Court when the cold gray fog of jet lag began to close in on my mind. Despite the crowd of rowdy Spaniards who shared my corner of the hostel I slept like a baby.

I woke late and by the time I had eaten breakfast and read the *Times* and the *Guardian* it was two o'clock. I spent the afternoon playing tourist at the Tower of London, which was perhaps not an excellent choice considering how blades and torture implements had featured heavily in my dreams of late and the Tower had an entire wing devoted to medieval instruments of death and agony. By the time I got to the Pig & Whistle the other four were already there.

They'd already bought me a pint. I sat and lit up a cigarette. Hallam opened his mouth to say something but I shook my head and waved him quiet.

"I just wanted to say," I said, "that I don't even know if I've done the right thing by asking for your help, and, honestly, I'll be almost as glad to hear nos as yeses. It's . . . I don't know. It's crazy. I know it's crazy. Maybe I'm crazy. But one way or another, I'm not going to stop, I'm going to go after him. Any of you who are crazy enough to want to help me are welcome, but anyone who isn't, believe me, I completely understand."

"Oh, stop torturing yourself, you angst-ridden lout," Lawrence said impatiently. "That sick fucking bastard needs killing, and I for one am very happy to help."

I turned to Hallam and Nicole.

"We thought this over pretty hard," Nicole said. "We wanted to come up with some brilliant alternative plan that would keep him locked away for life. But we can't imagine what that would be, and if you've been chewing on it for some time now and you can't think of it either, then I guess it doesn't exist. That old long arm of the law is too short for Morgan."

"He needs to be dealt with," Hallam said, "and it has to be us who do it, because nobody else will. Simple as that."

I turned to Steve. By now I was smiling.

He grinned back and said, "Course I'm with you, mate. Somebody has to keep the rest of you lot out of trouble. And next time come to us sooner. Bloody hell. Sounded like you could have used a little help down there in Indonesia."

"So we're off to Morocco," Steve said, a couple of pints later. "Bloody big place as I recall. Where did you have in mind for catching up with our old mate?"

"Todra Gorge," I said.

Four heads nodded slowly.

"Todra Gorge," Hallam repeated. "Perfect."

24

THE PILLARS OF HERCULES

Three days later Crown Air flew us from Luton airport, a little strip of a runway some distance north of London, to Gibraltar. It was the only flight that got us to the area for a reasonable price, and there was no need to pay two thousand pounds more to fly to Casablanca. We had plenty of time. Morgan had bought the special offer hook, line, sinker, and rod, and in two days' time he would fly into the country. Two days after that, if all went according to plan, he would arrive in Todra Gorge.

It had all been surprisingly easy to arrange. It helped that Nicole worked in a travel agency. We had put together a travel package that consisted of return airfare to Marrakesh, one night in Marrakesh, two nights in Todra Gorge, two days of camel-trekking in the desert, and two nights in Essaouira on the Atlantic coast. As far as the hotels knew, or Morgan for that matter, we were a new package-tour company called Marrakesh Express Holidays, which specialized in Moroccan packages for solo travelers or couples. I spent a few hours in a London copy shop using their computers to create official-looking documentation, using samples from real companies as a guide. It was Nicole's friend Rebecca, thinking that we were arranging a surprise birthday party, who called Morgan and gave him the last-minute cancellation story. He accepted on the spot.

Hallam, Nicole, Steve, and Lawrence had all managed to get one of the four weeks of vacation allotted to British employees despite their minimal notice. We were due to fly back from Gibraltar one week from today. If all went even remotely according to plan, that gave us ample time and opportunity.

Once in Gibraltar we got off the plane, picked up our bags, and hiked across the enormous military-sized runway, which actually had a traffic light on it to indicate when it was safe to cross. The Rock of Gibraltar loomed above us, taking up a good third of the sky.

"Remember the last time we got here?" Hallam asked.

"I remember being bloody happy to get here," Nicole said. "First place that wasn't bloody freezing. I'd had enough of sleeping in car parks for one life, thank you."

"Sleeping in Dover car park because of Steve's minor oversight," Lawrence added.

"Come on now, I think I've heard enough about that for one life," Steve objected. "How was I supposed to know that Australians need to get their visas in advance for bloody France?"

"That's true, how was he supposed to know?" Lawrence asked. "Nation of penal convicts, you can't expect them to be able to read."

"Well, at least we don't bloody well abuse our sheep for unnatural sexual practices the way you Kiwis do—"

The usual Anzac bickering continued well into town. We were in no rush; the ferry didn't leave for a good six hours yet. None of us wanted to climb up the Rock, we'd done it last time and it didn't seem worth a repeat. We made a few last-minute purchases, found a pub near the waterfront, and whiled away the afternoon with cigarettes and beer and a truckload of nostalgia.

I had met the Big Yellow Truck and its inhabitants for the first time within sight of the pub in which we now waited. The truck had set out from London, but Rick and Michelle and I had bypassed the first week and flown to Gibraltar. Rick and I did this in order to gain an extra week's worth of pay. Michelle, typically, had missed the rendezvous in London and had to scramble to catch up.

I had mixed emotions at first. The truck was older and creakier than I had expected. Its denizens had already bonded into a group, with their in-jokes and their newly formed couples, and I felt very much an outsider at first. But everyone seemed nice enough. Hallam and Nicole were friendly and easygoing and self-assured, and you could tell that there was steel beneath their laid-back exterior. Steve seemed like a stereotypical loud, boisterous, jovial Aussie lager lout at first. It took me some time to realize that that was only half his story. And Lawrence and I got on famously from the start, when I climbed onto the truck and he wordlessly offered me a beer. We fell into a conversation about the merits of San Miguel versus Kronenbourg. Then a dark-haired girl came over, draped an arm around Lawrence's shoulder, and smiled at me.

"Hi," she said. "My name's Laura."

The trip was supposed to go straight across Africa to Kenya, but we separated in Cameroon. War had broken out in the Congo, the border to Chad was reportedly closed, but those were side issues. Laura's death had been shattering for everyone. Me most of all, of course, but it took the spirit, the joy of adventure, out of everyone. We stayed together only long enough to arrange our flights out of Cameroon. Most of the rest of the group flew to Kenya. A few gave up and went back to Europe. I alone flew to Zimbabwe. Partly to visit my family there. Mostly to escape the memories of Laura that crowded around every corner of the truck, every familiar face, like an army of ghosts. I was drinking heavily, every night. It didn't help.

On our last night, camped beside a dirt road just outside Douala, after a while it was just me, Hallam, Nicole, Steve, and Lawrence. Everyone else had said their tearful good-byes and climbed into their tents for the last time. My mood was black despair, and when Nicole told me, gently, that it would eventually get better, I flared up angrily.

"How would you know?" I demanded. "How the fuck would you know?"

"You're not the only person to have a terrible thing happen to them," she said quietly.

"Yeah? What happened to you?"

There was a moment of silence as Nicole considered my challenge. She exchanged glances with Hallam, then she spoke.

"I had an older sister," she said. "Four years older than me. She had cystic fibrosis. You know what that is? It's when fibers grow in your lungs and slowly, over a period of many years, choke you to death. It starts young. Usually you're dead by twenty-one. But Helen was a fighter. She lasted until twenty-three. The last three years, the way she breathed, it was like living with Darth Vader. And she knew, of course, she knew all along that she was going to die soon. So she was angry. Furious. And sick, and weak, and demanding, and manipulative. And who could blame her? You know? Who could blame her? I'll tell you who. Her little sister. Try living in the same room as your dying sister for three years, trying not to hate her for dying and for being the center of everyone's life, especially yours. Will that do? Is that terrible enough for you?"

I had never seen Nicole lose control of her emotions,

never seen her even faintly aggressive before. "I'm sorry," I muttered, looking down. "I'm sorry. I'm really sorry."

"I am too," she said, immediately contrite. "Paul. That didn't come out right. I'm not angry at you. I'm not. I'm sorry."

There was a moment of silence.

"The worst thing that ever happened to me was in Bosnia," Hallam said. "Peacekeeping. This woman I knew in this little town I still can't pronounce, about fifty years old, the only one there who didn't go crazy, absolutely bugfuck crazy, about whether you were Serb or Croat or Bosnian. She lived all alone in this little house outside the village. I never really found out her story. We found her and her nephew both. What was left of them." He paused. "That's one thing I wish I'd never seen."

We all stared silently into the guttering embers of the fire.

"Lawrence?" Nicole asked, her voice barely audible.

"Sorry," Lawrence said, shaking his head. "I've been lucky. Never had anything that bad happen to me. Not even close."

"Steve?"

Steve shook his head. "I don't know, mate," he said. I didn't think I had ever heard him sound serious before. "I just don't know. There was this one time . . ."

He hesitated.

"What happened?" Lawrence asked.

"Well," Steve said. "There was this bit of a bloody misunderstanding, see? So I spent a couple years up in Darwin. And this one time, about midway through, there was another bloody cock-up, and they went and blamed me for it, so I went and spent a few weeks helping build this road across the arse end of the world up there. Bloody hot it was. And the flies, Christ. But I'd gotten to be mates, a bit like, with one of the overseers, see? Fixed up his bike for him on the side. Old Triumph, it was, classic piece of work. So this one time, I got him to take me out, before dawn like, and bring this eskie" — Australian for "cooler," — "full of ice cream to where they picked us up at the end of the day. Just as a treat for all the mates I was working with. And the whole day, I reckon it was the hottest fucking day of my life, I was telling them all about it, this bloody big eskie full of ice cream waiting at the end of the day." He sighed and looked forlorn. "But I'd forgotten to lock down the eskie, hadn't I? And something got in there. Roos or camels or I don't know what. And when we got there, all excited like, the eskie was open and all the ice cream had melted."

He fell silent.

After a moment Nicole said, incredulously, "That's the worst thing that ever happened to you?"

Steve nodded tragically.

"Losing your ice cream? That was your worst moment? Didn't you get stabbed once in prison? Didn't you tell me once that your father left you when you were eight?"

"Oh, sure," Steve said. "I've been in my share of scraps, and I took a shiv once, and my dad left me young, and my mum drank too much. But she was a good mum still, and he probably wouldn't have been much of a bloody father, so I reckon that all worked out all right. No, that wasn't so bad. But when I saw that empty eskie, after telling all my mates about the treat I had for them. Well." He sighed. "Bit of a disappointment, that was. Bit of a bloody big—what?"

For we had all started laughing. Once we started we couldn't stop, and eventually Steve joined in, and we all laughed until we had tears in our eyes. Looking back I guess it was the first time I had laughed since Laura's death. And the last for months thereafter.

The Moroccan ferry system had grown no more efficient in the two years since our last visit. "Welcome to Africa," Lawrence said dryly when we finally cast off, ninety minutes late. "Please drop your watches over the side, as they will only serve to confuse you for the next five thousand miles."

Most of the hundred or so passengers were returning Moroccans. Maybe coming home to their families from their backbreaking agricultural jobs in Portugal and Spain, maybe just returning after a day of shopping in Europe. There were a dozen or so backpackers, but no overland truck. I was relieved at that. It would have made the nostalgia so intense as to be actually painful.

We got our passports stamped by a bored official, maybe twenty years old, who was engrossed in his calculus homework. Then we crowded to the front of the boat to watch the sun set over the Atlantic. It was a glorious sight, a huge red disk disappearing beneath the endless ocean to the west, the pale half-moon rising to the east behind us, and the coasts clearly visible five miles on either side. Gibraltar and Morocco, Europe and Africa—the Pillars of Hercules. We stayed for a long time, the salt Atlantic wind in our hair, until the coasts were visible only as broken chains of light, we could no longer see the dark water that the ship surged through, and the sky had filled with stars.

We smoked incessantly. Lawrence made increasingly catty comments about it, starting with "I would have thought you were all smart enough to have quit by now," and moving up to "A filthy habit for filthy people." We knew it was mostly in good fun. Just like the old days.

It was nearly midnight when we finally arrived in Tangiers. A bad old town. Once upon a time it had been an International Zone with no real laws to enforce, and it still maintained a lot of that anything-goes, watch-your-back atmosphere. The moment the gangplank dropped, a huge shoving contest began, and continued all the way through customs, where an officer plucked the five of us from a scrum of grimly determined Moroccans and opened a desk just for us. I felt bad about the reverse racism, but not bad enough to turn down the special treatment. Which probably went for all of us.

Once outside, a sea of violently aggressive taxi drivers accosted us and demanded our business. We picked the first one who said "please." It's an arbitrary rule, but it beats no rule at all. He took us into the winding streets of the medina and to the Pension Palace, a crumbling but ornately majestic hostel near the Petit Socco crossroads. Naturally he initially told us it was closed and he knew another place at a very special price, but I think when we all broke out laughing he realized that that particular dog was not going to hunt.

We took four rooms, locked our bags inside, and went to the cafes of the Petit Socco.

"God, I forgot that about this place," Lawrence said sorrowfully as we sat down. "They're not going to have any beer, are they?"

"I'm sure if you ask nicely and wave a couple of hundred-dirham notes around they'll be more than happy to bring you a cold six-pack of San Miguel from somewhere . . ." I said.

"That's all right. I seem to remember they'll serve you in Marrakesh. One dry night shouldn't kill me," he said, as if trying hard to convince himself of that.

We shooed off all the would-be guides and ordered mint tea, in French. We could have used Spanish, and probably English if we had to, all three were tourist languages here. It tasted nothing like the mint tea in Nepal; the mint was the same, but here in Morocco the tea was so supersaturated with sugar that it is opaque even before they add the mint. It is no mystery why most Moroccan men of a certain age have rotting teeth.

"It feels so odd to be here," Nicole said.

"Always a bit odd to go back somewhere," Steve agreed.

"That's not really what I mean," Nicole said. "I mean it's odd to be here for . . . ah, hell. It's really *fucking* upsetting to be here to kill a man, even if he does deserve it. And Lawrence, don't you dare call me a weak sister," as he opened his mouth.

"No," he said. "I was going to agree."

"Cold feet?" Hallam asked.

Lawrence shook his head. "Not that. It's just, it's a serious thing, you know? I think our decision is well-taken, but it's a serious decision, and let's not pretend that it's not. It is upsetting."

"I've never done it before," Steve said. "I don't mind saying I'm not bloody looking forward to it either. I'm thinking of it as like pulling a bloody tooth."

"You won't need to." I hesitated, searching for the right words. "I brought you here. I'm the one he came after. I'm the one who should finish it."

"You didn't drag us off at gunpoint," Nicole said. "We're all in this together now."

"Right to the end," Lawrence agreed.

"It's . . ." Hallam began. We all fell silent as he found the right words. "It's not the end of the world. I reckon I'm the voice of experience here for . . . the deed in question . . . and the sad truth is it's not that difficult a thing. Either to do or to live with. Not saying that it's easy, or that it should be taken lightly, but . . . it's a lot easier than walking straight after a Dixcove spacecake."

We all laughed at that.

"A lot easier than finding a beer in Mauritania," Lawrence added.

"A lot easier than rescuing an abandoned cookpot full of lentils," from Nicole.

"A lot easier than crossing the border into bloody Nigeria," Steve said.

"A lot easier than the Ekok-Mamfe road," I threw in.

"A lot easier than climbing Mount Cameroon."

"A lot easier than shopping in Bamako."

"A lot easier than surviving food poisoning in Djenne."

"A lot easier than me trying to squeeze into a bloody trotro."

"A lot easier than spin bowling in coconut cricket."

"A lot easier than getting a new passport in Burkina Faso."

We raised our glasses and clinked our mint teas together, laughing. But when the laughter ended there were no smiles left on our faces.

The next morning we bought train tickets for Rabat. With a few hours yet to kill we went for a wander around Tangiers, to see what we could see. We saw sheep grazing peacefully on a hillside in the middle of the city; shoe shiners by the dozen; stairways and streets and tunnels and alleys branching at every angle and incline; the uttermost edge of Europe, seen through a salt-laden wind from the ramparts of the Casbah. We saw decay everywhere, crumbling walls and pitted roads, as if the city had been crumbling for a good fifty years. It probably had.

The train left only twenty minutes late. It was only three-quarters full, but there was little room, because most of the women carried enough goods to choke an army beneath their voluminous robes, doubling their width and making them waddle like overstuffed ducks. We rattled past rolling green countryside, farms fenced by walls of cacti, black bulls grazing so slowly they seemed like statues as we passed. We were paced by a flock of doves for a good half hour.

We changed at a station called Sidi-Kacem, where we had to wait for an hour because the connecting train was light. The station was in view of an oil rig, its highest spire topped by an eternal flame that burned away the runoff gas. There were orange trees all around, and Lawrence climbed up into one and picked enough for us all. The smell reminded me of Florida.

We nearly missed Rabat station, where we were told we had almost missed our connecting train to Marrakesh, and we ran to the wrong platform and then the right platform and frantically pulled ourselves into the train. "It's just so wrong to be in a hurry in Africa," Nicole panted. And indeed another fifteen minutes elapsed before the train finally shook off its slumber and began to trudge along its iron tracks. By the time we finally got to Marrakesh it was nearly ten o'clock, and we were all exhausted even though we'd spent most of the day sitting around waiting for something to happen.

We weren't up for wandering about the medina looking for a lodge so we took rooms on Boulevard Mohammed V, which was the main drag, just as it was in all the other towns in Morocco. It's always good civic policy to name the most significant street after your eternally beloved king. It was a very Westernized lodge, with clean sheets and wallpaper, very boring after the crumbling courtyard and ornate filigree of the Pension Palace the previous night. We had a beer apiece in the common room, more out of habit than need, and crashed.

I was woken by a loud banging on my door and I started out of bed, alarmed, and was frantically looking around for a weapon when Nicole called out from the other side of the door: "Time for your OJ, Mr. Wood! Stall Number Nine awaits!"

I groggily pulled some clothes on and joined the others in the hall. We crossed the street and headed straight for the heart of Marrakesh, the Djamme el-Fnaa, the great central square between the medina and the modern city. I was amazed by how well we all remembered the geography. None of us had been to the city since our visit two years before, which had only lasted ninety-six hours, most of which had been spent very drunk.

By night the Djamme was an intoxicating mélange of food stalls, sword swallowers, henna tattooists, snake charmers, dancers, gamblers, hashish salesmen, and buskers who were odd even by Moroccan standards—I wondered if Cigarette

Eating Man was still performing. But in the morning it was crowded by some thirty stalls selling fresh orange juice for about a quarter per glass. Stall Number Nine, we all remembered well, gave you an extra half glass for your ten dirhams. Unspeakable luxury. We added some fresh-baked baguettes and *pain au chocolat*, and breakfasted like emperors.

This was the day that Morgan was due to fly into Casablanca. Nicole's mate was supposed to watch for him at Stansted to see whether or not he was on the plane.

We went to the bus station and bought overnight bus tickets to Todra Gorge, which would give us a full day to prepare for him there. We spent the intervening time wandering around the medina, which as always reminded me of a line from that old video game Zork: "You are in a maze of narrow, twisting passages, all alike." Narrow, high-walled, cobblestoned streets, lined by countless alcove-sized shops selling leather, ornaments, carpets, spices, textiles, hats, daggers, food, medicine, musical instruments, live animals, every article imaginable. Kids played soccer, shopkeepers hawked their wares, hustlers attached themselves to us like leeches. It was dizzying and fascinating and a little bit frightening in its teeming, noisy, unmappable confusion.

We didn't talk much. I think we were all thinking mostly about what it was we had come here to do. We didn't want to talk about it directly, and it didn't leave room for much levity. Nobody bought anything or even tried to have some fun haggling with a shopkeeper. Mostly we just talked about things that we observed or nostalgically called each other's attention to some reminder from two years before. I felt impatient. I wanted it all to be over with. I think the others felt the same. I smoked more cigarettes than I ever had in a single day, and Steve and Hallam and Nicole were puffing away at a record pace too. *At this rate we'll all die of lung cancer before he even shows up*, I thought.

At one point we passed a tall pretty dark-haired European

girl in the medina, and for one crazy moment I thought it was
Talena come to join us. I couldn't help thinking that she
might come to find me the same way she had in Indonesia. I
imagined her sneaking up on me from behind as I walked
through the medina, tapping me on the shoulder, me turning
around to see her there with a fondly amused smile beneath
those mesmerizing blue eyes. A nice fantasy. But I knew it
would never happen. She had made it very clear that she
wanted no part of this. I wished I had some excuse to call her.
But I didn't really have anything to say, and I was far from
certain that she wanted to hear from me. *Later,* I told myself.
When it's all over. When I get home.

Laura and I had our first actual one-on-one conversation
on a rooftop cafe overlooking the Djamme el-Fnaa. I was sip-
ping a Coke and writing postcards, after which I planned to
go meet a gang of the others in the nearest hotel that served
beer. My subconscious must have recognized her when she
walked in, because I looked up for no reason and saw her
enter the cafe. She saw me, smiled, and sat down at my table.

"Hi," she said. "What are you writing?"

I looked down at the postcard and pretended to read.
"Dear Mom. I have been kidnapped by a strange cult of
African nomads who are starving me of meat and forcing me
to wash dishes and dig toilets. Please send military assistance.
P.S., I need more money."

She laughed. "Is that a dig at my strictly vegetarian cook
group?"

"It might be."

"I didn't notice any steaks the last time your group
cooked."

"That's different. We're vegetarian out of sheer laziness.
You guys do it out of principle. That's just wrong."

"It's not my fault," she protested. "Melanie's the only real veggie in our group. The problem is she's also the only one who knows how to cook."

"And whose fault is that?"

"My lazy parents'."

"Well, as long as laziness is involved in some way, all is forgiven," I said. "Where's Lawrence?"

She grimaced and waved her hands in a curt who-knows-who-cares-I-wash-my-hands manner.

"Uh-oh. Trouble in paradise?"

She sighed. "It's not . . . well. He's a good man. And, it seemed like a good idea at the time . . . and . . . and I vote we change the subject."

"Sure thing," I said, though I was very interested in the subject. I looked out at the Djamme for inspiration and saw one of the snake charmers. "You know what I think?" I asked. "I think the truck needs a pet. You know, a truck mascot. One of those big snakes ought to do nicely."

"That's a really good idea," she said seriously. "It can ride under the floorboards. Or in the locker space. We can feed it rats. I don't know if we have any rats yet, but we could start a rat farm too, where they keep the spare engine parts."

"Also we could feed it Michelle if she starts giving us any trouble."

"Good point. And I bet she will. That girl has trouble written all over her. Or at least she will when the henna-tattoo salesmen are finished with her."

"Let's do it," I said. "Sure, we could talk to everyone about it and have a vote, but like they say, easier to ask forgiveness than permission. We can go buy the snake right now and bring it back to the truck. I think Steve's on guard tonight. He'll never notice."

"Even if he does, he'll probably just think it's Michael," Laura said, and I barely managed to keep my expression rigid. "But what if it's shy? Then it will have to meet all these other people tomorrow. Poor thing will be psychologically scarred for life. I bet it's better off with small groups, so we should probably just go around tonight introducing it to people in ones and twos. You know, set it loose inside people's tents and hotel rooms."

"That's an even better idea," I agreed.

We nodded at each other in a serious, self-satisfied way before allowing two wide grins to creep onto our faces.

"Thanks," she said. "I needed that."

"No, no," I said, "thank *you*."

She stood up. "I guess I've wasted enough time. Not that this was a waste of time. But . . . I need to go find Lawrence and have The Talk." The capitals were clearly audible.

"Good luck with that."

"Thanks," she said. "And if I find a snake in my room tonight? You're a dead man."

At eight o'clock Nicole called London from a pay phone. She talked to Rebecca briefly, nodded, hung up, and emerged to give us the news that was supposed to be what we wanted. "Morgan was on the plane," she reported.

Nobody said a word.

The two buses to Todra Gorge were big and air-conditioned and populated almost entirely by backpackers saving a buck by spending their night on a bus instead of in a hotel. I felt ill from all the cigarettes. The seats were faded and torn and only reclined about ten degrees. I didn't feel as if I slept, but I must have, because once I thought I saw a big bald man at the front of our bus turn his head to stare at me, and it was Morgan. I shook myself and when I looked again there was no bald man there, just a Japanese couple.

We had a cigarette break by a gas station that was surrounded by a cedar forest. My watch told me it was two in the morning. The forest looked beautiful; no bushes or weeds, just a smooth carpet of grass beneath hundred-foot cedar trees, painted white and black by the bright moonlight, extending as far as the eye could see.

As we puffed away in front of our bus, Lawrence climbed down and walked over to join us. We waited for him to make the inevitable comment about filthy disgusting habits.

Instead, he said, "Give me one of those bloody things."

We stared at each other in shock.

"Lawrence," Nicole said, "have you ever smoked before?"

"Once," he said, taking a cigarette and a lighter from Steve. "I was eleven years old. I chundered"—Anzac for "threw up"—"like a champion." He gagged on the first puff. "Fucking things haven't gotten any better since," he coughed, but he kept at it. When he was three-quarters finished he stubbed it out and climbed back on the bus.

The four of us gaped at each other, speechless, before following him.

I must have slept again after that, because the next thing I remembered was looking out the window and wondering where the stars were. *Must be cloudy out there*, I thought. Then I realized, probably not. We had left the green, fertile, Mediterranean climate of northwestern Morocco behind and now we were on the very edge of the Sahara Desert, a land of camels and scorpions, raw jagged desert scrubland where only the hardiest and thorniest bushes and weeds survived the baking sun and flash floods, where entire mountains were a smooth uniform color unpunctuated by a single tree. Heavy cloud cover seemed unlikely.

I looked up farther and saw a crescent moon hanging off the shoulder of a colossal mass of rock that swallowed up most of the sky. The cliff edge gleamed pale as death in the moonlight. We were there. Todra Gorge, a narrow crevice perhaps a hundred feet across at this point and a good five hundred feet high. I nudged Lawrence beside me and his eyes opened as if he really had been only resting his eyelids.

"We're there," I said.

"Oh happy day," he said, and closed his eyes again.

A few minutes later the bus rumbled and wheezed to a stop, and after long minutes of confused disembarkation in the dark, we pulled ourselves and our things together and signed into the Hotel des Roches, a grand old dilapidated place, all faded tile and crumbling paint. We signed in under false names, which was easy enough. The hotel staff dealt with us and the three others staying here as if we were the first group of travelers they had ever seen, even though they must have been accustomed to receiving a new crowd every morning.

We napped in our rooms until dawn, then met in the common room for a quick breakfast of bread, omelettes, and mint tea. Lawrence turned down an offer of a cigarette. There were no jokes exchanged today. Morgan was due to arrive in Todra Gorge in twenty-four hours, on the same bus that had just brought us. It was time we started talking about the gory details of the ugly mission that had brought us here. It was time for a council of war.

25

CONAISSANCE

Todra Gorge runs for a good twenty miles, roughly east to west, a scar five hundred feet deep carved by the thin river that trickles down to the east. We were at the east and narrowest end, where a half-dozen hotels huddle in the shadow of a group of overhanging crags very popular with rock climbers. About a half mile beyond the hotels the river collects into a pond, and a shockingly green wedge of trees and farmland, home to maybe five hundred poor village farmers, sits amid a sea of red rock and blistering heat like a piece of Indonesia dropped into the desert. Between the hotels and the village a road switchbacks up a landslide scar to the top of the gorge, big enough for buses. When we had been here before, the river was a good two feet deep where the hotels were, and the buses had to get up a head of steam before splashing through it. But that had been spring. Now that it was autumn the river was only six inches at its deepest.

The gorge widened slightly and grew less precipitous as it climbed to the west. At the other end of the gorge was a youth hostel, and the adventure-traveler thing to do was to spend one day trekking up to the youth hostel, and the next trekking back, in the blistering heat of the desert sun. If you

have to ask why, then you will never understand. The trail
followed the riverbed for some time, but then climbed up into
the walls of the gorge. Sometimes the gorge widened, and
you could climb from top to bottom without using your
hands; but inevitably it narrowed again, sometimes for long
stretches, where the rocky trail was littered with boulders,
with a two-hundred-foot cliff to your right and a sheer two-
hundred-foot drop to your left.

That was why I had selected it. In the back of my mind I
had pictured it like this: We wait for Morgan behind a boulder, keeping an eye out with the binoculars; he arrives; we
waylay him and throw him over the edge; and by the time the
Moroccan police get around to investigating the death of
another clumsy traveler, we are back in Gibraltar. I guess
we'd all had it in the back of our minds. When I explained
this to them, they nodded as if I was stating the obvious.

"Sounds simple," Lawrence said. "Lot of things that could
go wrong though."

"Right. What if he's made friends on the bus, like he did in
Indonesia, and he comes up with a crowd?" Nicole asks.

"Or what if he decides it's too crowded and decides to
explore the other way?" Lawrence suggested. "Or what if
he's sick and doesn't even come here?"

"No battle plan ever survives contact with the enemy,"
Hallam quoted. "I think the real difficulty here is that we
have to keep ourselves hidden. If he sees any of us, the gig is
up. That will make it more difficult than I'd like to stay aware
of where he is."

"He might decide to take one of those extended camel treks
into the desert instead of hiking up here," Lawrence said.

"Or what if he's taken up rock climbing and he spends the
whole day going up those overhangs down at this end?" Hallam asked.

"We should have thought about this more," Nicole said,
shaking her head. "It seemed so simple in London, but now, I

mean, no offense, Paul, but this isn't a plan, it's just a hope
that he falls into our lap."

"I know," I said morosely. Hallam and Lawrence nodded.
I didn't know what to do.

Steve cleared his throat noisily and we all turned to him.

"Christ," he said. "A sadder lot of wet blankets I've never
seen. I reckon it's a bloody good plan. I reckon you lot are all
forgetting a couple of points here."

"What's that?" I asked.

"Well" — and here he switched to a Cockney accent —
"*basically* —"

We all chuckled. It was a truck in-joke.

"*Basically*, I reckon you're all forgetting that we're not
dealing with any kind of mysterious unknown stranger here.
It's Morgan. So one, I'm telling you, Morgan's going to come
up that gorge. You think he's going to go exploring and kiss-
ing babies in that village the other way? Not bloody likely, I'll
tell you that. And two, have you all forgotten just how bloody
fast that man moves when he's got a will in him? He's fitter
than I am, I don't mind admitting. He's not going to slow
down for any bloody group of mates he met on the coach last
night. Remember how he hated it when anybody slowed him
down? He might say, 'I'll save you a beer at the top,' but I
reckon that's the only concession there. And I reckon that's
only in the case there's no beer shortage up there."

For Steve it was an extraordinarily long speech. When he
finished the rest of us wore tentative smiles to match Steve's
grin. He was right. Morgan knew us, and that might be a
problem; but we knew Morgan, and that was our secret
weapon.

"I hear the ring of truth there," Hallam said.

"I'm convinced," Nicole agreed.

"Righto," Lawrence said. "Enough of this planning non-
sense. I always hated it anyway. Shall we go do a little recon
then?"

We pulled on our hiking boots, bought some water, donned our hats, slathered on sunscreen, shouldered our day packs, and began to hike up the Todra Gorge. We weren't going to go all the way up. Just high enough to find the perfect spot for an ambush. The perfect place to kill a man.

"Wish I had time to do some climbing," Hallam said wistfully, as we set out, looking up at the line of climbers crawling up the cliff face opposite to the hotels. "Precious little of that in England. Some indoor walls, some bouldering, but it's not the same."

"Maybe you could borrow some gear day after tomorrow when it's all over," I said, but I doubted it. I thought that when it was all over we would all simply want to get the hell out of Dodge and let our memories slowly heal over the mental scars.

We moved up the riverbed, dry gravel occasionally marked by a pool of water. Most of the gorge-trekkers had already left, and we had the trail to ourselves. The intense Sahara sun beat down on us, and we wrapped spare T-shirts around our necks to protect them. An anorexic creek trickled slowly down from the west end of the gorge, and the trail wandered drunkenly from one bank to the other. On either side were five-hundred-foot walls of red rock, scored into layers like rake marks on sand, each layer ten or twenty feet deep, the lines dipping and swaying like waves.

After about an hour the trail selected the north side of the gorge, stuck with it, and began to rise away from the base. The slopes had changed from sheer to steep but navigable. Goatherds who looked as if they had just stepped out of the fourteenth century coaxed their nimble herds down the sides of the gorge to drink at the river. Another half hour later we passed an old man with leather skin and black teeth leading a dozen camels to a pool of water. We gave the vile and violent creatures a wide berth.

A little while after that the edges of the gorge began to
close back in toward one another, as if magnetically attracted.
The trail was still wide, about twenty feet, but the rock face
to the right and plunge to the left gradually became steeper
and steeper, and the trail grew littered with boulders. I wondered how the boulders got here. Did they fall from above?
Or were they deposited by the flash floods that thundered
down the gorge once or twice each year?

We moved more slowly now. Steve detached his Walkman. This was it; this was the kill zone. We examined the
boulders we passed, the views up and down the trail, the cliff
face beneath us. Looking for the perfect spot to take a man
by surprise and throw him over the edge.

We found it about twenty minutes' walk from where the
walls grew sheer. About a two-hour walk from the hotel. The
trail bent to the left, on a crag that overhung the gorge floor
far below, went straight for about fifty feet, then bent back to
the right. The middle of this boomerang-shaped section of
trail was decorated by a few enormous boulders. It was ideal.
From the ends of that fifty-foot stretch we could see for a
long way up and down the trail, but what went on in the middle would be invisible to other trekkers. And it was a hundred sheer feet down to the canyon floor.

We would keep an eye for Morgan from there and wait
for him to arrive. Two or three of us would hide behind one of
the boulders as he walked past, and as he reached the middle
of that projecting stretch, the others would step out at the
other end, and his path would be blocked on both sides. It
would all be over with in a hurry.

That was the plan.

We returned to the Hotel des Roches for dinner.

"They need an extra letter in their name," Lawrence said
as he joined Steve and me at our table, in a corner distant

from the other diners. "Hotel des Roaches. They seem to expect me to support a tribe of thousands while I'm here. I'm not ready for that kind of responsibility. I'm not a family man."

"Maybe we could set up a Roach Refugee Camp," I suggested. "Rwanda-style. Roaches immigrate — but they don't emigrate!"

"That's a sick joke," Steve said seriously, and for a moment he had me, but then his smile returned, and he said, "Don't make me approach the bloody UN High Commission on Roach Refugees. They'll up and form a bloody working subcommittee, see if they don't."

"They might even issue a strongly worded press release," Hallam added, joining us. "A fact-finding tour sponsored by celebrity American roaches will be announced."

"Richard Gere will appear on the Oscars asking us all for a moment of silence for the roaches all over the world . . ." I said. "Where's Nicole?"

"Taking another shower." He shrugged. "What's for dinner?"

"Depends on how many of the menu items are actually available," Lawrence said.

"Cor, we're not in bloody Togo here," Steve said. "Morocco's nearly halfway civilized. I reckon the goods are pretty much as advertised."

"Your optimism does you credit," Lawrence said. "Unfortunately your judgment does the reverse. Hey, that's not just you, that's Australia as a whole. I've got myself a defining proverb there."

"Looks like eight different varieties of couscous," Hallam said, putting down the menu. "No camel though. Had rather a hankering for it."

"We don't eat camels," I said. "Camels eat us. I think they're the dominant species."

The waiter came by, and we all ordered vegetable stew on couscous with bread and Cokes. Hallam ordered one for

Nicole as well. None of us was vegetarian, but we all shied away from meat when traveling in the Third World. Across the room a small group of fresh-faced young backpackers dined on lamb and goat, risking a tomorrow spent sweating and huddling within thirty feet of a toilet instead of trekking up the gorge. Ironically, the five of us were probably more impervious to salmonella or whatever the meat might carry, as we were all heavily traveled, armed with cast-iron stomachs full of veteran kill-all-intruders bacteria recruited from at least five continents. But along with resistance to sickness came an increased reluctance to risk suffering it again.

We chatted and smoked for maybe twenty minutes. Nicole didn't arrive. She was still absent when the food came. "I'll go get her," Hallam said. "Probably fell asleep in the tub or something." But he didn't sound entirely convinced—that wasn't like her—and he left the room more quickly than was absolutely necessary. We began to eat.

Hallam came back about a minute later and after one look at his distraught face I forgot all about eating. He rushed up to us and dropped the scrap of paper held in his hand onto the table. He tried to say something, but no words came out, just a yelp, like a dog that has been stepped on. I'd never seen him like this. Cool, competent, calm Hallam had been replaced by a panicked animal.

I looked at the paper even though I already knew in my gut what had happened. A familiar scrawl.

HALLAM OLD BOY
YOUR WIFE LOOKS VERY PRETTY NAKED
WANT TO SEE HER AGAIN?
COME TO THAT PLACE IN THE GORGE
YOU KNOW
THE ONE YOU PICKED OUT FOR ME TODAY
RIGHT NOW, NO WAITING

BRING YOUR FRIENDS
TA

"He's here," Hallam managed at last. "He's got her. We have to go."

"Oh, no," Lawrence breathed, reading the note, and he stood up. As did Steve.

I remained in my chair. I needed to think. There was no time to think, but I needed to. Sometimes *don't think, do* is exactly what the situation calls for. But this time, I could tell, it called for *don't do, think*.

"Paul, *get up*, he's only fifteen minutes ahead of us, we can catch him," Steve urged.

"Not so fast," I said, forcing my voice to remain calm, dispassionate.

"What the *fuck*?" There was a dangerous note of hysteria in Hallam's voice.

"It's a trap," I said, thinking as I spoke. "Or a trick. One of the two."

"Paul, he *has Nicole*," Hallam said desperately, as if that justified walking into certain death. Of course for him it did. By taking Nicole, Morgan had effectively neutralized Hallam. Smart. Demonically smart.

"He's right," Lawrence said. "We have to think this through."

"We haven't got time," Steve said.

"It's a two-hour walk up the gorge," I said sharply. "Do you want to get there in two hours and be dead five minutes later, or do you want to get there in two hours five minutes, ready for what's going to happen?"

"We can talk on the way," Hallam urged.

"If we go there," I said.

"*If*?"

"How do we know he's taken her there?"

"It's in the note!" Steve exclaimed, as if it were the Ten Commandments.

"Exactly," I said. "So all we know is that that's exactly what Morgan wants us to believe. Which is a long fucking way from making it the truth."

There was a pause as Steve and Hallam absorbed this.

"So where do you think she is?" Steve asked.

"I think there're three possibilities," I said. I'd thought this through now, to something that made a kind of sense. "One. He told the total truth and he's taking her there right now because he's setting some kind of trap there and he's sure he'll be able to deal with us all. Two. It's a total lie, and he's taking her the other way, toward the village, and trying to send us on a wild-goose chase." I nearly continued *so he has time to finish her off*, but feared it might send Hallam over the edge of sanity. The thought shook me to the core—not Nicole, please, not her. "Three. He's being really fucking fancy and he hasn't taken her anywhere. She's right here in his room in one of the hotels and he's counting on us running around like headless chickens and going everywhere else."

"So *which one*?" Hallam asked.

That was the proverbial sixty-four-megabyte question, wasn't it? What would Morgan do? What was he after? We didn't know anything.

No; scratch that. We knew he was here, and that he'd followed us up the gorge today. (Unless one of us was in cahoots with him and had told him everything? . . . no.) We knew he had taken Nicole not more than half an hour ago, when she had gone to take a shower. Not an easy thing to do, even if he was twice her size; Nicole was stubborn as hell and wouldn't stop fighting unless there was no alternative.

And we knew who he was. Morgan Jackson. We knew him well.

"I think he told us the truth," I said. "I'm pretty sure. But I can't be totally sure. I think we should split up. One group goes down the trail. The other group stays here, checks the hotels and checks the road toward the village. But I don't think they'll find anything. I think I've got a pretty good idea what he's up to."

"What's that?" Lawrence asked.

"I think he's got a gun," I said. That explained a lot. It explained how he had spirited Nicole away without a scream or a loud battle. I couldn't see him ambushing her, clubbing her over the head, and carrying her away from the hotel — then he would have a hundred pounds of deadweight to carry, and if he doesn't judge the blow just right, he only stuns her or he hits her too hard and she's got blood streaming from her head, and we *are* in a fairly populated tourist zone, it's just too risky for him. And I couldn't see Nicole meekly giving in to him if he only had a knife, she would have screamed or kneed him in the balls or run for it or something, she knew we were only steps away. But a gun, that was different, that was a trump card. No sense screaming and getting us all killed right then and there.

"And he's just planning to lure us up there and shoot us all," Lawrence said.

"The simplest plan is most likely to be correct," I said. "And it doesn't get any simpler than that. Which is another good reason to split up, so that he doesn't just off us all."

"So he has a gun," Steve said. He sat down. So did Lawrence, and then Hallam. Hallam looked a little better. I think now that we had defined the terms of the engagement, had reduced some of the uncertainty, it was easier for him. And if I was right, Morgan still needed Nicole alive as bait, alive and ambulatory, and wouldn't have time to do anything awful to her. All good things.

"I think so," I said.

"And Nicole," Steve continued.

I nodded.

"And we don't."

I nodded again.

"Bit of a bloody problem, isn't it?" Steve said, and scratched his head.

"I don't think there was any struggle," Hallam said all of a sudden. "The note was in our room. I expect he got her coming in or out of the shower and took her back to our room to get dressed."

"So what do we do?" Lawrence asked me.

What am I, the Answer Man? I wanted to shoot back. I wanted to defer to Hallam. But he was too rattled to think clearly. And maybe I was the right man to ask. I felt that fury rising inside me again. Since we'd entered Morocco, I'd thought of facing Morgan with trepidation, thought of it as some kind of unspeakably awful chore that had to be performed, best done and finished and never thought of again. But now that it was at hand I felt very differently. Now I welcomed it. Now I relished the chance.

"We have to decide who stays back here," I said. "And then, then I have got a plan. It's not a very good plan, but it's all I've got. If anyone has a better idea, believe me, I would so much love to hear it right now."

"What's your plan?" Hallam asked.

I told them.

Everybody agreed it wasn't a good plan. But nobody had a better one.

26

SHOWDOWN AT BIG SKY

Lawrence and I left the hotel and began the long walk up Todra Gorge. To that boomerang-shaped bend in the trail between two sheer cliffs. To the kill site. That was what I had mentally christened it. Somebody was going to die there tonight. I could very easily become one of the night's victims, but that thought didn't trouble me unduly. It was the thought of Nicole and my friends being killed that frightened me. Killed because of me, because of what I had told them and where I had brought them.

We walked as fast as we dared. The moon was still hidden behind the towering walls of rock, and I illuminated our path with my Maglite flashlight. The same Maglite I had used to follow Morgan in Tetebatu, only two weeks before in Indonesia. I was glad I had bought new batteries in London. They would last all the way to the kill site. Not all the way back, I didn't think, but if dead flashlights were our major problem at that stage, I would be a happy man.

We had already done a good deal of hiking earlier that day, and adrenaline rushes don't last for two hours, but I didn't get tired. I could probably have trekked all the way to the youth hostel and back. The Annapurna Circuit had been

ideal training; my feet were hard as stone, blisters long since
replaced by calluses, and my legs were machines made of
iron. Lawrence didn't seem weary either. He was one of those
thin, wiry, indestructible types who never slow down.

I entertained vague hopes of catching up with Morgan
and Nicole before we got to the kill site. They probably only
had a twenty-minute head start on us, but I didn't think it
would really happen. He wasn't going to let her slow him
down. Nicole was tough, and capable, and maybe she could
get away from him in the dark. But I had my doubts. Morgan
was bigger and stronger and faster, and if I was right, he had
a gun. If it looked like she was going to get away, he would
shoot her without hesitation. And she knew that.

It was quiet, incredibly quiet, and incredibly dark. It's
easy to forget, living in a First World city where there is a
constant background glow of streetlights and office towers
even at midnight, just how dark the night can be. A thin ribbon of stars was visible high above, between the walls of the
gorge, but otherwise we might as well have been a mile deep
in a coal mine. There were no sounds save for the ones we
made; no wind, no animals, no trickle of water, nothing but
the noise of our rustling clothes and our boots scraping on
rock. It was cold, amazingly cold so soon after the egg-frying
heat of the day. The desert was blistering by day but bitter at
night.

We walked, fast and quiet. At first there was nothing to
talk about. But it was a long walk, I figured ninety minutes at
our quick-march pace, and there was plenty of time to think.
And the more I thought, the more a terrible suspicion began
to creep into my mind.

For a moment, back at the hotel, only a moment, I had
wondered if one of us might be helping Morgan. I had immediately dismissed the idea. The notion of Hallam or Nicole aid-
ing Morgan was simply insane. I was absolutely certain that
Steve, for all of his ex-con past, was more likely to French-kiss

a crocodile than do anything to unnecessarily harm anyone
else, especially Nicole. And I had figured that surely Lawrence
too was beyond suspicion. But now, as I walked and thought,
dangerous facts began to array themselves in my mind, and I
began to question that last conclusion.

There was a reason Lawrence had been one of my original
suspects. Not just because of his fling with Laura and his
almost-overwrought grief after she died. He was a quiet man,
closed off to the world. Funny and friendly, sure, but he had
never shown much of what lay hidden beneath that layer of
personality. I couldn't say that I knew what Lawrence was
like, what made him tick, the way I knew the other three.

Morgan could have sniffed out the threat to him here,
ambushed, and captured Nicole all by himself. He was quite
capable of it. But it would have been easier, much easier, if
one of us had fed him information, had been on his side.

In Indonesia, when Morgan and I found each other, when
he was briefly rattled by my presence, the only other trucker
he had mentioned by name was Lawrence.

The night Laura had died, Lawrence had gone off with
Morgan to the nearby town of Limbe. They had left together.
And Lawrence hadn't been seen until the next morning.

Nothing conclusive. Far from it. Suspicious. That was all.
Surely there was no reason, no conceivable reason, for
Lawrence to aid Morgan.

Unless Lawrence too was a member of The Bull.

For a moment I felt like my legs were marching along by
themselves, as if the connection between my muscles and my
mind had been severed. A cold trickle of sweat began to seep
down my back. It added up. I wanted to pretend it did not,
but it all added up. Nothing conclusive. But try as I might, I
couldn't think of any way to disprove my terrible new theory.
It was entirely consistent with the facts. And if it was true,
then we were walking straight into an inescapable trap.

I wanted to stop, think, change the plan. But it was too

late. We had to keep going despite my newfound doubts. There was no time to come up with some excuse to change things so that Lawrence stayed behind at the hotel. Not if we were going to save Nicole. The only thing I could do, the thing I had to do, was somehow try to work out whether Lawrence was trustworthy before we made it to the kill site.

I was tempted to just stop and ask him straight out. The surprise might force a revelation from him. But if it didn't, and if he was guilty, then he would be wise to my suspicion. Maybe it would be better to leave him guessing.

"Lawrence," I said.

"Yeah."

"How do you think he figured it out?"

A pause. "No idea, mate. No fucking idea."

"He must have been suspicious. Maybe he traced our company and found out it didn't exist. He must have been following us right from the start. It's like he was watching everything we did."

"Nothing we can do about it now. Hope and pray, mate, that's all."

"What about Steve?" I asked.

Lawrence's pace faltered. "What about him?"

"What if he gave us up?"

"*Steve?* What in Christ's name are you talking about?"

"He's an ex-con. I don't know half of what he's been involved in. Neither do you. He keeps it all pretty shady. What if he's working with Morgan? What if he's part of The Bull?" If Lawrence was guilty, he would be eager to deflect suspicion elsewhere.

"Your nerves are getting to you, mate," Lawrence warned. "Try and stay cool. For Nic's sake. There's no fucking way. You know that. Steve part of The Bull? That's as likely as—" He stopped abruptly.

I waited a moment, then said, "What?"

"You're a subtle motherfucker, aren't you?"

I didn't know what to say to that.

"You're not really asking about Steve." It wasn't a question.

I swallowed. "No."

Lawrence came to a full stop. After a moment so did I.

"Look at me," he said, his voice taut and intense. "Shine the light right in my fucking face."

I did so. Every muscle on his face was rigid, etched with tension and emotion.

"*I loved her too,*" he said. "At least as much as you did. At least as much."

We stared at each other for a moment.

"I'm sorry," I said, quietly, inadequately.

"Fuck it." He shook his head. "Let's move."

For the next hour we walked in silence.

"That's far enough, boys," Morgan called out, and we both started with dismay and took a few quick steps back. A bright light winked into existence, a flashlight beam, and I covered my eyes as he shined it at my face. This wasn't supposed to happen, we were supposed to hear them before we reached them and take at least partial cover behind a rock. I waited hopelessly for him to shoot.

He didn't, and I took advantage of the delay to unscrew the head of my Maglite, turning it from a flashlight into a lamp. Even after a ninety-minute trek the light was bright enough to illuminate the scene. We were about ten feet past the turn into the fifty-foot straightaway that we had selected. The trail here was about eight feet wide. About midway down the path there was a big boulder against the cliff face, maybe five feet in diameter, and Morgan leaned on the other side of it, using it for cover. He had his Maglite in one hand and, as expected, a sleek black handgun in the other. An automatic. We could barely see his face, it appeared only in outline, except for the whites of his eyes and his pale toothy grin.

A few feet in front of him, between him and us, Nicole sat

beside the boulder with her back to the cliff face, her arms tied behind her, gagged with some kind of rag. Like Laura had been gagged. Nicole seemed unhurt. She swiveled her head back and forth at us and Morgan, eyes wide.

"Hands up," Morgan said nonchalantly, and we complied. "Now where are the others?"

"They're not here," I said. My mouth was dry, but my voice was steady.

"Don't fuck around, Woodsie. You want to see her get a kneecapping and have this conversation over a nice soothing sound track of screams?" He aimed his gun at Nicole's knee. She froze and closed her eyes.

"They're not fucking here," Lawrence grated. "We thought you were lying, you fucking bastard *cunt*. We thought you'd gone the other way."

Morgan looked at us both, shined his light at our faces again, then nodded regretfully and lowered the gun. "Aye. Was afraid that might happen. The boy who cried wolf, hey? O ye of little faith. 'Tis a pity Hallam didn't join you. I had this delicious notion of making the rape and torture of his wife the last thing he saw in his life. Still, like Meat Loaf didn't say, three out of five ain't bad. Now why don't the two of you get down on your knees like good little boys? Don't like seeing you all ambulatory and all. You might get some crazy ideas in your heads about rushing me or running away and, well, you know, it's like a dinner party. After all this preparation you'd hate for some cunt to get stupid and ruin it all."

We dropped to our knees, encouraged by his gun.

"That's better," he said. "Bit surprised, were you? Bit shocked to get that note from your old mate Morgan? Old Hallam, old king of the heap, he was a bit taken aback, I reckon?" He laughed. "Don't think much of your old mate's mental capacities, do you? Figured I was a bit slow on the uptake, eh, Woodsie? Figured if some random stranger called me up and offered me a practically complimentary trip I'd just sign up and be damned? Didn't think a few alarm bells might start ringing in the old cranium, thinking, crikey, this sure is coming thick and fast after I nearly separated old Woodsie's head from his shoulders, isn't it? I reckon I haven't got your lightning computer mind, Woodsie, but I can put a thought or two together when I need to, aye? I can keep a step ahead of you when needs be."

"Did you bring the gun from England?" I asked.

"From England?" He chuckled. Clearly he was relishing every word of this. "Christ on a pogo stick, they don't have guns in England, Paul. I would have thought you would have known that. Really, if you're going to go shopping for a gun — an illegal gun, mind you — d'you reckon you'd seek one out in London or Tangiers? Pretty simple fucking question if you ask me. You wouldn't believe how easy it is to buy a gun in this country. But the haggling, that you probably would believe. The salesclerks in this country's supermarkets of sinful goods, Christ, what tossers. Almost wasn't worth it. Good quality though. Genuine original Glock manufacture, thirteen bullets in the clip. More than enough to play around with. I reckon you're both desperately praying for a misfire or summat. Well, pray on. Those Czechs make quality killing machines, I can assure you whole-fucking-heartedly."

"You are so fucked in the head," Lawrence muttered. Morgan's face tightened and he swung the gun to bear on Lawrence. I stiffened. Wrong approach.

"You were on the other bus, weren't you?" I asked quickly. "Last night."

Morgan glared at me, then back at Lawrence, then shook his head and lowered the gun again. "A moment, Paul," he said, "I pray your indulgence for a wee moment while I invite our other guest to the party. I have been unforgivably rude." He stepped out from behind the boulder, keeping the gun pointed in our general direction, and untied the gag from Nicole's mouth. His shaved head gleamed in the light, and he seemed absolutely enormous next to Nicole, like a member of a giant alien species. I wondered if even a professional soldier like Hallam could take him in a struggle. He retreated back behind the boulder as Nicole wrinkled her face and spat on the ground.

"I'm sorry," she said to us, dully. "I'm so sorry."

"It's not your fault," Lawrence said urgently. "Nic. It's okay."

"I'm so sorry," she repeated. She knew it was all over, I could tell. She knew that she was going to die in a few minutes. That we would all die in a few minutes, once Morgan was finished crowing and gloating. I thought she might be right.

But we still had a chance. I could see it from where I knelt near the edge of the trail. Twenty feet below me, up close against the sheer cliff face, about midway between me and Morgan, was a tiny spark of light. It moved slowly, in quick bobbing motions punctuated by periods of stillness, toward Morgan. It was Hallam. He had followed just behind Lawrence and me, and now he climbed sideways beneath us, illuminating each new hold with the mini-Maglite he held in his mouth, trying desperately to stay silent and invisible while up above a madman gloated about the upcoming rape and torture and murder of his wife. He was an expert climber but I knew this had to be fantastically difficult, climbing barefoot, without chalk or any gear, through the night. A single mistake, and he would plummet to his death.

"Now then," Morgan said. "Not to interrupt your spectacularly dull conversation, but the question was, my whereabouts last night, and yes indeed I was on the other bus. Actually I thought you might have seen me, Woodsie. Was a little concerned that my master plan had been rumbled. When your bus passed mine I looked out the window and I thought you were looking straight back and I was more than a little concerned. Most relieved that you didn't see me."

"Not consciously," I said, thinking of the dream I had had.

"Any more questions, Woodsie, old boy?" he asked. "Any more facts you desperately need cleared up before I dispatch you to the great hereafter? Time's a-wasting, you know."

"One or two," I said, desperately trying to think of some. We had to keep him talking long enough for Hallam to climb past Morgan and come up behind him. Out of the corner of my eye I saw Lawrence reaching out along the ground, closing his fist around a baseball-sized stone while Morgan's attention was on me. "Those notes you leave, they're not in your writing."

"Oh, please," he said dismissively. "Write them with my left hand. Little detail to keep the authorities off the trail. It's the details that tell in the end. Anything else?"

As he said "end," I saw movement below me, and I looked down, and I saw that little spark of light tumble down into the darkness and disappear. I gasped. Morgan didn't notice, or thought I was just panting with fear, as I had on that Indonesian beach.

"You're going to rot in hell," Lawrence said.

I heard two very faint clinks from below. I put together what had happened. A piece of limestone used as handhold or foothold had suddenly come loose, and Hallam had dropped the flashlight. That explained the two noises. But there had been no thud of anything large hitting ground. Hallam still clung to the sheer cliff beneath us. I wondered if he could make his way up to the trail in the dark. I doubted it. Rock climbing is hard enough when you can see what you're doing. Feeling your way up blind would be nearly impossible, even for Hallam. He would try, but I didn't think he would make it. He would make another mistake and fall to his death. We were on our own.

"Hell?" Morgan laughed again. "Heaven and hell. Really, Lawrence, I thought better of you. Such dreamy juvenile notions. Still, I can understand them at the moment. No atheist in a foxhole, they do say. Best you ready yourself for whichever one you're heading to in the very near future though." He sighed theatrically and came out from behind the boulder, shaking his head. "I do wish that Hallam had come though. Still, best-laid plans go oft astray, hey? Me and Nicole here will have to have some fun without any appreciative audience to watch." He reached down and ruffled her hair fondly, like a child's. "You're a tomcat, aren't you, girl? You're not going to beg for your life and offer to do anything I want if I just stop hurting you. Not like that cunt Mason. You know how I talked her out of that tent of yours, Woodsie, that night in Cameroon? I told her you had a surprise for her. And a surprise she got. She sucked cock like a two-dollar whore, she did—*down*, boy!" as I came to my feet at those last words, snarling. Morgan leveled his gun at me and took two quick steps back from Nicole, who had tensed for action. For a moment I was going to rush him, but I got hold of myself and crouched back down.

"That's better," Morgan said. "See, I just don't think they'd make up the appreciative audience we deserve, hey, Nic, old girl? But don't you worry. Even if you're going to be stubborn and uncooperative there's still a good deal of pleasant shenanigans we can get up to. Makes it even better, I must say, a girl who won't give up the fight. It's a rare treat."

"You *demented motherfucker*," Lawrence said.

Morgan shone a big shit-eating grin in his direction and I knew he was only seconds away from shooting us.

While he looked away Nicole adjusted her position slightly, moving from a sitting position to a crouch.

"It doesn't matter whether you shoot us or not," I said, trying to keep him distracted. "We've told the whole fucking world about you. FBI, Interpol, everyone."

"Oh, come on, Woodsie," Morgan said. "Now you're just being boring. The eighth deadly sin, old boy. I could give them my fucking autobiography and they wouldn't be able to touch me. You know that. And I'm sad to say, but you won't be much more than a footnote, mate." He raised the gun. "Now it's time to write your final—"

Nicole launched herself into the air and drop-kicked him like she was a professional wrestling star. It very nearly worked. A shot exploded from his gun but went miles over our heads. The flashlight flew from his hands, and he staggered almost to the edge of the trail before recovering his balance. He tried to stop the rolling flashlight with an outstretched foot, but he was a fraction of a second too late.

Lawrence grunted as he flung the stone he held at Morgan's head. He just barely missed.

For an instant, as Morgan's flashlight fell, it illuminated Hallam against the cliff face. He reached for it, but it was just too far away.

Morgan started to raise his gun toward me.

Three thoughts flashed through my head. I now held the only light; Lawrence and I, facing Morgan with a gun, would be far better off in complete darkness; and Hallam needed a light desperately. The solution was simple and obvious.

I lobbed the flashlight underhanded and dived forward onto my belly, scraping my hands hard enough to draw blood. As the light fell past the level of the trail there was another shot. I was sure that one had been meant for me.

Then the darkness was absolute.

I tried to figure out what to do next. My indecision was interrupted by a thump and a muffled grunt from ahead of us. He was struggling with Nicole. I was about to rush him when another shot rang out. For a moment I was terrified he had killed her. Then there was a light shining straight in my eyes, from above the boulder, and when I covered my eyes against the glare I saw Nicole lying doubled over in front of the boulder. She was gasping for breath, but there didn't seem to be any blood. I glanced over my shoulder.

"Now you two just remain exactly where you are for the

moment," Morgan said, his voice amused and casual. "Down on your bellies where you're good and harmless."

Nicole finally sucked in a long, loud breath and started to breathe normally again. She'd had the wind knocked out of her, nothing more. The third shot had been fired only to keep Lawrence and me away. I glanced at Lawrence. He was crouched, ready to spring, but it was too late. We exchanged a look and slowly followed Morgan's orders.

"Nice one, Nic," Morgan said. "Well done, fair play, all of you. Throwing that torch away, a stroke of genius, Woodsie, truly it was. It's a pity for you I was a Boy Scout. I reckon it's that fine organization's training that led me to bring another torch. Be prepared, they did tell me, time and time again. Speaking of which, sad as I am to say, it's time for you three to be prepared for one of the two great inevitables. And I reckon you all know I'm not talking about taxes."

"Fuck you," Nicole said. "Talk all you want, torture us all you want, do what you like, Morgan, it doesn't change a thing. You are fucked in the head. And you're a dead man. Hallam is going to find you and kill you."

Morgan yawned ostentatiously.

"Who do you think you are, Morgan?" I asked abruptly. We had to play for time, and I had a new game in mind. "You crazy motherfucker. You think you're the Great White Hunter, don't you? Tracking the most dangerous game? You're a sick deranged asshole, that's all you are."

"Boys," Morgan said, aiming the gun as Nicole closed her eyes, "I fear the time of your useful existence has come to its—"

"You're no better than NumberFive," I said.

There was a long pause. Then Morgan said incredulously, "*What* did you say?"

"NumberFive," I said. "The one who does the hookers in Bangkok."

There was silence for a little while and then he began to

laugh. "Woodsie, Woodsie, Woodsie. For a man so stupid you can be so smart. How the fuck did you find out about that?"

"I know all about The Bull," I said. "Tracked it down from that computer you used in Tetebatu." I wished I could see him, judge from his expression whether my ploy might be working, but all I could see was the blinding orb of his flashlight, bright as the sun, and the gleam of the gun barrel.

"I cleaned that up," he said.

"Not clean enough. The Bull isn't near as secure as NumberOne thinks. Holes the size of Mack trucks in your security."

"Is that so? You're a marvel, Woodsie. Almost a shame to kill you. Ought to leave you alive to plug those holes. Pity it isn't practical now."

"How'd it start?" I asked. "That's what I really want to know. I know Laura was your first, but how'd it start? How did they get in touch with you? And why?"

"What do you want, Woodsie, my life story?"

"If you'd be so kind as to oblige," I said.

He laughed. "You're a good sport, Woodsie. I always did like you. Playing for time, hey? Trying to extend your existence by a couple of minutes by any means possible? Well, can't say as I blame you . . . In a nutshell then. I mean, you understand my position. I still have to kill the two of you, deal with Nicole—and these things always take longer than you expect, time flies hey?—dress the bodies with the knives, snap a few photos, then get back to town and see what I can do about Hallam and Steve before I leave on the morning bus . . . what I'm trying to convey is that it's a busy night ahead and I haven't much time to spend dictating my autobiography. So. In a nutshell."

He cleared his throat and began. "Laura wasn't actually my first. Year before the truck, I was in Vietnam and I did two girls there. In Saigon. A couple of whores is all. I'd brought them back to my hotel for every man's fantasy, you know, and, Christ, what happened was almost an accident, truth be spoken. If they hadn't tried to relieve me of my money belt it would never have happened. But it did happen, and you know, I felt I had a knack for it. Felt I'd found my calling, see? Various, you know, difficulties, moral confusion, repression, various psychological conundrums that I won't trouble you with. Wrestled with those for the next year. And it was really Africa that brought it all back out to the surface again. All that raw primal kill-or-be-killed life all around us, see? Brought it back to the old forebrain. Three weeks into the trip I was thinking every night about killing one of you, believe that?

"And why Laura? Well, why not? I was quite sweet on her, see? Wanted to see her die like the bitch-cunt she was too, but the two aren't so totally incompatible as the likes of you might imagine. And at that monkey ranch in Nigeria, when the two of you were having a bit of a spat, we had a little chat and she made it quite clear that the one was never going to happen, so I figured, why not the other, hey? And I'd been in touch with The Bull before I came. All that confusion and torment and so forth, I went hunting around on the Net, spent a fair bit of time there if truth be told, and they got in touch. So it all came together very conveniently, see? Very conveniently for me too. I was an unhappy man before, I'll tell you that. I'm sure I seemed pleasant enough, but I was desperately unhappy. But now, now I'm doing what I was born into this world to do. That's all a man needs to do to be happy. Very simple really."

He shrugged. "And that's the story, my story, that's the long and the short of it. And now, if you'll all excuse me, and even if you won't, I'm going to pursue my happiness in my own inimitable way."

He leveled the gun for the last time. He must have seen something in our expressions, for at the last moment the flashlight wavered, and he lowered the gun and began to turn. He never made it. Hallam rose up behind him like vengeance incarnate, and with an animal's roar he grabbed Morgan and flung him over the edge of the cliff like a rag doll. Morgan was so surprised that he didn't even scream.

For a few seconds nobody moved. Nobody said anything. Nobody breathed.

We heard the wet crunch of impact, and that seemed to galvanize us into motion. Hallam dropped the flashlight he carried and rushed to Nicole, cradled her in his arms, tugged at her bonds with clumsy fingers, then gave up trying as both of them began to weep like children. Lawrence and I exchanged relieved glances and moved to stand at the edge of the gorge.

Morgan's flashlight had miraculously survived the fall, and his body had landed in its cone of light. He lay curled in a mostly fetal position, with a single arm outstreched. A pool of blood seeped and collected around him.

"Good riddance," I said, and spat.

A long silence followed.

"Christ," Lawrence finally said. "I don't know about you lot, but I could use a beer."

That broke the silence, and all four of us laughed.

"Good throw," Hallam said to me.

I smiled back. "Nice catch."

We walked slowly back down the trail to the hotel. Hallam and Nicole clung to each other as if they had been Krazy Glued. Lawrence, wonder of wonders, produced a pack of Marquise cigarettes. Locally manufactured filth. We smoked them all on the way back, once we stopped shaking enough to light them. The gorge seemed warm now, warm and welcoming.

Steve was half mad with anxiety by the time we finally returned and nearly crushed the four of us to death with his welcoming embrace. "Next time," he kept saying, "somebody bloody else can stay behind."

27

FARE-THEE-WELL

It was past midnight by the time we had all reunited, swapped stories, demolished a six-pack of San Miguel, and soothed ourselves enough to make sleep a possibility. The morning bus left at five-thirty, which didn't leave much time for shut-eye, but better five hours than none. We set our alarms, group-hugged for a full minute, and went off to our respective beds.

We made it onto the morning bus with time to spare. I wasn't at all groggy. A few seconds after I woke up, the memory of the previous night shocked me fully awake. The others seemed pretty sprightly too. Hallam and Nicole sat at the back of the bus with their arms wrapped around each other, Steve took the two seats in front of them, and Lawrence and I sat in front of him. This time I took the aisle seat, as I had discovered the hard way on the way to the gorge that the Moroccans do not build near enough legroom into their window seats.

We didn't really talk. But it was a good kind of silence. A comfortable kind. It was an awful thing that had happened, but we had come through it all right, and we had come through it together. I thought to myself more than once, on that bus trip, that these were just the people I wanted on my side when push came to shove, and that it was good to be around them. I think maybe they thought the same. I had crazy fantasies of moving to London. Well, the London part wasn't crazy. It was the part about Talena coming with me that didn't seem fully grounded in reality.

In four days Crown Air would fly us from Gibraltar back to London, which meant that even allowing for the inevitable travel delays we had a couple of days to kill. We spent them in Essouaira. A town by a gorgeous windswept beach on the edge of the Atlantic, popular but not *too* popular with the Lonely Planet crowd. Moroccan kids played soccer on the beach. Hash was cheap and only technically illegal. A chain of old watchtowers that dated back to practically the Roman Empire lay along the beach, staring down the chain of shipwrecks that littered the ocean, and we spent our days beach-hopping from one tower to another.

It was a good time. Hallam and Nicole barely left one another's side. They weren't distant, exactly, but Steve and Lawrence and I could tell that they were so wrapped up in one another's world that there wasn't really room for anyone else, so we gave them a lot of space. Lawrence made it clear that my brief suspicion of him was forgiven and forgotten, and Steve radiated his usual good cheer, and the three of us ate and drank and smoked and swam and played soccer with the Moroccans. It was a good time. I didn't feel at all bad about Morgan. I don't think any of us did. It was like Hallam said, a lot easier to deal with than we might have expected. He was a monster, and we had rid the world of him. Not so hard to look in the mirror after that.

We weren't worried about the authorities. I strongly doubted that anyone would find Morgan's body anytime soon. The hotel would just keep adding to his tab for another few days before wondering where he had vanished to. We had signed in under false names and could not be traced here.

And the Moroccan police were, well, not exactly the sort to strike fear into the heart of evildoers everywhere. And even if they did find the body, then find us, what evidence did anyone have? We would simply deny everything. I understood how getting away with murder had been so easy for Morgan for so many years.

So easy for Morgan and the others.

"So what about those other four?" Lawrence asked me, our second night in Essouaira, as he and Steve and I sat around a table smoking. Lawrence had become quite a heavy smoker, although he assured us that he'd give it up the moment he set foot back in England, that it was a travel thing only. I even believed him.

"Which other four?" I asked. His question had come out of nowhere.

"Numbers One, Two, Three, and Five."

"Oh, them." I'd nearly forgotten the other Demon Princes. "Not my department."

"Aye," Steve said. "Get some other lot to handle them. I reckon we've done our bloody bit and then some."

"I suppose I'll send out that article," I said. "After I edit out all the Morgan references. Can't hurt. Warn people that they're out there. Maybe make them sweat a little, make Interpol try a little harder to find some way to go after them. But that's the end of the story for me."

"For us," Steve said.

"I'll drink to that," said Lawrence, and we clinked our San Miguels together.

But that conversation spurred an idea. Maybe I wasn't quite finished with The Bull after all. Maybe there was one more thing I could do.

The picture was the hardest part. I'm a programmer, not a graphic designer, and Essouaira's sole Internet cafe was not exactly well equipped with all the latest software. Eventually I tracked down some freeware graphic-editing software called LView and worked out how to put it through its paces. At least the picture itself was a good one, from the archive of Africa pictures I kept on my Unix account. Morgan wearing his shark-tooth hat, in Todra Gorge no less. There were others in the picture, Carmel and Nicole and Michael, but I used LView to cut Morgan's head out and then expand it to passport-picture size. The Swiss Army knife pictures I took straight from Victorinox's Web page. A little cutting, pasting, rotating, and reflecting, and voilà: two Swiss Army knives, blades extended, crossed in an X over Morgan's smiling and still-recognizable face.

I accessed The Bull via Safeweb so they would never be able to track my access back to Essouaira. I doubted that they had the necessary technical expertise in the first place, but then again when dealing with a group of psychopathic murderers there is no such thing as too paranoid. I went to their registration page and chose "Toreador" as a password. And voilà, I was NumberSix.

```
Entry #: 58
Points to date: 0
Entered by: NumberSix
Entry date: 1 Dec 2000
Kill date: 28 Nov 2000
Kill location: Todra Gorge, Morocco
Victim specifications: NumberFour aka Morgan
Jackson
Kill description: Capital punishment.
Media files and URLs:
    Photo here.

        This is your only warning. Stop hunting,
        or be hunted.
```

An empty threat, of course. But they didn't know that. I thought it might make a few twisted hearts beat a little faster. It might have the other four killers looking over their shoulders, staying up late at night, blaming one another for the security breach. It might even save a life or two. And that was good enough for me.

On the ferry back to Gibraltar I was unaccountably nervous, fearing that some crack Moroccan detective was about to tap us on the shoulder and ask us a few questions, that we would be sent back to serve life sentences in Tangiers. Visions of *Midnight Express* floated in my mind. But instead our passports were stamped at Gibraltar customs without so much as a single question, and we were waved onward onto that barren hunk of English rock. We found a hotel, and slept, and at noon the next day I looked out from my window seat on our Airbus A318 and saw London spread all over the landscape like a carpet of civilization. It was a curiously moving sight. No one should ever call London a beautiful city, but it is homey in its own sprawling, awkward way.

"When do you head back to California?" Nicole asked me, as I waited on the tarmac.

"Tomorrow afternoon," I said.

"D'you want to stay with Hal and me tonight?"

"I . . . yeah, I would," I said. I was surprised by the question. I would have thought the two of them wanted to be alone. But both Lawrence and Steve had true bachelor pads with no room for another, and I didn't particularly want to stay in another Earl's Court hostel surrounded by drunken students.

We had a farewell meal and a few pints at the Pig & Whistle, and Lawrence and Steve went back to their flats after a round of backbreaking hugs and promises to stay in touch

and hopefully visit me in California. Hallam and Nic and I
had one more round and retired to their flat.

"Ah, Christ, it's good to be back," Hallam sighed as he fit the
key into his door. He opened it, tossed his bags on the floor,
walked straight to the couch, plopped down on it, and turned
on the television. Nicole, laughing, followed him and leaned
back into his arms, and I pulled up a chair and sat next to them.

"You're a good man, Mr. Wood," Hallam said after a little
while, apropos of nothing.

"Thanks," I said, surprised.

"I mean it," he said. "Nic and I have the good fortune to
have lots of people that we're *glad* to call friends, but you're
one of those we're *proud* to call a friend."

"Thank you," I said, and I meant it. "I'm glad to hear you
say that. Especially what with me just almost having gotten
us all killed and everything."

"Don't feel bad about that," Nicole said. "Please. We
came with you with our eyes wide open, believe me. We
knew what we were getting into. It was the right thing to do.
And it all worked out for the best."

"Few tense moments in there," I said.

"There were," Hallam said. "There were indeed."

"And they've gotten us to thinking," Nicole said. "Hal and
I. We're not getting any younger, you know."

"And when I thought I might have lost her—" Hallam
shook his head and gave her a squeeze. "It's the kind of thing
that makes you reevaluate things, you know?"

I looked at them carefully. "I suppose so. Where are you
going with this?"

"We decided," Nicole said. "We're going to try to have a
baby."

"Really?" I asked.

"Really," Hallam said. "It's time. You can't go gallivanting
around forever."

"And even if you could, you still shouldn't," Nicole added.

"Wow," I said. "Wow! That's . . . that's terrific! That's great! Congratulations!"

"Now save the congratulations until there's an actual bun in the oven," Hallam said.

"Well, thanks for telling me, anyway," I said. "Do Steve and Lawrence know?"

"We're not telling anyone but you, for now," Nicole said.

"Don't particularly want to run into a wall of crude jokes about how the baby-making's going every week down the pub," Hallam explained, and we all laughed.

"No smoking or drinking," Nicole said with a sigh. "For *either* of us," to Hallam.

"Life is full of terrible sacrifices," Hallam said mock-seriously, and kissed her. "Let's see what else is on the telly."

That night I slept on their sofa, and when I woke in the middle of the night and heard the urgent sounds of their lovemaking from the other room I suddenly felt terribly sad and alone. They were my friends, and I loved them and wished them nothing but the best, wished them days of happiness until the ends of their lives, and I was happy for them, I was delighted to see them so happy building a future together. But I couldn't help but contrast that with my own life. I had no future to build, no one to go home to. I had found no Nicole, and maybe I never would. Hal and Nic fitted together perfectly, an example to everyone. As if they were the two pieces of life's simplest jigsaw puzzle. But simple as it was I thought I might never figure it out. That happened to people. They never found their other half. Thinking of the couples I knew I thought it might happen to *most* people. I felt a terrible certainty that I would spend my life being one of them.

Maybe I had found my Nicole. Maybe her name was Laura Mason.

Enough. Laura was dead. I had to get on with my life.

But I *had* gotten on with my life. I realized that for the first time. I *had* put Laura behind me, at least as far behind as she was going to go. It wasn't because of Laura that I had been unhappy for the longest time, that I had felt like my life had turned to shit even though half the people I knew envied it. Laura hadn't helped, but she wasn't the real reason. The real reason was me. I couldn't blame Laura anymore. She had been a cheap excuse for everything that went wrong in my life for long enough. I had to face up to the truth. I was the problem. The problem was me.

Nicole and Hallam and I said our good-byes after Nicole made us a full-on English breakfast, guaranteed to triple your cholesterol levels if you so much as blinked at it. The Piccadilly Line took me back to Heathrow, where I had landed ten short days before. It was December. In all the excitement I had almost forgotten that. Christmas was coming up. I didn't know where I would spend it. My family didn't really celebrate together anymore. It occurred to me on the flight back that there was no one I had to buy presents for. Lots of people that I *could* buy presents for, who would be happy to receive them from me; but nobody who would *expect* one, nobody in the whole wide world.

At San Francisco International the bored woman at Immigration asked me if I was coming to America for business or pleasure, and I was about to say "business" when I realized that I didn't work there anymore, my job had been terminated, my work visa was invalid. Everything was changing. I had no job. In a couple of months my apartment lease would expire. I had nowhere to go for Christmas.

Maybe I should go to London after all. But what would I do there? Could I really change my life by changing its setting? Was there something wrong with me that a mere shift in venue could not repair? I thought that there was. I wished that I knew its name.

It was a cold and foggy day. I took a taxi back to my apartment and fell into my own bed with a great sigh of relief. But I didn't really feel relieved. Now that I was back, now that Morgan was gone, what was I supposed to do? Where did I turn next?

After a little while I called Talena, even though it was late, past eleven.

"Hello?" she answered.

"Hi," I said. "It's me."

"Paul! Where are you?"

"I'm back," I said. "It's all over. Everything's finished."

"What? Tell me what—"

I hung up and winced as I replayed the conversation to myself. I must have sounded like an idiot. Like I was on drugs. I felt like I was on drugs. Downers.

I sipped Scotch and watched TV. It helped a little. Outside it started to rain.

Then at about midnight there was a knock on the door. I answered it. I didn't have a clue who it might be.

It was Talena, dressed in a black raincoat.

I stared at her.

"Did you leave your manners over in England?" she said, but kindly. "It's considered good form to invite a girl in from the rain."

"Yes," I said. "Sure. Sorry. Come in."

She came in and joined me on the couch. I turned off the TV.

"Tell me all about it," she said.

And I did. The whole thing, omitting no detail. I spoke in a dry monotone but she hung on every word. It didn't take that long, it had only been ten days, albeit action-packed ones, since I had last spoken to her. And right at the end, when I was telling her about Hallam and Nicole's decision to have a baby, to my own great surprise and shame, I burst into tears.

I don't know how long it had been since I had last cried. Ten years at least. Maybe more. I thought I had forgotten how. But I broke into wracking sobs, clutched at my head and cried like a baby, loudly, sobbing and shaking and sniveling as if it was the only thing I knew how to do. After a moment Talena was next to me, her arms around me, lifting my head onto her shoulder, whispering soothing words into my ear. I cried for a long time. I felt inexplicably and terribly sad but somehow relieved. As if I was releasing something awful that had been pent up inside me for years and grown toxic.

When I was finally finished, my face and Talena's shoulder were soaked with my tears and snot. I sank back into the couch, exhausted, and looked up at her.

"I think I'm done," I said, banally, and nasally.

"Okay," she said gently, producing a package of tissues from her purse, which she used to wipe my face and her shoulder relatively clean. I didn't move. I felt utterly humiliated, but somehow that was okay. As if I knew I had finally hit bottom, and at least there was nowhere deeper to sink.

"Come on," she said. "Let's go to bed."

"Let's?" I didn't think I had heard her correctly.

"You shouldn't sleep alone tonight," she said. "Come on." She led me to my bed and under the covers. We kept our clothes on. We held each other, at first tentatively, and then as if we had always been together. She was very warm.

"It's going to be okay," she whispered in my ear. "Everything will be okay."

At some point during the night we both stripped down to our underwear, it was too warm to keep our clothes on, but we didn't kiss, didn't touch except to hold one another. Once she murmured in her sleep, something anxious, in a harsh foreign language, and I held her tighter, and she woke up and her eyes opened and she smiled to see me there.

When I woke up she was gone from the bed, and I was afraid she had left, but she was only in the kitchen, making coffee. She was fully dressed and she smiled at me in my boxers and told me to take a shower. When I came out of the shower she had toast and coffee ready and we ate it on the couch, watching TV, sitting at opposite ends but with our legs overlapping in the middle.

"I should go," she said eventually. "I have to get to work."

"All right," I said, following her to the door. "I'll call you tonight."

"Call me today. Tonight you can buy me dinner."

At the door she kissed me. Our first kiss. It went on for a long time. I saw stars.

"I'll see you soon," she whispered, breathless.

"Not soon enough," I whispered back.

I watched her walk down the stairs and disappear into the San Francisco fog. After a little while I decided to go for a walk myself. I always liked the fog. It makes the whole world seem beautiful and mysterious. And that's what we all really want, isn't it?

Beauty and mystery. And somebody to share them with.